MW01680417

INTRIGUE

Seek thrills. Solve crimes. Justice served.

Protective Warrior

Janie Crouch

Custody In The Crosshairs

Barb Han

MILLS & BOON

First Published 2026
First Australian Paperback Edition 2026
ISBN 978 1 038 98252 0

First Published 2026
First Australian Paperback Edition 2026
ISBN 978 1 038 98252 0

FSC® www.fsc.org MIX Paper | Supporting responsible forestry FSC® C001695

Published by
Harlequin Mills & Boon
An imprint of Harlequin Enterprises (Australia) Pty Limited (ABN 47 001 180 918), a subsidiary of HarperCollins Publishers Australia Pty Limited
(ABN 36 009 913 517)
Level 19, 201 Elizabeth Street
SYDNEY NSW 2000 AUSTRALIA

Printed and bound in Australia by McPherson's Printing Group

Protective Warrior

Janie Crouch

MILLS & BOON

Janie Crouch writes passionate romantic suspense for readers who still believe in heroes. After a lifetime on the East Coast—and a six-year stint in Germany—this *USA TODAY* bestselling author has settled into her dream home in the Front Range of the Colorado Rockies. She loves engaging in all sorts of adventures (triathlons! two-hundred-mile relay races! mountain treks!), traveling and surviving life with four kids. You can find out more about her at janiecrouch.com.

Books by Janie Crouch

Harlequin Intrigue

Warrior Peak Sanctuary

Protective Assignment
Protective Lawman
Protective Refuge
Protective Warrior

San Antonio Security

Texas Bodyguard: Luke
Texas Bodyguard: Brax
Texas Bodyguard: Weston
Texas Bodyguard: Chance

The Risk Series: A Bree and Tanner Thriller

Calculated Risk
Security Risk
Constant Risk
Risk Everything

Omega Sector: Under Siege

Daddy Defender
Protector's Instinct
Cease Fire

Visit the Author Profile page at millsandboon.com.au.

To Harlequin. Thank you for giving me my start and for seeing me through over twenty-five books.

CAST OF CHARACTERS

Lawson Davies—Former CIA agent and co-owner of Warrior Peak Sanctuary. Runs the tactical unit.

Sarah Peterson—Resident psychologist at Warrior Peak Sanctuary.

Xavier Michaels—Runs the day-to-day operations of Warrior Peak Sanctuary.

Hannah Davies—Lawson's little sister and longtime employee at Warrior Peak Sanctuary. Engaged to Xavier.

Cade Thatcher—Former soldier who now works at Warrior Peak Sanctuary and helps with tactical missions there. Engaged to River.

River Robertson—Works at Warrior Peak Sanctuary as an assistant to the counselor. Engaged to Cade.

Aaron Ward—Former cop at Kings Mountain PD and was Bailey's training officer; now handyman at the lodge. Engaged to Bailey.

Bailey Masters—Former cop at Kings Mountain PD; now cop in Blue Ridge. Engaged to Aaron.

Chapter One

"Those are only going to last for a few days you know," Lawson Davies pointed out to his sister, Hannah, as he leaned against the wooden doorframe of the lodge's entrance, watching as she fiddled with her most recent flower bed additions. "What's the point of spending so much time pruning them?"

"Because I enjoy it!" she protested, shaking her head at him as if she could hardly believe how obstinate he was. "Just because the flowers aren't going to last long doesn't mean there's no point in doing it at all."

He cocked an eyebrow. "You've been obsessed with those flowers all year."

She paused her pruning, rounding on him with the shears. "Yeah, so I'm going to enjoy them when they're actually in bloom," she pointed out, jabbing the shears toward him demonstratively.

He held up his hands in surrender. "Hey now, show mercy. It was just an observation," he protested.

She laughed. "If you keep bad-mouthing my flower beds, you're going to get it," she warned him. "What are you even doing out here, anyway? Did you just come by to annoy me?"

"Keeping an eye on you," he replied. "I don't trust you with those shears. I've seen how clumsy you are."

"When I was a kid! You really think I'm as bad as that now?"

"Yeah, I do," he retorted.

She let out an irritated snort. "Well, guess you better keep your distance, then," she warned him playfully, holding up her shears. "I might trip and stab you with these."

"And you'd still care more about your flowers," he teased her.

"You're damn right I would!" she replied. "I've worked hard. I want to enjoy the fruits of my labor."

He grinned as she turned her attention back to the blooming flowers running alongside the path that led from the main building to the residential cabins in the woods beyond. He really didn't mind that much that his sister was so intent on spending her time making the flowers look perfect. After everything that had happened in the last couple of years at Warrior Peak, he couldn't blame her for hanging on to something she had total control over.

God knew, he'd been doing the same thing. Working on the lodge had been a relief these last several months. It helped ground him from all the recent troubles they'd endured here, and the fact that he was one of the people who got to call the shots was just a bonus.

He was all about structure and order and balance, which went back to his military and CIA days. And seeing all the employees working hard on the rebuilding, and all the improvements they'd done, made all of the hard work worth it.

Warrior Peak Sanctuary had been a safe haven and dream come true for Lawson and his best friend and business partner, Xavier Michaels. It had become something they could really be proud of. Over the years they'd helped military and law enforcement, and, more recently, domestic-abuse survivors find themselves and their strength again. To be able to rest and recuperate from injuries and refresh their bodies, minds and souls in a peaceful, safe environment did wonders for a person's overall being. They had also been able to bring in more professionals and add a variety of different activities to aid in the healing process. They'd seen large improvements with all the new additions they'd made available to their guests.

Since the last attack on the lodge, they'd decided to do an overhaul on certain aspects of Warrior Peak. The main one being the addition of a small separate building next to the main lodge for Sarah Peterson, the lodge psychologist, to have her new office. They'd also added a small cabin next to it and turned that space into new living quarters for her. The section in the lodge that had been her office before had been renovated and turned into additional rooms for guests.

He hadn't been as sold on having the two spaces next to each other, but after Sarah had rattled off the list of benefits it provided her with them being side by side, who was he to argue? She loved it, and that was what mattered.

Seeing that the residents enjoyed the space separation was a good thing, too. They seemed to feel a little more comfortable being able to go to a separate space and not feel like they were being watched and judged when they went to their therapy appointments. It lifted a small weight off their shoulders and that was important. Lawson wanted them to feel safe and secure in their sessions and everything they did for their recovery.

Lawson had also noticed that Sarah had seemed a bit more hesitant to use the makeshift office they'd originally done up for her in another part of the building while they were constructing the new space. It was farther away from the main entrance and all the hustle and bustle of activity in the lodge. He had his suspicions that she felt isolated being farther away from everyone, and closed off from getting fast help, should she need it. Lawson hoped that would not ever be the case again.

He knew she had been struggling since Jed's attack on her previous office. He'd terrorized her and torn her safe space apart in front of her eyes in a fit of rage. A large man ranting at a petite, sweet, fragile woman like Sarah… It set Lawson's blood boiling every time he thought about it. He'd do whatever he could to make sure she felt safe at the lodge again, to help get her back to the happier, more carefree and confident woman she used to be.

The plunge tub had also been a good addition. It added a bit of excitement to the place. It had many therapeutic benefits—that was why Lawson had suggested adding it in the first place—but it had turned into more of a challenge for those staying there. It had become a test for people to see how long they could last in it and then rush back inside to warm up.

Those who did manage to use the tub for its benefits seemed to enjoy it, though. Lawson had even tried it himself a few times, but he wasn't sure he entirely saw the benefits of freezing your ass off for the sake of your mental health. Damn, at least it woke you up in the morning, better than a coffee ever could. That had to count for something, right?

And even though he loved picking on his sister, he had to admit, the flowers she'd been working so hard on around the lodge looked nice. The bright blooms popped against the soft green of the grass, especially in the sunlight that streamed through the trees beyond. Times like this, he could see why the lodge worked as well as it did. Why it was a place where people were able to actually leave behind the horrors of what they had endured before, and relax in the peace of this environment.

A peace that was suddenly shattered. The door to Sarah's new office slammed open and raised voices sounded inside. Suddenly, Toby Miller, one of her new clients, came storming down the path, his eyes blazing with anger.

"Hey." Lawson stepped out onto the path with his hands held open at his sides. "What's going on?" He looked worriedly between the angry man and the open door.

"She's freaking crazy," Toby snapped, jabbing his finger back toward the office.

Lawson followed his gesture, and saw Sarah standing in the doorway, her face pale, blue-green eyes wide, her shoulders tensed up toward her ears. She looked stiff enough to crack in half.

Lawson sighed. "Go inside," he told Toby. "Cool off for a minute. I'll talk to her, alright?"

"Fine, but I don't know how I'm supposed to accomplish anything with her acting the way she is," he growled as he stomped down the path and back into the lodge. Lawson turned his attention back to the therapy office, where Sarah had already ducked back inside.

"You want me to check on her?" Hannah asked, eyes wide and hands clenched into fists at her sides.

Lawson shook his head. "No, it's fine, I'll handle it," he assured her. He had been feeling particularly protective of Sarah lately, after everything that had happened with Jed a few months ago. He imagined that she was seriously spooked by the encounter she'd just had with Toby because of it. He squeezed Hannah's shoulder lightly as he walked by her down the path.

He reached the door of the therapy office and noticed it wasn't completely closed. He pushed it open and stepped inside, glancing around. Sarah was slumped on to the small couch opposite her desk, her shoulders still drawn up toward her ears, and her whole body trembling.

"Hey," Lawson murmured to her softly.

She jumped, her head snapping around like she was suddenly looking for danger to strike. When she saw who it was, she let out a long sigh of relief.

"Oh, Lawson, it's you," she replied, pushing a hand through her ponytail, and patting her blond hair back into place. "I—I'm sorry, I don't…"

"It's okay," he assured her. "I sent Toby back to the lodge. He's going to be fine when he cools down. Are you alright?"

She chewed her lip and stared straight ahead. She looked like she was trying to decide if she was going to tell him the truth or not. But if it impacted her work for the lodge and its residents, he needed her to be honest about what was going on. It was the only way they would be able to support her.

She knew that better than anyone, having worked as the resident psychologist for as long as she had. If her clients weren't honest with her, she couldn't effectively help them to heal and overcome their issues. The same thing applied to her in this situation. Lawson wanted to help her, but he needed all of the information first.

"I don't know what came over me," she admitted in a small voice, shaking her head and getting to her feet to pour herself a glass of water. She lifted it to her lips and took a long sip, swallowed and then spoke again, a little more clearly this time.

"I can't discuss specifics, you know that. But…it was just like any other session," she explained. "We were talking about some of his stuff, you know, and it brought up some triggers for him. He started to get agitated, totally normal for a guy in his position, but when he got up and started pacing around… it—it just pressed some button inside of me. I didn't know how to handle it."

Her face was pale, her normal bright eyes dim, as she recounted the incident to him. He could tell how spooked she was—it probably triggered her flight response. Even though it had been months since everything that had gone down with Jed, she was still clearly carrying the trauma from it, whether she wanted to admit it or not.

"I'm sorry," she told him, finally lifting her gaze to meet his. "I should have… I should have been more prepared for something like that in sessions. It's normal. I didn't mean to freak him out." She sighed, rubbing her temples. "Damn, I feel like I've put our sessions back with this."

"It's okay," he assured her gently. He didn't like seeing her like this. He reached his hand out to touch her shoulder in support, but drew it back and dropped it to his side. He needed to keep his emotions in check and be professional here.

"I don't know what's gotten into me recently." She sighed and closed her eyes, shaking her head.

Lawson cocked an eyebrow. Really, she didn't? It seemed pretty clear to him, even if she wasn't willing to admit it yet. She felt like she needed to be the strong one, always taking care of others and listening to their problems while ignoring her own needs.

Jed Baxter, one of her previous patients, had turned out to be a double agent trying to get close to Xavier, Lawson's business partner, to collect information he was convinced he had. In a session with Sarah, he had smashed up her old office, destroying it right there in front of her eyes. It was a miracle she hadn't been hurt, and Lawson couldn't even imagine how terrified she must have been when it happened.

So, yeah, it made perfect sense to him that she would struggle with someone else coming at her with the same anger, the same fury, the same harshness. Even if she knew she was safe here, even if she knew that nobody would ever have allowed something like what happened with Jed to happen to her again, psychological wounds didn't heal just like that.

He knew that better than anyone.

"You have nothing to worry about," he promised her. "Why don't you take a break? Go for a walk, get some fresh air, clear your head." He paused and looked her over. "How long has it been since you've had any food? You want to come over to the lodge, get something to eat?"

"I probably should," she told him. "I was running a bit late today. I didn't have time for breakfast."

"Then, yeah, you should," he replied firmly. "It'll do you good to get some food in you. Let's close up and I'll walk you over."

"Thanks," she agreed with a small smile. She flicked her gaze up to meet his, her eyes lingering on his. Like there was something she wanted to tell him—something on her mind she didn't know quite how to put into words.

Whatever it was, she thought better of it, and pulled her jacket from the back of her chair and slipped it over her shoulders. Even though it was warm outside these days, Lawson hadn't seen her without a jacket in several months, almost as though it was a protective layer between her and the rest of the world.

"I'll lock up. I've got the spare keys on me. You have your keys?" He looked over to her for confirmation and saw her pat her pocket, then nod her head.

Lawson got the place locked up, and stole a glance at Sarah out of the corner of his eye. There was something he had been meaning to ask her, something he had wanted to suggest. He hadn't been sure how to bring it up, but he guessed now was as good a time as any under the circumstances. He doubted she was going to take it well, though, but maybe she would come around eventually. He needed to stop beating around the bush and just say it.

"Okay, all set. Let's go." He slipped the keys back into his pocket and placed his hand at the small of her back to get her walking.

"Have you thought about taking a break?" he suggested to her.

She immediately stopped walking and frowned at him. "What do you mean? I'm taking a break right now."

"No, not that kind of break," he replied as he shoved his hands into his pockets.

"So, what, then?" she asked, clearly confused.

He knew Sarah was dedicated to her work; hell, he was pretty sure it was the only thing that was keeping her grounded right now after the attack. But surely, she could see that she wasn't going to be able to help anyone else in a meaningful way until she focused that attention on herself first.

He took a fortifying breath before speaking again. "A longer break," he said. "Take some time to figure things out."

She stood stock-still on the spot. The corners of her mouth turned down into a frown. In her eyes, he could see the shock and it gutted him. This was the last thing she had expected him to say, and he could tell how deeply it stung.

"I'm fine," she said, forced out the words, and crossed her arms over her chest defensively.

He sighed, jerking his head down toward the lodge. "Sure you are, but maybe think about it?" He paused, waiting for her reply. Her frown deepened but she eventually nodded. "Right now, you still need something to eat," he pointed out. "Come down and get something with me?"

"Fine," she muttered, but the discomfort was evident in her tone. This, he got the feeling, was going to be a problem, but he wasn't going to give up that easily. Just because she was normally the one who took care of everyone else didn't mean that she didn't need someone to look out for her sometimes, too.

Chapter Two

Sarah stuffed her hands into her jacket pockets as she followed Lawson down the path toward the lodge. She felt like an unruly child being put in a time-out for something they weren't truly responsible for. Internally, though, she was reeling. Did she really hear him correctly? She wasn't sure. She felt as though she must be reading in to what he'd said the wrong way, but what else could she take away from his words?

A break. Not just a few hours away, a full-blown break. That was what he had suggested. That was what he wanted her to do. No, there was no way… There was just no *way* she could take that much time away from her work. She would be climbing the walls with boredom.

She had a hard enough time as it was, tossing and turning all night long, replaying the day of Jed's attack over and over again in her head. Given more time to sit with her thoughts, how was that going to make things any better? Be any easier? She would lose her mind.

Besides, this job was her life. This work, it had been her dream since she was a little girl. She had known, even then, that it wasn't going to be easy—known that it was going to demand a lot from her—and she had been prepared for it. She had been aware, from when she had started her training, that it was going to throw some tough situations at her, and she had told herself that she could handle it. She was going to be that safe place, that port in a storm for people who needed it.

"Is this about what happened with Jed?" she demanded, hurrying to catch up with Lawson.

He glanced at her out of the corner of his eye, and nodded. "I just think you could use some time to process it, that's all."

"I don't..." she protested. "I... It only happened a few months ago. I'm still dealing with it—"

"Yeah, and having some space to dedicate to that might do you some good," he replied. "Getting away from here will help you clear your mind, get a better perspective on things."

She shook her head. "No way," she retorted. "I'm fine. I'm just being hard on myself because I was working with him, and I should have seen there was something going on..."

She trailed off, distinctly aware of how it sounded. Like she was still stuck in the process of blaming herself. Hell, if she was, would anyone be surprised? She was supposed to be able to get a good read on people, not—not let a traitor into their midst, a spy who intended to upend the whole place.

She'd always considered herself an intuitive person who could sense the needs and intentions of others. But after what happened with Jed, she didn't trust her own intuition as much anymore. She had let down herself and other people by not seeing through Jed sooner.

Even though the warmth of the summer sun was beating down on her face, she couldn't help but shiver slightly when she thought about everything that had happened. The look on his face when he had gone into a rage in her office, the way his eyes had darkened and his features had twisted into someone who was unrecognizable. The charming smile he had used to deceive them had disappeared.

She'd seen plenty of people working through serious issues before, vanishing into dark memories or bad self-belief, but she had never, in her whole time working as a psychologist, seen a transformation so consuming and so terrifying.

And that—that had stuck with her. Knowing that someone could just flip on a dime like that, go crazy in that way, terrified her. And crazy was the only way she could describe it. The people she treated, they weren't crazy, they were just damaged, trying to navigate the reality of what they had been through as best they could. But Jed? He was deranged…with evil intentions and a darkened soul. And she prayed she was never going to have to deal with someone like that again.

"I can't expect myself to go back to normal that quickly. It takes time," she continued, and she could feel him watching her out of the corner of his eye. They passed Hannah, who offered Sarah a sympathetic smile. Sarah hated people looking at her like that, as though she was some kind of victim, in desperate need of help. She was fine. She just…needed a moment of fresh air and something to eat, that's all.

"Sarah, there's nothing wrong with taking a break," he remarked to her gently. "How many times have you told that to one of your clients?"

She pressed her lips together. Well, she couldn't argue with that, she supposed. Damn the man! He was sneaky, using her own methods against her. And maybe he had a point, but she didn't want to admit that to him, not so easily, anyway. He offered her a kind smile, but she still wasn't reassured. The words he'd said to her about taking a break were swirling around inside her head and she felt a knot forming in her stomach.

All at once, Lawson stopped in his tracks and reached into his pocket. Checking his phone, he frowned, and glanced over at her.

"I have to take this," he told her apologetically. "We can talk more about this later, okay? Please make sure you eat something soon and get some fresh air."

"Yeah, sure," she replied, though she secretly hoped that he was going to forget they'd had this conversation. She knew she should take his concern to heart, and truthfully, she probably did need some time off. She just couldn't entertain the thought of that right now. She needed her work and this place to help keep her grounded right now.

She was proud of what she did here, helping people to find their balance, their footing again. She felt that canceling therapy sessions or shifting her clients to someone else in town would do more harm than good. She needed them as much as they needed her right now.

"You sure you're okay?" he asked her, lingering for another moment before he left.

She nodded, forcing a confidence she didn't quite feel. "I'm fine," she assured him. "You go. Your text seems important."

He paused and looked her over, seemingly trying to gauge the truth in her words. Her skin tingled from each place his gaze landed, but then he nodded and headed back inside the lodge. She hoped it wasn't anything serious. God only knew that this place had been through enough as it was.

"Hey, you want to give me a hand with these flowers?"

Sarah turned to see Hannah sitting back on her heels, a smile on her face. Sarah couldn't help but return it. Hannah always had the brightest, bubbliest energy, especially when she was outside working on her flower beds. She was so proud of the blooms she had managed to bring out this summer, and Sarah could hardly believe that time had passed so quickly as to see them in full bloom like this.

"Is everything alright?" Hannah asked her gently, nodding back up toward the office. Sarah pulled a face. She didn't really want to talk about it again—she felt raw and exposed enough from Lawson's comments. She couldn't really talk about it, anyway, not with Toby being a client.

She knew Hannah had seen how he charged out of her office like his ass was on fire, though he had every right to be upset with her. The moment his triggers had kicked in and he'd started getting agitated, Sarah had started to panic. She'd withdrawn into herself and flashed back to Jed. She hated how scared she'd become when he had started pacing her office floor, clenching his fists at his sides. She'd felt useless, like all her training had suddenly vanished in a puff of smoke, and she had no clue what to do to calm him down.

Him seeing her frozen and pale, with a shocked look on her face hadn't helped, either. He'd given her a look of disappointment and then stalked out the door. This was her job, the one thing she was good at, and she'd failed him. Failing herself and the lodge in the process.

"Sorry, it's a doctor-patient thing. It doesn't matter, anyway," Sarah muttered, trying to shut down the conversation before it went any further. She knew Hannah was just trying to help, but it was hard to see it as anything other than prying into her private business.

"I wasn't talking about the client-thing, Sarah. I meant you. And you matter to me," Hannah told her, crossing her arms over her chest and hitting her with a serious look. Damn, at times like these, she really reminded Sarah of Lawson.

Hannah and Lawson carried themselves with the same seriousness, like they were ready and willing to take on the world given the chance. And neither of them was going to let Sarah get out of this situation without sharing the truth of what was going on in her head. Sarah pulled out the band from her hair and ran her fingers through the curly blond strands.

"I just… I feel like I've been floundering lately," she confessed. "After what happened with Jed, I mean. I thought… I felt confident in myself and my abilities, and now, it's like the ground was ripped out from under me and I've been sinking in quicksand. Like the ability to do my job and the security I've always known here are suddenly gone, you know?"

"Yeah, tell me about it," Hannah agreed, her brow furrowed. "It screwed me up for a while, too."

"I'm sorry to hear that," Sarah replied.

Hannah cocked an eyebrow. "Hey, we're not talking about me right now," she reminded her. "We're talking about what's going on with you. You could take some time off, you know, figure out how to handle it."

Sarah closed her eyes and sighed. "That's what Lawson said. I don't want to leave my patients like that," she remarked, shaking her head. "I don't think it's a good idea. They need stability and continuity for their treatment to really work, and that's not going to happen if I just vanish off the face of the earth."

"Yeah, but they're not going to receive proper treatment from you if you're freaking out all the time, either," she pointed out.

"I know, I know," Sarah conceded. "I feel like I'm more like my patients than a therapist right now. Normally, I'm in control, but now, I just don't know how to handle myself."

"You should consider seeing a therapist yourself," Hannah suggested. "You could find someone in town, I'm sure of it—"

Sarah shook her head again. She knew it was likely a good idea, but there wasn't a chance in hell that she was going to up and leave the lodge high and dry like that. Plus, what would it say about her and her ability to help others if she ran away? This was her job and Warrior Peak Sanctuary was her home. She wasn't going to be run off by her own insecurities. She'd find a way to deal with them.

"I just need to think about this logically," she replied. "I have all the skills I need to get this under control, I just have to find a way to implement them. Grounding exercises, breathing control, stuff like that. Techniques I'd suggest to my own clients."

She could sense the doubt in Hannah's mind before she even made eye contact with her, but she didn't want to deal with it right now, not when she had already been dealing with her own traumatic issues. Hannah was doing much better in her struggles. Sarah had seen tremendous improvement in her. She didn't want to set her back by pulling her into her own mess.

She was telling the truth, after all. She knew exactly how to work through trauma, at least on a technical level. She had served as the touchstone for so many people who'd come and gone through Warrior Peak's therapy program. People who'd relied on her for support and help in their hardest, darkest times. Why couldn't she just…do the same for herself now, too?

Maybe she just needed more exercise. Take a look at her diet, make sure she wasn't getting too much caffeine, which could be putting her on edge. There were plenty of steps she could take before she would have to look elsewhere for help, and she was determined to do everything she could to focus on them rather than allow herself to get involved with something outside this place.

"So, need help with the flowers?" she asked, nodding to the beds in front of them, trying to change the subject back to Hannah's initial question.

Hannah glanced down at them, as though she had almost forgotten they were there. "Sure, but I don't want to interrupt you getting something to eat."

"No, I'm good. I don't think I could eat right now, anyway."

"Then, yeah, I could use some help. But let me know if you change your mind about eating," she added, handing her the shears.

"You've done such a good job with these," Sarah remarked, shifting the conversation to something else. The more time she spent focused on her freak-out in Toby's therapy session earlier, the more likely it was that it would turn into harmful rumination, and she really, really didn't need that right now.

Hannah brightened up as soon as she mentioned the flowers.

"I know, right?" she replied proudly. "I thought it would take more for them to bloom this first time around, but I guess I have a green thumb."

"You do," Sarah agreed, and she stooped down to smell the peonies. Their sweet, rosy perfume filled the air around her, and she closed her eyes, trying to ground herself with a focus on the scent.

See? I'm fine.

She just needed to give herself a little more time, and focus her energy on the grounding and calming techniques she would have prescribed to any of her clients, and she would be back to normal in no time.

At least, that was what she had to keep telling herself. Because the thought of having to leave this place, for anything at all, was more than a little terrifying to her right now.

Chapter Three

Lawson strode down the main hallway in the lodge with purposeful strides. He went past Reception and the main gathering room, and was passing the dining hall, where he heard someone call his name.

"Hey, Lawson!"

He glanced around, and saw Xavier and Cade hanging out by the dining table in the center of the room, clearing out the plates from the recent meal.

"Can you give us a hand with all this?" Cade called to him. "Aaron's out at the paddock and we could use an extra pair of hands."

Lawson held up his phone and made an apologetic face. "Sorry, guys. I have to take this," he told them.

Xavier shook his head at him. "Anything to get out of dish duty, huh?" he teased.

Lawson held his hands up. "You got me," he joked. "See you guys in a bit."

Truth be told, he didn't have time to stick around and help out right now. No, he'd just gotten a text from someone he hadn't heard from in a hell of a long time, and something told him that if she was getting in touch with him, something had to be going on. Something bad.

The text from Lainey Daye had told him to get to somewhere

he wouldn't be overheard and call her. He knew she wasn't screwing around or being overdramatic when she'd typed that, either. Lainey had never taken a joking attitude. She always said exactly what she meant, and nothing more.

It was one of the many things that had made her such a good agent for the CIA. Lawson had trained alongside her, and she had worked in the agency for the better part of a decade before she'd left field duty and begun working as an analyst instead.

The two of them had kept in touch on and off, though they had mostly been focused on their own lives the last few years. Still, Lawson felt some loyalty to her, same as he was sure she did to him, and he wasn't going to leave her out in the cold if something was going on and she needed his help.

He reached his room and pulled the door shut behind him, double-checking to make sure it was locked. He dialed her back and lifted the phone to his ear, and it rang a couple of times before Lainey answered.

"Lawson?"

"Lainey. I'm alone," he told her. "What's going on?"

"Good," she replied, her voice taut.

Lawson could tell at once that something was up, and he didn't like it. They'd worked together for long enough that he could recognize when something was wrong, and when it came to Lainey, he knew it wasn't going to be anything simple. She had a knack for diving in headfirst when it was something important to her.

"What's happening?" he demanded. "Are you safe?"

"For now," she replied. "Can you meet me in town? I don't want to say much over the phone."

"In town?"

"I'm at a café, not far from the sewing shop," she explained.

He frowned. "Wait, you're…"

"Yes. It shouldn't take you more than an hour to get down here," she replied. "Can you make it? I need to talk to you. In person. It's really important."

"Of course I can," he replied without even really thinking twice about it. He was never going to leave Lainey out in the cold, and if she had come all this way to find him, she must have believed he was the only person who could help her. "I'll need to shift a couple things here, then I'll be on my way."

"Good," she responded. "Please, hurry. I'll see you soon, Lawson."

And with that, she hung up, leaving him even more confused than before. What the hell was happening? Why was she here? Why didn't she just come up to Warrior Peak? He needed to get moving if he was going to find out.

As he gathered himself, his mind drifted back to their time together in the agency. They had worked together well, their last mission a drug bust in Richmond that went off without a hitch. With both of their analytical minds in the game, they had managed to put together a plan that led to no casualties, the drug runners arrested and their stash in police custody, where it belonged. They'd gotten a hell of a lot of dangerous trash off the streets that day, and he was still proud of that.

Afterward, they'd gone to get a beer together. Well, he'd had a beer. He'd noticed at once that she wasn't drinking, and had wondered aloud what was keeping her from her usual post-work celebration. They had grabbed drinks together multiple times over the years and it wasn't like her to just order water.

"I—I'm pregnant," she'd blurted out.

His eyebrows had nearly vanished off the top of his head. "What the hell?"

She looked up at him, and he could see how torn she was, the pain written all over her face.

"I can't do this anymore, Lawson," she admitted. "I… This work, it's getting to me. I used to love the high I got after a job well done. But now, I have other things to think about. Other priorities, the baby…"

Lawson was stunned. She hadn't even told him she was seeing anyone, and now she was pregnant? Sure enough, though, that was the end of it for her. She wanted to leave fieldwork and focus on raising her kid with the love of her life, and he couldn't blame her.

Doing what they did, day in and day out, was tough on families, and he'd heard of way too many people who'd ended up divorced because of the amount of pressure their line of work had put on them. Lainey could see it just as clearly as he could—she would have to make a choice. And she chose her new life.

Of course, Lawson had missed her, but he wanted the best for her, and he trusted that she knew what that was. She had retired from the field to start working as an analyst, a much safer job with more manageable hours. He had asked about her in their mutual circles a few times over the years, and based on the small details he'd picked up, she seemed to be doing really well.

But this? This wasn't good. This sounded serious. What had happened to throw her back into the middle of the action like this? He knew she wasn't in town just to catch up with an old friend. Hell, she could just come up to the lodge for that.

His mind was spinning as he tried to put the pieces together, but he knew there was no point in guessing until he was in front of her and she could tell him herself what was going on.

He left his room and headed down to the entrance as he tried to keep his thoughts from running wild. She had said she was safe for now, so someone was chasing her? Looking for her? For what purpose? Information, or something worse?

He was starting to give himself a headache but he couldn't seem to stop the questions from forming in his mind. What had happened to her kid, her husband? He knew how much they meant to her and he doubted she would have been able to handle it if something had happened to them. Damn, the thought of it made the hair on the back of his neck stand up.

He'd learned what it was like to have the things he held close threatened these last several months, and it wasn't a good feeling.

He diverted down one of the side halls and headed downstairs. He knew he needed to let Xavier know he was leaving the property and what little he knew of Lainey's urgent request. They were business partners, but they were also best friends and they looked out for each other in all ways.

"Hey," Lawson said as he walked in the office door. Xavier glanced up from the papers on his desk, his brow furrowed. A far cry from the goofy guy clearing dishes just ten minutes ago.

"What's up?" Xavier asked, narrowing his eyes. "Everything okay?"

"Everything's fine," he assured him, even though he didn't know if it was truly the case. "I'm going down to Blue Ridge for a bit. I got a call from an old friend at the CIA. Remember Lainey Daye?"

Xavier's shoulders immediately tensed at the mention of the CIA. Lawson didn't blame him after everything that'd gone down a few months prior. "Yeah, didn't work with her, but I remember her. What's going on?"

"I'm not sure yet—she asked me to come meet her. Can you hold down the fort for now?"

"You got it," Xavier replied with a nod. "You need help? Backup?"

"Not right now," he answered, slipping his hands into his pockets. "I'll keep you updated as much as I can. But I need to go, it seemed pretty urgent. I'm not sure when I'll be back, either, probably later tonight."

A dark shadow flitted across Xavier's face, and Lawson could tell his mind was drifting back to the memories of what had happened with Jed just a few months ago. He'd blamed himself for that, for bringing that kind of danger to their door, even though Lawson had tried to tell him he had nothing at all to feel guilty about.

Everyone came to Warrior Peak with some history to their name, and sometimes, that history came back to bite them in the ass. It wasn't Xavier's fault that a deranged man was desperate for information about illegal weapons and would stop at nothing to get it.

"Oh, and can you keep an eye on Sarah for me while I'm out?" Lawson asked.

Xavier cocked an eyebrow. "I guess so," he replied. "Why, is something going on with her?"

"Something happened in her last appointment," Lawson explained. "She should be okay now, but she seemed pretty shaken up by it. I don't want her getting into her head about it, you know?"

"You got it," Xavier agreed, and Lawson nodded his gratitude before he turned to head out to his truck.

Even though the sun was shining above his head, he felt a

shiver run down his spine. Lainey reaching out to him like this wasn't exactly what he had expected. As far as he knew, she was living a quiet life as an analyst and enjoying her family life. Something told him that she wouldn't have been contacting him unless she felt as though she didn't have any other choice. When she had gotten out of the game, she'd been intent on making a new life for herself, a life that didn't revolve around the stress and danger of what she'd known before.

But, as he knew all too well, just because you wanted to leave something behind, it didn't mean it wasn't going to come looking for you at some point or another. So if he could help her get through this, then he would.

He owed her that much.

He jumped into his truck and pulled away from the sanctuary, watching the main building shrink in his rearview mirror. And he said a brief prayer to whoever might be listening that whatever was going on with Lainey didn't cause any more trouble at Warrior Peak.

Because God only knew they had been through enough lately as it was.

Chapter Four

Sarah took a deep breath as she hovered in the doorway to the dining room. This should have been a calm, relaxing part of her day, a chance to unwind with the people she cared about, and catch up with others about things going on at the lodge.

Instead, she knew she needed to talk to Toby after what had transpired earlier in his therapy session. The way she had reacted had been so unprofessional and she felt awful about it. He had every right to be upset by her behavior and she needed to make things right. She didn't want to be the cause of a setback in his recovery.

Smoothing down her skirt, Sarah walked over to Toby, who was serving himself up a generous portion of mac and cheese from the large pot on the table. He glanced over at her as she drew closer to him, and she could see the annoyance on his face. She didn't blame him. He'd come to her for help, after all, and she had freaked out on him. He was perfectly within his rights to be annoyed or angry at her for what had happened.

"Hey, Toby, do you have a minute?" she asked him and glanced around, making sure no one else was approaching. She wanted to apologize to him but she didn't want everyone else to know what was going on.

He sighed and put down his plate, turning to face her. "Sure," he replied. The current residents at Warrior Peak were a small enough group of people that, if someone wanted to talk, it was better to just get it over with and have a conversation with them. It was useless to try to avoid them, and he knew that as well as anyone.

"Thanks," she murmured, and she twisted her hands into a knot in front of her, trying to remember what she'd practiced in her head before she'd come over. "Um, I wanted to apologize about what happened earlier," she explained. "In your session."

"Right," he replied, eyeing her with obvious doubt.

She took a deep breath, and forced herself to keep going. "When you got emotional," she continued. "It triggered something in me. And I know that's not fair. I know you come to me for help because you want guidance and to work through everything that's happened to you. It's not your fault that some of what we were talking about brought my unpleasant memories to the surface."

She realized she was rambling, and slowed herself down, taking a deep breath, trying to ground herself in the moment. The smell of the food around her, the chatter of people filling the room. See? She was okay. She could do this. She wasn't going to start freaking out again, not a chance in hell.

"It triggered my flight response and that's why I shut down like I did," she went on. "I had a panic attack, and I know that's not helpful for you in the work that you're doing. I should have been able to handle my own triggers better, but I need you to know that they had nothing to do with you. It was all on me. Your emotions are completely valid, and I apologize for how I reacted."

He nodded slowly. She could see some of the doubt and irritation starting to edge away now that she had explained it to him.

"I know that wasn't an appropriate interaction for us to have as a patient and a therapist, and I understand completely if you'd like to seek care elsewhere," she said. "There are a few great therapists I can put you in touch with if that's how you'd like to move forward. But, if you're willing to give me another chance, I would love to pick up where we left off."

Finally, a smile crossed his face, and he shook his head. "I don't want to work with anyone else," he replied. "I'd like to keep working with you, Sarah. If you think it's going to be okay for you."

"It will be," she promised him, a flood of relief washing through her. She wasn't sure how she would have felt if he had accepted her offer to set him up with a new therapist, but she was relieved he was willing to let her try again. He clearly had some level of trust in her, despite how messy things had gotten before.

"Thanks, Sarah," he told her. "Now, if you don't mind, I want to have some dinner."

"Of course," she replied. "Don't let me stop you."

And, as she stood there, she realized that her stomach was grumbling. After the messed-up session and the way the rest of her morning had gone, she'd lost her appetite. But now, it seemed to be coming back. The food smelled so good.

She grabbed herself a plate and started to load it up, and then went to join the rest of the staff sitting with the current guests at the long table that ran down the center of the dining room.

She slid in next to Hannah, who was sitting beside Xavier, as she always was these days. Opposite her sat Aaron, and then Cade and River, who were chatting about something that caused River's cheeks to flush. Sarah smiled at the love that shined brightly from the couple. They deserved it after what they'd been through the year before at the lodge.

There were a couple of people missing, though. Bailey would still be down in Blue Ridge finishing her shift at the police station, but Lawson seemed to be absent. That was unusual. Sarah glanced around, wondering if she was missing something, but if she was, she couldn't figure it out. Maybe he had just gotten called away for something more important than a meal?

She tried to focus on the food in front of her, not letting her mind wander off in too many directions. Her thoughts drifted back to the text he'd received. Hopefully, it wasn't bad news and Lawson was just busy with something around the property. She'd have to catch up to him later.

She wanted to check in with him, though, and tell him that she'd smoothed things out with Toby and that he still wanted to work with her. That would prove that she didn't need to take a break, right?

Sarah ate quietly, glad to just be surrounded by people she knew she could trust. She was starting to feel a whole lot better compared to the mess that she was earlier in the day and she could almost convince herself that she was already putting it behind her. That was what she had to believe, anyway.

"Yeah, I mean, I've seen it reported in a couple of places..."

Sarah turned her head to tune in to the conversation happening down the table. Kieran Abbott, one of the new arrivals, had his brow furrowed as he recounted it to Xavier, sitting next to him.

"And how many people did you say had gone missing?" Xavier asked, sounding concerned.

"I think it was a half-dozen women in the last few months," he replied. He pulled his phone out of his pocket and tapped it a couple of times to pull up an article. "Yeah, look. This is the piece I saw on it..."

Kieran handed his phone to Xavier, since he was in the center of the group chatting. Everyone close leaned in to get a better look at what was written on the screen in front of them. The article, it seemed, covered a spate of vanishings along Highway 50—one of the roads that ran by the Warrior Peak Sanctuary. The highway ran from California to Maryland and was a primary state highway in North Carolina; actually, it was known as NC 50 there.

The pictures of the women who must have been among the missing, looking innocent and free, smiled out from the screen.

"I had no idea," Hannah muttered, and Sarah could hear the fear in her voice. They had all seen so much darkness, so much pain this last year or so, it must have been hard for Hannah to hear about something like this. Sarah gave her hand a quick squeeze under the table, silently comforting her.

"Yeah, I saw it covered in a few places," Kieran replied with a shrug as Xavier handed his phone back and Kieran tucked it back into his pocket. "A bunch of women have gone missing along that road. I don't know if they think it's the same person, or maybe just the weather that's taking them out, but..." He trailed off, leaving the possibilities hanging in the air.

"Isn't there a section of it somewhere called the loneliest highway in America?" Hannah remarked. "I mean, if someone was going to pick a place to hunt for vulnerable women, that would be the one to go for."

"That's Nevada actually. But, I agree," Xavier added. "It's still pretty secluded up in these mountains. Not a lot of places to stop on the winding roads. It could just be the weather, but the fact that it's mostly women going missing...it sets off my alarm bells. I'm going to do a little research, see if there's anything else going on that we might not know about."

"I'm sorry for bringing the mood down," Kieran replied, shaking his head. "I just thought you guys should know."

"No, it's good for us to know," Xavier assured him. "We'll be extra careful from here on out. Keep an eye out for any women traveling by themselves, and make sure they're safe. If they're planning on coming here to the lodge and they're alone, maybe offer them lifts so they're not driving alone."

Sarah glanced over to River, whose face had paled. Cade had found River on the side of the road not too far from there, and Sarah could tell from her expression that she was pondering the possibility of what might have happened if she hadn't been so lucky as to meet him. Would she have ended up being a target? The thought of it made Sarah's stomach twist into a knot. She had become so fond of River since she had arrived here, and the very idea of her getting hurt was more than she could take.

"Everyone, keep your wits about you if you're out there by yourselves," Xavier added, looking around the table. "It's probably nothing, but I don't want any of you getting hurt."

The conversation moved on, as Hannah shifted to something more upbeat—talking about her flower beds and the horses. Soon enough the dour faces turned into smiles, and laughter carried through the room. Leave it to Hannah and her bright personality to turn things around.

Soon, dinner was through and Sarah hung around to help Xavier clean up. As they were collecting and stacking dishes, her skin started to prickle. She could feel him watching her.

"How are you doing?" he asked her. "I saw you talking with Toby earlier."

She sighed, and glanced over at him. "Did Lawson tell you talk to me?"

"He told me to keep an eye on you while he was out."

"Where is he, anyway? I haven't seen him since this morning," she asked, frowning.

"Running errands in town," he replied vaguely. Did he know what Lawson was really doing, or did he just not want to tell her? Either way, she knew that was all he was going to say.

"Okay, well, I'm fine," she replied firmly. "I don't need Lawson telling everyone else my business—"

"He wasn't telling me your business, Sarah," he said, shaking his head like he was disappointed in her that she thought that way about Lawson. "He was just worried about you. Wanted to make sure you were doing okay, that's all."

Now, she felt properly chastised. "I'm okay," she sighed. "I… It's just been a difficult few months, that's all."

"I know," he agreed. "It has been for all of us. But you know you can always speak with one of us if it's getting to be too much for you, right? You don't have to keep it to yourself. No one will fault you. Everyone needs a helping hand now and then."

"I know," she responded, and she managed a smile. "Thanks, Xavier. I'm alright. I needed to clear something up with Toby, but everything's good now."

"You're a great therapist, never doubt that," he told her. "He's lucky to have you. We all are."

She smiled again, this time more sincerely. "Come on, stop trying to butter me up and let's get these tables cleaned," she said playfully, and they began moving the dishes to the kitchen, where River and Hannah were on wash-up duty.

When they were all done, Xavier headed down to the office to finish up some work he'd started before dinner, and Hannah and River walked Sarah back toward her little cabin. It was nothing special, but she enjoyed it much more than the room she stayed in at the lodge. She was glad to have a place just for her, that she could call home.

"It's such a beautiful night," Hannah remarked, tipping back her head to catch the last rays of the sun before they dipped behind the mountain.

"It really is," Sarah agreed, and she glanced over at River. She could tell just from the look on her face that she was preoccupied with the conversation they'd had earlier, about the missing women.

She nudged her gently, pulling her back into the moment. "You okay, River?"

River blinked, and then nodded, wrapping her arms around herself. "I'm fine," she assured them. "I just… I can't stop thinking about those poor women who went missing. It could have been me, if Cade hadn't been there to find me."

"But it wasn't you," Sarah reminded her. "You're okay. You're safe here."

"I know." River sighed, kicking at a loose rock on the ground as they walked. "But—but so many of those women weren't. It doesn't feel fair, you know?"

They reached Sarah's cabin, and she paused, looking at River with a concerned furrow in her brow. She could tell when her friend was struggling, and it was obvious from the look on her face that she was having a hard time holding herself together right now.

"Xavier said he's going to look into it," Hannah reminded her. "If there is anything going on out there, we'll know about it soon enough. And then we can handle it. Right?"

"Right," River agreed, though she sounded far from sure about it. Sarah unlocked the door to her cabin, but before she stepped inside, she felt a cold shiver run along her spine.

She wasn't sure what it was, but all this talk of what had been happening with those missing women had her feeling out of sorts. She couldn't put her finger on exactly what it was that was going through her head right now, but she knew she didn't like it.

And she knew, all too clearly, that it reminded her of what she had felt when she had been sitting opposite Jed in those therapy meetings. And look at how that had ended.

"Anyway, you should get some rest," Hannah told her, leaning over to give her a hug. "I'll see you tomorrow."

"See you tomorrow," Sarah returned, trying to match Hannah's bright smile. She didn't want to be a downer, and she didn't want it getting back to Xavier or Lawson that she seemed twisted up about anything, either.

Or else they were going to make her take that break that she wanted to avoid more than anything in the world. And the thought of giving up—or even taking a break from—her work, the one thing that was keeping her distracted right now, was more than she could bear.

Chapter Five

Lawson sat opposite Lainey in Reed's Café, as she clung to a cup of cinnamon-scented decaf coffee like it was a buoy in the middle of a stormy sea. Her gaze darted left and right, and Lawson eyed her with sympathy.

"Nobody's going to come looking for you here," he assured her. "You have nothing to worry about. Okay?"

"I don't know if I believe that," she admitted, shaking her head and chewing her lip.

"You trust me, right?" he pointed out. "That's why you came here in the first place. So, talk to me, Lainey. Tell me what's going on."

She sighed deeply, and he could tell it came from some place deep down in her soul. She was clearly carrying the weight of something enormous on her back, and she was struggling to keep herself upright underneath it.

"I trust you," she admitted. "I just… I've kept all of this under wraps for so long, or at least, I've tried to. I'm not used to talking about it."

"You called me, remember. Talking about it is the only way we're going to be able to help you," he told her gently. "You've got to tell me what you're running from."

She nodded, taking a sip of her coffee. He couldn't help but notice that her hands were shaking. Damn, he had seen her handle a whole lot when they had been working at the agency together, so for something to spook her this badly, it had to be big.

"I came across something strange on one of the recent accounts I was responsible for running a financial analysis on," she explained. "I kept running across this one particular name and the name kept popping up in some unusual places. He wasn't connected to the accounts I was working on, but somehow, he seemed to be paying in and withdrawing from one of the connected accounts, then different kinds of accounts branching out from it."

Lainey took a deep breath before continuing and Lawson sat back and crossed his arms as he processed her words.

"I know it wasn't part of my job, but I started following the different trails and some dead-ended but others continued to branch off into other accounts owned by him or shell companies disguised as legitimate businesses. The man was apparently running several different schemes and had his hands in a lot of illegal stuff—everything bad you could think of, and probably more."

"Were you able to find a name? Or a main account where all the funds were flowing through?"

Lainey glanced at him again and lowered her voice even more. "I couldn't find them all, but I found some. And the man's name is Victor. Victor Granger. He's the head of a big crime ring and runs pretty much everything you can imagine. Drugs, weapons and…trafficking, Lawson. He has all these young women and even girls working for him. He's brutal and sadistic in his punishments and revenge."

His eyes widened and tension ran through his entire body. It didn't surprise him that she had caught on to something like that.

She had always been smart and observant, and able to spot when something was off. She was the last person he'd want looking into him if he was trying to pull off crimes of the magnitude she was describing.

"So what did you do?" he asked, leaning forward with interest.

"I collected everything I'd found and took it to the higher-ups," she explained. "Presented a case. Told them that we needed to put together an operation to bring him down before he did any more damage than he already had, or hurt any more people. I even offered to organize and lead the operation if they wanted me to."

"And what did they say?"

"They told me in no uncertain terms to back off," she sighed, shaking her head.

He frowned. "Why the hell…"

"Said that I was paranoid and looking for problems where there weren't any because of my past as an agent. Some thought I was actually looking to be in the spotlight," she continued, and he could hear the venom in her voice. She didn't like being pushed off a case for any reason, and this—this sounded big.

"So what are you doing here?" he demanded. "If they told you to back off?"

"When the hell have I ever been good at leaving anything alone?" she pointed out, giving him a wry smile.

"True. You never knew how to back off or to let someone else take over," he replied with a smirk, shaking his head.

"I continued looking into him. He's running a trafficking and kidnapping ring along a highway not far from here, Highway Fifty. His crew is grabbing unsuspected women off the road and he's forcing them to work for him or selling them to clients. I've even tracked a few missing women to a couple of ports to the east and then they've disappeared. I assumed they'd been sold overseas. He's got twin sons, Lyle and Nelson, who are in on it, too. And he's been getting away with it for far too long. Too many people have been turning a blind eye to it all. I couldn't just sit back and pretend I hadn't seen what I did. Know what I know."

"And, let me guess. He figured out that you'd been tracking him?" he asked.

She nodded. "And it's put a target on my back." She sighed. "And my family, too. That's why I'm here. My tires were slashed, my house was vandalized. My husband took the kids to Florida to stay with his family. I just have to hope that I can keep their attention on me. I couldn't handle if something happened to my family."

Her voice cracked as she spoke, the pain evident. Lawson could see how much this was wearing her down. Her eyes looked lifeless with dark circles underneath, and she appeared a lot older. And not just because ten years had passed. This was something else, something heavier, a weight that she wasn't going to be able to shift from her shoulders until she knew the threat to her family was over.

When she said she wasn't going to be able to leave this alone, he knew she was telling the truth. He hoped he would be able to provide the help she obviously needed.

"This has bad news written all over it, Lainey," he muttered.

"And Granger's not going to take kindly to someone trying to put themselves in the middle of it," she continued. "I know. And I'm sorry to bring this to your door, I just didn't know if there was anyone else I could trust. I can't help but think that there's at least a few leadership in his pocket, or they've at least been threatened by him in some way to just turn a blind eye. I can't see any other reason they'd ignore my information."

"I understand. You were right to come to me," he promised her. "I'll do everything I can to help you with this and to protect you. You have my word on that."

She closed her eyes and leaned back in her seat. "I knew there was a reason I came to you," she murmured, and a small smile crossed her lips. "We always made a good team, right?"

"Agreed," he replied, and he lowered his voice and leaned forward. "So what can you tell me about this guy?"

"Hell, I don't know where to start," she replied. "I think the most pressing thing is the kidnappings he's been doing along Highway Fifty. From everything I've been able to find out about him, he's been laying traps with his goons along the most isolated parts of the roads, and waiting for a woman to come by—hitchhiking, driving alone, something like that—and they offer them help."

"Stopping them someplace isolated like that highway would definitely work. Not a lot around and no one to see or hear anything to report it," Lawson mused.

"Sometimes, they don't even seem to use traps, they just grab them as long as they're alone. Then they sell them off or set them to work doing who knows what. I don't even know what to think about what that might involve. Those poor women."

He grimaced. He was pretty sure he'd heard some talk about women who'd gone missing along the highway lately, and this might explain what had happened to them. The thought of it... God, it made him sick. He'd dealt with a lot of evil people in his time as an agent, but the human traffickers were the lowest of the low, as far as he was concerned.

Abusing the vulnerable to make money, forcing them out into the streets to earn for them... And if this guy was targeting young women, then they could be almost certain that it was sex trafficking, too.

"I want you to pass on to me all the information you have, as soon as you can," he told her. "I'll go through it and see if there's anything we can do. We're in touch with law enforcement here, and I'm sure they'll be willing to help us."

"You think you can trust them?" she asked doubtfully.

He nodded. "I know we can," he replied firmly. "We've worked with them on several cases around the area over the years. And in the meantime, you need to lay low. Have you got somewhere to stay in town?"

"Yeah, I have a room at a local motel," she replied. "It's not much, but it's got what I need to work on this."

"You need to get rid of your phone," he went on. "I'll get you a burner. Let me know the room number you're staying in and I'll get it delivered—"

"Who do you think I am?" she joked, raising her eyebrows. "Of course, I already got rid of my phone. Here's the number for my burner and the info I've got right now." She slid a small piece of paper with her number scribbled on it and a thumb drive across the table.

He grinned as he reached for them. There she was, the woman he had known all those years ago. The badass who would stand up for herself and others and always do what was right, no matter what the world threw at her.

"Of course, you have," he replied. "I'll contact you after I look through everything, okay?"

"Right," she answered, her voice a little shaky, as though she didn't entirely believe that he would be able to help her. He knew this must have been a last resort for her. They hadn't spoken in years, but he was glad she had reached out to him. Especially since it affected the area he now called home.

"It's going to be alright, Lainey," he told her with a confidence he didn't quite feel.

The truth was, he didn't know exactly what they were in for. The last thing he wanted was to bring trouble back to the lodge again. They'd only just finished rebuilding from their last couple of dangerous events—the fire and Jed's destruction.

But when someone came to him looking for help, he was never going to turn them down. That was why he and Xavier had started Warrior Peak Sanctuary in the first place—because there were so many people out there who needed some form of help. They wanted the lodge to be that place, a safe haven where those in trouble could turn to for assistance, or stay.

"You'll get back to your family in no time," he promised her. "We'll bring this Granger asshole and his sons down, and he's not going to have a chance to hurt anyone else. You hear me?"

"I hear you," she replied, and she grinned at him. "Maybe I can introduce you to my kids when all of this is over, huh?"

"Maybe you can," he replied, smiling back at her. He liked that thought. Just because they had both moved on with their lives didn't mean that their friendship couldn't be rekindled. They had been through so much together back in the day. And he'd love for her to meet the others and see the lodge, too.

But right now, he couldn't focus too much on the future. No, he had to think about what was right in front of him, and that was making sure that they did whatever they could to protect her and shut down this crime ring.

Because he would be damned if he let someone else get hurt. He'd seen enough of that the last year or so, and if it was in his power to do something about it, then he definitely would.

Even if going after someone like Victor Granger, someone with the power to scare off the biggest agencies, was probably going to put one hell of a target on his back.

Chapter Six

Sarah closed her office door and turned to walk the short distance to her cabin, inhaling the fragrance of Hannah's peonies on the pathway. Today had been a good day.

A much better day than the one before, anyway. She'd had another session with Toby this afternoon, and though she had initially been a little worried about how it was going to go, it had been far easier than she had imagined. He had been willing to work with her, willing to hear her out, and the two of them actually seemed to get along better than they had before. Like he could see her vulnerabilities now, and had connected to them in some ways, especially after everything he had been through.

Yesterday had been nothing more than an off day, and she was more than happy to leave it behind her for good. On a day like today, it was hard to be in anything but a good mood, with the way the sun was shining down above her. Summer was always the best time of year—the bright days, the long evenings, where you could sit around and talk late into the night without getting too chilly. And, after the year they'd had, they deserved a chance to really kick back and unwind.

She looked up and caught sight of Lawson standing outside the front of the lodge, frowning down at his phone. She could tell even from where she stood that he looked tired. She hoped he hadn't been worrying about her, given how much better she was already doing. She hadn't had a chance to talk to him again since the morning before, when Toby had stormed out of her office upset.

She changed direction and headed over to speak to him, and he tucked away his phone when she approached and met her gaze. She could see dark rings under his eyes, and wondered if he had gotten any sleep last night. She hoped there was nothing going on with the lodge, nothing dangerous…

"Everything okay?" she asked him.

He nodded. "Fine," he replied, his voice a little more curt than she was used to.

She blinked at him in surprise. "I just wanted to tell you I'm feeling so much better," she said, gushing to him. "I had another session with Toby today, and it went really well—"

"I think it'd be good for you to take a break."

She stopped dead in her tracks.

"Wh-what?" she stuttered. "What are you talking about? I just told you I'm fine."

"I still think you could do with some time away from the lodge," he replied. "Let me get you an apartment in town. And a therapist. Somewhere you can really unwind after everything that happened."

She parted her lips in surprise. What was he talking about? First, he had just been suggesting a break, not moving out of the lodge, but now…

"It would do you good, having a quiet place where you could work through your trauma," he continued.

"Trauma?" she asked. "Who said anything about trauma? I've just been having a hard time lately, that's all—"

"Sarah, you know I only want what's best for you. You may not see—or want to see—it as trauma, but that's exactly what Jed did. He terrorized you in your own safe space. It's normal for you to feel uneasy after that. Anyone would. You're a therapist, you know this," he told her firmly, his eyes locking on to hers with a serious expression.

She had no idea what to say. She was completely caught off-guard, and didn't know how to navigate this conversation he'd sprung on her. She'd been so happy with her progress earlier today and wanted to share it with Lawson. Now, he was trying to get rid of her. But why?

"You're just trying to get rid of me," she retorted, practically daring him to argue with her.

He sighed. "That's not what I'm trying to do. I just want you to be safe."

"And I'm safe here!" she protested. "Unless—unless there's something you're not telling me about?"

He didn't reply, letting her words hang heavily in the air. Her eyes widened. *What the hell?*

"Lawson, is something going on?" she asked, her voice shaking slightly.

He shook his head at once, but she could tell from the look on his face that he was lying to her.

"Is someone threatening the lodge again?" she persisted.

"No," he replied. "I'm just… I'm trying to do what's best for you. To protect you."

She locked her eyes on to his, tension strung tight between them. Tension that she tried her best to ignore. Because he was one of the owners of the lodge, and her boss. It would make things way too complicated if something happened between them—even though she truly wanted it to.

But now, as he stood before her, she couldn't help but notice the way his eyes burned into hers. The way his body shifted to be closer to her.

"I don't know how to explain it all to you right now," he told her. "But I will. I promise."

"You better," she muttered. "Because right now, it seems like you just want me gone."

"That's not it at all. Please believe me."

"Then tell me how you really feel," she demanded. She wanted him to acknowledge what was between them. She wanted to know that it wasn't all one-sided on her part. Didn't she deserve that? Or, more to the point, didn't they?

"You know how I feel about you," he murmured.

She shook her head and took a step toward him. The warm air around them seemed to be holding its breath, waiting to see how this was going to turn out.

"I don't, not really," she protested. "You've never told me."

"You're good at your job," he told her.

"And is that it?" she asked. "I'm good at my job and that's why you want to keep me around?"

"That's not what I'm saying."

"No, I can see that," she said. She knew this wasn't fair, this wasn't the smartest way to go about this conversation, but right now, she didn't give a damn. She just wanted him to admit it—to admit what they had been dancing around for months now.

She continued. "You want me out of your hair, so you can, I don't know, focus on someone else?"

His eyes drilled into hers, a flash of anger passing across his face. "That's not true," he growled. His voice dropped, the emotion finally showing. That was what she needed to see from him—the proof that whatever was happening here, it wasn't just in her head. There was something between them. No matter how complicated that might make things.

"So what is true, then?" she asked. "Why are you trying so hard to get me to leave?"

"Because I can't stand the thought of anything happening to you," he responded through gritted teeth. Normally, Lawson was so careful in how he carried himself, but right now, she could see the restraint cracking—she could see him giving in to this feeling between them.

"You're being selfish," she protested. "You just want me gone so you don't have to deal with whatever this could be between us."

"That's not it at all," he replied, moving closer to her, hands coming to her arms, like he was holding her in place. Making sure she wouldn't slip through his fingers. Her breath caught in her throat, and her eyes flicked to his mouth and the stubble across his strong jaw. Her fingers itched to reach out and touch it, to feel it beneath her fingertips.

"Then tell me to stay," she breathed. "Show me that you don't want me to go."

Those words hung between them, almost a dare—she was pleading with him to show her just how much he needed her there. Hopefully, as much as she needed to be there with him.

He was the grounding force that had kept her on her feet these last few months, and she couldn't bear the thought of being somewhere without him.

But, instead of speaking, he drew her close to him and pressed his lips onto hers for the first time.

The moment their lips touched, she melted into him. This was what she had been waiting for all this time—his kiss, his promise, the knowledge that he felt this need between them, too. Though they had both pretended not to notice it for the sake of keeping things professional, there was no denying it.

His arms slid to her waist and he gripped her tightly, like he didn't want to let her go. She reached up, her fingers finding purchase in his hair, the feeling almost surreal after all this time. They were outside the lodge, where anyone could see them, but she didn't care. It felt like the world stood still to give them this moment. It felt right.

When he held her, she felt safe in a way she hadn't in a long time. That sure, strong sense of certainty, knowing that nothing could hurt her as long as she was right here, in his arms. This was where she belonged, whether she had been willing to admit it or not. She was just glad they were finally having this moment between them.

Then, all of a sudden, he pulled back. She let out a small gasp, not ready for it to be over yet. He dropped his hands back to his sides and drew his gaze away from her, as though looking her in the face would have ignited something he knew he couldn't control. She stared at him, willing him to look at her again, to acknowledge what had just happened, but he didn't.

"That didn't change anything, did it? You still want me to go," she demanded, her voice low. Her breath hitched in her throat as she silently begged him to respond to her. She desperately wanted him to say it was all a misunderstanding. That he needed her like she needed him. But the words never came.

Instead, he just stood before her, not saying a word. Her heart thudded in her chest and tears gathered in her eyes, but she refused to let them fall. Not here, not in front of him. She'd shatter later, when she was alone and could process it all.

She was hoping admitting their feelings would change things

for the better. They'd be able to move past this bump in the road and be together. But she got it. He couldn't risk having a liability like her around after the way she freaked out at a patient. They had a reputation to uphold and she'd been anything but professional in her behavior that day. He couldn't trust her.

"Fine," she muttered. "You don't have to say anything. I get it. I'll go."

And with that, she turned on her heel and started to march back toward the cabin. The tears were blurring her eyes now, but she blinked them back, not wanting him to see how much all of this had hurt her. She couldn't let him know how long she had been aching for that kiss—or how painful it was to know that it still wasn't enough for him to want to keep her around.

She swiped away the tears as she stepped through the door to her cabin, the pressure of that kiss still lingering on her lips. She had dreamed of kissing Lawson like that for a long time, but she had never imagined she would be reduced to tears after it happened.

Something was off around here; she was sure of it. But, right now, it wasn't her business to stick around and find out what it was. Lawson wanted her gone? She was gone.

And she wasn't going to waste another minute thinking about him.

At least, that was what she had to tell herself.

Chapter Seven

"You've looked over the files I put together for you?" Lawson inquired as he strode into the office where Xavier, Cade and Aaron were waiting for him.

All three of them nodded.

"It's a lot to take in," Cade admitted, as Lawson took his usual seat at the other side of the desk.

"I know," he agreed. "But I want you to be as prepared as possible. Granger's got a serious reputation and the last thing we want is to be walking into this situation without everything we need to know."

"How did you even come across this case, anyway?" Xavier asked, as he leafed through the papers of the file Lawson had delivered to them that morning. He'd called a meeting with the guys, not giving many details at the time, and he was glad to have them here and ready to go. He always felt better when he had a team in place, ready to take on whatever was out there waiting for them. Especially a team like this one.

"It's a long story, but the shorter version is Lainey," he replied, clasping his hands in front of him.

"Lainey. As in *Lainey Daye* Lainey? This is why she contacted you?" Xavier inquired with a furrowed brow. Aaron and Cade looked at the men, waiting for more details.

Aaron spoke up. "For those of us not in the know, who's Lainey?"

"She's someone I partnered with over a decade ago in the CIA—we were good friends. She left the active side of the agency and went on to become an analyst when she started a family. This came across her desk while she was doing research on a case." Lawson rubbed a hand down his face. "It's blown up into a big deal for her, put a target on her back, so she came here looking for my help."

Cade's curt voice cut in. "So she stirred up a hornet's nest and brought it to you for us to help clean it up?"

"It wasn't really her fault—"

"Lawson, seriously," Xavier interrupted. "What you're not saying is she was told to stand down for whatever reason and she kept digging, got herself in trouble." He shook his head. "I didn't work with her, but I remember how she did things."

Lawson sighed. "She didn't do it deliberately, Xavier. If something like this crossed your desk, would you ignore it? It's missing women, trafficking young women, maybe even girls…in our backyard."

"I've been thinking about this since Kieran showed us— and sent Lawson—that article last night. It made everyone at the table uneasy with possible danger so close. I think we should help," Aaron offered. "I mean, our women drive these roads all the time. What if it ended up being one of them? You'd be kicking your own asses or worse if something happened."

Lawson nodded his head toward Aaron in thanks. He appreciated him voicing his thoughts on the matter, because that's exactly where his own had gone. Aaron was a former police officer and engaged to Bailey, who currently worked as a cop down in Blue Ridge. She and the other women there at the lodge traveled to town on these roads all the time. If something ever happened to any of them when the guys could help prevent it…

"What I need to know is whether or not you think you're going to be able to handle it." Lawson directed his comment to the other two men.

Xavier and Cade exchanged a glance. For the first time in a long time, Lawson saw some doubt on Xavier's face.

"Problem?" he asked.

"From this file, this is a large crime ring and this guy sounds pretty dangerous," Xavier remarked. "You sure it's something we can handle?"

Lawson frowned. If there was one person he always expected to jump into a new mission feetfirst, it was Xavier.

"Yeah, I know we can," Lawson replied. "Unless you've got your doubts."

"It's not doubts, exactly." Xavier sighed. "It's just…this guy sounds like seriously bad news and we have no idea how many men he's got working for him. I don't want to bring that kind of trouble here to the lodge. Again. We built this place as a safe haven for people who needed it. To help them recover and find their way after the hell they'd seen and been through. And this place has seen more danger than it ever should have over the last year. We're still recovering from the last. And… Hannah. Now there's something here I know I need to protect."

Lawson grimaced. He should have expected this. Xavier and Hannah had fallen for each other hard and fast these last several months, and Xavier wasn't the guy he had been when they had first started Warrior Peak and the tactical unit. He was more settled now, more focused on what was good for him, instead of what would give him a thrill in the moment.

"I don't crave the excitement or need the adrenaline rush the way I used to," he continued, gesturing down to the file in front of him. "Justice? For sure. But danger? I don't know if I can handle that again. Or handle putting Hannah in the middle of that. I'm still dealing with what happened last time."

"Agreed," Cade echoed. "This really hit home for River. She's been more unsettled since Kieran mentioned the missing women at dinner. She could have been one of those women. It took her a long time to feel safe again after all she went through and it's brought a lot of that back up for her."

Lawson could see why Cade would be particularly protective of her. A crazed cult leader had chased River hundreds of miles to kidnap her, planning on taking her home to marry him. Cade had actually picked her up hitchhiking on the side of the road on his way to the lodge a few years ago. So, yeah, he understood. Everyone there at the lodge had demons of some sort they dealt with and this would stir a lot of them up.

He got it on a more personal level, too. Because there was someone here he cared about, more than he could put into words. Hell, when she had asked him to elaborate earlier, he hadn't been able to. He could still remember, all too clearly, the way she had looked at him, the pain in her eyes when he hadn't been able to come out with what he needed to say.

He should have told her a little of what was going on. She'd asked if there was danger, and instead of ignoring her question, he should have offered something. Anything, so she'd understand that he was just concerned about her safety, that he wasn't trying to kick her out or get rid of her for good. It was for protection…because he cared and he didn't want her in the line of fire. Knowing what a man like Victor was capable of, if he got his hands on Sarah…

"I don't get why the cops can't handle this, anyway," Cade remarked, interrupting his thoughts.

Lawson shook his head. "That's the problem," he explained. "When Lainey brought this to me, she said she took her findings to the higher-ups and they shut her down. Told her to drop it immediately. She thinks a few might be looking the other way deliberately or involved in some way. Shortly after that, she was targeted. Had to move her family to Florida and she came here for help. She's determined to finish it and she can't go home until she knows her family is safe and the threat is gone."

"And she came to you because you worked together?" Cade asked.

"Because she knows she needs this dealt with by people outside law enforcement," he replied, narrowing his eyes. "And by people who aren't going to get tangled in red tape."

"And you think we can trust her?" Xavier wondered aloud.

"I know we can," Lawson said. "She needs our help. If she could have dealt with this on her own, she would have. But she can't. And if this guy gets to her…" His gut clenched at the thought. He didn't even want to let his mind go there.

Xavier rolled his shoulders back, nodding. "Then I guess we have to do something about it," he said, his voice certain.

"And you agree with her assessment that this Granger guy and his sons are responsible for the women who've been going missing on the highway?" Cade asked.

"It makes sense from the information she collected on the guy. I would be shocked if that wasn't mostly him," Lawson replied. "All the more reason to get this under control. I don't want him operating close to us, when we've got so many vulnerable people coming here. If he picked up someone who was looking to get to the lodge, I don't think I would be able to forgive myself." He shook his head, trying to eliminate the thought from his mind.

"So how exactly do we move forward with this, then?" Cade asked, flipping through the file on Granger once more.

"We need to get our hands on one of the guys working for him," Xavier suggested. "The file said he had a bunch of guys stationed out along the road. They likely aren't heavily armed or well-defended. It wouldn't be too difficult to shake one of them loose, get them talking to us. I doubt they're all that loyal to him."

"I wouldn't be so sure," Lawson warned. "This guy's got his hands in everything. There's probably no limit to what he'd do to keep his thugs loyal to him. Threaten families, hook them on drugs."

Or maybe that was just what Lawson had to believe. Because if he was honest with himself, and admitted that there were people out there willing to do stuff like that without any good reason, it would have messed with his mind.

"Either way, we can't afford to wait around. Aside from your friend being in danger, think of all the innocent women they've already grabbed or plan to. Our women here," Aaron reminded them.

"We have to find his base of operations in the area, and we need at least one of Granger's guys to give us a location. And we need to do it fast before another woman goes missing," Cade confirmed.

The thought of it set Lawson's teeth on edge. He knew they were right. He still couldn't wrap his head around the fact that this had been going on in their backyard and he hadn't known.

It could have continued happening right under their noses and he would have had no clue.

Until it came to Warrior Peak. Until it hurt someone he cared about.

Until it came for Sarah.

He shifted in his seat, turning his attention back to what mattered here. They needed a tight plan, and the guys were right—they needed to act fast.

"Alright, let's do this then. We also need to call Sheriff Willis and go over all this with him when we have an idea of how we're going about it," Lawson declared. "We know for a fact he's on our side, and he'll be aware of the disappearances since it's outside Blue Ridge. We'll need his help officially, if we manage to catch anyone."

They went through the file again, running over every detail to make sure they were all on the same page. It was a lot to take in, Lawson knew that, and he didn't want to risk anything by not making certain that the guys were clear on the task at hand.

They tried to figure out where Victor's base of operations might be, derived from the information that they already had, but there wasn't much to go on. There were a lot of isolated areas up in the mountains where they could be hiding. There had clearly been a concerted effort to make sure nobody could gather too much intel on this guy. Who did he have in his pocket? And how much harder was that going to make their job?

Much as Lawson was trying to stay focused, he found his mind drifting back to Sarah. He couldn't stop thinking about the way she had looked at him before, the pain in her eyes when she had called him out and asked him if he really wanted her to stay.

If he'd had any sense, he would have told her yes, of course, he did, that he needed her here. That he would do anything to keep her around. But he couldn't, not right now, not with everything that was going on.

And now, she was going. He had passed her cabin earlier, and had seen an open suitcase sitting on the bed, half-filled with her clothes. It had made his chest pang with regret, and he wished he could take it all back, wished he could just tell her how sorry he was and that he didn't mean for it to happen like that, didn't mean for her to actually leave.

Since everything that had gone down with Jed, he had been extra protective of her, and aware of just how vulnerable she was. Aware of just how much it would have hurt if something had happened to her.

When he had seen her right after the attack, the rage he'd felt had caught him off guard. He could normally control himself, even in the most impossible of situations, but with her, it was different. With her, his emotions took control, and he would have done anything to get revenge on the person who had done that to her.

Thinking back to their earlier conversation, he should have handled it better. Told her a little about the situation and asked if she'd be willing to take a short break. Hang out in town and concentrate on herself for a bit. Not make it seem like he didn't want her around. Like he was kicking her out.

He knew it wouldn't have been forever, but *she* hadn't. Not the way he voiced his concerns. When they were done with their meeting, he could seek her out and try to explain. Because if something else happened to Sarah, he would never forgive himself.

But right now, he needed to stay on task. Finish going over the information with the guys and figure out a plan to take down Granger and his crew. Then he'd see where things stood with Sarah. The stakes were too high to get distracted right now.

Chapter Eight

As Sarah stuffed her clothes into her bag, she tried to ignore the women who were standing in the doorway, watching her pack.

"You don't have to just pack up and go right this instant," Bailey protested.

Sarah didn't pay attention to her. She folded up a top with shaky hands, then tossed it into the pile. "Yes, I do," Sarah replied through gritted teeth. "Lawson made that very clear."

"He didn't tell you to pack up and go today, did he?" River asked her.

Sarah paused. Okay, he hadn't said *that* to her. In fact, after the kiss, he hadn't said anything to her. But that had been more than enough for her to wrap her head around what he wanted, and she wasn't going to hang out and pretend like she was fine being in a place she wasn't wanted. "No, but—"

"Then you need to sit down for a second and take a breath," Bailey told her as she put a hand on Sarah's shoulder and guided her to the edge of the bed. "Talk to him. Figure this out. He probably didn't mean it the way it sounded. You know how men can be…"

"Pigheaded?" Sarah retorted. "Arrogant? Mean?"

"I was going to say poor communicators," Bailey replied, chuckling slightly. "I'm sure Lawson didn't mean it to come across the way it did."

Sarah took a deep breath and sighed.

"I know he really cares about you," Bailey continued, as Sarah put her head in her hands. "There has to be something more to this than what it seems on the surface. He wouldn't just kick you out like that, with such little warning."

"He thinks it's for my own good," Sarah said, rolling her eyes. "So I can recover from…you know, from everything that happened with Jed."

"So he's got the right intentions, then?" River asked.

"Yeah, he just wants you to get better," Bailey told her.

Sarah frowned. "By leaving this place?" she asked. "I don't see how that would work. I don't want to go. This is my home."

Both of the women fell silent for a moment, and then, River cut in once more.

"I don't see why you should have to leave to do that," she pointed out. "I mean, the internet is a thing. You could do therapy online. You shouldn't have to leave if you don't want to."

"My thoughts exactly," Sarah replied, smiling up at River thankfully.

"And, I don't know about everyone else, but I'd miss having you around," River added. Bailey put an arm around Sarah and gave her a squeeze.

"I would, too," she agreed. Sarah leaned her head on her shoulder for a moment, feeling another rush of emotion.

She'd never be able to cope with being away from her friends. The support and comfort she got from them was irreplaceable. She had never felt more accepted and safer than she did there at the lodge. The thought of leaving them and her home, even if only for a little while, made her chest ache. It just didn't feel fair. No matter what Lawson's motivations might have been for trying to encourage her to leave, they felt cruel to her.

"Thanks," Sarah mumbled a little sadly. No matter what they thought about her, if Lawson had decided that she needed to leave, what choice did she have? He co-owned the place, after all, and if he wanted her to take a break, that was that.

She just still couldn't believe he wanted her gone. One little freak-out and he was pushing her out the door. No! No. It just wasn't right. There had to be more to it. She'd worked too hard to get where she was and she wasn't going to let him tell her she had to go. She couldn't abandon all the people who came to her for help, all the progress she'd made with them in their recoveries.

"You guys are right," she told them, suddenly feeling a surge of certainty in her chest. That kiss had thrown her for a loop and scattered her brain, but now she was thinking clearly. Her mind was back on track. She knew what she needed, and she needed to be here; she wasn't about to let Lawson just kick her out. This was her home and she wasn't going anywhere.

"You're going to stay?" Bailey asked, her face brightening.

Sarah nodded with a smile. "I'm going to stay," she replied. "There are too many people who depend on me for guidance and I don't want them to have setbacks. I need to stay busy, too, keep to a routine. I can work on my own stuff while still helping others with theirs, right? I don't have to leave to deal with my own problems."

"Exactly what I was thinking," River agreed. "You've got the right idea."

"Yeah, I don't know why Lawson was trying to chase me out of here," she remarked, shaking her head. "I work with so many of the residents, what would they have done while I was away? Bring in someone unfamiliar? That could cause other issues and setbacks. Honestly, sometimes, I don't know what's going on inside his head."

River and Bailey exchanged a look, which Sarah noticed at once.

She furrowed her brow and glanced between them. "What is it?" she asked, confused.

"You really don't know, do you?" Bailey asked, with a slight laugh.

"I really don't," she replied. "You want to fill me in?"

"You know, for a smart woman, you can be really dense sometimes," River teaser her gently.

"I have no idea what you're talking about," Sarah protested. "Why are you looking at me like that? What am I missing?"

"You really don't know how Lawson feels about you?" Bailey asked.

Sarah frowned at her. Had she seen the kiss? She hoped not. She felt like she didn't want that exposed to anyone else. She was hurt and embarrassed about what had happened after the kiss, and she didn't want to have to explain all of that to anyone.

"I mean, I know… I guess he… But he wants me gone," she replied.

"He wants to keep you safe," River said gently. "He's protective of you. That's what this is all about."

Sarah shook her head in denial. "I don't know if I can believe that," she muttered, looking down at her hands. It was a sweet thought, him caring about her like that. But if he really wanted her, then he would have told her that after their kiss. Instead, he just stared at her, jaw set tight, unable to come out and say what she needed to hear.

"You should," Bailey laughed. "Everyone else can see it. Including us."

"Yeah, well, until I hear it from him, I think I'll play it safe," she insisted.

She could sense that the two of them were still not entirely convinced by her protestations, and she felt heat rising in her cheeks.

"Wait, you're blushing," River pointed out all of a sudden.

Sarah ducked her head, willing her cheeks to stop giving away her thoughts. She hoped her friends would just drop it.

She should have known better.

"You're blushing because you're thinking about Lawson, aren't you?" Bailey teased.

"No, it's not that!" Sarah protested. "I just… I don't know."

"Did something happen between the two of you?" River asked eagerly, planting herself on the edge of the bed and looking at her expectantly.

Sarah parted her lips, considering what to say. Maybe it would do her good to share what was going on with them, and get it off her chest. These women were her friends, and she knew she could trust them.

"I mean, I guess you could say that," she admitted.

Bailey clapped her hands together. "Okay, now you totally have to spill," she urged her. "What happened?"

Sarah pushed a hand through her curls. She had been doing her best to keep the memory of the kiss from her mind, but having them bring it up like this, it was impossible not to remember the pressure of his fingertips on her hips, the way he pulled her into him like he needed to be as close to her as possible. The way his hair felt between her fingers.

"It was…it was just a kiss," she told them finally, dropping her chin to her chest. She couldn't believe she was talking about this with them. She knew they were going to demand the details.

"Oh, my God, finally!" Bailey exclaimed, tossing her hands up in the air. "I think that means I win the betting pool."

"Tell me you're kidding," Sarah replied.

Bailey laughed. "Yeah, yeah, I'm kidding," she assured her. "But what was it like? Was it everything you hoped it would be?"

Sarah bit her lip. "It was…a lot," she admitted. "It came in the middle of an argument. He was telling me that he wanted me to go, and I was making it clear that I didn't want to leave. We were arguing about it, and I kept challenging him, getting in his face, and then all of a sudden, we were just…kissing."

"Whoa!" Bailey exclaimed. "That sounds kind of hot!"

"It was intense," Sarah said, biting her lip. She remembered the feel of it, the heat moving from his body to hers, like they were silently communicating something between them. She couldn't help but wonder what would have happened if they hadn't been arguing, had just been having a regular conversation, and not in public. Would they have kissed more? Taken their desire in a different direction?

"Did it feel good to get everything out in the open like that?" River asked.

Sarah sighed. "I guess it would have, if it hadn't come in those circumstances," she replied. "I can't figure out what he wants from me, if anything at all. And that kiss, it just made everything way more confusing. It's just such a mess."

"I can imagine," Bailey told her kindly. "But you should cut Lawson some slack. All the time I've known him, he's been friendly but a little closed-off. He's more serious, overly cautious. Of this place and the people he cares about. With everything that's gone down lately, I think it's brought out the more protective side of him. He just wants to keep everyone safe and thinks it's his responsibility to make sure that happens. Not get wrapped up in feelings."

"I guess so," Sarah admitted. "But I feel like I shouldn't have to put up with all this back and forth. If he wants me here—if he wants me at all—he should come out and tell me. Even if he doesn't want to act on it now. I have a right to know and for him to not push me away."

"In a perfect world, for sure," River mused. "But think about everything he's been through in the last year. What we've all been through. It's not that much of a surprise that he would struggle to share his feelings. He might think it would make him too vulnerable to open up like that."

"Yeah, him trying to send you away could be his way of telling you that he wants to keep you close," Bailey suggested.

"And how would that work?" Sarah asked skeptically.

"Hey, I can't read the mind of any man," Bailey protested, holding her hands up. "Maybe you just have to give it time. Talk to him about how you feel."

"And maybe kiss him again?" River suggested.

Sarah couldn't help but laugh. "I'm pretty sure that would just make everything more complicated," she replied. But, at the back of her mind, she felt a tingle of excitement at the thought of feeling his mouth on hers again, feeling his hands wrapped around her, that strong, protective grip that made everything make sense.

"Well, whatever happens, I'm staying," Sarah announced as she started to pull some of her clothes out of her bag. "If he thinks he's getting rid of me that easily, he's going to be in for a surprise."

"Agreed," Bailey replied. "We'd stage a protest if he tried to get rid of you, don't worry."

"Good to know you guys have my back." She laughed, and she got up to give River a hug. Honestly, she didn't know what she would do without these women. They were her family just as much as this place was her home.

Chapter Nine

"I'll catch up with you in the morning, alright?" Lawson told Xavier as they stepped out of his office. "We can figure out exactly what we're going to need to pull this off. And how many favors we're going to need to call in to make it happen."

"Sure. And don't forget the sheriff," Xavier replied. His eyes were filled with certainty and focus. He might have been reluctant to get involved with this in the first place, but now that he was in on it, Lawson could tell he wasn't going to let anything get in the way of seeing this through.

"Right," Lawson confirmed. "After we run through everything one more time tomorrow, I'll give him a call and fill him in on what we're doing. Maybe he can make a few inquiries of his own. That way they won't lead back to us."

It had been a long day of planning. Cade and Aaron had left a short time ago to handle a couple of things they needed to tend to, then go spend time with their women. Lawson and Xavier had continued working on the case, jotting down a few details to follow up on the next day. Afternoon had rolled into evening and now, it was time to take a break. They needed to rest and clear their heads for what was to come. And Xavier was anxious to get back to Hannah, check in and spend some time together.

Which meant there was just one person Lawson needed to speak to now.

Sarah.

She had been on his mind all night, that kiss replaying in his head more times than he could count. More than that, though, the pain on her face when he had stayed silent at her demand to know how he felt about her. He had frozen, torn between wanting her close to him and wanting her to leave for her own safety. He couldn't find the words to express that. Now, he could see how much it must have hurt her, and he would do everything he could to put that right.

Because she was his priority right now. Everyone else on staff at the lodge was coupled up, and they all took care of each other. They could deal with their own stuff on their own terms. But Sarah? Sarah was out on her own, and still struggling with the impact of what had happened with Jed, whether she was willing to admit to it or not. And he intended to do everything in his power to help her.

And sending her away, he could see now, wasn't going to actually do anything to aid her in that task. He was just scared—scared about what might happen if she got caught up in the middle of their takedown of Granger and the trafficking ring. What might happen if she was targeted. That thought was more terrifying than anything else.

Instead of thinking with his head, he'd led with his feelings. That worried him, too. Knowing he cared so deeply for someone to be scared down to his bones for their well-being. He wasn't sure how to deal with that. His sister was one thing… she was family. But now, she had Xavier to look after her. But, Sarah… She was something entirely different. He was having a hard time processing it all.

And the kiss.

He wasn't sure what had come over him in that moment. The way she was looking at him, it just lit a fire inside him—something urgent and demanding he couldn't ignore. Like that might have been the last chance he had to kiss her. And he was sure as hell not going to pass it up.

Normally, at this time in the evening, she was reading a

book somewhere outside, enjoying the longer evenings with a glass of wine. Now he didn't know what she was doing. He had seen her at dinner, but she had ignored him, refusing to so much as make eye contact. He couldn't blame her. He'd been an insensitive jerk.

Wandering out to the back porch, he found her reclined on one of the lounge chairs, next to the cold plunge tub. She had a book in one hand and a glass of white wine in the other, condensation forming on the glass.

She glanced up at him, and her eyes narrowed as she laid down her book on her lap. "If you've come to talk to me about leaving, save your breath," she told him. "I'm not going anywhere."

"That's not what I came here to talk about—"

"I'm not leaving my home," she went on, as though she hadn't even heard him. "And before you say anything about the trauma, I've signed up for an online therapist group I got from the recommendation of a colleague I went to school with. The group is going to match me up with a therapist as soon as possible."

"I'm glad to hear it," he replied. "But I don't want you to leave, Sarah."

She stared at him like he had grown an extra head. "But you said…"

"I know what I said," he admitted, shoulders slumping down. "Do you mind if I sit?"

"Go ahead," she murmured, not taking her eyes off him. She seemed to have softened slightly, now that he'd told her he wanted her to stay, and he sank down into one of the seats beside her, wishing he had his own glass of wine to take the edge off this conversation.

"I—I'm sorry about the way I spoke to you," he explained. "I know it wasn't right. I was just trying to wrap my head around some stuff that's been happening around here, and I thought you would be better off somewhere else."

"What's been happening?" she asked, tensing slightly.

He knew he had to level with her. She was perceptive, and if he tried to keep anything from her, she was just going to figure it out in her own time, anyway...and then be even more hurt that he had hidden it.

"We've been presented with an urgent case and we're running a tactical operation out of the lodge," he explained. "The guy we're taking on, he's...a big deal. Influential. And we need to act fast."

Her jaw hung open. "I thought you guys were done with all of that?" she asked, dumbfounded.

"I thought we were, too," he admitted. "But I can't walk away from this one. I have to try to help, if I can. A friend of mine, she's in danger, and the guy who's after her... I can't in good conscience just let him continue on with the level of destruction he's causing. He needs to be stopped so she and others can be safe."

"And what about you?" she asked softly. "Are you going to be okay?"

He straightened his shoulders. "I'll be fine," he replied. "The guys and I are good at what we do. Besides, this is who I am. This is what I've always done."

"It doesn't have to stay that way, though," she whispered.

He sighed. "I don't know about that," he replied. "I just know I have to deal with this. No matter what. I can't let this guy get away. And I just... I didn't want you around when it happened. I thought he might target this place if he gets wind of what we're doing, and I wanted you gone so you wouldn't be in his line of fire if that happened."

"You could have just told me that," she pointed out, but he could see the flicker of a smile on her face. He might not have gone about this the right way, but at least she could see that his intentions were pure.

"I know, and I should have," he agreed. "I should have come clean from the start. I know this isn't my decision to make, and you can't make a choice for yourself unless you have all the information you need."

"Thank you for telling me," she replied, and she reached over to give his hand a squeeze. "Can you tell me anything about this operation? Why it's so important to you?"

"I can't tell you too much," he responded. "There's only so much information we have access to right now."

"I'll take whatever you can give me. I assume it has to be pretty major to have you guys involved?"

"Yeah, this guy's into a lot of illegal stuff. But the main thing we're focusing on are the kidnappings happening in this area," he admitted to her. "They could be related to sex trafficking by this guy and his crew."

The blood drained from her face and she lowered her gaze, clearly shocked by what he'd just said.

"Oh," she murmured. "You think the recent kidnappings off the highway are related to that?"

"We think so," he said. "We're still trying to piece everything together, but it looks likely. We're going to get to the bottom of it, though. We're going to stop it. I promise."

"I know you will," she acknowledged. "I know this is your area of expertise. Sorry for pushing for more information. I didn't mean to overstep."

"It's okay," he assured her, rubbing his thumb along her fingers. "I get it."

"And I'm sorry…" she began, hesitating before she forced the words out. "I shouldn't have put you on the spot and demanded to know how you felt about me." She shook her head when he tried to speak. "You should be allowed to share your feelings in your own way, your own time. And the kiss…"

His eyes darkened at the mention of their kiss and his gaze dropped to her mouth. "Oh, I'm definitely not sorry about that," he replied softly.

She bit her lip, staring at him with hopeful eyes. "Really?"

"Really," he assured her, and he moved closer, kneeling on the porch beside her chair. She was so small, he was at eye level with her right now, and those sweet blue-green eyes were softening.

"I've been thinking about kissing you for a long time," he continued, interlocking his fingers with hers. "I'm just sorry it wasn't how I pictured it."

"It wasn't?" she breathed.

"No, I always pictured it…softer," he murmured. He drew

even closer to her, their breath intermingling in the space in front of them.

"You want to show me?" she asked, a smile curling up the corners of her lips.

"If you'll let me," he replied, his gaze burning into hers.

Instead of replying, she nodded and closed her eyes.

So he leaned in the rest of the way, closing the last of the gap between them. Finally, their lips came together again, and this time, it felt far softer, far sweeter.

He reached his hand up to cup her face, and she slid her hands to his arms, holding on to them as though for dear life. He knew just how she felt. There was something about her that felt steady and strong, and as he deepened the kiss, he knew this was what he had been waiting for. Not the two of them, overwhelmed by emotion, but the two of them choosing to give themselves to each other. To accept that want between them, and finally act on it.

His tongue slipped into her mouth as he grazed his fingers down her cheek and moved his hand to the back of her neck to hold her in place. He felt the goose bumps rushing across her soft skin in the process. Her perfume filled the air around them, something sweet and with a hint of vanilla, like fresh cupcakes. And she was just as tempting.

She moved her hand up his arm, sweeping it over the nape of his neck and into his hair, her fingertips digging slightly into his scalp as she pulled him in closer. He felt her touch tingling all the way down his spine, lighting up every inch of his body.

She turned to face him fully, swinging her legs off the lounge chair to the ground. She kissed him harder, her teeth catching on his lip as her book tumbled out of her lap and onto the ground, not giving it a second thought. A damn meteor could have hit the lodge right now, and Lawson doubted it would have been enough to break them apart.

When they finally pulled away from each other, both of them laughed, a tension breaking between them, their argument completely forgotten. For so long, he had done his best to ignore the desire he felt for her, to keep things on a more professional level. But now? This was what he wanted from now on. No hiding. No pretending it wasn't there. Just giving himself over to her, to this desire between them.

"Is that more like you had imagined?" she asked coyly.

"Hmm, much closer," he replied, leaning his forehead against hers. "But I think I need a little more practice to get it right."

She giggled as he leaned into her and kissed her again, the taste of white wine on her lips. He couldn't help but smile into the kiss. He knew there was still so much he needed to worry about, so much he needed to take care of, but right now, all that mattered was how she felt in his arms.

And how certain he was that he would do anything it took to keep her there.

Chapter Ten

Lawson woke with a smile on his face. He was tired and a little stiff from sitting out on the porch with Sarah so long the night before, but it had been worth it. They'd cleared the air and he'd finally told her he had feelings for her. And kissing her… He could kiss her all day and never get tired of her sweet sighs, her pink cheeks and the feel of her skin. She'd made him feel like a teenager again.

It was nice to let everything else fade away and just concentrate on her. On them. Seeing her radiant smile at breakfast made it even better. They sat together, arms and hands brushing as they ate, and conversation flowed easily around them. He couldn't wait for this mission to be over, for Granger to be behind bars, so they could move forward.

After breakfast and cleanup, everyone went to their respective work locations to check in and take care of their immediate duties. Cade and Aaron had a few things to handle around the property while Xavier and Lawson holed up in the office. Xavier had some paperwork to finish up while Lawson spent time on the phone with the sheriff, filling him in on their plan. They had a lot to get done in a short amount of time before putting their plan in motion later that day.

Since the men would be busy all day and into the evening with their mission, the women had decided to drive down the mountain to Blue Ridge that evening for a much-needed break. Lawson was glad to see Sarah feeling better, more like her old self. Having her friends close definitely helped.

After the women left for town, Cade, Lawson, Xavier and Aaron gathered in the office, which had become their war room as they planned their attack against Victor and his men.

Lawson was all too aware of just how much was on the line. Not just Warrior Peak, though that was part of it. Mostly, it was just Sarah. After spending time together last night, his need to protect her had skyrocketed, and he knew he was going to do whatever it took to ensure she didn't have to face any of the trouble this operation might bring to them.

"Are we almost ready to move out?" Xavier asked, glancing around the room. The other men replied with nods. They were all armed, all ready to take on whatever came next. Each of them was taking a different rest stop to keep watch for the comings and goings of Granger's men, and, if the opportunity arose, to grab them before they could do any harm.

Really, it was a reconnaissance mission, but Lawson could tell that the rest of them, like him, were itching to take it to the next level and actually snatch up one of the evil bastards involved in this trafficking.

"It's nearly dark, so we should get stationed at our rest stops as soon as we can," Cade replied.

Lawson nodded in agreement.

Xavier glanced over at him. "You alright?"

"I'm fine," he lied quickly. Truth be told, he'd been worrying a whole lot in the last day or so about what they were getting themselves involved in. Playing back their earlier conversations in his mind, Lawson could understand the others' true fears of setting out on this mission. He didn't want to share his own concerns, though, because he knew that would break the morale.

Even though this was the place he usually felt the most comfortable—working with the guys to come up with a plan to take down someone vile and dangerous—this was more intense than what they had faced off against before, and there was just no avoiding that fact.

Granger was a big fish and capable of bringing down hell on

their heads if he decided to, for their interference in his business. One slip would be all it would take to have him and his thugs on their trail.

Then there was Lainey to think about, too. He knew he would never be able to forgive himself if something happened to her or her family because of his failure to act. It made Lawson so mad when he thought of all the people who had failed to lift a finger when she'd brought it to their attention.

But he couldn't let his emotions get the better of him. He needed to keep himself under control. Now, more than ever, there were so many people relying on him to see this through. Not just Lainey, but all the women whom Victor had already targeted and was using and abusing for his business and his own perverse needs, and those still yet to be taken. But not on his watch, if he could prevent it.

Lawson rose to his feet and looked around the room. If there was anyone in the world he trusted to pull off an operation like this, it would be these men in front of him.

"Last chance to back out if you don't want to get involved," he warned them. He wouldn't blame anyone for deciding they didn't want to be part of this. Hell, if Lainey hadn't asked for his help, he wasn't sure he would have put himself in the line of fire at all.

But all three men looked back at him steadily, and Cade answered for the group, with confidence. "We're all in."

None of them wavered for a moment. They really were in—all in.

Lawson nodded back. For the first time since Lainey had brought this to him, he felt hope rise in his chest. They were going to do this.

End Victor Granger's reign of terror once and for all.

AN HOUR OR so later, Lawson pulled his truck to a halt in the desolate rest stop he was using as his stakeout position. The small building was set back from the road, surrounded by thick trees, with a restroom door at each side of the structure lit with a single flickering bulb between them, and a broken snack and soda machine in the center. It was dark and gloomy. It felt as though the whole place was holding its breath, waiting for something to happen.

After killing the engine, Lawson climbed out of the truck and looked around. No vehicles coming either way—this place was empty. An easy hunting ground for anyone searching for women in trouble. He doubted there was CCTV out here, and even if there was, it likely hadn't worked in years, anyway.

Lawson flicked on the warning lights in the truck, a sign that something was wrong and that he was in need of help. He knew that if Granger really had his men working up and down this highway, it wouldn't be long until one of them showed up to check it out. And, when they did, he needed to make it look as though he was a woman.

He sighed as he strung some pearls from the rearview mirror and slipped a pink, fuzzy cover over his wheel. Then he scattered some feminine paraphernalia around the cab—colorful notebooks, a shiny pen, a hairclip, a bright pink backpack and a pair of high heels—where it would be seen. Luckily, he'd been able to borrow some stuff from the women—actually, they all had. The others would be setting up their vehicles like this, too.

Then he got out and leaned a spare tire against the truck and placed a couple of tools on the ground. To anyone driving by, they would think there was a woman in trouble and in need of help…provided they didn't see him.

The trap was set. Now, he just had to wait for someone to take the bait.

He headed over to the restroom and knocked on the women's side, making sure it was empty. When no one responded, he pushed open the door and leaned up against the wall, pulled out his phone and fired off a text to the others to let them know he was in position.

Along the highway, Cade, Xavier and Aaron would be taking up their positions, all of them prepared to snare one of Granger's men as soon as they got the chance. It might not have been the most foolproof plan, but they needed to get their hands on one of the boots-on-the-ground guys to figure out exactly how his operation worked.

Their texts came in one after the other, letting him know

that they were ready to go. Lawson glanced out toward his truck, sitting there by the side of the road, and wondered if this had been the right call. He pushed down those thoughts. He couldn't let any doubt get into his mind—he needed to keep a clear head. He knew the guys were all relying on one another to pull this together, and he wasn't going to be the weak link to bring it all crashing down.

Soon enough, one of Granger's men would see a vehicle on the side of the road, broken-down and apparently belonging to a woman. They'd pull over, ready to snatch up another innocent, and instead, they'd be faced with a highly trained ex-cop, former military man, or former agent for their troubles. Lawson hoped they picked his rest stop to come to. He wanted to see the looks on their faces when it happened.

He listened to the road outside. Nothing, just stillness. Damn, he hoped an actual woman didn't turn up looking to use the restroom—it would be hard to explain what he was doing in here if they did.

He needed something to pass the time, to keep himself from overthinking. Then, he thought of Lainey. It had been a few days since he had last spoken to her, and he'd told her he'd update her once they got their plan in motion. Now seemed as good of time as any.

He dialed the number of the burner phone, and she answered a few seconds later.

"Hello?"

"Hey, Lainey, it's me," he greeted her. "How are you doing? Everything okay?"

"So far." She sighed. "What about you guys? Have you had any luck yet?"

"Not yet," he admitted. "But we're working on it. We're stationed along the highway now, all four of us, waiting for one of Granger's men to take the bait. As soon as we have one in our custody, we'll get back to you. We're going to use him to get all the information we can about the man himself and his operation."

"You be careful," she warned. "They're violent men, Lawson. They don't hold anything back. He must do something to ensure their loyalty because they're completely devoted to him."

"I will be," he promised her. "You don't have to worry about us, Lainey. We can handle ourselves."

"I just wish there was more I could do to help." She sighed. "I hate hiding out here, having you and your friends risk your lives for me and my family."

"You just focus on staying safe. Stay inside, keep your door locked, keep a look out for any trouble," he told her firmly. "That's the most important thing right now. And keep your phone close."

"I will," she acknowledged. "I just don't like feeling useless."

"You're not useless," he assured her. "If you hadn't brought this to us, we would never have known who was causing all this trouble, right? You've given us a break. And now, we can use it to bring these guys down for good."

"I know you're right," she replied. "Just…look after yourselves, okay? I'll never forgive myself if something happens to one of you for helping me out."

"No worries, just stay sharp," he reminded her. "I should go. I need to keep focused on what's happening here. But with any luck this will all be over soon."

"I hope so," she murmured, and he could hear the smile in her voice at the mere thought of it.

"I'll speak to you later," he promised her, and they said their goodbyes, leaving Lawson in the quiet of the night once more. He tucked his phone back into his pocket, and pushed the door open another couple of inches. How long were these guys going to make them wait? They had laid out the perfect honey trap for them, and now, they just needed them to take the bait.

When he thought of all the women who'd been lured into this nightmare, all the girls who had been kidnapped and forced into doing God only knew what for that man, it was hard for him to keep his cool. He'd seen a lot of nasty stuff over the years, but this? This might be the worst of it.

But he could handle it. They all could if it meant stopping this criminal organization. His thoughts drifted back to Sarah, their kiss. He had something good going for him now. Lawson knew he'd do anything to protect her, keep her safe. No matter what.

No matter whom he had to take down in the process.

Chapter Eleven

A harried waitress greeted Sarah and the other women as she passed them with a loaded tray of drinks and food. “Welcome, gals. Have a seat wherever you can find one.”

“Thank you,” Sarah replied, then turned to Hannah. “I’ll see if I can find us a seat and you three get the drinks.” She nodded toward the bar, then glanced around the packed room before seeing a small group leave a table off to the side by the window, and hurried in that direction.

As she waited, Sarah tilted her head to look at the clear sky above her, lost in thought. The moon was half-full and glowing, not a cloud in sight, and the stars were twinkling in the distance against the dark backdrop of the night. She wasn’t sure she would ever get used to being this far out in the middle of nowhere, but it was worth it just for the scenery.

She was startled out of her gazing as Hannah, Bailey and River walked up to their table and set down the drinks.

“Oh, you grabbed a good spot,” Bailey cheerfully acknowledged as they settled around the table.

While Sarah and the others reached for their glasses of wine, River scooped up her lemonade. She’d volunteered to be their designated driver for the night, and Sarah was glad she was off the hook and could have a little fun. She wanted to talk to them about everything that had been going on in her head lately, and she knew that she wasn't going to be able to muster up the courage until she'd had a couple of drinks.

"It's a beautiful night." Hannah sighed as she glanced up at the moon above them. Many of the patrons of the bar were sitting outside, enjoying the balmy weather. The low buzz of conversation was comforting to Sarah and she felt like she could finally relax for the first time in forever. She liked knowing that this place was full of people who really seemed to be enjoying themselves, so she wouldn't have to worry about being overheard. She had a lot she wanted to share.

"Yeah, it really is," River agreed. "Shame the guys couldn't join us."

"You know what they're up to tonight?" Hannah asked.

Bailey shook her head. "No idea. As far as I know, they're up at the lodge, making plans for something important."

Suddenly, all eyes at the table turned to Sarah, like she might have a better idea of what was happening.

She cocked an eyebrow. "Why are you all looking at me?"

"Because if anyone knows what Lawson is planning, it's you," Hannah teased her with a laugh.

Sarah felt her cheeks flush with heat. "I don't know what he's up to right now," she admitted. "He did mention that they were going to help look into the kidnappings that were happening around here."

Bailey tilted her head. "You guys haven't talked yet?"

"Not about what they're doing, really," she replied.

"Oh, so about other things, then?" Hannah asked. She always had a nose for gossip, and there was no way she was going to let this go.

"We did clear the air about me leaving," Sarah replied, trailing her finger around the bottom of her wineglass. God, this felt weird. She wanted to share with her friends, but it suddenly occurred to her that she didn't know if she was risking things with Lawson by talking about everything. But she knew she couldn't hide it. Plus, they all talked about their relationships with her and it didn't seem fair to keep hers from them. She wanted to be honest with them and she did need to talk to someone about it all.

"Oh, okay. Now, you have to spill," Bailey announced.

Sarah bit her lip, but couldn't keep the smile off her face. She told them about the kiss they had shared, and how he'd wanted a redo after the way things had gone before.

Hannah made a playful grossed-out face. "Wow, who knew my brother had it in him to be romantic?"

"Holy hell." River laughed. "You guys…you're finally doing it, huh?"

"I'm not really sure what we're doing right now," Sarah replied. She'd hardly allowed herself to follow that train of thought, and had been too spooked at the notion of what might be happening between them to ask more questions about them or go any further than she already had.

Things had been so tense between them for so long, and now, something had actually happened. She felt like one wrong move would be enough to blow it all up, and there was no way in hell she was going to let that happen.

"You're not?" Hannah asked. "You didn't have any type of relationship conversation? Come on, you have to spill. You can't keep us hanging here."

"Hey, it's my love life, not yours," Sarah protested, shaking her head. "I just… I know Lawson has a lot going on right now. And I don't want him to have to drop all of that just because we have feelings for each other or something."

"Not 'or something,'" Hannah corrected her. "You definitely have feelings for each other. It's written all over your faces whenever the two of you are together. I think you two are the last ones to notice."

"Oh, trust me, I did notice signs," Sarah replied. "I just didn't want to push and end up pushing him away. I figured, when he was ready, something would happen."

"And you think he's ready now?" River asked.

Sarah paused for a moment. She hoped he was ready. She wasn't sure she would ever be able to stop thinking about how good their kiss was, or how badly she craved the man. How much she wanted even more.

"I hope so," Sarah responded. She'd been single for a long time now, and she'd be lying if she said she didn't miss having someone special to share her life with. She had done plenty of dating when back in college, but all of the guys she had wound up with had been totally incompatible with her. None of them understood her drive, her dedication to getting her degree or working as hard as she did. They expected her to do what was important to them, not follow her own dreams.

She had stuck with her useless dating life until her PhD, when she'd had to take a long, hard look at herself and accept that she wasn't going to be able to give people helpful advice on their own lives if she was still making the same mistakes in hers. She had sworn off dating, focusing on her career instead, until she was in a place where she could feel confident.

And now, she was. She had a job she loved, was living in a place that felt like home and was surrounded by people she really cared about, who really cared about her. There couldn't have been a better time to start dating again. Not just start dating, though. To build something, with Lawson.

After all this time waiting for the right person to come along at the right time, there were things she wanted to catch up on. Falling in love, building a real life with someone, maybe even having kids, if the time was right.

But that was something for "future" her to consider. She needed to focus on the present, and not put too much pressure on Lawson or herself to jump into this relationship feetfirst. They'd shared a couple of amazing kisses, and that was about it so far, even if the thought of them sent a shiver of delight down her spine.

"I don't want to jinx it," she told the women around her as she shook her head. Hannah opened her mouth, clearly about to hit her with another question, but before she could, a waiter appeared beside them.

"Some drinks," he told them, distributing a few glasses of wine on to the table.

"Oh, we didn't order anything," Bailey remarked, but the waiter nodded over to a table just across from them.

"Those guys ordered them for you," he replied, and all of the women turned around to see whom he was talking about.

Sure enough, there were a couple of guys sitting a few tables away, sipping on beers, grinning in their direction.

"Well, I'm not drinking, so I don't want this," River told the waiter.

"I'll take the free drinks!" Hannah replied, grinning.

The waiter shrugged and backed off, leaving the women alone once more.

"You think that's a good idea?" River asked warily. "We don't want to give them the wrong idea."

"They're just drinks," Hannah replied, waving her hand. "It's not like we're accepting a marriage proposal."

"Do you recognize those guys?" Bailey muttered as she stole another glance toward the men who had purchased the drinks.

Sarah shook her head slowly, looking over her shoulder at them again. They were still watching them as though waiting for a reaction.

"They must be from out of town," Sarah added.

"And they're just trying their luck with some women they thought might be single," Hannah pointed out. "It's not a big deal."

"I don't know," River replied. "It feels…off."

Sarah nodded. She wasn't sure exactly what it was, but there was something nagging at the back of her mind, a warning that something was wrong. In this small town, everyone knew everyone, and it wasn't exactly the kind of place that got a lot of tourists.

"It's fine," Hannah said, trying to assure them. "Come on, it's busy here tonight, it's not like they're going to try anything."

Sarah tried to shake off the doubt in her head. Hannah was likely right. They didn't owe these guys anything for accepting the drinks, right? Maybe they were just trying to be friendly.

The guys kept an eye on them all night, while the women gossiped, laughed and enjoyed each other's company. As the evening wore on, the crowd thinned out, and the women headed back to their car. Sarah noticed the men walking out the door right as they pulled away from the bar.

While driving out of town, Hannah and River chatted about chores that needed to be done the next day at the lodge—guests checking out and vendor calls that had to be made. Bailey chimed in occasionally as she checked her phone for any urgent messages from the police station that required her attention.

Sarah was a little more subdued on the drive, unable to stop thinking about the men who had bought them the drinks earlier. Maybe she was just on edge knowing everything that was going on in town at the moment, but she couldn't help but wonder if there might have been something more to it.

They had been driving on the winding mountain road leading up to Warrior Peak for about fifteen minutes when a pair of headlights flashed in the rearview mirror. Bailey and Sarah were riding in the back and whipped their heads around when the light flooded the back window so they could see what was happening behind them.

"Damn it," Bailey muttered. "There's someone on the road behind us."

River gripped the wheel a little tighter while she glanced in the rearview mirror. Sarah knew she was thinking about the women who had been taken from the side of the road. It was all Sarah could think about, too.

"You recognize the car?" Hannah asked.

"I can't see anything but bright lights," River replied.

Bailey's lips tightened. "What if it's the guys who ordered us drinks?"

"I did see them leave right after us," Sarah volunteered.

All the women exchanged nervous looks. "Maybe we're just being jumpy? You know, from the article and what the men told us at the lodge," River offered.

"Probably. But we're still about forty-five minutes away from the lodge, I'm calling Lawson," Sarah replied, and she dug for her phone in her pocket. She had no idea who was behind them or what they wanted, but she sure as hell wasn't going to sit around waiting to find out. Better to be safe than sorry. As she pulled out her phone, she realized her hand was shaking, and tried her best not to let the others see. She didn't want them noticing how freaked out she was at the situation.

Not until she'd had a chance to speak to Lawson, anyway. He and the others had been in the office when the women had left to go to town. Surely, they'd be done with their meeting by now, right? A couple of the guys could drive down to meet them, and just like that, this whole mess would be over. They would laugh at how paranoid they had been and forget about it. Because there was no way the car behind them could have anything to do with the men Lawson and the others were after right now, they were just feeling out of sorts.

At least, that was what she told herself, as she listened to the phone ring and silently pleaded for Lawson to pick up.

Chapter Twelve

Lawson snatched up the phone as soon as he saw it was Sarah calling and lifted it to his ear.

"You okay?" he asked, concerned.

"Not really," she blurted out.

His heart dropped as soon as he heard the tone of her voice. He knew she would never fool around about something like this. If she sounded that scared, it was because she had a real reason to be, and he hated the thought of her struggling like that.

"What's going on?" he asked, wishing he had somewhere to pace. Right now, in the confines of this restroom, he was stuck in one spot.

"We…we're just coming home from the bar," she told him. "Some guys there had the waiter deliver us drinks. We didn't talk to them and they didn't look familiar, but they left right after us and there's a car behind us on the road right now. We can't help but wonder if it might be them following us."

She paused and took a deep breath, and his gut clenched. *Damn.* Someone was possibly tailing them. Could they be related to the guys they were after tonight? They tended to focus on women driving alone, but he wasn't going to take that chance.

"Listen to me," he told her firmly. "You go straight back to the lodge, okay? Don't slow down and don't pull over. If it is someone following you, they won't try and cross the property lines. Especially if they don't know who else might be around."

At least, he hoped not. Truth be told, he didn't have any confirmation that they wouldn't. This wasn't something they'd anticipated. He hoped that the surveillance there might be enough to scare them off, but if they had come this far, there was a chance they were going to take it even further.

"Okay, we've still got a ways to go," Sarah replied, her voice still trembling. "I… Are you at the lodge?"

"Not right now," he admitted. She let out a small whimper. He hated being so far from her when she was clearly struggling so much, but there was nothing he could do about it.

"Where are you?"

Before he could reply, he heard a noise outside. He cracked the door open and saw a black SUV pulling to a halt next to his truck. Talk about bad timing…

"I'll explain later," he muttered to her, dropping his voice so it wouldn't carry outside the restroom.

"Lawson, I—"

The men stepped out of the SUV—two of them. One of them whistled, calling out to anyone who might have been nearby, and they paced around the truck he'd left there as a lure.

"Listen to me, Sarah," he told her urgently. "Tell Hannah to call Xavier and fill him in on everything that's happening. Do it now. I'll stay on the line with you until you get through."

"Why?"

"Please, just trust me on this," he begged her. "I know how it sounds. Just get her to call him, okay?"

"Sure, okay."

She did as she was told, and, a few moments later, she told him that Hannah had Xavier on the line.

"Okay, good," he replied as he nervously ran a hand through his hair. He glanced outside once more. One of the men was motioning toward the restroom, clearly sensing there was someone inside. "Now, get her to tell Xavier to call all the men back to the lodge. They'll meet you there."

"All of them? Who else is out there?"

"Everyone," he replied. "And tell Xavier that I have our

target. I'll handle business while they make sure all of you are safe."

"Target?" she whispered. "Lawson, are you in danger right now?"

"No," he said quickly. "But I'm looking at two guys who are about to be. You have nothing to worry about, Sarah. You just make sure you're safe, okay?"

He hung up before she could answer. He knew she was going to be pissed at him after she found out the details of what he and the others had done, so would the other women, but that was a problem for another time. What mattered was making sure that he pulled this off. They finally had these guys right where they wanted them, and he would be damned if he'd let them slip through his fingers.

He turned on one of the restroom taps, and then dived into a stall, stepping up on to the toilet so they wouldn't be able to see his feet. He wasn't going to give them the slightest heads-up as to what was going on here. There were two of them, after all, and he would need every advantage he could get.

His heart was pounding in his chest, and he wondered how long it had been since he'd last seen action like this. The adrenaline was rushing through his system, lighting up every part of him, and he clenched his fists at his sides. He was going to make them pay for what they had done, for everything they had pulled on his stretch of road. If he'd known about this before, he would never in a million years have allowed them to get away with it. But this was his chance to bring it to a close.

Or at least, start the process.

"Hello, miss?"

One of the men called out to the supposed damsel in distress as they approached the restroom. They sounded innocent in their inquiry. Helpful. Almost kind. It was a damn good ruse, he had to give them that, even if he hated that they were clearly so well-practiced at it.

The door to the restroom opened. Lawson could see the two men entering through the crack in the stall. He braced himself. He didn't know if they were armed, or what they were packing if they were. But he had the element of surprise, and that had to count for something.

"We saw your vehicle outside. Do you need a hand with a tire change?" one of the guys asked. The sound of the tap running was his only response.

Lawson bided his time. He needed to wait until they were right outside the stall before he made his move. He couldn't risk missing his chance. He couldn't risk screwing this up.

"Check the stalls," one of the men muttered to the other, and they began to make their way along the grimy stalls. First, the one farthest from Lawson, and then, the one next to him.

And finally, both guys were standing right in front of his stall. He planted his hands on each side of it for leverage, as one of them tried the door.

"It's locked," one remarked. "She must be in—"

Before he could finish what he was saying, Lawson swung his legs toward the door with all of his might and slammed his feet into the flimsy wood panel. It crashed off its hinges, and smashed into the two men standing on the other side.

He sprang down on to the floor and quickly surveyed the situation: one of the men had been tossed against the far wall and slammed his head into the dirty tiles, while the other was half-pinned by the door on top of him. He shoved it off his chest and scrambled to his feet, reaching for a weapon at his side.

"What the hell—" he blurted out, but Lawson took advantage of the obvious shock written all over his face. Lawson lunged for the assailant's gun and grabbed it out of his hand, then took his arm, twisted it up roughly behind his back and slammed the man into the wall. The man let out a cry of pain, then Lawson tossed the gun aside and pulled out a pair of cuffs he'd brought with him. He snapped one of them around his wrist and attached the other to a metal pipe hanging on the wall above him.

The other man had gotten to his feet, and Lawson rounded on him. Using the man's dazed state against him, Lawson grabbed his arm, then slapped a second cuff on his wrist before he knew what was happening. There was a wound on the man's head, dripping blood down his face, and Lawson doubted he would have been able to put up much of a fight, anyway, even if he had wanted to.

Lawson pushed the guy back against the wall and lifted the man's cuffed arm above his head, attaching the other end of the cuff to the metal pipe running along the ceiling. He checked the man for weapons and didn't find any, so Lawson pulled out his phone.

While he was dialing the sheriff, he leaned back against the wall and took a deep breath, waiting for the other man to answer. After a few rings, the sheriff picked up, his voice a little groggy.

"Sorry to wake you, sheriff," Lawson greeted. "But I have a couple of guys with me here I thought you might want to meet."

"You got them?" Sheriff Willis asked, his voice sounding surprised.

"I got them," Lawson replied, unable to keep the grin off his face. Yeah, maybe he shouldn't have been celebrating so soon, but any win was one he would welcome right now.

"Tell me what happened, exactly," Willis demanded. "I need to know what I'm dealing with here."

They had talked a few times about what they intended to do, but the guys had ended up making a few alterations at the last minute. Lawson stepped out of earshot and swiftly filled in the sheriff on the plan the guys had put together, with the broken-down vehicle on the side of the road as a lure. The guys who had turned up expecting a helpless woman were now cuffed to a metal pipe in a public restroom in the middle of nowhere.

Sheriff Willis let out a sigh.

"You bring them down to the station," he told him. "But like I said before, if you don't have anything we can pin on them right now, we're going to have to let them go. You hear me? I'm not intentionally bringing this kind of trouble into my town."

Lawson nodded, even though the sheriff couldn't see him. He got it. They couldn't just lock up these guys and throw away the key, no matter how much he would have liked to do just that. No, they had to go through the proper judicial process.

And if that meant Lawson needed to get a confession out of them before they could lock them up, so be it. He couldn't risk having to cut them loose, and allowing them to run back to Granger and tell him about their trap and that someone else was on their trail.

"I'll meet you at the station in an hour," he told the sheriff, and Sheriff Willis muttered his agreement, still clearly in the process of waking up.

Lawson turned his attention to the two men opposite him. Both of them were scowling, muttering curses at him with hatred in their eyes. If he was going to do this, he was going to have to get the information he needed from them quickly. He had about the length of the drive back to Blue Ridge to squeeze some of the truth out of them, and he hoped he'd scared them enough to get them to spill, one way or another.

He smirked, looking between them. "We've got a lot to talk about, boys," he told them, then went about undoing the cuffs from the pipe and dragging them to the truck waiting outside.

Chapter Thirteen

"We're here," Sarah breathed as she saw the lights of Warrior Peak come into view. This was what she needed right now—that sense of safety, that sense of calm. No matter how tempting it might have been to let the fear get the better of them, as long as they had made it to the lodge in one piece, everything was going to be okay. It had to be.

River turned the car off the main road and onto the connector road that led up to the lodge. As soon as she made the turn, she pulled over to the side and shut off the car lights; all the women held their breath as they waited to see what the car behind them was going to do. Sarah stared out the back window and, much to her surprise, the vehicle continued on up the road, without so much as slowing down.

Thank God. Maybe they had just been paranoid after all. She felt a little guilty for letting her nerves get the better of her, but she figured she was way better off being safe than sorry when it came to all of this. She didn't want to take any chances or make it easy for anyone to get close to them. Not when she knew what kind of danger was out there waiting for them. Much as she wanted to believe they'd already had their fair share of turmoil these last few months, she knew that life didn't work like that.

"Come on, let's get up to the lodge," Hannah said.

River turned on the car lights and they continued up to the main building. As soon as she parked in the gravel lot, River turned off the engine, and they all headed inside. Sarah could tell they were all lost in thought, wondering if they had been foolish in overthinking the possible threat, but it didn't matter. What mattered was that they were back now, and nothing was going to happen to them as long as they were here.

A few minutes later, as Hannah hung outside the front door with Sarah, Xavier's truck rushed up the driveway. Hannah breathed a sigh of relief, and she ran over to Xavier to give him a hug as soon as he stepped out. He wrapped his arms around her tightly and surveyed the area, making sure it was safe.

"You guys alright?" he asked as he led Hannah back toward Sarah.

"Yeah, we're fine," Sarah assured him. "We just got a little spooked by some guys at the bar, that's all. Thought they were following us, but whoever it was just continued down the road after we turned off. Guess they must be staying at one of the ranches nearby."

"Maybe seasonal workers," Xavier suggested as he pushed open the wooden door and led them inside.

"Maybe," Sarah agreed, chewing on her bottom lip. If she was being honest, there was only one thing on her mind right now and it was Lawson. She felt as though she would only be able to get her feet under her again when he was close to her.

"Where's Lawson?" she asked Xavier as she followed him. She tried to keep her voice neutral, but it came out a little more insistent than she had intended.

"He's surveilling at a rest stop about thirty miles away," Xavier replied. "Cade and Aaron were, too, but they're on their way back now."

"Why not him?" she asked, her stomach dropping. She knew it was silly, that Xavier never would have been so calm if he thought Lawson was in real danger, but she hated the thought of him not being here with everyone else. She was spooked and shaken, and she felt like his presence was the only thing that would ground her again.

"Hey," he murmured to her, seeming to sense how worried she was. "He's going to be okay. You know that, right?"

"I know that..."

"He's tough as nails," he reminded her. "And he can handle himself. Those guys who are going to run into him, they're the ones in danger. Not him."

Sarah thought back to what he said on the phone, that he wasn't in danger, but the men he was up against were about to be. She smiled slightly. She knew she should trust him on that. She knew he was good at what he did. She'd watched him and the others training before and knew he could handle himself.

And yet, she still wished he was here by her side more than anything right now. Not exactly the right attitude to have, and she knew it was selfish, given how important what he was taking on happened to be, but she couldn't help it.

They headed into the main greeting room and joined River and Bailey, who both looked tense. Xavier assured them that Cade and Aaron would be back soon, and she could see the relief on both their faces. She was happy for them, but she clutched her phone in her pocket, willing Lawson to call her so she could hear his voice and know he was fine.

Cade and Aaron arrived back a short time later, and the other women practically jumped on them in relief. Bailey scolded Aaron for not telling her about the mission they had been on, but Sarah could tell there was no real malice to it. Her face looked relieved and happy, not angry.

"Heard anything from Lawson?" Cade asked Xavier, his arm around River.

Xavier glanced over at Sarah, who shook her head.

"Just what Hannah relayed earlier," he replied. "He had a couple of them approaching the truck."

Cade's jaw tightened. He was trying to contain his concern, but Sarah was attuned to people's expressions and emotions because of her job. She could tell he was worried, and that had her feeling even more panicked. She tried to calm herself, digging her fingernails into her palm to ground herself, but it wasn't working.

All at once, her phone buzzed in her pocket, and she let out a yelp of surprise. She was so on edge, the noise had really startled her. She practically ripped her jacket pocket trying to get it out before the sound stopped, and she stared down at the screen. Lawson. Thank God.

"Is it him?" Xavier asked, and she nodded, lifting a hand to the group and stepping away so she could take the call in private.

"Lawson?" she answered, her voice a little shaky.

"Hey, Sarah," he replied. He sounded calm, and the soothing tone eased some of the tension in her. His voice was the best balm to her nerves right now.

"You guys okay?" he asked her. "You get back to the lodge?"

"Yeah, we're here now," she assured him. "The guys who were following us…well, they weren't following us. They carried on up the road after we pulled in. I guess we were just being jumpy, I'm sorry—"

"Hey, you've got nothing to be sorry about," he promised her. "It's better to be safe. The stakes are high right now and we're all on edge. I'd much rather you were too cautious than anything else, you hear me?"

She smiled. He was so damn sweet. Even when she felt silly for making such a fuss, he was there to ground her, remind her that she was right to look out for herself.

"What about you?" she asked him. "When are you going to be back?"

He sighed, and suddenly his voice sounded tired. "It's going to be a while," he warned her. "Tell everyone not to wait up."

"Really?" she asked, trying not to let the disappointment sound in her tone. She didn't want to spook him or act entitled, but everyone else had their person right now. She didn't know exactly where they stood, relationship-wise, but she knew she wanted him there with her.

"I have two of these bastards in custody," he told her, and she could hear the proud grin in his words.

"You do?" she gasped.

"Yeah, the ruse worked and I nabbed a couple of them at the rest stop," he explained. "Some of the sheriff's men went up there to bring their car back down and they searched it. Found enough in there to keep them locked up for a while. Hopefully, as long as it takes to get to the answers we need."

Sarah heard the pride in his voice, and he had every right to feel that way. One step closer to taking down these men was exactly what they needed right now, even if it meant he was going to be at the police station all night.

"You going to be okay?" he asked her gently.

"I'm going to be fine," she promised him. "Everyone else is back and safe. I'm just anxious to see you. All that talk of missing women was just…surprising and unsettling."

"I understand. It's unsettling for all of us," he replied. "You just need to stay there and get some rest. Hopefully, this will all be over soon."

"I can tell how tired you are, Lawson. Are you sure you can't come back soon?" She hated the needy tinge in her voice but she still felt off and she was concerned about him.

"No," he said, sounding regretful. "I have a lot to deal with here at the police station. I don't want to leave until I know we have everything under control. Let the others know what's going on, okay?"

"Sure, I'll tell them," she agreed. "Just…don't push yourself too hard, okay? You take care of yourself."

"I will," he promised her softly. He lingered on the line for a moment, as though there was more he wanted to say. She knew how he felt.

All the stress from what had happened earlier in the night was still rushing around her head, and she knew she wasn't in a good state to be blurting out anything that might cross the line this early on in their budding relationship.

"I'll see you in the morning," he told her finally, and she bid him farewell, listening until he hung up the phone.

She stood there, phone pressed to her ear, recalling Lawson's voice, and holding it in her memory. She couldn't wait until she could see him again, give him a hug. To know for certain that he was as good as he claimed.

Sarah was ready for all of this to be over, to be able to move forward and figure out where they stood with each other. To be happy.

Together.

"What's going on?" Xavier asked her, snapping her back to reality.

"He's got a couple of the guys in lockup," she explained as she tucked her phone back into her pocket. "He said they got enough evidence from their vehicle to keep them locked up for a while. So that's good news, right?"

"That's great news," Xavier replied, breathing a sigh of relief. "I was worried that we were going to get them and they wouldn't have anything incriminating on them."

"You didn't have a plan in place?" Bailey asked, her eyes widening. She was a cop, so, of course, she was stressed at the thought of them not having something ready to go, but Sarah put a hand on her arm, trying to calm her down.

"It's okay," she reminded her. "They're in custody. That's all that matters."

"We had a plan," Cade offered. "We just had no way of knowing if whoever we caught would have anything illegal on them to keep them in jail."

"Come on, you guys need to get some rest," Aaron interrupted whatever else Bailey might have said, grabbing her hand. She glanced over at him, obviously still a little doubtful about the approach the guys had taken, but what mattered was that they had gotten the result they wanted.

Even if the guys should have been more careful in the way they went about it, two of Granger's men were in jail right now, and they would be able to get information out of them.

Or, at least, that was what she hoped.

Sarah headed back toward her cabin, counting out her footsteps, the stars still glittering in the night sky above. She knew she was going to have a hard time getting to sleep without Lawson back on the property, but she had to trust he knew what he was doing.

He was good at his job. Always had been. He could handle this.

Even if there was something nagging at the back of her mind, telling her that this Granger person and his organization were worse than the men they had taken on before. And she hoped she never had to find just how right she might be.

Chapter Fourteen

Lawson lifted his head from the pillow with a groan. It felt like there was a drill going off behind his eyes, as his head was pounding painfully. He wasn't a young man anymore, and he couldn't get away with pulling all-nighters, like he had last night.

Well, he'd gotten an hour or two of sleep. By the time he had finished up at the police station for the night, leaving the sheriff and his deputies to get the two guys locked up and ready for interrogation, his head had been reeling from the chaos of the day behind him, and he hadn't been able to get any rest.

He needed to figure out how he could get the information out of the thugs about Granger and his operation. He had hoped they might have been Granger's sons, but no such luck. They were just a couple of lackeys, Jim Adams and Paul Donner, and they each had a rap sheet about half a mile long.

The sheriff's men had dug through their car and found enough drugs and unregistered guns to keep them locked up for a while longer, and the sheriff had promised Lawson that they weren't going to see sunlight unless it was to go to court.

Lawson was planning on going back down to the police station later in the day to speak to them himself. Since they were on that highway with the intention of grabbing a young woman, he knew they had to have some knowledge of Granger's operation, at least a location to deliver whomever they kidnapped. The question, though, was how loyal the two men were to their boss.

Would Lawson be able to rattle them enough to share information, or were they too scared of Granger and whatever he would have threatened them with to keep their mouths shut? He'd have to wait and see how it played out after he got there and started asking them questions.

He swung his legs out of bed and massaged his temples, knowing he was going to have to fill in Xavier and the others on what had happened the night before. He was sure they'd want to know details—the same ones he wanted to know himself that he obviously didn't have—but he could at least tell them the basics of what went down and provide the rest once he knew more.

The only way any of this operation was going to work for them, and to prepare his friends for whatever came next, would be to keep everyone updated on each step forward. No matter how small a detail was, it could end up leading toward the bigger picture.

Lawson was never big on postcase reports, and much rather preferred to be in the action and leave someone else see to the specifics, but he needed his team as strong and prepared as possible, and having all the necessary information to more forward would be the best way for that to happen.

He pulled the door open and was about to head downstairs to grab a coffee to wake himself up when he found Sarah standing in the hall, a couple of steaming mugs in her hands, and a smile on her face.

"Hey," she murmured, handing him a cup. "I figured you could use some caffeine after your late night."

He hesitated for a moment before taking the cup. He was sleep deprived and not really up to talking, and he knew she would have questions about what had gone down. He didn't want to worry her further.

"I can go, if you want," she told him, seeing his hesitation. "I know you must be exhausted."

"No, it's okay," he replied, and he gestured for her to step into his room. "Come on in."

He held the door for her, and glanced down at her face as she passed by him, noticing the dark rings around her eyes. Had she been up worrying about him all night? He hoped not. He didn't want her spending all her time concerned about what was going on with him when he knew he was well and truly capable of handling himself.

Plus, she had been so freaked out about the encounter with those guys last night at the bar. He knew she was right to be cautious, but he could tell that her previous experiences had left a stain on her psyche. She was hyperaware, jumping at every little noise. After everything she had been through, he couldn't say he blamed her.

She slipped into the seat at his desk and he planted himself down on the edge of the bed. Her eyes slipped to his hand, wrapped around the coffee cup, and she noticed a few grazes on it.

"Your hand…" she murmured, reaching out to touch it.

He winced and drew back, but shook his head quickly. "Nothing to worry about," he assured her. "They got it a lot worse than I did, trust me."

She smiled at him. "Good. I was so worried about you last night, I…"

She trailed off, and then shook her head. "I'm sorry, we don't need to talk about that," she told him. "I'm just glad you're okay."

"Not to worry. I'm just tired," he reassured her. "It was a late night and I feel like I just closed my eyes."

She glanced around his room, and raised her eyebrows at the sight of a few plants sitting on a shelf next to the window.

"I didn't take you for much of a gardener," she remarked. "Especially with how you talk about Hannah's flowers."

"I'm not," he replied, chuckling. "Xavier just bullied me into having something in the rooms other than the bare minimum when we started this place."

"How do you mean?" she asked, cocking her head with interest.

"I just wanted this place to be simple," he explained. "I thought that would make things easy for the people who were staying here. The rooms were pretty bare back then, until Xavier said it looked like a prison, and we actually needed to make it more homey."

"And that's how he convinced you to put some plants up in your room?" she asked.

"Well, sort of," he said. "He had to show me a few studies about how improving our living space can have an impact on our mental health. And then I decided I could use some greenery around here."

"You'd make a great interior designer," she teased him. "Prison chic. I can see it being the next big thing."

"Maybe in another life." He laughed. Even though he was still exhausted, there was something about her company that sent a jolt of energy through his system. Well, that and the caffeine. That helped, too.

She got to her feet to admire his plants, and then, casually, sat down on the bed next to him. After their kiss, it felt like a far more pointed gesture than it might have before. He shifted his leg so it was pressed against hers, his coffee cup resting on his thigh.

"So how are you doing? How's therapy going?" he asked her.

She sighed. "I'm doing okay, I guess. I'm still processing everything, I think," she responded. "I haven't been assigned a therapist yet, but should be soon. I'm worried I'm going to have trouble opening up to someone I don't know. Putting it all into the right words and having it make sense."

"Oh, yeah?" he prompted, frowning. "Why do you think that is?"

"Part of it, I think, is because of what I do. It's hard to be on the other side of the desk, you know? And also, with everything else happening around here, it's hard to know where to start," she admitted. "Especially when there's so much…other stuff going on now."

She glanced up at him, a small smile on her face.

He cocked an eyebrow. "Other stuff?" he asked her.

She nodded. "Other stuff," she repeated, as though daring him to ask her what.

"And what other stuff might that be?"

"Oh, well, that will be between my therapist and me," she replied playfully.

"You planning on talking about me in therapy?" he asked her.

She flashed him an impish smile, her cheeks flushing slightly. "Wouldn't you like to know," she retorted, shifting so she was pressed against his side.

This was comfortable, in a way Lawson wasn't sure he had felt in a long time. He decided then and there that he wasn't second-guessing this attraction he had to Sarah. He wasn't questioning if he was doing the wrong thing, for once in his damn life. He was just enjoying her company, the memory of their kiss and the new closeness it brought.

"I'd very much like to know," he replied, turning to face her and putting aside his coffee cup. "But I'm not going to pry," he murmured, reaching over to take her cup out of her hand, placing it next to his, then resting his hand on her cheek.

Sarah gazed up at him, leaning her head into his hand slightly, letting her eyes soften. She seemed to finally be able to relax after the chaos of what had happened the night before, and he was seriously glad for that. The last thing he wanted was for all of this to trigger more fear in her, to give her more trauma to deal with.

Slowly, he closed the distance between them, planting a soft kiss against her lips. She reached up to grasp his shoulder, her fingertips digging into his skin. God, she felt good. Even that kind of touch was enough to make the hairs on the back of his neck stand on end. He pulled back, brushing his nose against hers, and rested his forehead against hers.

"I can't wait until all of this stuff with Granger is behind us," he told her softly. "So I can put all my attention where it matters. On you."

She sank into him, letting a smile spread across her face. He loved seeing her like this, happy and relaxed, and just enjoying the moment with him. No matter what was going on outside his room, all he wanted right now was to lose himself to the feeling of the two of them together. Of her being in his arms and how perfect it felt.

"You have my attention right now," she murmured to him, her eyebrows raising, her teeth resting on her bottom lip.

He knew at once what she was suggesting. It had taken them a long time to get to this place, to acknowledge the way they felt about each other. To be in a place where they could finally act on their feelings. And damn, he wanted nothing more than to enjoy the stolen moment that they had been given right then.

He leaned close again, but this time, when their lips touched, he deepened the kiss. She parted her lips, allowing him to get closer, and he wrapped his arms around her, breathing in her scent. He felt the desire stirring inside him, and the need that he had tried to hold down for so long was rising up to take control.

And, in the soft morning light pouring through the window behind them, he knew he was finally ready. They were both finally ready.

He sank down into the bed with her, grinning into the kiss.

Chapter Fifteen

Sarah gazed up at the ceiling, a dizzying smile on her face. She could still feel the pleasure tingling through every inch of her body as she lay beneath the covers in Lawson's bed.

That had been…*whoa.* So much better than her fantasies of them together. Her head was still spinning from their intense connection—it was more than she could ever have expected. They had been dancing around their feelings for each other for so long, she had been starting to think it would never happen.

From the moment their lips had touched, she felt herself give in to him, her body accepting this closeness for the first time. No, more than accepting it, she *needed* it, craved it from some place deep inside her.

He glanced over at her as he buttoned up his shirt, flashing her a sexy grin.

"You good?" he asked her.

"Better than good," she replied with a sigh, flipping over to face him. "You sure you can't stay a little longer?"

"I would love to, trust me," he admitted, pulling a face, and planted himself down on the bed next to her. He took her hand and drew it to his lips, placing a kiss against it softly. If she hadn't already been lying down, she would have swooned on the spot.

"But I have to go into town and talk to the sheriff about what we're going to do next with those assholes he's got in jail." He sighed, running a hand through his hair.

She propped herself up in the bed and shrugged. "How about I come with you?" she suggested. "I have some groceries to pick up in town and Hannah asked me to grab a few items for the kitchen, too. I was going to ask one of the guys to go with me, but I'd much rather go with you. If I wouldn't be in the way, that is?"

He paused for a moment, then smiled and nodded. "You know what, I'd love that," he replied.

"I'll get dressed," she said coyly, flashing him a playful little grin. As much as she knew she would have enjoyed lounging around naked with him, they had stuff to take care of, and she wasn't going to be the one to hold him up.

"While you're doing that, I'm going to call Xavier really quick and tell him we're running to town and that I'll fill them in on everything when we get back." He gave her a quick kiss on the forehead, then stepped in the hall to make the call.

When she was dressed, they walked down to his truck. He looped his little finger around hers, holding on gently, like he was making sure she didn't drift away. She could hardly keep the grin off her face. She knew the other women would have a ton of questions for her if they saw the two of them together, but honestly, right now, she was finding it hard to mind much. Maybe she wanted people to see them like this, just to make sure it was real.

He offered her a hand to help her into the truck, and she rolled down the window as they pulled away. It was another beautiful day, and the sunshine filled the cab. Sarah snuck a look at him out of the corner of her eye, and felt her chest flutter slightly again. It felt so damn good to be with him like this.

"It's gorgeous today," she remarked, holding her hand out of the window and swimming it through the cool air.

"It really is," he replied, his eyes lingering on her for a second longer than necessary.

She laughed, her cheeks flushing slightly. It was like he could hardly keep his eyes on the road, the sight of her too exciting to deny. As he drove, he reached over to rest a hand on the inside of her thigh. His touch was strong and grounding, and she couldn't stop stealing glances at his hand. It was so new, but at the same time, his presence was so familiar, as though this was where the two of them had always belonged.

For a moment, even though she knew it wasn't going to last long, she felt as though the weight of everything that was going on around them was lifting from her mind and she could finally relax. Of course, she knew it wasn't that easy, but she was happy, and with Lawson, and she just wanted to take a moment to enjoy it.

He pulled the truck to a halt in the town square, and he offered her a hand to help her out. He dropped a kiss on her cheek before he looked over toward the jail.

"You going to be alright?" he asked her, concerned.

"I'm just going to the store." She laughed. "I'm going to be fine."

"You better be," he warned her playfully, and she kissed him again. She couldn't get enough of him right now. "I'll see you in a bit."

She watched him walk toward the station, then turned and headed in the direction of the store. As she made her way across the street, her attention was drawn to the bar she and her friends had been to last night. She paused when she reached the sidewalk. Maybe she could just pop in for a minute and ask about those guys from last night? See if they were regulars or passing through. Help put her mind at ease.

Even though there was a Closed sign in the window, she knocked on the door, and a moment later, an older woman's face appeared through the glass before she opened the door to greet her.

"Everything alright?" she asked.

"Sorry to bother you," Sarah blurted out. "I just… I wanted to ask you about a couple of guys who were in here last night?"

"The ones who ordered those drinks for you and your friends, you mean?" she asked, nodding knowingly.

"You've got a good memory. Yeah, those guys," Sarah replied. "Have you seen them around before?"

"I have," she responded. "They pass through here on their

way to work a few times a year. Not exactly the most clean-cut guys you'll ever meet, but they're harmless enough."

"Right," Sarah said, breathing a sigh of relief. "Sorry to bother you. Thanks."

"Sure," the woman replied, and she closed the door again and set about taking care of whatever she had been doing before Sarah had interrupted her.

Sarah closed her eyes for a moment and inhaled deeply. See? There was nothing for her to worry about—those guys had just been trying their luck, hitting up her and her friends in the hopes they might turn out to be single. She didn't have to read anything else into it.

She hooked her bag over her shoulder and headed off toward the store, feeling a little lighter. She knew that last night had just been her fear and anxiety getting the better of her, and she was a little embarrassed about it. Even though Lawson had told her there was no problem with her playing it safe, she couldn't help but wonder if he was secretly rolling his eyes at her behind her back.

No, he would never have done that, and she knew it. He just wasn't that kind of guy. What you saw was what you got with him. It was one of the reasons she liked him so much.

"Sarah?"

She startled, then grinned when she saw Lawson coming toward her, then cocked her head, a little confused.

"I thought you were interviewing those guys today?"

"I was supposed to, but Sheriff Willis is out right now. I guess I should have called first," he replied. "You need a hand with that grocery shopping?"

"Oh, I could always use a big strong man to help carry the bags." She laughed, handing him the reusable ones she had brought with her. "Here, you take these."

They walked to the grocery store, and she hummed along to the tinny music playing over the speakers as they picked out dinner together. It felt almost surreal, doing something as mundane as this with him, but in a good way. She'd love to repeat it as often as she got the chance. Maybe that was a little selfish, but hell, who could blame her? She loved having him all to herself.

As they checked out, she felt eyes on her and looked over to see Lawson watching her. She glanced up at him with a smile and he winked back, causing her to blush. They made small talk while the cashier continued to ring up their groceries and it felt like the most natural thing in the world. They seemed to share an easy rhythm between them and Sarah had to reach out and touch his hand just to make sure she wasn't dreaming. He squeezed her hand back, and then they gathered the bags and headed back to the truck to load them up.

"I think this is going to be enough to keep us going all summer." He laughed.

She shrugged. "Hey, not all of it is for me. Plus, I like to think ahead," she replied as they climbed back into the truck. But, before they could drive off, Lawson got a text on his phone. He looked down at it and grimaced slightly.

"What is it?" she asked.

"The sheriff," he replied. "He says I should head over there now. They're ready for me." He glanced over at her. "You want me to drive you back up to the lodge?" he asked. "I can come back down afterward, it's no trouble..."

"Don't be silly," she answered, shaking her head. "You don't need to go all the way up there and back again. You'll spend two hours just driving. It's daytime and I'm perfectly capable of driving myself. How long do you think you'll be?"

"A few hours, at least."

"Text me when you're done," she suggested. "And I'll come pick you up."

"You don't have to—"

"I know I don't," she replied softly, reaching over to touch his arm lightly. "I want to, Lawson. I want to help."

"Okay, well, if you're sure," he said as he handed Sarah his keys.

"I'll go up and drop off the groceries and check in with everyone, then I'll come back down and grab myself a coffee while I wait," she suggested. "I don't have any appointments today and I could use the change of scenery."

"You going to be alright on your own?"

"Of course, I will," she replied. "I might have been a little out of sorts last night, but I can handle myself. You don't have to worry about me."

A weight seemed to ease from his shoulders when she said that, and she was so glad to see him give in and stop worrying about her for a change. It wasn't that she hadn't given him reason to be concerned over these last few weeks, but the last thing she wanted was for him to neglect other things he needed to focus on to hover around her.

There was only one main road up the mountain to the lodge and she knew it like the back of her hand. Plus, it was the middle of the day, so she knew there'd be no trouble on the road right now. The men Lawson and the others were after, including the two locked up at the police station, skulked around in the dark of night. No way would they try something in daylight, on a well-traveled road where anyone could drive by and see. Those kind of men preferred the shadows to keep them safe.

Sarah sat and watched as Lawson crossed the street to the police station. He turned to wave at her before he went inside, and she waved back and then put the truck in gear and pulled out on to the road. A truck full of groceries, a sky full of sunshine and a sweet man waiting for her to come pick him up. Did it get any better than that?

Chapter Sixteen

Lawson entered the police station, where Sheriff Willis was waiting for him, arms crossed, a terse expression on his face.

"Finally, you're here," he muttered. "Kept me waiting long enough."

Lawson stopped in his tracks. "You weren't around when I first came by," Lawson pointed out, cocking an eyebrow at the sheriff. If there was one thing he had never credited the sheriff with, it was a short temper.

Sheriff Willis rubbed a hand over his face. There were dark rings beneath his eyes, and Lawson couldn't help but feel a little sorry for him. Clearly, it had been a long-ass night, dealing with those two prisoners in lockup, and it looked as though it was taking its toll.

"You good?" Lawson asked him.

The sheriff nodded. "Sorry. Just wish they weren't in my station, that's all," he replied, nodding in the direction of the cells that held the two prisoners.

"They been giving you trouble?"

"They've been talking a big game," Sheriff Willis muttered, sighing. "Giving my officers plenty to think about. Seems like Granger taught them to be as difficult as possible while they were under lock and key. Probably thought it would get them released sooner that way."

"Sorry you had to be involved in this. Thanks for dealing with them," Lawson replied grimly. He could only imagine what kind of trash talk the thugs had been saying to the police officers who worked here. All the threats and taunts they were probably maliciously spewing to get a reaction, or cause the officers to drop their guards so they could get the upper hand.

"I understand why they're here. I just hope this can get wrapped up quickly. They're both causing such a ruckus, none of my officers are comfortable being around them," the sheriff remarked as he went to grab the keys from behind the counter. "When you're done, we'll get them transferred over to the FBI and it can become their headache. Our small town isn't set up to handle something of this magnitude."

Lawson couldn't help but feel bad for the man, especially with all the danger that had surrounded the lodge over the past couple of years. Normally, Blue Ridge was a quiet, peaceful town that didn't see much action in terms of criminal activity. There had been a lot the sheriff had to step in and deal with concerning the lodge that no one had expected or been prepared for. None of them at Warrior Peak had any idea of the constant danger they would face.

They were all ready for it to be over and done with, so they could get back to their normal day-to-day without having threats and danger constantly hanging over the heads. They were all due a break.

"Have you already contacted the FBI?" Lawson asked as they made their way to the interrogation rooms. He knew there was a chance the FBI would step in immediately, but he was hoping he'd at least be able to take a quick stab at the suspects before they were taken into FBI custody.

"I did," Sheriff Willis replied. "I filled them in on everything you told me and sent what information I had over to them. They've got some agents on the way, said they'd probably be here tomorrow."

"So what you're saying is I've got one shot to talk to them both, see what I can find out before they're gone," Lawson confirmed, and the sheriff nodded with a grim smile.

"Sorry I couldn't give you more time. I just want them out of here. All this trafficking stuff is too dangerous for our small-town police station." Sheriff Willis gestured down the hallway. "Donner's in the first interrogation room," he told him. "You ready to get started?"

"Yep, let's do this," Lawson replied, steeling himself for what lay ahead.

Lawson had looked over Paul Donner's rap sheet the previous night while he'd been at the station, and it was pretty impressive, he had to admit. Impressive in a way that he was surprised Donner had been able to set foot outside a prison at all. Assault, drug charges, illegal possession of a weapon, attempted murder…the list went on. Obviously, Granger had the right kind of connections to keep his guys from doing hard time.

Sheriff Willis unlocked the door, and Lawson led the way inside. Donner was cuffed to the table, and he shook his chains demonstratively as soon as Lawson stepped inside.

"Let me out of these," he snarled, and Lawson ignored him. The man was going to throw as much nonsense as he could at them to avoid dealing with the real questions at hand, and it was up to Lawson to keep his cool. He'd handled plenty of people like Donner over the years, and if the man thought he was going to get under his skin, he didn't stand a chance.

Lawson sat down opposite the perp, while the sheriff stood behind Lawson, hands clasped before him, like a security guard.

"I don't know what I'm doing here," Donner snapped. "This is false arrest!"

"Really, Mr. Donner?" Lawson asked. "Because I've had a look at your file. And with the stuff they found in your car alone, you'd go down for many years. Not to mention the attempted kidnapping charge."

"What kidnapping?" the man retorted. "I didn't kidnap anyone." He leaned back in his seat smugly, locking eyes with Lawson. "I think you should be the one on this side of the table," he remarked. "You're the one who assaulted us. When we hadn't done anything wrong. We were just going to use the bathroom."

Lawson steadily held the other man's gaze and raised an eyebrow at his comments. Donner could try to spin the arrest any way he wanted, but Lawson wasn't stupid. He knew exactly what the thug and his buddy were out there to do. And it certainly wasn't to use the facilities.

Sheriff Willis snorted with amusement, and Donner's eyes darkened.

Lawson calmly clasped his hands in front of him on the table. "What can you tell us about Victor Granger and his operation?" he began. "If you share what you know, we can see about cutting you a deal, like Mr. Adams."

For the briefest moment, Lawson could see the doubt in the other man's eyes, as he wondered if what Lawson had said was true. Lawson stared back at him, poker face in place, keeping up the act, but then Donner's lip curled into a sneer.

"Yeah, no way has he said anything about anything," he replied. "Nice try, man. You have any clue what Victor does to snitches? Worse than anything you could think of."

"So, fill us in. Tell us what we need to know," Lawson said. "Give us his location. Tell us about his operation. We won't let on that you gave anything away. It's your best chance for a lighter sentence. If you show some kind of cooperation."

Donner barked out a harsh laugh, shaking his head. "You people… This little backwoods town has no clue the nightmare he'll rain down on you all. You'll never be able to sleep again, wondering when he's coming for you, or what he'll do to you and anyone you care about."

Lawson felt his muscles tense at Donner's words, and he saw the sheriff shifting uncomfortably from the corner of his eye. Sheriff Willis was already unsettled enough about these two men being in his station, and he didn't need to hear this. It would only make his apprehension about the whole affair worse.

Watching Donner across the table and seeing the fear flickering in his eyes at what his boss might do to him had Lawson wondering exactly what kind of horrors Granger had drilled into his men's heads about the consequences of snitching if they were caught. He almost didn't want to know.

Suddenly, Donner's eyes went flat and darkened, his gaze locked on Lawson with what looked like madness.

"You go after Victor, it'll be the last mistake you ever make," he warned Lawson, his eyes burning. “You and everyone you know. You have no idea how dangerous he is.”

“Why don’t you tell us, then? Help us and yourself.”

“You don’t have a damn clue.” He laughed again, the sound bouncing off the walls around them. “I’m going to enjoy seeing you find out.”

Lawson could see why the sheriff had looked so exhausted when he had arrived today. All the crap Donner was spouting off, and he assumed Jim Adams would be the same.

“You’re going to get yourselves killed and you’re going to deserve it,” he continued, an evil grin spreading over his face. “I wish I could be there when it happens. You’ll find out soon enough who you’re dealing with.”

“We’re not getting anything out of him. Come on, Lawson, let’s go,” Sheriff Willis muttered behind him.

Lawson rose to his feet and tried not to react to the sheriff saying his name in front of this thug.

A thoughtful look crossed Donner’s face, then he grinned. “Lawson, huh?” he remarked. “Not a common name. Especially around these parts. You think he won’t be able to find you? You’re a walking dead man, Lawson.”

Lawson glared back at him, trying not to let the fear that gripped his chest take hold.

Normally, he’d let this kind of threat bounce off, but now? Now, he had something to lose. All he could think of was Sarah and all she’d been through recently. Then his thoughts quickly shifted to his sister and the others at the lodge. The thought of Granger and his men coming after any of them had a chill racing down Lawson’s spine. He had to admit to himself it spooked the hell out of him and he couldn’t even try to deny it.

They stepped out of the interrogation room, Lawson shutting the door behind them, and the sheriff grimaced and rubbed a hand down his face.

“I’m sorry for dropping your name back there. Rookie mistake,” he apologized. “I’m tired. I wasn’t thinking.”

“It’s okay,” Lawson replied, though his gut was churning. “They would have found out who I was one way or another, anyway.”

Sheriff Willis lowered his voice and looked over his shoulder, like someone might be eavesdropping on their conversation. “These guys have me rattled,” he admitted. “I’ve had some rough types in here before, don’t get me wrong, but this…the way they’re coming at us, it’s just different. Like they know they’ve got the devil on their side, and they’ll do anything they can to turn him loose on us.”

“I get it. Don’t let them get to you,” Lawson warned him. “That’s what they want. Until they give us reason to think otherwise, they’re all bark.”

The sheriff nodded, but there was still a wariness to his expression, as though he didn’t entirely believe Lawson’s claim. Lawson had to hope it was just because the older man was exhausted, not because he was actually letting these guys get to him.

“Where’s Adams?” he asked, steeling himself for round two. His rap sheet hadn’t been as impressive as Donner’s, but he still had plenty on it to keep him locked up.

The sheriff nodded to the cells lining the end of the corridor. “Down there,” he replied. Lawson gritted his teeth. He silently swore to himself that no matter what this guy threw at him, he would be able to deal with it. These weren’t the worst of the people they’d have to handle if they were going to take down Granger, and Lawson wasn’t going to let these thugs throw him off his game.

The moment they reached Jim Adams’s cell, the man was on his feet, pressed against the bars.

“Where’s Paul?” he demanded.

“None of your business,” Lawson replied. Adams gripped the bars, his hands holding on so tightly his knuckles looked nearly white.

“Tell me what you’ve done with him,” he continued, practically spitting out the words.

“You don’t trust him?” Lawson asked. “You think he might have spilled something? Or sold you out for a plea deal?”

Unlike his buddy, Adams didn’t even seem to consider that as a possibility for a moment. He snorted with amusement.

“You think that he would sell out Granger like that? For a

speck on the map like you?" he demanded, jabbing his finger through the bars at Lawson. Lawson took a step back, not wanting this creep to lay a hand on him.

"You know what he's going to do with you the moment he finds out about this?" he continued, his voice rising with each word out of his mouth. "He's going to wipe you off the face of the earth. There's going to be nothing of you left! Do you understand that? There's nothing you can do to stop it! He's coming for you right now!"

Adams kept babbling, barely pausing to take a breath. Spittle was flying from his mouth as he spoke, and the cell bars rattled as he shook them. He was getting more agitated and animated over the words he threw at them. The churning in Lawson's gut intensified as he watched the man become more unhinged.

Lawson was starting to get a clearer picture of the hold Granger had on his men. Apparently, it bordered on the extreme, and Lawson in no way wanted to know what the man had done to his crew to have this Adams go off the rails like this. If all of the men in Granger's operation held this kind of loyalty, Lawson and his team were definitely going to be in for the fight of their lives when it came time to face him and his gang of thugs.

"And you're going to end up dead. You and everyone you care about." Adams spat at them, then fell back on the bench and started cackling gleefully.

Lawson's heart dropped. *Sarah.* Once again, she was the first person he thought of when Adams said that. He would never forgive himself if something bad happened to her as a result of them going after Granger and his crew. He could still remember the terror he'd seen in her eyes from the fire and its aftermath, when Bailey and Aaron's past caught up with them at the lodge all those months ago. The thought of her being dragged into more danger because of her connection to Lawson made him feel sick.

Adams seemed to realize he'd landed a blow that actually hurt. His eyes drilled in to Lawson's, total certainty on his face, as though there wasn't a doubt in his mind that he was telling the truth.

"Tick tock. It's only a matter of time now," Adams said, tapping a watch that wasn't there.

Lawson gritted his teeth. He had told the sheriff not to let these guys get to him, but Lawson wasn't sure he could take his own advice.

Chapter Seventeen

Sarah lifted the decaf coffee to her lips and took a sip, enjoying the last of the late afternoon sunshine as the day began to shift into evening.

She had been back to the lodge, dropped off the groceries, checked in with Hannah and Xavier, and returned a few emails before she made the hour-long drive back into town to pick up Lawson from the police station. She sent him a text when she arrived, telling him to meet her at the corner café across the street when he was done. He hadn't responded so she had no idea how long he would be, but that was just fine by her. She was happy to relax, sip on her coffee and nibble at the carrot cake she had ordered. It wasn't often she got a chance to come to town and people-watch like this, but there was something really fun about observing the townsfolk going about their business.

Her interest in people, after all, had been what had gotten her into her line of work in the first place. She was always curious about what was going on in people's lives and in their minds, and how she could help them deal with their problems and emotions. She found the human brain so fascinating.

As she watched couples chatting and kids running around, she smiled. It was hard to believe that a town like this could have a possible sex-trafficking problem, though she doubted anyone she was currently observing here would know a thing about it.

And she hoped it stayed that way. Now that Lawson had gotten those two guys into custody, it was surely only a matter of time before they got the information they needed to take down Granger and shut down his operation.

Finally, as she finished up her coffee, she spotted Lawson coming out of the police station across the street. Even from here, she could tell he had a grim expression on his handsome face. He must not have gotten the information he needed, she thought. She tossed her trash and walked out to meet him.

"How did it go?" she asked him softly, reaching for his hand and giving him his keys back.

He frowned. "Not as well as I'd hoped," he admitted. He switched the keys to his other hand, then entwined his fingers with hers.

"You didn't get much out of them?"

"We didn't get anything out of them," he replied, shaking his head. "But I expected that. It was… They seemed like they were enjoying themselves and weren't worried at all about giving anything away."

"What do you mean?" she asked, frowning. That didn't make any sense to her. Why would they have enjoyed being interrogated? They had to know that the business they were involved with was seriously dangerous, and they would be facing years, maybe even decades, in prison if the truth of everything they had done came out.

"Instead of answering questions they were taunting the officers, making them uncomfortable, and spewing threats. Just trying to get a rise out of everyone," he admitted, as they walked hand in hand toward the truck, which was parked in the town square. "One thing they both kept saying was that Granger was going to come after us. Going to…"

He trailed off, shaking his head as he reached the truck and unlocked the door, like he had all at once decided that she didn't need to hear the rest. A shiver ran down her spine. She didn't want him keeping things from her, but judging by the look on his face, she had to trust that she was better off not knowing.

"It's okay," she told him softly. "You did your best, right? And what matters is that you have them locked up. They aren't out there trying to take more young women. That has to count for something."

"You're right," he acknowledged, but the furrow between his eyebrows told a different story. She knew that he wanted to get to the bottom of it all. She wished she could help in some way. But she had learned the hard way that nothing came that easy—

All at once, the quiet of the town square was shattered by a noise. A popping sound. Then another.

At first, Sarah thought it was a car backfiring. But, as Lawson spun around to step in front of her, she realized what it actually was.

Gunshots. Someone was shooting.

"Get in the truck and get your head down!" Lawson ordered her as he yanked open the driver's-side door and grabbed something from underneath the seat. She stood there for a moment, frozen, unable to move.

"Sarah, now!" he yelled at her, and it snapped her out of her fugue state. She dived into the truck, ducking down on the floorboard, and wrapped her arms around her knees as her heart pounded in her chest. Her mind was racing. What the hell was going on out there? Why was someone shooting? It had been so peaceful, so safe, and now…it was shattered by the sound of gunfire.

She jolted as a bullet hit the side of the truck, a dent appearing in the door just a few inches from her. Her eyes widened, panic flooding her system.

Another bullet hit the metal, and another, the dents pushing inward, like the side of the truck was about to buckle in on itself. Was Lawson okay? If the bullets were hitting the truck, then they weren't hitting him, right?

She heard another gunshot, this time sounding closer, and wrapped her arms around her head, trying to block out the noise. She was shaking and started to whimper, but could hardly pay attention. Loud. It was all so loud and terrifying. She wanted to see what was going on but was scared to move. She couldn't believe this was happening right now. And Lawson… Where was he?

Suddenly there was silence. It was almost deafening—it had gotten so quiet so fast. Sarah's heart thudded in her chest and she held her breath, praying that Lawson was going to call her name. She needed to know he was okay. If something had happened to him, she didn't know what she would do…

And then, all at once, the door next to her opened. She jerked back and screamed. But instead of some would-be attacker, Lawson stood there, staring down at her with fury in his eyes.

"You okay?" he asked urgently.

She pulled her arms away from her head and looked up at him slowly, and then nodded. "I think so," she breathed. Her mouth was dry and her body felt numb. She'd been crumpled up on the floorboard and she wasn't sure she could get her limbs to cooperate. She didn't think she'd been hit, though there had been a lot of bullets pinging off the truck's frame. She couldn't be sure until her body was completely functioning again.

And the same couldn't be said for Lawson.

Her eyes widened when she saw a red stain on his right side. She reached out to grab his shirt and pulled it up, revealing a bloody gash on his skin.

"What happened?" she exclaimed, terror flashing in her eyes. She tried to squirm her way off the floorboard.

"It's fine, just a graze," he assured her, gently brushing her hand away. As he shifted, she noticed that he had a gun in his other hand. So the shots she'd heard from nearby had been from him.

"Just a graze?" she exclaimed. "You're bleeding!"

"I'll be fine," he promised her. "Can you step out of the truck? I want to get a look at you."

With Lawson's hand under her arm, and Sarah pushing up on the seat, she managed to get herself up and stepped out of the truck.

First thing she noticed was that the square was empty—everyone who had been here before must have scattered when the gunfire started. She knew this incident would change the fabric of the town entirely.

She craned her head around as Lawson looked her over and

her heart dropped when she saw someone sprawled, not moving, on the ground next to the police station.

Lawson saw her staring, and shifted so that he was blocking her view.

"Hey, you don't need to see that," he told her gently.

"Who is that?" she demanded, voice trembling. "The sheriff?"

"No, the sheriff's okay."

"Well, who is that? What happened?" she asked again.

"I don't know exactly yet," he admitted with a sigh. "But Donner and Adams were both rushing out of the station firing, so I'd guess somehow they managed to get weapons off a couple officers inside and made a run for it. The sheriff and his guys are not used to dealing with men like these."

"They both had guns?" she gasped. "And they—they were shooting at you?"

"Yeah, trying to make good on their threats, I suppose," he replied as he gazed down at her. She could feel the tension radiating off him, and she knew he must be unnerved by what happened, though he was doing everything he could not to let her see it.

"So the dead guy is one of them?"

He gestured behind him, toward the unmoving body on the sidewalk. "Jim Adams."

"Oh," she replied. A bad guy was dead. And Lawson, if she was guessing right, had been the one to kill him. The thought made her stomach twist into knots. He'd done what he'd had to do, of course, but she had never imagined she would see something like that, and definitely not here in Blue Ridge.

"And what about the other one?" she asked.

"Donner made a break for it," he admitted.

Her eyes widened. They hadn't recaptured him. The other man was gone. Sarah wrapped her arms around her middle. The thought of that man running back to Granger and then him setting his sights on this town… The danger around them had just multiplied tenfold.

A few officers emerged from the station to deal with the mess that had been left outside their building and to take care of Jim Adams's body. The sun was fading now, bringing a dark night. A cold chill ran through Sarah's body, though she knew it was nothing to do with the weather.

"They said they were going to come after you," she muttered.

Lawson nodded. "They did," he replied.

She could tell by his posture that he wished he hadn't told her that. But that didn't matter now. She already knew they'd all be in danger when the guys first set out to find the men kidnapping women on the mountain road.

"So, what now?" she asked as they continued to glance around the damaged town square.

"I've got to go back over and give a statement and check in with the sheriff," Lawson told Sarah. "Do you want to come with me, or go back and wait inside the café?"

Sarah shivered again and shook her head. No way was she staying here by herself, not after what just happened. "I'll come with you," she said quickly and latched on to his hand.

Lawson nodded and wrapped his arm around her as they made their way across the square and back into the police station, meeting Sheriff Willis at the door. He left Sarah in the waiting area and followed the angry sheriff back to the interrogation room.

After what felt like forever, Lawson reemerged looking more haggard and holding his side like he was in pain.

He walked right up to Sarah and drew her into his arms, then kissed her forehead.

"Come on, we need to get you back to the lodge," he told her. She didn't speak as he steered her gently back toward the truck. Gun smoke still lingered in the air, the scent of it cloying in her nostrils. She wanted to forget this had ever happened, but she knew it wouldn't be that easy. Especially with Lawson being hurt.

"You should have had someone look at your wound while you were in there," she gently chided.

He shook his head, opened the passenger door, and helped her inside. After sliding into the driver's seat, he palmed the wheel and glanced over at her. He must have noticed her expression and knew how much the situation was getting to her.

"It's going to be okay, Sarah," Lawson told her, putting a hand on hers and giving it a tight squeeze.

And, as much as she wanted to believe him, she had no idea if she actually could. Not with one of those men on the loose, and not when he was likely running back to his boss to tell him all about them.

Chapter Eighteen

Lawson gently pressed the cloth against Sarah's arm as she perched on the edge of his bed. She was staring off into space like she had no idea at all where she was.

The lodge was quiet except for the raised voices Lawson could hear drifting up from downstairs. He knew the guys were arguing about what had happened in town and what the best course of action would be now that Adams had escaped.

As soon as Lawson and Sarah had arrived back at the lodge, he'd asked her to wait for him in his room while he talked to the guys. After she went upstairs, he had filled Cade, Xavier and Aaron in on everything that had happened since the previous night. The rest stop bust, Adams's and Donner's interrogations, their escape, and Adams's death by Lawson's hand.

The guys were just as concerned about Donner's words as Lawson was. Even though the man only had Lawson's first name, if someone had the right resources it wouldn't take them long to find out his last name, as well as information about Warrior Peak and the others there. Victor Granger could easily be that someone.

Lawson left the guys discussing plans while he went to check on Sarah. His mind kept turning to her while they were talking and he needed to reassure himself that she was truly okay.

"You should be down there with them," she mumbled.

He lifted his gaze to meet hers. There was a long, thin cut on the side of her arm from where she had dived into the truck to take cover. Neither of them had noticed until she mentioned the sting on the drive back, and he was cleaning it up before he walked her back to her cabin to get some rest.

"They can deal with it for now," he replied, though he knew she was right. These guys relied on him to lead their team, and he needed to be involved in whatever plans they were making next, so he did need to get downstairs and meet with them soon.

But Sarah had been trembling like a leaf when they had arrived back at the lodge, and he knew he needed to take care of her first. He couldn't even imagine how terrified she had been when she had heard those gunshots going off in town. He was used to this, to some extent, between the military and his stint in the CIA, even if Blue Ridge town square had been the very last place he had imagined having to fight off attackers.

But her? She wasn't used to this. She needed help. The adrenaline would still be coursing through her system right now, and he couldn't leave her alone.

He smoothed the cloth over her arm, and she twisted it around to look at the angry red mark on the back of her forearm.

"It's not that bad," she told him.

"I hate that you got hurt at all," he muttered. At least she hadn't been shot. His side had been grazed, but he could barely feel it. He would likely start to feel that all-too-familiar sting soon, but he didn't care about that at all when she was so scared and needed him to comfort her.

"What about you?" she asked, nodding to his wound.

He glanced down at the stain of blood on his shirt and shrugged. "It's fine," he replied. "I doubt it even needs stitches."

"Let me have a look, at least," she insisted, peeling up his shirt and wincing when she saw his side.

"That looks bad," she murmured, and he grabbed a bandage from the first aid kit and slapped it on to appease her. He didn't want her worrying about him. She needed to focus on herself and her own mental health. He could tell on the drive back to the lodge that she was starting to withdraw into herself from stress and fear. He wanted to help her calm down and he hoped that reassuring her that he was alright would help with that.

"It'll heal in no time," he assured her. "I've had plenty worse, trust me."

She managed a small smile. "That doesn't make me feel better," she said, and he kneeled before her, hands on her legs.

"What would make you feel better?" he asked her.

She took a deep breath. "I want you to be honest with me," she replied. "What happens now that one of them has gotten away?"

He sighed. He knew he owed her the truth, after what she had just been through, but he wasn't sure she would be able to handle it. She looked down at him, kneeling in front of her, her eyes full of certainty. She deserved to know what came next, and he believed she was strong enough to take it in stride.

"It means that Donner will be heading back to Granger," he explained. "And that we don't have the element of surprise on our side anymore. Or time. He'll do his research on us, find out who we are and where we are. Then he's going to make a move. It'll be fast. Now that he knows what went down and that we're trying to disrupt his operations."

She nodded, letting out a shaky breath.

"That's pretty much what I thought," she said. "What—what are we going to do?"

"I don't know yet," he admitted. "I need to talk with the guys, and fill Lainey in on what happened earlier."

In the chaos of everything that had been going on, he had almost forgotten about Lainey, which he felt guilty about now. What if they knew where she was and went after her? He didn't think that was possible, since no one knew she had been there. But if Granger really had the connections all over the place like Lainey claimed he did, she could be in more trouble than she realized.

"Why don't you give her a call to tell her what's happening?" Sarah suggested.

"Good idea," he agreed, and he pulled out his phone and dialed Lainey's number, resting his arm on the bed next to Sarah as he did so. She rubbed his shoulders gently, as though she could sense how tense he was.

No answer. He ended the call and tried again…and again, and again. But nothing. His jaw tensed. He didn't like this, not one bit. Especially not after the events of the day.

He put his phone away, and Sarah slipped her arms around him, searching his eyes. For what, he wasn't sure, but decided not to ask. He knew she was concerned for him, just as he was for her.

"She's probably fine," she assured him. "Maybe she's in the shower or stepped out for a minute or something. I bet she'll call you as soon as she sees she missed your call."

"I hope so," he said, though he wasn't sure he entirely believed it.

She leaned her head against his for a moment, and he closed his eyes. He just wanted this to be over. Maybe he never should have gotten involved with this in the first place, but he knew there was no way he could let Lainey face this on her own. She was his friend, after all, and he stood by his friends, no matter how hard it might be, or what dangerous situations they needed help with.

"I've got this…feeling," she murmured, her voice tinged with worry. "Like something bad's going to happen."

He opened his eyes and pulled back, gathering her in his arms.

"It's going to be fine," he promised her with as much certainty as he could muster. "Try not to worry, I'll do everything in my power to protect you."

"I know. I trust you."

He planted a kiss on her lips, sealing his promise. He didn't care what happened next, he didn't care what kind of danger he had to face to keep her safe—he would do it.

"Come on, let's get you back to your cabin. I'll tell the guys we'll meet in the morning. I think we could all use a good night's rest." He held on to her hand as they walked down the stairs and out of the lodge.

When they got to her door, he gave her one more kiss and

waited until she was inside before heading back to the lodge to tell the guys they'd meet tomorrow.

He wasn't sure what would come next, but he did know they all needed to be alert and ready.

"SO LET ME GET this straight. You were almost shot dead in the town square?" Hannah asked Lawson, raising her eyebrows at him in horror.

"He was never going to get me from that angle," he protested. "And besides, I had a gun. I could protect myself."

The air was tense this morning while all eight of them gathered in the main greeting area of the lodge and went over everything again from the last couple of days.

Lawson and Sarah had both been exhausted and the guys had been too wound up to deal with the day's events last night. Everyone needed a clearer head and a good night's rest to process what had happened and come up with their next course of action.

Facing Granger and his men sleep-deprived would do none of them any good in the end.

"In Lawson's defense," Sarah rushed to add, "there was no way to know something like that would happen. We were leaving one minute, then the next, shots were being fired. Lawson did what he had to do to protect us both."

"I thought we could trust Sheriff Willis and his men," Xavier muttered, clearly disappointed. "But if they couldn't even keep those two under lock and key—"

"Hey, now that's not fair," Bailey chimed in. "That is the first time since I started working at the station that something like this has happened. Those two creeps were making all kinds of noise and had everyone uneasy. Everyone—"

"Xavier. They're not used to dealing with people like that," Lawson protested, interrupting Bailey. He didn't want their discussion getting off-track. "They didn't stand a chance. It's a miracle none of them got hurt."

"No, they came right after you," Cade pointed out. "They could have killed you. In the middle of the town square. In front of everyone."

Lawson felt the wound in his side throbbing at him again. It wasn't bad, but it was a reminder of how close he had come to taking a bullet in the gut.

"But they didn't," Lawson replied urgently. "And we don't have time to talk about what might have happened. We've got to focus on what we're going to do now that one of them has gotten away."

"Yeah, and where do we start with that?" Xavier asked. "We don't even know how long it's going to take Paul Donner to get to Granger—"

"Or where he even is," Cade added.

Before Lawson could reply, his phone buzzed in his pocket and he turned away to take the call. The others were so lost in the intensity of their conversation, they hardly even noticed he'd stepped away. He glanced down at the screen: *Unknown number.*

Lainey calling him back?

He'd tossed and turned all night, silently willing her to return his call so he could stop worrying about where she was or what might have happened.

He answered the call, expecting to hear Lainey's voice on the line. But instead, he froze to the spot when he heard a man's smooth, low voice filling his ear instead.

"Lawson Davies," the man said.

He immediately knew whose voice was on the line.

He swallowed hard, but before he could say something in return, Granger spoke again.

"I hear you and your friends have been looking for me," the man continued, his voice calm, unbothered. "I'm a little disappointed that it wasn't more of a challenge to find you. But I'm also delighted to learn a former CIA agent somehow ended up on my tail. I made sure to thank our nosy mutual friend with her help in that."

Granger paused and gave that revelation a moment to settle in Lawson's gut. Then he made a tsking sound, like he was scolding a wayward child, before he continued. "Poor Lainey Daye cracked like an egg. It was such a surprise to come up on her in that small little town. And my man Paul—the one you had unlawfully arrested—confirmed her whole story before he took his last breath. He was decent help, but he was also responsible for them getting caught and Jim getting killed. I couldn't let that go unpunished."

He chuckled darkly. The sound of it sent a shiver down Lawson's spine. The others seemed to have noticed something was wrong and turned to see what was going on.

"Is Lainey okay? What have you done with her?" Lawson demanded, finally managing to force out the words. He already knew what the answer was going to be.

Granger barked with amusement. "Who do you think I am, Mister Rogers?" he retorted. "No. I'm sorry to report that she is most definitely not okay." He paused briefly. "And for the record, you and your friends won't be, either, when I get my hands on you. I don't appreciate people sticking their damn noses in my business, Mr. Davies."

"If you hurt her—"

"Your words don't mean anything to me," Granger interrupted sharply. "Ms. Daye already understands the repercussions of not minding her own business. However, I will be visiting her again shortly and I'll make sure to give her your regards. Oh, and do say hello to that pretty little therapist of yours, will you? What's her name… Sarah Peterson. I look forward to meeting her soon. Maybe she can help me work out some of my kinks. I bet she's good at that."

And with that, the line went dead. Sheer rage coursed through Lawson's body at the sound of Granger talking about Sarah. He could have crushed the phone in his hand, but he knew he had to keep it together. Behind him, silence filled the room, and he turned to face everyone again.

"Who was that?" Xavier asked, frowning at the phone in Lawson's hand.

Sarah stared at him from the other side of the room, her face white, as though she had sensed that Granger had been talking about her.

"Granger," he replied bluntly. "He's got Lainey and he made her talk. He knows about us. And the lodge."

"Damn it," Cade muttered, reaching for River and putting his arm around her protectively.

"He's going to be coming here. We need to make preparations," Aaron replied, reaching his hand out toward Bailey. She gripped his hand hard enough that her knuckles turned white and Aaron pulled her to his side.

"What we need to do is get the guests to safety," River replied, pressing into Cade's side for support. "I know what it feels like to be trapped in a place under siege and not knowing if you're going to survive. It's not fair to everyone here to have to go through that."

Sarah walked over to stand beside Lawson, nodding at River to acknowledge her concerns.

"I agree with River. We need to get everyone off the property now," Sarah insisted. "We have a duty to everyone here. We can't let them stay now that Granger knows about the lodge. They'll be sitting ducks. They come here to recover and find peace. They don't deserve to be thrown back into a war."

"No. No way," Xavier replied, shaking his head. "This place is my home. We just got everything almost back to normal. I'm not leaving this place defenseless. I'm not going to be run off it by some two-bit—"

"We don't have a choice, Xavier!" Sarah protested.

"We all live here. It's our home too," Cade gruffly corrected.

"I agree with Xavier. I don't want to go," Hannah replied, her voice filled with anxiety at the situation they faced. "I—We need to provide stability for everyone who stays here, we can't just kick them out."

"We're not kicking them out," Sarah argued. "Think about it, people. This is supposed to be a place of healing, of safety. We can't provide stability for them if we're…" She trailed off, letting that unspoken word hang in the air between them all. She didn't need to say it out loud—everyone knew what she meant.

"They're right, Xavier, and you know it," Lawson said, stepping forward and nodding. "We can't risk leaving these people here as prey for Granger and his men. Everyone here could be hurt or worse. Do you really want that on your conscious? We need to get them out. Now."

Xavier gritted his teeth and fisted his hands down at his sides. Lawson could tell from just a glance that he was furious at the situation and wanted to put up more of a fight. Lawson couldn't worry about that now, though. Granger and his men would be coming for them soon and he just wanted to get the guests out of here before that happened.

And do everything he could to keep Sarah safe in the process.

Chapter Nineteen

"I don't get it," Chuck protested. "Why do we have to leave?"

"It's just for a few days," Sarah replied quickly. "You'll be back on the property before you know it. Is your stuff packed? We have another car leaving in a half hour."

Chuck crossed his arms over his chest and narrowed his eyes at her. "I'm not going until I get an explanation as to why we have to leave," he said.

Behind him, milling in the entrance hall to the lodge, were a half-dozen other guests who were equally confused as to what was going on. Sarah ran a hand through her hair, trying to pull herself together. She understood their reluctance to leave, especially without really knowing why they were asking them all to go. Unfortunately, though, she didn't have time to offer explanations right now. They were on a tight deadline to get the property cleared…fast. None of them could say for sure when Granger and his men would attack, the guys just knew it was going to be soon and they didn't want to get caught unprepared.

All the staff at the lodge were in the process of moving the guests to a motel in town, where the sheriff said he would have a few of his men standing guard until the threat from Victor Granger was neutralized. It wasn't much, but it was the best they could do for now. Sarah just knew there was no way they could stay here. All of them had been through so much to bring them to Warrior Peak in the first place, and she would never forgive herself if staying at the lodge now brought even more trauma into their lives.

Spinning a story to get them out of here had been tough, though, and Sarah felt guilty for uprooting them from their safe space without a good explanation. She had been trying to coax them into gathering their stuff and leaving, while the other women helped clear out their rooms and a couple of the guys shuttled them to town.

It had been an all-day job so far, and she could feel the exhaustion making her hazy around the edges. She wanted to curl up in bed and sleep, but she doubted she would be able to get any rest, even after all of the guests were safely at the motel.

"There's been a threat against the property," she told him finally. "We need to get you out of here until we can be sure that it's been dealt with."

Chuck's face dropped. There was a murmur of surprise among the other guests. Hopefully, that would be enough to hold them for now, and convince them it wasn't safe for them to be here.

"I'll finish packing up," Chuck muttered, and he rushed back toward his room, followed by the other guests who had overheard. Sarah closed her eyes and leaned back against the door for a moment, breathing a sigh of relief. This was the last group they had to get down to the motel, then the only ones left on the property would be the eight of them. The remaining staff would be staying in town, too.

Not that she imagined it was going to be much easier then, given how much Xavier had been digging in his heels about this. He and Lawson were in the office right now arguing. She'd passed by a half hour ago and heard raised voices, but she understood it. Though it was home to all of them, Xavier was the most attached to this place. It had, after all, been his family's property before they'd turned it into Warrior Peak Sanctuary. He had to feel like he was losing part of himself and his past by leaving the lodge to be threatened, possibly even destroyed, by Granger and his men.

Sarah shivered when she thought about that evil man, and

when she remembered the look Lawson had given her when he had gotten off that call with him. His eyes had landed on her immediately for a moment, and she had known without him having to say anything that Granger had said something about her.

Finally, when the last group of guests were shuttled out of the lodge, Sarah stepped outside to the porch and inhaled a big lungful of fresh air. It was nearly ten, and she could feel the raw exhaustion getting the better of her. From the moment the sound of gunfire had first filled the air in the town square yesterday, she hadn't had a moment to pull herself together. She wasn't even sure if she could at this point.

Especially with so much tension between the guys in the lodge right now. None of them had eaten all day, and she doubted that was helping much with their frazzled nerves. She had thought about going to the kitchen to cook something up, but with how shaky she was right now, she wouldn't have trusted herself around a hot stove.

She stared off to the edge of the property, where the trees that lined the horse paddocks in the distance had started to cast long shadows on the ground below. She shivered as she looked at the trees. They would provide good cover for someone looking to sneak up on them. She could almost feel eyes on her now, like Granger and his men were watching her from the shadows, ready to make their move at any moment.

"Hey."

She nearly jumped out of her skin when she heard a voice behind her. Turning, she saw it was Lawson.

"Oh, it's you," she murmured, sighing with relief.

He nodded, stepping out on to the porch behind her and slipping his arms around her waist. "Sorry to scare you," he said, placing a kiss on the side of her neck.

She closed her eyes, trying to let the comfort of his presence ground her some. It did, a little. It seemed like a miracle that anything could break through the weight of the fear in her system right now, but Lawson could.

"You finally get Xavier to agree with you?" she asked him, and he let out a small chuckle.

"The day I get Xavier to admit he's wrong about something

is the day hell freezes over," he said wryly. "I don't think I'll ever manage that. But he's not fighting me on it anymore, at least. He's with Hannah right now. Calming her down."

"She okay?"

"As much as she can be." He sighed. "I don't think any of us are exactly at the top of our game currently."

Sarah leaned against him and nodded in agreement. Right now, it felt as though they were on the eve of war, just waiting for the battle call to sound. It would be a miracle if they all made it out of this in one piece. Tensions were high, and everyone was scared, but dealing with it in their own way.

"Have you checked in with Sheriff Willis?" she asked him, and she felt him sigh against her neck.

"I tried to get through to him, but all the lines are busy and our cell phones don't seem to be working, either."

She turned to him, her brow furrowed. "Why do you think that is?"

"I think it's Granger trying to isolate us," he admitted. "This is his way of making sure we can't get anyone up here to help us."

"I guess it's a good thing that you spoke to the sheriff earlier when you were arranging protection for the guests. At least he's aware of what's happening up here."

"Yes, he's aware. He was dealing with the FBI when I spoke to him. Handling the Donner and Adams situation. And as soon as he's done, they'll all be heading this way." Sarah breathed a sigh of relief from his words.

"That's good news, then. Do you think they'll make it up here in time to help?" she asked hopefully.

Lawson searched her face, like he was committing her features to memory. "I'm not sure, but it would be great if they did. At least we know they'll be coming. Sarah…"

He stopped talking, and stared at her for a long moment. She knew, before he said anything, what was going to come out of his mouth. She had been ready for it, from the moment they had started moving people off the property.

"I need you to go, too, Sarah," he told her gently.

She shook her head. She had been preparing what she was

going to say to him since that morning. She could help them at the lodge, and she'd rather be in danger with the people she cared about than safe and alone, wondering what was happening.

"No. I need to be here," she replied firmly. "With you. And the other women, they need me. I know this place, I can be a help—"

"Sarah. You know you can't stay. It's too dangerous. I can't focus on what needs to be done if I'm worried about you," he pointed out. "I care too much about you to have you here when all hell breaks loose. I'd never be able to forgive myself if something happens to you."

Those words knocked the breath from her lungs. She knew exactly what he meant. It felt like such a twisted joke, for all of this to have happened now that they were together. It was so unfair.

"I can't leave you, Lawson," she breathed, and he closed his eyes, resting his forehead against hers for a moment.

"I don't want to be apart from you, Sarah, believe me," he murmured. "But I need to have a clear head going into this. And I can only have that if you're safely away from here. You need to go with the other women, and you can look out for each other. Bailey knows how to handle herself. You'll be safe with her."

She gazed at him. She knew there would be no changing his mind, but she still asked him one last time to reconsider.

"I don't want to leave you to take this on alone," she protested, even though she was certain it was futile.

"I'm not going to be alone," he assured her. "I have the best damn backup in the country. If anyone can end this, you know it's going to be us."

She smiled slightly. Well, he had a point there. Victor Granger might be scary, but he didn't know what he was dealing with—three former military, two being former CIA, too, and a former cop. Or the other things the past couple of years they'd had to face down together.

"Will you please go?" he asked her. "For me?"

"Yes, I'll go," she replied. "But promise me something, Lawson. Promise me you're not going to do anything crazy."

He kissed her, the kind of urgent, needy kiss that told her just how high the stakes were.

She grabbed his face, holding him there longer, not wanting this moment to be over.

He pulled back and smiled at her, a little sadly.

"You know I can't promise that," he replied. "Come on, pack your stuff. You need to leave."

Chapter Twenty

Lawson lifted a hand to wave off Sarah and the rest of the women, who were departing the lodge in Bailey's car. His heart twisted in his chest as he stared at Sarah, the sadness at leaving written all over her face. He wouldn't have expected anything less, but as long as she was going and would be safe, that was all he could ask for right now.

He thought she'd put up more of a fight to stay, but she seemed to understand how important it was that she left with the others.

When Granger had made that threat against her, Lawson knew there wasn't a chance in hell he could have kept her here without being out of his mind with worry the entire time. He wouldn't be able to focus and it would end up costing them all.

As soon as the car was out of sight, he turned to the team of men behind him—Cade, Aaron and Xavier stood next to the door, each of them with a grim expression on their face. They knew they were about to take on the fight of their lives, and whether they made it out in one piece was going to be down to their skills and their instincts. With their women safe, they could now focus on taking down Granger. For good.

"Come on, let's get geared up," Lawson instructed them. He had taken the lead, as he always did at the lodge. It was his tactical unit and he knew he couldn't let any of them think he had any doubts about how this was going to go. Sometimes being a good leader meant showing confidence you might not really feel in order to keep your team strong, assured and focused.

The guys headed inside to the dining room, where they had gathered everything they had in the way of weaponry and firepower—well, what was left after setting the various traps around the property.

In silence, the guys got themselves ready—guns holstered, bulletproof vests on, knives strapped to their thighs and various other smaller ones on their bodies. The air was crackling with tension as the reality of what they were preparing for set in, and Lawson could tell they were all lost in thought. Probably thinking about their women, and wondering if they would really survive this. Just like Lawson was.

"We have the home-field advantage," Lawson reminded them, and the guys lifted their heads to look at him. "Remember that. It's the biggest bonus we have on our side, and we have to use it against them."

"You think Granger's going to make his move tonight?" Xavier asked.

Lawson nodded. "I can't see why he wouldn't," he replied. "He knows that he has us right where he wants us and he's already cut off our communication. The faster he strikes, the less time he gives us to prepare. And he's arrogant. He thinks he can easily take us down."

Cade nodded, sliding a serrated knife into a thigh sheath.

"But his arrogance can easily be his undoing," Lawson went on. "He's used to having the upper hand. All his lackeys are scared of him, their fear rules them. And he's accustomed to having that kind of control. If we can lure him out here, get him on our territory, it might be enough to throw him off."

Might be being the crucial part of that, though he didn't say it out loud. All of them were thinking it, but the last thing they needed was to start letting their nerves get the better of them. If their confidence wavered for a single minute, all of this would be over before it really even started, and there was no way Lawson was going to let Victor Granger and his men win that easily.

When he thought of everything they had been through, everything they had survived up until this moment, he knew he couldn't—wouldn't—let the other man win. They had fought too hard for this place, to make it safe for the people who needed it, and he would be damned if he allowed that evil man to take it from them.

Which was why the guys had spent the better part of the last hour setting up traps all around the property. Trip wires that would trigger flash-bangs, grenades and smoke bombs. Enough to give the guys a warning as to where they were approaching from. These guys were criminals, at the end of the day, and likely hadn't dealt much with enemies who had tactical knowledge like Lawson and his friends. Granger and his men didn't know what they were up against.

"How many do you think there are going to be?" Aaron asked.

Lawson grimaced. "I don't know exactly," he admitted. "But I would guess somewhere in the realm of twenty or thirty. I doubt Granger will be able to move all of his men out here on such short notice, but he likely travels with a large crew in case of situations like this..." He trailed off.

A crew, he had to admit, who had Lainey. If she was even still alive. He hadn't been able to hear her voice on his call with Granger, and Lawson had a bad feeling that the man had either killed her or hurt her badly. Men like Granger didn't like leaving loose ends. Especially ones that caused him trouble and brought attention to him and his operation. He cursed himself for not being more careful, not keeping a closer eye on her, but it was too late for that now.

Right now, they just had to deal with the threat in front of them. If they were able to take down these guys, then hopefully, Lawson would be able to get Lainey out of his clutches and back to her family.

He pushed down those thoughts. No distractions. He couldn't let his emotions get the better of him. If there was one thing he had learned from his time in the field, it was that the people who let their hearts get in the way of their heads usually ended up dead as a result.

Lawson looked around at his friends. If he had to take on a man like Victor Granger and his crew, he was damn glad he was doing it with these men standing beside him. After all the time they'd spent together over the years, working together, trusting each other, becoming a team. He would do everything in his power to make sure they all walked away in one piece.

"Thank you for standing with me on this," he told them gruffly. He wasn't good at saying what was on his mind at the best of times, but now, he needed them to know how much confidence he had in them.

"I know there's only four of us, but we can do this," he continued, as Cade, Aaron and Xavier nodded. "We have the advantage. And they have no idea what they're coming up against. We can win this. I know we can."

"You ready to do this?" Xavier asked, and Lawson nodded. He reached for the control panel next to the door and pulled the switch. The whole property was plunged into an eerie darkness.

"Let's do this," Cade said.

"I'm ready," Aaron answered.

"Then let's get into position," Lawson replied. "Cade, Aaron—upstairs, split up. Each of you take a side. You'll have the advantage through the upper windows to see out over more of the property. Take the front side. Concentrate on taking them out before they get close enough to infiltrate the lodge. You got your rifles?"

They both held them up.

"Good," he replied. "Xavier and I will cover the downstairs windows, out the back. Okay, guys, let's move."

They got into position. Xavier and Lawson crouched in different areas at the windows that looked out toward the back of the property. Any minute now, they knew the place would be lit up by some sort of explosion, and then their fight would truly start. But, for now, they had to hold out in silence, waiting for something to happen.

"You ever thought this was how it would go?" Xavier muttered to him wryly. "When we opened this place?"

Lawson chuckled, glad for something to break the tension.

"I had a lot of plans for the lodge, but this wasn't in them," he admitted. "What about you?"

Xavier shook his head. "Same," he replied. "Not exactly how I pictured it going. But I guess we should have known our pasts would come back to haunt us."

"This is where it ends," Lawson replied firmly. "After this, we'll implement some new safety procedures and protocols so the lodge will never come under threat again."

Xavier glanced at him out of the corner of his eye. "Guess you've got more to protect now, too, huh?" he remarked.

Lawson nodded, his mind flashing once more to Sarah. He was glad she left with the other women, but at the same time, he wished she was beside him. When she was close, it was like everything else just fell into place. Even though he knew he had made the right choice by asking her to leave, he missed her already.

"Yeah, I guess I do," he replied.

"You think we'll get backup in time?" Xavier asked, glancing at his watch, then looking out the window across the yard.

Lawson grunted. "Wish I could say yes, but I think we'll mostly be on our own. The sheriff and FBI had a lot to wrap up, so I guess it really depends on how long it takes them to do everything they need done."

"Maybe the women will get to town and let Willis know what's happening. That they've blocked our communications. That should help speed up the assistance," Xavier offered while moving to another window.

Both of them fell silent again, ears straining for any sound outside. Upstairs, there was a creak on the floorboards. Cade and Aaron were getting into position to look out over the grounds.

"Remember, don't show them any mercy," Lawson told Xavier, shifting back to battle mode. "You know they wouldn't give any to us. We need to strike hard and fast. Take out as many as we can, as fast as possible. If we're lucky, they'll hit some of the traps first and that will help improve our odds."

Xavier nodded. Lawson knew he didn't need to tell him twice. He was gripping the gun in his holster tightly, ready to take a shot at a moment's notice, but there was still nothing. After a few more seconds of silence, the grounds lit up in a burst of light. An explosion echoed from the right side of the lodge.

"Here we go. Let's get it done."

Chapter Twenty-One

Sarah stared out of the window as the last view of the lodge disappeared out of sight. Bailey had just pulled off the property and onto the winding mountain road that would lead them down to Blue Ridge. Sarah's stomach tightened with worry, praying they would make the hour drive to town unscathed.

Normally, going for a drive made Sarah feel so free and alive—the wind in her hair, feeling the sunlight on her face, and the smell of clean forest air wafting through the windows. But tonight, under cover of darkness and fear, she felt as though the car's exterior was shrinking around her.

She didn't want to leave Lawson, and she could tell the other women with her felt the same. How could they just up and drive away from the men they loved? Even if it was for the best, it felt wrong. Logically, Sarah knew Lawson was right. She and the other women, except Bailey, would be a hinderance to the men. They'd be a distraction, splitting their focus and possibly getting someone killed. That was the last thing she wanted on her conscious. She'd never forgive herself if she was the cause of one of her friends being hurt, or worse. But her heart? Her heart was demanding she return and stand by his side. Help protect him as he would protect her. As senseless as it sounded, that's all she wanted to do.

"I can't believe we have to leave," River muttered, breaking the silence as she stared out of the window.

"It won't be for long," Sarah assured her, slipping at once into therapist mode. "And we all know it's for the best. We want the guys to be able to focus on what they need to do instead of worrying about us, right?"

"Exactly," Bailey agreed. She had that confident tone to her voice that made Sarah start to unwind slightly. If there was anyone she could trust with all of this, it was Bailey. She had a good head on her shoulders, and she knew exactly how to handle herself in situations like this. After all, Bailey was a cop down in Blue Ridge. Sarah was thankful for that knowledge.

"We have to concentrate on what's in our control right now, not what's out of it," Sarah continued. There was something comforting about sliding into this familiar role, telling them what she knew they needed to hear. It might not be easy, keeping calm when she felt so terrified, but she knew they needed to stick together to make it through this.

"Yeah, agreed," Bailey replied. "The guys are relying on us to keep ourselves safe. That's what we need to do right now."

Hannah was sitting in the passenger seat, staring silently out the window like she couldn't even hear them. River had her arms wrapped around herself and was shivering slightly. They were all dealing with their fears in their own ways, but Sarah hated seeing her friends so lost and upset. She gritted her teeth. She needed to stay strong, and pass that strength on to the other women.

They would all survive this. Their men would be fine. And they'd all be together again soon.

"We're going to be back at the lodge tomorrow," Bailey announced as though she could sense the tension in the car. "And Granger and his goons are going to be where they belong. Behind bars."

Sarah noticed how tightly Bailey's hands gripped the wheel as she spoke and how her eyes constantly checked the review mirror, looking for danger. Of all the women in the car, this had to be worse for her. With Bailey being a cop and having the knowledge and skills she did, it had to be hard for her to be there escorting the women instead of helping their men defend their home.

Sarah tried to think of something positive she could add to Bailey's words. Something that might help ease the tension but nothing came to mind. Normally, she had many reassurances she offered her clients in times of stress, but right now her mind was blank. Her thoughts buried behind her own unease and terror.

All at once, Sarah stiffened as headlights appeared behind them. Bailey's eyes suddenly darted to the rearview mirror.

"Was there anyone else coming down from the lodge?" she asked, concerned.

Sarah shook her head. "Not that I know of. We should have been the last ones to leave."

"Well, there's another car—"

"Bailey, look out!"

River screamed just in time to alert Bailey to the car heading directly for them up the mountain road. Bailey slammed her foot on the brake and twisted the wheel to avoid a head-on collision, sending them grinding into the dirt and grass at the side of the road. Sarah jerked forward, grabbing the back of Hannah's seat in front of her to hold herself steady.

Bailey cursed to herself as she glanced around, trying to figure out what they should do. The bright lights behind them suddenly revealed another vehicle slowing to a stop a short distance away.

There was no way out. One car blocked the road heading down the mountain, and another blocked their way back to the lodge.

They were trapped.

River whimpered and hugged herself tighter, Hannah sat frozen in her seat and Bailey and Sarah were each watching a set of headlights, waiting to see what would happen next.

Sarah's stomach twisted in fear. It had to be Granger or some of his men. They must have already been watching the lodge while everyone was planning to leave, waiting for the perfect time to strike.

They were too far away from the lodge now, for Lawson or

the others to know they needed help. Besides, if these cars were here, Sarah was sure they were at the lodge too. Help wouldn't be coming for them. They would get out of this on their own. One way or another.

The vehicle behind them was a black SUV with dark-tinted windows, making it nearly impossible to see anyone inside. The women sat in terrified silence and waited as the front passenger door opened, and a well-dressed man stepped out. The moment Sarah laid eyes on him, she knew he had to be Victor Granger.

There was nobody else who would have carried themselves like that, she was sure of it. He exuded a cold, calculated confidence. His head was shaven, and his face radiated a fury Sarah had never seen before. She felt like a helpless animal trapped by a ferocious predator, ready to swallow her whole.

Granger made his way toward the car, and his eyes seemed pinned to Sarah's. He gave her a dark, cruel grin that sent a shiver down her spine. But it told her exactly what she needed to know. He was there for her, not any of the other women. He had singled out Sarah with that one look. Now, she could use that knowledge to her advantage and get the others out of there.

She quickly turned to the other women, lowering her voice and speaking urgently.

"Listen to me," she ordered them. "He's here for me. He's trying to get leverage over Lawson, I'm sure of it. If I make a break for it, then he's going to send his men after me. And you can get out of here."

"We're not leaving you here," Bailey said sharply, sounding angry at the very suggestion.

River and Hannah shook their heads emphatically to agree with Bailey.

"You're leaving for me, because I'm asking you to," Sarah assured them. "You all need to get to safety, then you can get me help. But you have to get out of here in order to do that."

"Sarah, no." Hannah reached back and grabbed her hand.

"There is no way this car is leaving without you in it. I will not leave you here for these men. Lawson is depending on me keeping you safe, Sarah. I won't do it," Bailey said, all but growling at her.

"It's the only way, and you three know it. He won't hurt me, he'll take me back to the lodge to flaunt me at Lawson. To show him he couldn't keep me safe. When I make a run for it, you need to hurry. He won't be expecting it, you can get away. I can't…"

Her voice hitched at the back of her throat as the reality of this situation began to sink in. She was going to have to get out of this car and put herself in grave danger, to ensure her friends could get away. The thought was terrifying. But she knew it was the only way to help her friends. To give them a chance.

It seemed Granger had been making his own plans on how best to get to Lawson, throw him off his game. Apparently, she was his trump card. The man knew Lawson would do anything to keep her out of harm's way, and that would most likely get him and the other guys at the lodge killed. Sarah couldn't let herself be used like that. Against the man she loved.

Granger stopped a short distance from her side of the car, holding his hands up, trying to seem nonthreatening.

"Sarah Peterson, my dear," he said with a smile curling his lips. "We've been looking for you everywhere."

She reached for the door handle, her heart pounding in her chest. River shot her a panicked look and squeezed her leg tightly, as though telling her to stay right where she was, but she knew she couldn't. She couldn't risk her friends getting caught, too.

Hannah turned in her seat and pinned Sarah with her watery eyes. "Sarah, please—please don't do this. We need to stay together."

Sarah shook head and turned to Bailey, giving her a hard look.

"You need to get out of here, get to Sheriff Willis," she firmly told her.

"Sarah—" Bailey replied, but Sarah just cut her off.

"Bailey. You know this is the right move. Get to town as fast as you can."

Bailey gritted her teeth and took a deep breath, then nodded and pinned Sarah with a determined gaze. "Fine. We'll go," she replied. She seemed to know as well as Sarah did that there was no other way out of this. She would do her part, and she had to trust that her friends would do theirs.

"You stay alive out there. Lawson will kill me if anything happens to you. You hear me?"

For Lawson. For her friends. She had to run. She had to put as much distance between herself and these men as she could. She doubted she would be able to outrun them, but she was going to give it everything she had.

Sarah sucked in a deep breath, trying to slow the terror gripping her insides, then nodded once to acknowledge Bailey's demand. "I will."

Then she threw open the door and bolted into the trees, heading back up toward the lodge.

"After her!" Granger roared, and Sarah heard doors being thrown open, heavy footfalls behind her. Her heart slammed against her ribs and her breath tore from her lungs, the humid summer air already starting to make her sweat.

She didn't exactly know where she was going, she just knew she was pointed in the general direction of the lodge and she had to get as far from these men as she could. She ran with everything she had, even though her legs were like rubber beneath her. She forced herself to keep moving.

She heard men's voices calling after her, and the squeal of tires on the pavement. She prayed her friends would get away. Get to town and get help and rescue her before anything horrible happened. She was sure a man like Victor Granger wouldn't think twice about using the other women as leverage, too, and the thought of something happening to them… It made her sick to think about it.

Twigs snapped beneath her feet as she ran, as she darted away from the trees and back toward the road, knowing she would only get lost in these dark woods. She felt the same fear she had on that fateful day back in her office with Jed, when everything had fallen apart as she watched his vicious destruction. All the safety she'd felt up to that point was suddenly ripped away. She was now faced with the brutal reality of how much danger she was in.

She just needed to make it to the lodge, to Lawson.

She curled her hands into fists, arms pumping through the air, pushing her legs as fast as they would go as she heard cars on the road behind her. She glanced around to see Bailey's car closing the distance between them. Damn it, she'd hoped Bailey would take her advice and get help, but at the same time, there was a part of her that was beyond relieved that her friends hadn't left her after all.

"Sarah! Get in!" Bailey yelled to her as she drove alongside Sarah. Sarah reached out for the car door, but missed. Sarah cried out in frustration. She was too slow and they were too fast; they couldn't make another pass or slow down for fear of being caught. There was another car closing the distance behind them.

And then, she felt a pressure at her back. Someone grabbed her shirt and pulled her back toward them. She screamed out in surprise and tried to break free, but the grip was too strong. There was no way she could escape.

Sarah was yanked to a halt and fell back to the ground. All of the adrenaline she had coursing through her veins suddenly fled, and her body felt like a sinking weight in quicksand. This was the end for her. She was well and truly caught, and she had no clue what would happen next. Tears suddenly blurred her vision and she let out a terror-filled scream that cut through the night air.

Dark, shiny shoes suddenly stopped in front of her, and she shrank back, bumping into the legs of the man behind her.

"Stand her up." A low, menacing voice practically growled the words. Two sets of rough hands grabbed her and pulled her to her feet.

She stood there, surrounded by several men, her panicked gaze darting around until it landed on their leader.

Victor Granger.

She waited for what he would say. Would he order her killed? Or keep her to use against Lawson?

Out of the corner of her eye she saw Bailey's car race by with Hannah's and River's faces plastered against the windows, eyes wide in fear for her. At least her friends got away. Sarah had no clue what would happen next, but she knew she had to be strong. For the same reasons she had to run—for Lawson, for her friends—she had to survive.

Chapter Twenty-Two

Flash-bangs and men's startled yells sounded around the lodge from Granger's men trying to breach the perimeter of the property. From the sounds and multiple bright lights, Lawson knew they were surrounded and the first wave of men were closing in. He glanced at Xavier to see him peer out the window, seeking his first target. Lawson repositioned himself, lifted his weapon and looked out to find his own.

Just as Lawson locked on the first man breaching the trees, a terrified scream rent the air, causing the hairs on his neck to stand on end. Every muscle in Lawson's body tensed.

He looked over at Xavier, checking to see if he'd heard it, too. Xavier's eyes were wide. And he looked just as worried as Lawson about what that sound meant.

Whose voice that had been. But Lawson knew.

He was on his feet before he could argue with himself. He knew better than to do what he was about to do. He should stick to the plan, no matter what. But there was no way he could ignore that agonizing, terror-filled scream.

He knew beyond a doubt that that scream was Sarah. He couldn't leave her to face whatever Granger had planned for her alone.

Xavier grabbed his arm and pulled him back down, and Lawson tried to shake himself free. He couldn't think about the plans they'd put in place or how much danger he'd be putting himself in by going out there. He had to make sure Sarah was safe. It was the only thing he cared about.

"You can't go out there," Xavier warned him. "The plan's in motion. None of it is going to work if you blow this for us now, you know that."

Lawson gritted his teeth. He knew Xavier was right, but he had to make sure Sarah was okay. He knew he shouldn't have let her leave without him. He should have escorted her to town, then come back to face off with Granger. Now, with more worry for her on his mind, he didn't know if he'd be able to clear his head enough to focus on what he had to do.

"It could have been anything," Xavier told him, his face grim, and Lawson knew what he was not saying. He was reminding Lawson that it was as likely to be Hannah as it was Sarah, that all of the men had loved ones out there tonight. But Victor was relying on them losing their cool, and they had too much riding on this to let that happen.

Lawson crouched down beside the window again, that scream ringing in his ears. Granger must have ambushed them leaving and grabbed Sarah. So what did that mean for his sister and the other two women? He knew Granger would have singled out Sarah because of him. He even implied as much when he'd called Lawson to boast about Lainey.

But before he could linger on that thought any longer, a sharp explosion of light filled the sky. Another flash-bag, at the front of the lodge.

Aaron spoke through his comm a moment later.

"Six men coming up the driveway," he told them. "Flash-bang has them staggering about blindly."

"Take them out," Lawson replied without a second thought. A moment later, gunfire filled the air, breaking through the silence, echoing through the quiet night—the men were being picked off with ease.

"More are coming," Aaron warned them. "You guys ready?"

"Roger that," the other three men replied in their comms simultaneously.

Another flash-bang went off at the opposite edge of the property, and Xavier and Lawson ducked down beneath the windows on the ground floor, both of them leveling their weapons, ready to take the shot whenever they could. There were several more men staggering around, trying to regain their sight, weapons dangling from their shoulders or hands. They needed to deal with these men now, before their vision cleared and they could return fire.

Lawson lined up his weapon, and fired: one, two, three. He'd picked off three guys in a row, while Xavier took out the other two. Bodies littered the front and back of the property, and Lawson knew it was far from over.

"How many more do you think we're going to be dealing with?" Xavier asked as he steadied his gun on the sill of the open window before him.

Lawson shook his head. "I have no idea," he replied, voice tight with worry. He still couldn't clear the scream from his mind, even in the midst of a gunfight.

His thoughts kept circling back to the women and what Granger would possibly do. He knew the man would want to use Sarah against him, force his hand to surrender. But what about the others? Bailey was a cop and she had her gun. Had he captured them—or worse?

All at once, several rounds of gunfire sounded from the front of the lodge, jolting Lawson back to the present. One of the windows behind them smashed, exploding inward in a hail of glass and bullets. Xavier and Lawson dropped down on instinct, not making themselves any more of a target than they needed to be.

He heard Cade's voice over the comm about several more men approaching, followed by more gunfire, then the sounds of men yelling and thuds of bodies hitting the ground outside. Good. They were clearing these guys out quickly.

Lawson couldn't help wondering how many more men Granger would end up sacrificing to get his hands on him. Would he continue until his last man? Or would he realize it was hopeless and give up or make a run for it?

A loud boom drew Lawson's attention, and he spun around, ducking below the window. A couple of guys had been blown off their feet and one was scrambling for cover while the second lay unmoving on the ground. Xavier took the shot and took the man out before he made it far. At the same time, they heard more windows being shattered and more gunfire sounding from outside. Those men were determined to get in, no matter what it took or how many lives were lost in the process.

Cade and Aaron were also consistently firing from the second floor. Every once in a while, one of them would make a mumbled comment over their comms, but with all the noise and explosions, it was hard to make out most of what they were saying. He and Xavier just had to rely on the fact that Cade and Aaron were both skilled with weapons and would have each other's backs with whatever came at them. If they really needed help, they'd definitely let Lawson and Xavier know they were in trouble.

Lawson turned his attention back outside. Both men had their weapons balanced in the window, waiting for anything that moved in the darkness.

"There," Xavier muttered, pointing out a dark figure moving at the edge of the grounds. "You see him? He's next to the path—"

"Got him," Lawson replied, and he fired a shot. It smashed off the concrete path below, and the man sprang to the side, dodging the bullet. Lawson cursed, and quickly reloaded, lining up another shot.

He exhaled as he pulled the trigger, squeezing down on it in time with his breath, and this time, the shot landed, hitting the man in the leg. He let out a howl of pain that filled the air around them, and Lawson let out a sigh of relief. Thank God. He couldn't get sloppy, not now, when every shot could mean life or death for him and his friends.

Silence filled the air once more, then another flash of light from outside. Aaron and Cade picked off the few who were approaching from the front of the lodge, and Lawson ran over to one of the shattered windows to get a better look at what was happening. There had to be at least twelve dead by now, maybe even more. Granger couldn't have many more men with him to send in now.

"How many more does he have?" he muttered almost to himself, running a hand through his hair.

"We must have evened the playing field a little by now," Xavier agreed. Lawson could hear the hope in his voice.

"I'm not sure. It'd be nice if this was almost over but it's doubtful. We haven't seen Granger yet. So he must have something else up his sleeve for us," Lawson added.

And Lawson couldn't help but think that it had to do with that scream. And Sarah. Granger had singled her out when he'd called Lawson to boast about finding them, so he knew the man would make a play for her at some point. That was why Lawson had wanted her down in town instead of there with him. There was no way to know for sure, though, until it was all over. And Granger played his final hand.

A long quiet surrounded them, as they waited for the next attack to come. But it didn't. Lawson and Xavier glanced around the property again, looking for movement, but everything was calm outside.

"Clear up here, for now. You guys good?" Cade's question crackled over the comm.

"Good here," Xavier replied warily.

Lawson and Xavier glanced at each other, concern crossing both their faces. Was this it? Had Granger decided to change tactics and leave instead? Move to another location and use these men as decoys while he got away free and clear? Not the best-case scenario because he'd still be out there preying on the unsuspecting and vulnerable, but at least Lawson and his team would be free of the danger surrounding them. They could step back and let the FBI take over.

What about Lainey, though? Lawson's gut clenched at the thought of his friend. She'd been a constant worry in the back of his mind and he felt guilty he hadn't tried to find her yet. He wanted to keep his promise, to get her back to her family. For them to all be safe. First, he had to deal with the immediate danger to him and his friends. To Sarah. Then he'd focus all his attention and resources on finding Lainey and bringing her home.

All at once, the comms crackled to life again.

"Heads up," Aaron warned them. "There's a car down the main road, looks like it's headed toward the lodge. And it doesn't look like Bailey's."

"It's Granger," Xavier stated. "Has to be."

Both Lawson and Xavier rechecked their weapons, readying themselves for the next round. Lawson called through his comm for Cade and Aaron to do the same. He wanted them all to be loaded up and ready for whatever came next.

With Victor Granger's arrival, this would be it. The final showdown. Lawson and Xavier shared a look of determination. They were ready to do whatever was necessary to protect the lodge and their women, including putting themselves on the line. Their women's safety and happiness were all that mattered to them in the end.

Chapter Twenty-Three

Sarah couldn't stop staring at Victor Granger's hand on her knee. He'd placed it there the moment she had been pulled into his car, making it clear to her that there was no way she was going anywhere. As if she didn't know that already. She felt like she was going to throw up. Her entire body was wracked with tension and fear as she continued to stare at his hand.

She glanced out of the window and realized they were on the connector road to the lodge. At the rate of speed the man behind the wheel was driving, they'd be there in a few minutes. She'd be able to see Lawson. A part of her was relieved that she would be able to see him again. But another part of her was terrified at what Granger would do to her as soon as he had her in front of Lawson once more.

"I can't wait to see the look on his face," the man in the front seat said as he smirked in amusement. "That ex-CIA bastard, he's going to see what he gets when he messes with us—"

"Shut your mouth, Lyle," Granger told him bluntly. It was clear he was not in the mood to listen to the younger man's gloating. "I'll do the talking. Keep your thoughts to yourself."

The man's face fell, and he turned back to look out the windshield, concentrating on the road in front of him. The man beside him in the driver's seat, who looked just like him, let out a snort of amusement.

"Shut up, Nelson," Lyle mumbled to his look-alike, then punched him on the shoulder.

Sarah gripped the door handle tightly, wondering if she could throw open the door and jump out and escape. But she knew the car was going too fast and she wouldn't survive.

Even if Granger and these other men were going to flaunt her capture in front of Lawson before they decided what to do with her, at least she'd be able to see the man she loved again.

Sarah knew the women would have driven down to Blue Ridge by now to alert the sheriff, but she had no idea if the cavalry would make it back up to the lodge in time to save her or help end the attack. She just wanted all of this to be over.

She wished everything could go back as it was before they were aware of the kidnappings and Granger's arrival in the area. Everything had been so chaotic lately, Sarah couldn't even recall what a normal day was supposed to be like for her now. It all just felt so hopeless.

For a moment, Sarah even thought about trying to reason with the man beside her.

She could tell him that Lawson was a good man, and that he just wanted Granger and his operation out of the area. That Lawson would look the other way, leave him to his business, if he just left the lodge and its people alone. No harm, no foul.

She could try to feed him all those lies, but she knew she wouldn't be very convincing. And he'd never believe her, if she tried. He'd probably laugh in her face. Lawson never would have looked the other way when it came to what Granger was up to, not in a million years. He wanted to see the man behind bars, maybe even dead. If that was what it took to get him out of the picture.

Sarah shut down those thoughts at once. She couldn't believe she was actually considering bargaining with the evil man sitting beside her.

Granger grinned at the side of her face, but Sarah refused to so much as glance in his direction. Instead, she kept her eyes trained out the front windshield. She wasn't going to give him the satisfaction of knowing he had gotten under her skin in any way. She was sure that was part of his plan.

He might be used to getting everything he wanted, but that didn't mean she was going to hand it to him without a fight. She clenched her jaw in determination as they drew closer to the lodge, praying that Lawson was ready for whatever was about to happen.

"He's going to be ready for you," she told them, the first thing she'd said since she had been bundled into the back of this car. The confidence in her voice caught even her off guard, and she finally looked at Granger, who seemed slightly thrown by the way she spoke to him. Apparently, he seemed to expect her to be scared and cowering away from him instead of speaking her mind.

"I hope he is," he replied, quickly gathering himself again. "I want to see the look on his face when he sees that I've got his girlfriend, and when he hears the plans I've got in store for you."

"You're going to make us a pretty penny, Sarah," Lyle told her, grinning at her. There was something lecherous about the way he looked at her, and she couldn't help but shiver. She tried not to let her mind stray too far down that path. She didn't want them to see how afraid she really was.

"Us?" She couldn't help but ask the question. Were the two look-alikes related to Granger?

"Oh, forgive my rudeness," Granger replied cordially. "These are my sons, Lyle and Nelson. They help with certain areas of my operation."

"A family business. What a wonderful role model," she muttered under her breath.

Granger's grip tightened on her knee, causing her to wince. "You've got a smart mouth. You should watch your words before they get you into more trouble."

"You're not going to make a cent from me," she told them, ignoring the man's threat. "You should turn around now. Get out of here while you still can. Hand yourselves over to the cops and hope they take it easy on you."

Lyle and Nelson laughed, but their father, for a moment, was quiet. Had she struck a nerve? She stole a glance at him out of the corner of her eye, but he wasn't giving anything away. He just watched her with his dark, soulless eyes.

Finally, they reached the entrance to the lodge. Sarah couldn't help the gasp that escaped her lips at the sight before her. Smoke still lingered in the air like a thick fog and the ground was littered with bodies. She clenched her hands into fists and her stomach dropped. *Please, please, let those be Granger's men.*

As the car slowed down more, and some of the fog began to clear, she could see what looked like a dozen men on the ground around them—some of them dead, unmoving, others dragging themselves along the ground to safety.

Granger cursed under his breath, then rolled down his window and yelled to them. "Hold your positions!"

His voice was cold, hard, but she could hear the hint of uncertainty behind his words, as though he hadn't been prepared for this sight to greet him when he arrived.

Suddenly, hope rose in her chest. They really were doing it. Lawson and the others were really defending the lodge and taking down Granger's men. The proof was right before their eyes. She hated that she'd had any doubt, but with the army of men they'd been facing against their mere four, she couldn't help but feel the initial helplessness of it all. But now, maybe, just maybe, the guys could end this.

"Stop here," he ordered Nelson, and the vehicle jerked to a hard stop. Sarah clung to the handle of the door, praying that this would be over soon. If she could just find a way to get away from this evil man and his sons…

Granger reached over her and pushed open the door, then shoved her out onto the gravel. She gasped and tumbled to the ground, unprepared, putting her hands out to catch her fall. Gravel bit into her palms as she landed, tearing her skin.

Granger climbed out of the vehicle behind her and grabbed her arm, yanking her to her feet, and held her in front of him like a shield. He must have known Lawson would be quick to take the shot if given the chance, but with Sarah standing in front of the man, he was probably more cautious to do so.

"Lawson Davies!" Granger yelled, his voice booming in her ears. She winced and squeezed her eyes shut at the sound. She wanted to wrench herself away from him, but he had too tight of a hold on her for her to move. She was going to have to bide her time and look for an opening she could use to get away.

"Davies, can you hear me? I've got your woman out here!" he continued, clearly enjoying the power he held in that moment. "You better show yourself unless you want something to happen to her." Granger paused, lifting some of her hair and running his fingers through it. "Nice and silky, and she smells good, too. I bet I could make good money off her. I've got plenty of clients who'd pay well for a chance to take her to bed."

Sarah shuddered at the thought, fear and anger coursing through her. This was what he had done to so many other unsuspecting young women and girls they'd grabbed off the highways. Forced them to work for him, using their bodies and selling their souls to survive.

She looked around, searching for something…anything that might help her escape. A gun dropped by one of his fallen men, a knife, even a big rock. But there was nothing. She knew Lawson and the others were within hearing distance, knew he was biding his time and making a plan.

She just had to hope that he wouldn't do anything that would end up getting her or both of them hurt in the process.

Chapter Twenty-Four

Lawson growled as he rose to his feet, then strode toward the door the moment he heard Victor Granger's voice. If it hadn't been for Xavier grabbing his arm, he would have been out there before he had realized it.

"Lawson. Hey," Xavier told him. "Stop. Take a breath. Think."

"He's got Sarah," he snarled to Xavier, jerking on his arm to break his hold. But Xavier tightened his grip on Lawson's arm.

Xavier nodded, eyes dark with worry. "I know," he replied. "And I want to get her away from him as much as you do. But you have to keep your head. Victor's relying on you for an emotional reaction so he can take you out. You know that. You have to keep your head, you hear me?"

Lawson yanked his arm free of Xavier's grip, fury racing through his veins. Whether he liked it or not, he knew his friend was right. He couldn't just march out there and confront the man, no matter how much he wanted to. Granger was trying to taunt him into making a mistake. Likely after he had seen the mess they had made of his men.

If anything, this was a good sign, a sign that Granger was a little concerned about what had happened here and what was yet to happen between them. It was hard for Lawson to process any of that right then though. It still felt like Granger had the upper hand since he had Sarah.

He moved to the window, keeping low to get a look at the situation outside. And, sure enough, there they were—Sarah and Granger, outlined against the headlights behind them, his grip on her arm giving her nowhere to go. Her eyes were wide and terrified, a rabbit caught in a snare, and his heart ached seeing her like that. He needed to get her away from him before he and the others could make a move on Granger and what was left of his men.

"We can't get a good shot from up here," Cade muttered through the comm. "The headlights are obscuring him. There's no way we would be able to make sure we wouldn't hit Sarah."

"Hold back then," Xavier replied, seamlessly taking the lead when Lawson needed him to. "Don't take the shot unless you're sure you can take him out without hurting Sarah."

Lawson's mind raced, trying to think of a solution where Sarah could get away from Granger without being hurt. He hated feeling helpless. He could tell from the look in her eyes that she was silently pleading with him to get her out of this in one piece. He had to save her.

The only way Lawson could do that, he decided, was to do what Granger expected him to do, knowing the guys would have his back.

"Xavier, look at me," he ordered him. "I'm going to turn myself over to Granger."

Xavier's eyes narrowed. "Lawson—"

"No. Listen," he said, his voice low as he tucked a gun into the holster at his side. "I can't let anything happen to her. So if that means letting Granger think he has me, I can deal with that. I'm going to surrender on the porch. It's the only way to move this forward."

Xavier frowned but nodded. Lawson could tell his friend didn't exactly like this approach, but it wasn't as though they had any other choice right now. Granger had the upper hand at the moment.

The two of them headed out onto the front porch, the headlights from Victor's vehicle obstructing their view of the man and his goons standing in front of them. If Lawson could just lure Granger away from the lights long enough for Cade or Aaron to take the shot…

And there was Sarah. Granger still held her in front of him, blocking most of his body. Lawson could tell she was trying to be strong, but her pale face and wide eyes gave her away. He wanted nothing more than to rip her out of the man's grasp, pull her into his arms and reassure her everything was going to be okay. He just needed her to hold it together a little longer.

Lawson shifted his gaze back to the man responsible for all of this. Xavier had been right when he told Lawson to keep his wits about him. If he went off half-cocked now, they'd all be dead, and God only knew what terrible fate Sarah would suffer by Granger's hands.

He agreed with his friend's assessment that the man was expecting Lawson to make an emotional decision, and he couldn't let himself fall into that trap. This all would go to hell in a second if he did.

Lawson held his hands out to his sides, showing Granger he wasn't holding a weapon. "I'm here," he told the man.

Granger sneered at him, clearly not buying it. "And what about the rest of your little buddies?" he asked. "Where are they?"

"I sent them away," Lawson lied quickly. "There's no one here but Xavier and me."

Granger took a step toward them with Sarah, the headlights outlining them both as one. Her eyes were pinned to Lawson's, but she didn't acknowledge him or make a sound. That was smart. They only needed one slip from Granger and maybe she could get away and take cover. If Lawson could hold the other man's attention on him, he could give her that chance.

Suddenly, two identical men climbed out of the car behind Granger and Lawson's eyes darted to them. Lyle and Nelson, his sons. They were both armed. Lawson steadied his breathing, hoping Cade and Aaron had clear shots of them from the top floor of the lodge.

"I don't believe you," Granger replied simply. "Lyle, Nelson, clear out the building."

The two men strode forward to do their father's bidding.

They had their father's build, and the same dark, hateful eyes. Both carried themselves with a sleek swagger that was powerful and confident. They were overconfident, hopefully. But before they could reach the porch, Granger changed his orders.

"On second thought," he remarked, almost casually, "shoot them both in the head first."

"No!" Sarah screamed and started fighting Granger's hold. Lyle and Nelson rounded on Xavier and Lawson, but before they could lift their weapons, gunfire exploded from the floor above them.

The goons in front of Granger and Sarah scattered, bullets from Cade and Aaron's guns following them as they ran. Nelson cried out a curse as he threw himself toward the porch for cover to avoid the bullets raining down. Xavier was there to intercept him, and grabbed him by the collar of his shirt and slammed him roughly against one of the pillars outside the front door.

The bullets poured down from above, driving Granger back toward the safety of the car, one arm still wrapped around Sarah, like he knew he wouldn't leave the lodge alive without her in tow. Lawson could hear her fighting him, trying to get free.

"No! Let me go! Lawson!" Her frightful cries pierced his heart. He couldn't go to her yet, though, they still had to take care of the brothers first. They were too much of a threat to them all. Even though Lyle and Nelson were both dodging bullets, they were still armed and it would only take one lucky shot to disable or kill Lawson and Xavier. He prayed she could just hold on a little longer.

Nelson was sliding down the pillar as Xavier landed a kick to his gut, the crack of a rib sounding from the strike. Lyle was a little smarter, trying to raise his gun at Lawson before he darted for cover.

Lawson managed to dive out of the way in the split second before Lyle fired his weapon. Lyle raised his gun to fire again and Lawson jumped up, surprising him. Lawson grabbed Lyle's arm and twisted it up behind his back, forcing him to drop his weapon. Suddenly, Xavier was there pulling Lyle away from Lawson, and forcing him to the ground. Xavier punched him in the face, then slammed his head back into the hard earth a few times until Lyle went limp beneath him.

"Go after Sarah!" he exclaimed. "I've got him!"

Lawson didn't need to be told twice. He turned on his heel and sprinted toward the car, where Granger was dragging Sarah to escape. If he managed to get her off the property, Lawson would likely never see her again. Lawson couldn't let that happen. He had to stop Granger now.

He came in hot, rushing around the back of the car, where he was sure Granger had taken Sarah. But before he could get his bearings, a fist slammed into his stomach, knocking the wind out of him and sending him stumbling backward.

"Lawson!" Sarah screamed, her voice sounding shrill and panicked. He wanted to reassure her that he was okay, but he couldn't speak. He tried to suck in a long breath, but doubled over in pain. For a man as old as he was, Victor Granger knew how to throw a punch.

Before Lawson could stand up fully, Granger was there, knocking him to the ground. His eyes flashed with fury as he pulled back his arm and slammed his fist into Lawson's face over and over. Lawson shoved his arms between them to block the punches and tried to roll to the side to throw him off. Before Lawson could get his legs under him, Granger shoved Lawson onto his back and put his knee on his stomach, the full weight of him pressing down on to his chest as he tried to choke the life out of him.

Lawson tried to get his arms up to grab Granger's hands at his throat, but the man forced them down with his own arms, shifting his grip on Lawson's neck. Even as the darkness started crowding the corners of his vision, Lawson's only thought was of Sarah. And the hope she'd been able to get away.

Chapter Twenty-Five

Sarah stared in horror as Granger attacked Lawson. He never even had a chance to defend himself. That first hit was enough to take his breath and Granger took swift advantage. Now, she stood there frozen, watching as Lawson lay helpless on the ground with Granger hovering over him, choking him to death.

She was terrified, but she had to do something. She couldn't stand there and watch Lawson die and not do anything to try to help. But what? Maybe Xavier would come?

She shifted her gaze to where Xavier had been fighting with the sons. Apparently, Lyle had gotten his second wind. He and Xavier were still throwing punches and from the look in Xavier's eyes, she could tell Lyle didn't stand a chance. She also noticed that Cade was standing off to the side with his weapon pointed at Nelson, who was still groaning on the ground holding his leg. Aaron seemed to be checking Victor's men scattered around the grounds and restraining those still moving.

That left Sarah herself. It was up to her to help Lawson in any way she could.

At first, she leaped on Granger's back, hoping that would surprise him enough to release his hold. The man let out a growl and threw her off to the side. It gave Lawson the opportunity to get his legs free from under Granger and he was using them to kick him wherever he could land blows, hoping to release his grip.

Sarah jumped up and ran to the vehicle beside her, looking around to see if there was something inside it she could use. Quickly scanning the interior, the only things she could see were a half bottle of water and a thin towel on the floor. No. She ripped open the glovebox and shuffled through the contents. Tears filled her eyes. There was absolutely nothing. She angrily swiped at her eyes, clearing her vision, listening to the grunts and groans and gasps filtering in the car from outside.

She chanced another look outside the vehicle and noticed Granger no longer had Lawson pinned to the ground. They were rolling around trading punches, but Granger still seemed to have more of the upper hand, landing more hits than Lawson was able to return. Sarah could see the marks around his neck and knew that had something to do with it. If Lawson was in full fighting form, she knew he'd take the man down with ease.

Her eyes shifted again between the microfiber towel and the water bottle. She couldn't believe these were her only options. Trying not to think about what she was going to do, she grabbed both items and scrambled out of the car.

Granger was back on top of Lawson, holding him down and punching him in the face, the chest, anywhere he could land a blow. Sarah cringed when she heard a crunch and Lawson's painful groan. She clenched the bottle of water in her hand and raced over to them. After uncapping the lid, she threw the water in Granger's face, startling him enough to shift his eyes to her, giving Lawson the opening he needed.

Lawson slammed a fist into the man's side, throwing him off balance long enough for Lawson to draw a full breath, and then he followed it up with another punch to Granger's nose, a spray of blood leaking down his face. Granger let out a grunt, his head flopping to the right, and she felt a pulse of triumph. Lawson locked his hands together, and then smashed them into Granger's face. The man spat blood, his eyes darkening with a pure malice.

He shoved away Lawson's arms and pressed his own to Lawson's throat again, this time bearing down with all of his weight.

He was going to kill him for sure this time. That snapped Sarah out of her daze. She rushed forward again and climbed onto Granger's back, wrapping her arms around his neck and tugging. She kept jerking and jerking with no effect. Granger's rage had completely taken over—he didn't even acknowledge her presence.

Sarah quickly wrapped the towel around his neck, grabbing each end and pulling back with all the force she had. She pushed off his back for leverage and kept tugging on the cloth with all her might. A grunt and gasp were music to her ears. It was working!

She let out her own grunts of frustration and exertion as she tried to pull the man away from Lawson. At last, he lifted his hand and clawed at the cloth around his throat.

Granger stood up, far too easily, and tossed Sarah back toward the car. She slammed into the side, letting out a cry of pain as he rounded on her. She had never seen such unfiltered hatred in someone's eyes before, and she did her best to scramble back and away from him.

Granger dragged a hand across his bloodied nose, smearing scarlet across his face. He looked like a demon, covered in blood, eyes nearly black with fury.

"You're not worth the cash I could make from you," he told her, spitting a mouthful of blood at the ground next to her.

He moved toward her, a maniacal grin spreading across his face, as though he was going to enjoy exactly what he planned to do next. She scrambled backward, whimpering with fear, trying to kick at him, but her legs felt like jelly. She didn't have any more fight in her.

But a second later, she realized she wasn't going to have to fight. Lawson lunged at him, sending Granger slamming into the side of the car with a sickening crash. He let out a cry of pain, and Sarah tried to crawl away as fast as she could so he couldn't grab her again.

Lawson was on top of him, his eyes wild and his face already starting to bruise. Cuts were scattered across his lip and his brow, dripping blood down his face, but he didn't seem to notice.

Lawson landed punch after punch, slamming his fists without mercy into Granger's head, the forceful hits snapping his neck left and right as he tried to lift his arms to get a blow in. But it was over.

"Stop!" Granger cried out, his mouth bubbling with blood. Lawson was like a machine, delivering jab after jab. He was practiced and skilled enough to render Granger useless. The man tried to lift his arms to cover his head, but Lawson pinned them to the ground beneath his knees, giving him no room to escape.

Her plan worked. She had given him just enough time to react, to recover, and now, he was winning. She watched, unable to speak as she took in the sheer intensity of his brutal assault. And she knew, deep down, that this was for her—this was because Granger had threatened her, threatened them. It was for everyone else, too—the trafficking victims, the lodge, their friends, the future they all wanted. But mostly her.

Police sirens shrieked in the distance, making Sarah jump, as Xavier rounded the corner of the car to grab Lawson's shoulder.

"Hey. Lawson!" he called to him. "It's over, Lawson. Stop. You can stop."

Panting hard, Lawson drew his fist back one last time, and then turned to look up at Xavier. His eyes, which before had seemed so distant, snapped back to reality. Although it was clear he wanted to end Granger right then and there, he had to go to jail. It was the only way his victims were going to be able to get justice for everything he had done.

Lawson rose to his feet, and Xavier flipped over Granger and snapped a pair of cuffs on to his wrists. Lawson's eyes finally found Sarah, and he grinned, a smile so wide it looked as though it could have split his face in two.

"We've got this," Xavier assured him. "Go, your girl needs you."

She really does, Sarah thought as she scrambled off the ground.

Lawson made his way toward her and wrapped his arms around her in an embrace that made the world fall away for a moment. She knew they had been through hell, but right now, all she cared about was feeling safe in his arms, where she belonged.

"Is it over now?" she breathed. She wouldn't be able to believe it until she heard those words come from his lips.

He nodded against her neck. "It's over," he promised her, and he pulled back, looking her up and down. "Are you alright? Did he hurt you?"

"I'm fine," she replied, though she could feel some of the pain from her torn-up hands and bruised back as the adrenaline started to fade from her system. Her body was going to make her pay for this tomorrow, she was sure of it, but right now, she was grateful that she was here with Lawson, that they were both safe.

And most of all, that Victor Granger seemed to have finally been brought to his knees. Hopefully, he would never see the outside of a prison again so he could never hurt another innocent woman.

"You look just as pretty as your sons right now," Xavier taunted Granger as he stood over him. The man's head turned to the side so he could see both his sons bloodied and bruised, sitting cuffed on the ground with Cade and Aaron standing guard over them and Granger's few men who had survived the attack.

He knew it was over and he was going to pay for everything he had done.

"Hope nobody you're in prison with finds out what you're in for," Xavier continued, a grin spreading across his face. "They don't take too kindly to sex traffickers."

Sarah sank into Lawson's arms again, closing her eyes and focusing on the feel of his chest rising and falling against her ear. She was sure what came next was going to be chaos, but she didn't care. She was where she belonged right now.

And nothing in the world could take that away from her.

Chapter Twenty-Six

The moon was high in the sky above as the front of the lodge was suddenly lit up with multiple glowing lights. Several cop cars screeched to a halt around them, swiftly followed by the paramedics. Lawson held Sarah close, trying to block out all of the noise and activity around them and just concentrate on how she felt in his arms.

He could feel her tears against his shirt, and he hated that she was so upset right now, but he reminded himself that things could be so much worse.

"I'm so sorry," he murmured to her, brushing his lips over the top of her head. "I thought I was protecting you by sending you away from the lodge but I should have known that the safest place for you to be is by my side."

"It's okay," she replied, lifting her gaze to meet his. "I know you were just trying to do the right thing. I don't blame you."

He smiled at her, and leaned down to plant a kiss against her lips as the sheriff hopped out of his car behind them.

"Sorry it took us so long to get here, but it looks like you guys have it handled. Granger had a few surprises set up for us along the way and the FBI is dealing with that. SWAT is currently securing the outer area," Sheriff Willis volunteered, as Lawson pulled back from Sarah. "So what's the status here? Who do I need to cuff?" he demanded.

"We're just glad you made it, Sheriff. Xavier has them," Lawson replied, directing him to the other man, who was still standing over Granger. "He'll tell you what you need to know."

"Good," Sheriff Willis replied, nodding sharply and walking toward the two men. "This way, men! Let's round them up," the sheriff added, directing his deputies to Granger's men scattered around the ground.

Just then, Bailey's car pulled up behind the sheriff's vehicle. All three women sprang out and rushed to Sarah's side

"Are you oka—" Hannah began.

"What happened?" Bailey asked, speaking over her.

"Where are—" River began at the same time, but Sarah just pointed them back toward the lodge.

"Over there," she replied. "They're waiting for you."

River and Bailey ran off toward the lodge, while Hannah rushed to where Xavier was standing, talking with the sheriff. She practically leaped into Xavier's arms when she reached him. Lawson couldn't help but smile, glad that they had all found each other again. He still felt guilty for sending Sarah away in the first place, but that line of thought would have to wait. There was so much more they had to take care of before he could replay everything that had happened.

Once Hannah had extracted herself from Xavier's arms, she took his hand and came over to talk to Lawson and Sarah.

"Are you okay?" she asked her brother, fussing over him as she took in the bruises and cuts on his face. He knew he would be looking rough come the morning, but right now, he could hardly feel it. He was sure the paramedics would want to give him a once-over to make sure he was okay, but the important thing was Lawson had survived. Hurt like hell, but he would make it.

"Yeah, I'm fine," he replied.

"And you, Sarah?" she asked with concern. "Oh, God, I was so scared when you got out of the car like that."

"You did *what*?" Lawson asked, confused. He thought Granger had intercepted the women and forced Sarah to give herself up to him.

"I knew they wanted me," she said softly, shrugging. "I

thought it would give the others a chance to get away if I pretended to turn myself over to them, but I had to run instead."

He stared down at her. He could hardly believe it. He squeezed her closer, hating the thought of her sacrificing herself like that, but even more in awe of her than he had been before, which he hadn't thought was possible.

"I thought we might never see you again," Hannah blurted, her voice wracked with emotion. Lawson tensed. There it was, the horror that he had almost faced.

He had almost lost her. And the thought of it made him feel sick. It was worse than any of the physical pain he had endured that night, by a long shot. He closed his eyes and pressed his face into her hair, reminding himself that she was safe. That was what he needed to remember, above all else, and he was never going to let any threat get that close to her again.

But there was someone else out there who needed his help right now. Lainey was still out there somewhere. Granger wanted him to think that she was dead, but there was no way Lawson would give up until he knew for sure.

"Are you going to be okay?" he asked her.

"Yeah, I'll be fine," she murmured. "What about you?"

"There's something else I need to do," he told her. "I'll meet you at the hospital, alright?"

"Don't get hurt," she pleaded with him, and he kissed her cheek.

"I promise I won't," he replied. "But there's someone else I need to get back to their family in one piece."

She squeezed his hand, and then one of the paramedics led her away so she could get checked over. He watched as she went, feeling a pang at the thought of leaving her again, but he promised himself it wasn't going to be for long. Soon enough, he would be back by her side.

He stalked over to Granger, who was being held along with both of his sons inside a cop car. All of them were cuffed and looked worse for wear, though what they had waiting in front of them was far worse than anything Xavier or Lawson could have inflicted on them with their fists and weapons.

Lawson yanked open the door, startling the men inside.

"Where's Lainey?" he demanded, reaching inside the car, grabbing Granger by the collar.

The man grinned at him, teeth smeared with blood. "You really think I'm going to tell you where that bitch is?" he asked. "Let her rot. If we're going to prison, she can stay in hers, too."

Lawson grimaced. Okay, so he wasn't going to get the information out of Granger, but maybe his sons would be quicker to crack. He looked at them.

"Lyle, Nelson," he snapped. "You want a couple of years cut off your sentence?"

"Yes," Lyle blurted out. His face was pale where it wasn't marked with blood or bruises. They were looking down the barrel of a long life in prison for helping their father with his crimes, and he figured they would want to do anything they could to try to shorten their time behind bars.

Though Lawson knew damn well he couldn't cut them a deal like that, he was willing to try anything he could to get them to hand over Lainey's location.

"Then you tell me where she's being held," he continued, lowering his voice so it didn't travel beyond the back seat and the three men inside. He didn't want them trying to use what he had said to wheedle their way out of the sentence they deserved, and he was going to use everything he had at his disposal to get them to talk.

"Don't say a damn word," Granger warned his sons.

Lawson watched the two brothers closely. Indecision flickered across both their faces before their eyes darted to their father's. Lawson's pulse jumped in anticipation. One of them was about to crack, he could tell. Granger could tell too, if his face turning a concerning shade of red was any indication. Looked like whatever power the man once had over his sons was gone.

"There's a compound, just outside of town," Lyle said quickly, like he wanted to be the one to tell him. "And I… She's being held in a back room there. The code for the building's main door lock is two-six-three-one."

"Address," Lawson ordered. "Now."

"It's where the old dairy farm used to be," Nelson revealed. "It always stunk of old milk."

Granger growled, trying to tell them not to say anything else, but that was all Lawson needed to hear from them. He slammed the car door shut and headed over to Sheriff Willis.

"You know where the old dairy farm outside of town is?" he demanded.

"Yeah, about an hour from here," the sheriff replied. "Why? You got a craving for cheese all of a sudden?"

Lawson managed to let out a laugh, despite the circumstances. He shook his head. "They're holding my friend Lainey there," he replied. "I need to get to her."

"I'll take you there myself," the sheriff replied. "My officers have this under control. They're taking this personally, after what happened at the station."

Lawson nodded in understanding. He knew the horror of what had gone down that day would live long in the memory of the town. Blue Ridge had never had any incidents of that magnitude.

Sheriff Willis and Lawson climbed into the sheriff's car and sped away from the lodge. Time was of the essence since they didn't know how long Lainey had been held or what condition she was in. The sheriff radioed in what was happening and a few other vehicles joined them on the road. Lawson looked over his shoulder to see who all was following them.

"Who's with us?" Lawson asked warily.

"A SWAT unit and the FBI," the sheriff replied. "When the women came racing into town for help, they busted in the station while I was finishing up with the FBI. They filled us in on what they knew, that Granger and his men would be attacking the lodge soon and about Sarah. We had already devised a plan and were about to split up to put it in motion. I tried to reach you guys, but they must have already taken out the communications."

Lawson grimaced. They could have used them earlier at the lodge, but at least they were helping with the cleanup now, and to get Lainey. Might not be a bad thing to have them along in case Granger had any more men hanging around their base of operation. Lawson hadn't thought to ask the man's sons. He was just concentrating on getting to his friend as fast as possible. He had no idea how long they'd actually had her or what had been done to her.

One thing he did know, though, was now her superiors had to take the information she'd given them and do something about it. Pass everything along through the proper channels to see that Victor Granger and his sons got the punishment they deserved. And Lainey would be free to return to her family.

They just needed to find her alive. Lawson knew she was a fighter, since that's what had gotten her into this mess in the first place. Not being able to let something go or someone else take the reins. He just had to hope she'd kept a level head through it all so Granger hadn't felt the need to get rid of her.

Eventually, the sheriff pulled the car to a halt outside a run-down factory; there were several fresh tire marks outside, a sure sign that it had been used recently. Lawson climbed out of the car cautiously, eyes darting around to make sure there were no men left over to guard the place, but it looked like all of them had been sent to the attack on the lodge.

The SWAT team and FBI vehicles pulled up behind them. Agents fanned out to search the grounds and the building. Before Lawson could offer them the code Lyle had given him, they blasted the door. Lawson rushed in behind them, glancing around, calling out for Lainey. For a moment, a dark, unsettling silence hung over the place.

As the group he was with moved farther into the building, they heard more gunshots echoing around. Apparently, there were some men left there after all. A voice sounded over their comm unit, relaying that everything was clear, and the team Lawson was with proceeded.

Nothing but an eerie quiet greeted them the deeper they went. Then suddenly, he heard it. A pounding noise and a muffled voice called through the door at the end of the corridor.

Relief flooded him all at once. It had to be Lainey.

"I heard something. Check down there," he told the SWAT leader standing beside him, and the men raced forward and busted the door down.

Sure enough, there was Lainey.

"Oh, thank God," he muttered as he pushed through the small

crowd to reach her. She was chained up to a chair, her head lolling down to her chest, her face riddled with bruises and cuts.

She lifted her head up when she heard Lawson's voice, and a couple of the team set about trying to free her from her chains. Her dull eyes lit up and she tried to grin, though it turned into a grimace. Lawson could tell she was in a lot of pain.

"You found me," she muttered through her swollen lips, her voice weak. Looked like they might have broken her jaw. Her face was so swollen and bruised, her eyes looked like a couple of seeds in a watermelon.

"I would never leave you behind, Lainey," he promised her. "Come on, let's get you out of here and checked out. Then we can get you back to your family."

Still sitting, she fell forward into Lawson as soon as she was free. She was beaten up pretty badly and was holding her side, but she was alive. That was what mattered.

"Victor Granger's done?" she asked him.

"He's done," he promised her. "You're never going to have to deal with him again, except to testify against him in court and put him behind bars for the rest of his life."

She squeezed her eyes shut, and a tear leaked down her face. With Lawson's help, she got to her feet and gave him as much of a hug as she could, groaning through the pain it caused her.

"Thank you," she breathed. "I wouldn't have been able to do this without you, Lawson."

"You're welcome," he replied sincerely as he put an arm around her and helped her limp toward the door. After being tied up for so long, he was sure her legs were starting to ache just from moving again.

He raised an eyebrow at her. "Just promise you haven't got any more cases you're going to drag me into, yeah?"

She tried to laughed. "I promise. After this, I think I'm done for life. I don't want to look at another case again."

"Let's get you to the hospital," he told her.

"Yes, please. Some type of pain meds sounds really good right about now," she replied.

He chuckled and shook his head. "I'm sure the doctors can hook you up with some good stuff," he replied firmly.

"I don't want to put you out—these guys can take me," she offered.

Lawson shook his head. "I think I'll make sure you get there in one piece." Besides, he needed to go there, anyway. He had his own injuries to get looked at.

And because that was where he'd find Sarah. He wanted to hold her, and tell her that, at last, it was all over.

Chapter Twenty-Seven

Sarah paced back and forth in the waiting room as she counted out the minutes since Lawson had arrived. She wasn't sure exactly how much longer it was going to take him to get patched up, but she felt as though she was going crazy while she waited.

He had arrived at the hospital nearly two hours ago with a woman she assumed was Lainey. They'd both been surrounded by medical personnel and taken back to the treatment area as soon as the staff got a look at them.

Sarah had already been looked at and patched up. Her hands had been tended to and disinfected, but she couldn't go anywhere until she knew that Lawson was okay. She kept watching the doors they'd disappeared behind, willing Lawson to walk out.

"I'm sure he's fine," Hannah tried to reassure her. She was sitting on one of the hard plastic chairs that lined the wall, leaning into Xavier's side.

"Yeah, I'm sure most of his injuries are superficial," Xavier agreed. "You know he'd want you to go back to the lodge and get some rest."

She shook her head. "I can't go yet," she replied firmly. "I need to know he's okay."

"Who's okay?" a rough voice behind her asked.

Sarah's head snapped around when she heard Lawson's voice.

She breathed a long sigh of relief when she saw him standing there and went over to wrap her arms around him.

"Oh, my God." She sighed, leaning against his chest. "You're okay?"

"Pretty much," he replied, but she could hear the wince in his voice.

She sprang back from him at once. "Oh, sorry, I didn't even think," she blurted out, scanning him for injuries. "What's the damage?"

He reached out a hand to Sarah and drew her back to his side. "A couple of cracked ribs," he responded. "Throat contusion, some cuts and bruises, and a broken finger."

He lifted his hand, to show the splint on his finger. His face had been cleaned up and patched, and it looked a lot better now that it wasn't smeared in blood.

"Really. That's all?" she asked. She had been so scared he'd end up with serious damage after his fight with Granger. She was so relieved all his injuries seemed mostly minor. His neck, though… She shuddered at the swift memory of Granger with his hands wrapped around Lawson's throat.

"Hey, that's nothing to sniff at." He tried to laugh, wincing again, and raised his injured hand to his neck.

"I'm sorry. I mean, I'm just glad it's not worse," she replied, taking his good hand and giving it a squeeze. "What happens now?"

Lawson and Xavier exchanged a look. "Well, I gave my statement to the FBI while I was being fixed up. They're still back there talking to Lainey. They'll be contacting the rest of you to get statements in the next few days. I told them they'd find us all at the lodge."

"How's Lainey," Xavier asked. "Did she mention how she ended up at the old dairy farm?"

"Apparently, Donner grabbed her after he escaped and was leaving town. Just dumb luck he ran into her and recognized her from a photo Granger had been passing around. She'll need some time to heal, but she'll be fine," Lawson replied with a smile. "Once she's released, the FBI will see she gets back home to her family."

"Speaking of family," Xavier interjected. "We should get back to the lodge and see the damage. There's a lot that needs to be done."

"Yeah, the others are back already," Hannah added, rising to her feet. Xavier draped an arm around her protectively.

"There's going to be a lot in the way of repairs and cleanup. Again." Lawson sighed.

"You need to rest," Sarah protested, but he just smiled at her.

"I'm okay," he replied. "I want to know what we're going to be dealing with. Then I'll be able to relax."

"The sheriff has a couple of his guys ready to run us back to the lodge," Xavier explained. "Come on, let's get out of here."

ON THE WAY back to the lodge, the sun had begun to rise. Sarah sat plastered to Lawson's side in the back of the police car, not leaving any room between them. Not that either of them minded. He wrapped his arm around her and pulled her closer.

It was a new start, a new opportunity for them to turn the lodge into the safe space it was always meant to be. With Victor Granger gone, it felt like the way was finally clear for Sarah and Lawson to be together, like they had wanted to be for so long.

Arriving back on the property, Sarah was surprised to see that there were already a few cars scattered around, parked in the driveway. She frowned, worried.

"What's all this?" she muttered as they climbed out of the car. Bailey waved to her from the porch, grinning as a few people walked past her into the building.

"What's going on here?" Lawson asked, sounding confused.

"When we got back from the hospital we noticed the bodies had been removed, and the FBI were packing up their evidence, ready to leave," Aaron replied. "Told us we could start cleanup whenever we were ready."

"And apparently, while the guests were in town, word got around that the lodge had been attacked," Cade called back to Lawson as he emerged from inside. "After the FBI cleared out, people started showing up with supplies. Seems like we have a lot more friends than we thought."

Sarah's lips parted with surprise. "They came to help?" she asked.

"Excuse me!" someone called behind her, and she turned to see a man heading toward them with a large pane of glass under one arm. She stepped aside for him to walk past her, staring after him until he disappeared through the entrance.

"Yeah, Sheriff Willis also called in some help from the officers," Bailey told them as she headed down from the porch. "And a few other people from town also wanted to give us a hand, when they found out what happened and that we'd helped stop the criminal organization that had been terrorizing the roads around here. This place is going to be back on its feet in no time."

"That's amazing news," Sarah replied, a rush of emotion rising through her chest. This was so kind of people who were basically strangers to come up and help put the place back in order. It was such a great feeling, knowing people cared enough to help get the lodge back up and running again.

"You want some coffee?" River asked as she popped her head through the front door. "I just got a pot on. I figured it's going to be too noisy to get any sleep, at least anytime soon."

"Sounds good to me," Hannah replied, tugging on Xavier's hand to lead him inside. Sarah followed behind them, and smiled when she saw the industrious hard work taking place around her. It was seriously incredible; she could hardly believe what she was seeing.

Several hours ago, this place had been a complete disaster. And although it still had a long way to go, it already looked better.

They all walked through to the kitchen, where River and Cade were passing out coffees. Sarah wrapped her hands around hers gratefully, inhaling the scent. She was tired, sure, but too full of excitement to go to bed yet. And the feel of Lawson's strong arm around her shoulders was enough to ground her and give her all the peace she needed. Bailey and Aaron laughed about something at the far end of the counter, both of them practically giddy with relief.

"Where do we even start?" Xavier asked.

Cade shook his head. "I think they're determined to take care of everything for us," he replied, gesturing around them. "I mean, we'll probably still be picking bullet fragments out of the main building for the next year..."

"But the hardest part is already dealt with," River insisted. She looked so relaxed, and it made Sarah so happy to see her unwinding after the stressful few weeks they'd had. Stressful months, if she was being honest.

"Yeah, and then we'll have to think about putting Victor Granger and his sons behind bars," Bailey added as she joined the group.

"We can handle that when we have to. The FBI has it under control," Aaron replied, shaking his head. "For now, I think we deserve to celebrate. Right?"

"Well, I don't know if coffee has quite the same ring to it that champagne does." Hannah giggled. "But how about a toast? To the lodge?"

"To the lodge," Lawson agreed, and he lifted his mug. Around him, everyone repeated the sentiment, tapping their mugs against the others and then taking a long sip.

Afterward, the couples drifted off to see where they could help out, and Sarah finished up her coffee and sighed.

"I guess I should find some way to make myself useful, huh?" she remarked, smiling up at Lawson.

He gazed down at her for a moment, and then pressed a kiss against her forehead. "I'm so proud of the way you handled yourself last night," he murmured to her.

"What do you mean?" she asked, slightly confused. She had succeeded in getting herself kidnapped by Granger. She didn't see how that was anything to be proud of.

"I mean, you were willing to sacrifice yourself to keep the rest of the women safe," he replied. "Not many people would have the nerve to do that. You're the bravest woman I know."

She leaned into him for a moment, and then he cocked his head at her with a playful smile on his face.

"By the way," he remarked. "Was that a towel you attacked Granger with?"

She let out a slightly shaky laugh. "It might have been."

He laughed. "You're crazy, woman," he replied. "And I love you."

Those words hung there between them. For a second, Sarah froze. There's no way he just said what she thought he did, right? She locked her gaze with his.

"You…?" She couldn't get any other words out.

"I love you," he repeated, not wavering for a second as he gazed at her. "I love you for your strength, your bravery and your kindness. How you keep surprising me. And because you were willing to wait for me, even though I took my damn time getting my head out of my ass. I love you, Sarah."

She giggled, the sound light and magical to his ears, and cupped her hand gently around his cheek.

She leaned in slowly to plant a kiss on his lips, not breaking eye contact. "I love you, too, Lawson," she replied.

Before she could say another word, he moved into her and deepened the kiss.

All at once, the chaos surrounding them seemed to fall away, leaving nothing but the two of them, in their embrace.

She wanted to stay there forever.

Epilogue

"Here, let me help," Lawson told Sarah, offering her a hand to climb down on to the rocks next to the clear blue natural pool below the waterfall. She picked her way down toward the water in her sneakers, the sun gleaming off her legs beneath her shorts. He tried not to let his gaze linger on the sight of her like that, but damn, it was hard not to feel like a teenager around her.

"Made it!" she told him happily, as she sank down on to the edge of the rocks, kicked off her shoes and dipped her feet in the water. "Mmm, that feels so good."

He grinned as he sat down next to her, taking out the contents of the bag they packed full of food and fresh lemonade from the kitchen.

When he'd woken early on that Sunday morning and saw the late summer sun pouring through the window, he'd known he wanted to finally take her up to his favorite spot, just the two of them.

Now, here they were, by the pool at the bottom of a waterfall that stood high in the mountains above the lodge. It was a bit of a hike to get there, but the peace and quiet was exactly what he wanted for her.

"This is exactly what I needed." She sighed, closing her eyes and leaning back on her elbows as the sun bathed her face. He looked down at her for a moment. It was these instances, just the two of them in the quiet, where he realized how much he loved her. How safe and settled he felt when she was around.

Of course, they'd known each other for several years, but it was only now that he was able to be truly and totally honest with himself about his feelings for her.

"Good," he murmured, pushing a glass of lemonade into her hand. "Here you go. I think we could both use a drink after that hike."

"Thanks," she replied, smiling at him as she took a sip of the tart, sweet lemonade Hannah had made earlier that week.

"So how's therapy going?" he asked her.

She paused for a moment, considering the question, and then replied, "Overall, it's been good, I think. Not easy by any means, especially since we moved it up to three times a week. But I want to make sure I have my head straight for Granger's trial."

"But you're coping with everything okay?" he asked. "It must be intense, working through all that happened."

"It is," she admitted. "But it's not impossible. And besides, it's not going to be forever. The trial's finally in a couple of months, and I can step back some after that. Refocus on other things and move past all this once and for all."

"Good point," he agreed. "You're doing great, Sarah. You should be really proud of yourself."

"I'm a therapist—of course, I'm good at therapy," she joked.

Suddenly, she jumped up, pulled off her shirt and wiggled out of her shorts. She flashed Lawson a flirty grin, slipping into the water below. "Come join me, it's so nice in here…" she said, flipping to float on her back.

He didn't need to be told twice. He quickly stripped off his own clothes and dove into the water alongside her. He used to come to this spot all the time last summer, to think through problems and reflect on what all they'd been through and where he'd like to see them going. But there was something about sharing it with her that was a million times more special.

He used to think that he wouldn't be able to let anyone get close to him. He was scared to be vulnerable with someone and to let them see the real him, underneath the tough-guy exterior. But he had never once doubted that letting Sarah into his life was the right call. He just hated that he'd waited for so long to make it happen.

He was just grateful that Sarah was patient and that she loved him, despite his tendency to be hardheaded. He intended to keep her in his life forever.

She swam toward him, resting her arms on his shoulders and smiling at him. He pushed her hair back from her face, gazing into her eyes. Sometimes he still couldn't believe that after all this time, she was his.

"What about you?" she asked, brushing her nose against his.

"What about me?" he replied.

"What are you going to do after the trial?" she said.

"What do you mean?" he asked, confused. He would have to testify, too, of course, but he didn't expect it to be that big of a deal for him. He'd dealt with plenty of people like Victor Granger over the years, and standing up against them in court wasn't new to him. In fact, he was eager to tell the truth about Granger and to get him locked up for good.

"I mean…" she began, trailing off for a moment, like she wasn't quite sure how to put it. "Do you have any other missions you might take on? Anything else that Lainey has asked you to do?"

He shook his head. Lainey was back home and settled with her family again and she was doing well. She'd invited him and Sarah down for a visit at the end of the year, around the holidays, and they had already made a pact not to talk business.

"Nothing that I know of," he replied. "Why do you ask?"

"Just…curious, that's all," she replied coyly, a little smile on her face. "I want to know where you see your life in a year. Or two years. Or ten."

"And why might that be?" he asked her, though he already knew the answer. Though the two of them hadn't actually discussed what was coming next for them, their love for each other was obvious. If he could spend the rest of his life waking up next to her, he would, and he hoped she knew that.

They had moved into one of the resident cabins together down by the others, and his sister and the other women were thrilled at having Sarah closer for them to hang out and gossip with. They decided to leave her separate cabin empty and usable for any of their residents who might need more intensive therapy, or couldn't handle being in closer quarters with others.

Lawson loved being able to see her first thing in the morning and last thing at night before he closed his eyes. To spend more quality time together just enjoying each other's company, or sipping on coffee every morning before they went about their daily tasks at the lodge—which had been completely fixed up and repaired by the folks who had shown up in the aftermath on that fateful day last year. Now, thanks to all their help, the lodge was better than when they first started out and thriving more than it ever had before.

He and Xavier finally had their dream come true for Warrior Peak Sanctury. It was truly now a safe place for people to come to for help and treatment and to find themselves again. No danger or destruction or old ghosts reappearing. It was a place of calm and reflection and caring and safety.

"Because I want a real life with you," she confessed. "A family. I want to be a mom one day. I want us to raise kids together, Lawson. But that's going to mean a safe life. You know? Not one where you're running off on tactical missions all the time."

"Hmm. I like the sound of that," he murmured, sealing his mouth over hers once more.

"You mean that?" she asked softly as she pulled back, brushing her nose against his. "It's not going to get too boring for you?"

"Are you kidding?" He chuckled. "Having a life with you? That sounds like the most exciting mission in the world to me."

She giggled, and gazed up at him. "Well, that's a hell of a lot to live up to," she pointed out.

"Yeah?" he replied, slipping his arms around her waist and pulling her as close as possible, so there was no space between their bodies.

"I think you can handle it." He kissed her again, smiling into the embrace. She let out a long breath against his mouth, as though this was what she had been waiting to hear all this time. He would make it clear to her every way he could, every time she asked.

"I love you, Sarah," he told her softly.

"I love you, too," she whispered back, and she kissed him again, the taste of lemonade on her lips. He might have waited too long to make her his, but now, she belonged to him and he belonged to her. He knew he was going to spend the rest of his life making up for lost time, and he was looking forward to every moment.

They had all the time in the world to enjoy together now. To enjoy building a life and a family with one another, and he could hardly wait to get started.

With the love of his life in his arms, everything felt possible.

* * * * *

Custody In The Crosshairs

Barb Han

MILLS & BOON

USA TODAY bestselling author **Barb Han** lives in north Texas with her very own hero-worthy husband, three beautiful children, a spunky golden retriever/standard poodle mix and too many books in her to-read pile. In her downtime, she plays video games and spends much of her time on or around a basketball court. She loves interacting with readers and is grateful for their support. You can reach her at barbhan.com.

Books by Barb Han

Harlequin Intrigue

Wilde Country

Custody in the Crosshairs

Marshals of Mesa Point

Ranch Ambush
Bounty Hunted
Captured in West Texas
Escape: Big Bend Canyon
Lone Star Country Protector
Twin Threats in Austin

The Cowboys of Cider Creek

Rescued by the Rancher
Riding Shotgun
Trapped in Texas
Texas Scandal
Trouble in Texas
Murder in Texas

Visit the Author Profile page at millsandboon.com.au.

All my love to Brandon, Jacob and Tori, my three greatest loves.

To Babe, my hero, for being my best friend, my greatest love and my place to call home. I love you with everything that I am.

And to all the readers who are on this journey with me.

I am eternally grateful for you!

CAST OF CHARACTERS

***Blaize Wilde*—**He inherits a crumbling Texas ranch—and an unexpected mystery in the form of baby Lark.

***Carys Aldric*—**A young Child Protective Services agent with fierce moral courage and a heart too big for her role's boundaries.

***Lark Wilde*—**A three-month-old infant at the center of a dangerous mystery.

***Stephanie Cross*—**Mysterious mother of Lark, believed to be deceased.

***Leah Mendez*—**Guarded, anxious neighbor of Stephanie's.

***Kit*—**Grandmother who stands to lose her home.

***Silus Vexler*—**Small-time crime boss on the hunt for Stephanie.

Chapter One

Blaize Wilde walked outside the broken-down barn at Wilde Cattle Ranch taking mental inventory of the shitshow he and his two brothers had just inherited. The weathered wood planks and rusted metal roofing sheets with pieces missing wouldn't be complete without peeling paint and cracked walls. How was he supposed to get this place up and running without a bank load of cash?

"No one would blame you for selling to get what you can out of it." Kit, his grandmother, ambled up, catching him off guard while he'd been deep in thought.

You would. Kit had built this small cattle ranch with Blaize's grandfather. Her son had drained the place of money and spirit. Selling now meant his beloved grandmother would have to move from the only home she'd known for more than fifty years. Not happening. Period.

"There's work to be done to get the place back in shape." Blaize stood in front of a barn in need of far more than a coat of paint. It could use a torch. Starting from the ground up might be easier than attempting to salvage what was left of this rickety old, neglected building. "Nothing we can't handle."

He forced a smile.

"Have you found your brothers yet?" Kit asked, slipping her

bony fingers through the crook in his arm and then holding on to him like she needed him for balance.

"No, ma'am."

"Well, you got the news about your father's passing last night and showed up before the sun," she said. "You should try to get some rest after driving all night." Blue eyes stared up at him, still bright.

"I'm good."

Cormac's death was no loss to the world. A few liquor manufacturers might feel the drop in sales, though. When your last name was Wilde, the jokes wrote themselves. They also got old real quick. Cormac did his best to live up to the family name. His sons couldn't stand the man for it.

Blaize glanced down into serious eyes framed by wrinkled skin.

"How are you doing with it all, by the way?" She waved her free hand like she was presenting paradise, but the twinge of sadness mixed with helplessness in her gaze told the real story. She was afraid for her future. Yet she would never put pressure on the grandsons she loved.

"Me? Like I said, I'm fine." Cormac had never been much of a father. The irony there being Blaize had wanted the whole wife-and-kids package, figuring he could do better than his father. "The world is better off without a person like Cormac in it, as far as I'm concerned."

Another glance told him that he'd struck a raw nerve.

"I'm sorry, Kit. I didn't mean to say your son was a—"

She clucked her tongue, stopping him mid-sentence. "Nonsense. There's nothing to apologize for." She squeezed his arm. "He gave me three incredible grandchildren. It might have been asking too much for him to be good, too."

Three grandchildren from three different mothers, married to none. Cormac was a real piece of work. Kit had hinted there was a time when he wasn't like that. As far as Blaize was concerned, there was no excuse good enough to cover the man's lies and reckless behavior.

"Thank you, by the way," he said, wanting to change the

subject. He smiled and patted her hand. "I'm pretty sure you just gave me a compliment."

"I meant every word." She looked up at him with a devilish grin. "I'd keep throwing out compliments, but you'll accuse me of brown-nosing to keep my bedroom at the ranch."

Blaize laughed for the first time in a very long time.

"You don't have to worry about being evicted as long as I'm around." He wanted to offer reassurance even though he couldn't be certain his brothers would agree to keeping the place. If he could locate them. Since neither were on social media, preferring to stay off the grid, he was limited as to how he could reach his brothers. All he had was phone numbers, no addresses.

"Speaking of you boys, did you get a hold of Raiden or Phoenix?"

He shook his head.

"They'll turn up," she said. "They always do."

"I'd settle for them answering my calls."

Not that they had a reason to. Blaize had been living in his own hell for the past couple of years. Losing the person you promised to spend the rest of your life with had a way of obliterating every piece of you and causing you to go dark with everyone you knew or cared about. Your world shrank. You cut people out of your life. Lashed out. Blaize couldn't blame his brothers for not answering his calls or texts anymore. He'd been a jerk to them, and they had no idea why.

"They will," Kit said, turning toward the farmhouse that was in almost as bad a shape as the barn. "But first, what should I cook for dinner? Something nice to celebrate your homecoming."

"Don't go to any trouble on my account."

She batted her free hand at him playfully. "You coming home qualifies as special, Blaize."

"Fine." He knew better than to start an argument with Kit despite some of her spark dimming with every passing year. There was enough flicker there to light a fire when provoked. "A special occasion calls for steaks on the grill."

"Now you're talking," she said as her eyes lit up. "The corn on the cob at Harden's stand up the road is the best. We'll pick up some of that along with a pair of potatoes. We can do 'em up with sour cream and the works."

"It'll be a feast."

Blaize liked the excitement in her eyes and the hope in her voice.

The cattle ranch was in dire straits. He'd stayed up part of the night driving and the rest looking into the books. He hoped like hell he didn't let her down the way he'd disappointed his wife. *Former wife.* The reality of those words struck like a physical blow. Blaize was no longer married. He was thirty-five years old. No kids. Very little money. And now he needed to save this small cattle ranch or watch his grandmother lose her home.

Life sure as hell knew how to kick you in the teeth when you were down.

Gloomy gray clouds rolled overhead. A couple of rain drops splatted on his forehead. Lightning streaked across an ever-darkening sky. Thunder boomed a few seconds later.

He ducked his head down. "We better head inside before this gets worse."

In Blaize's life, it always did.

CARYS HOLMES HELD a three-month-old baby in her arms, gently bouncing up and down in a feeble attempt to stop the little girl from crying. *Hopeless.* Carys was hopeless. This attempt was hopeless.

In times like these, she seriously questioned her career choice. Holding an inconsolable baby definitely fit into the downside category.

Her office door opened. Harrison Tucker poked his head inside.

"What is that baby still doing here?" her coworker asked, frowning, practically yelling over the noise.

It didn't help. The little one screamed louder.

"I think she's sick."

He stared at her like ... *And?*

"It's just hard to throw her in a car seat and then drop her off at an orphanage when she's this upset."

The air stilled as the baby sucked in a breath before launching another ear-splitting wail. The kid had a good set of lungs on her.

"That's the job, sweetheart." The frown lines on Harrison's face softened.

"She's a baby, Harrison. Sister's Love is severely understaffed right now. They had two people quit last week alone." Carys looked down at the baby, who was winding up to belt out another loud cry. "They won't have time to hold her like this."

He pursed his lips. "Some days, this job is the worst and you go home wondering if you made any difference at all. Other days, you see a once-troubled teen now making straight A's in school and on a better path because you intervened and they listened to your advice."

That still didn't answer the question of how she was supposed to drop off an innocent child at an understaffed orphanage. There were no available foster families and her babysitter's husband said the baby couldn't stay with them.

"She's already lost so much already," Carys said. "And there's at least some hope the woman the vehicle was registered to had loaned out her car. It is possible the baby's mother wasn't the one driving." The fiery crash made it difficult to positively ID the female driver.

"There's no proof she wasn't, either. And the mother hasn't shown up, so she still needs to be taken in."

Fair point. Carys didn't have a comeback for that.

The baby belted out another shrill. Did she know her mother might be gone? *Is gone, Carys. There's no reason to hold out hope the mother is somehow still alive.*

"Sorry about knocking, but I have a raging headache and these walls are paper thin," Harrison said as soon as she sucked in a breath.

"I have aspirin in the top drawer if you'd like some." Carys needed to figure out a plan to quiet the crying. Her heart was cracking in half at the pitiful sounds—sounds that she could relate to for the same soul-deep reason. Loss.

He shook his head. "Took some a few minutes ago." He paused for a beat, resigned. "You'll locate and notify the father or a family member, and she'll be picked up in no time. She might not even spend the night at Sister's. You know how that goes." He squinted like it hurt to look at anyone. "Plus, it's Friday and you probably have a hot date tonight."

Everything he said made sense, except the last part.

She almost laughed. Instead, she cracked a smile. "You know it."

"Wait. I was kidding. You do?" His face scrunched. More pain?

"No. Nothing." His reaction caught her off guard. It was likely the pain of his headache causing his face to twist with concern when he believed she had a date. Why would he care?

She chalked it up to curiosity and nothing more.

At twenty-four years old, she'd been on the job for two, going on three, years following college graduation. Harrison had worked here for six. Clearly he had more experience—and was probably right.

"We can't wear a red cape for everyone who comes through the front door, Carys." With those words, he waved and closed her door.

He might have had more time on the job, but that didn't mean he had as much compassion. Did those extra three years harden him?

Harrison would agree—this job was difficult. You were exposed to child abuse and neglect that made you lose faith in humanity. Carys decided on day one of the job that when the bad days outnumbered the good, it would be time to move on. While she was occupying this desk, however, she would do everything in her power to help kids and families.

Did that mean bending a few rules when necessary?

Carys gently placed the baby in her carrier seat, then strapped her in.

Phone. Wallet. Keys.

Once Carys had all three, she grabbed the carrier's handle and then headed out of the office. Taking the baby to her nearby rented two-bedroom bungalow wasn't a big deal. Her home was warmer than this sterile office environment. Two years on the job already, and Carys had yet to make the space hers. There were no pictures sitting on her desk. Nothing personal on the walls.

No wonder the little girl couldn't get comfortable.

After securing the carrier in the back seat, Carys made the short drive. Halfway there, the little one quieted.

"Do you like car rides?" Carys whispered. She should have thought of the move earlier. It would have saved her ears and the baby's lungs. She glanced at the rearview mirror. The girl's face was still red. Her forehead had been warm earlier. Carys couldn't decide if the baby was sick or just overheated.

She pulled the sedan onto the parking pad next to her house and then cut the engine. She took a deep breath and waited a few seconds for the screaming to kick up again.

It was quiet.

A small win. Carys was more convinced than ever that she'd made the right call in taking the baby out of the office. The office kept a loose work-from-home policy following the pandemic, so her absence shouldn't raise any alarm bells. Her boss might even think Carys was on her way to the orphanage. Good. That could buy more time. She could reach out to the director, Rosie Baumgarten, after lunch.

As a bonus, now that there was peace, Carys could log into the work computer via her laptop and take a deeper look at the baby's file. Locating next of kin before the workday ended was her primary focus before she had to drop off the little girl at the orphanage. The little one had stayed overnight at her babysitter's house and the change in routine had probably added to her fussiness.

After taking the carrier inside and setting up at the kitchen table, she made a cup of coffee and checked the time. Eleven thirty. Good. She had plenty of daylight hours left to locate next of kin once she looked up the birth certificate.

Storm clouds had rolled in on the way home. Rain splatted against the windows.

Thankfully, Ruby Lark was still out. She must be exhausted.

Carys wondered if the baby girl was called Ruby, Rue, or Lark. Then again, it wouldn't surprise her if she was called by her full name, Ruby Lark. This was Texas. Two names weren't out of the question. Since Carys had always liked the name Rue for a nickname, she decided to go with that one for the time being.

Fingers tapping on the keyboard, she glanced at the intake form. There wasn't much there she didn't already know.

The vehicle owner's name was Stephanie Cross. The deputy on scene's name was Levi Liu. Carys made a mental note of the names as she skimmed down the page. There wasn't much else.

Huh.

Thankfully she'd requested a court order to give her access to the child's birth certificate before taking custody of Rue. The permission should be granted before end of day if all went well.

What was she supposed to do until then?

She tapped her fingers against the table, waited.

An hour passed by while getting caught up on paperwork from other cases. Then another.

Her stomach growled.

As she reached toward the laptop to close it down, an update dinged. The permission to access Rue's birth certificate came through. Curiosity got the best of her, so she immediately accessed the TxEVER system, a secure database, and got a name.

Blaize Wilde. She rolled her eyes. *Now that sounds like a stable person.*

Taking note that the last names didn't match, Carys located his cell number and made the call, hearing the first ring and waiting for voicemail to click in. No one ever picked up calls from strangers.

"Hello?" Blaize's deep masculine voice caused a visceral reaction in her body.

"Mr. Wilde?"

"Speaking."

Carys mentally shook off the shock of hearing his voice. "My name is Carys. I'm afraid I have bad news. Are you sitting down?"

"Don't need to," he said on a loaded sigh. "Go ahead and get it over with. Tell me the reason you called."

"I work with Child Protective Services, and your daughter, Ruby Lark Wilde, is in my custody."

"Excuse me?" The degree of shock in his voice said this was likely the first time he was being told about his daughter. And now he was going to have to learn someone he cared about might be dead.

"My apologies if this is the first—"

"You have the wrong person," he said. "I never fathered a child."

"Your name is listed on the birth certificate, Mr. Wilde. And I'm quite certain that—"

"Sounds like someone has been drinking from the outside hose too long," he said and then hung up.

What kind of irresponsible jerk fathered a child and then walked away, leaving the mother to raise a child on her own?

That bastard.

He was also Rue's only hope of not being turned over to an orphanage tonight since there was no other next of kin to be found.

Biting back a slew of curses, Carys tapped the phone icon on her screen. She hit *Recents*, tapped the number at the top of her screen, and clamped her mouth closed.

When he answered this time, he would get an earful. The call rolled to voicemail. *Of course it did.*

"Listen here, you total piece of..." She took in a deep breath, reminding herself that she was leaving a recorded message that could be used against her later. "I have a sick baby in my custody who needs her father to step up to the plate or she'll be left at an understaffed orphanage after losing the one parent who loved her enough to stick around." Realizing she'd gone too far, she ended the call and prayed those words wouldn't be the reason she was fired.

As she set the phone down, it buzzed.

He was calling back.

Chapter Two

“I just saw that you’re leaving a message, so you might as well tell me what it says.” Blaize barely got the words out before a grunt came through the line. It was quickly followed by an apology along with a plea to delete the voicemail without listening to it.

He said he would.

“Here’s what I know so far—I have a baby girl in my custody who I’m about to be forced to take somewhere that won’t be a good place for her right now, and you’re the only parent I can locate.”

“What happened to her mother?” He wasn’t a jerk. He might not have the first clue how his name ended up on the kid’s birth certificate, but he cared what happened on a basic human level.

“There was a car accident.”

“Oh.” He sat with that for a moment. “Hold on. You said that I’m the only parent you can locate. To be clear, the kid isn’t mine. But what happened and how did you get my—”

“The car caught on fire, and the driver hasn’t been positively ID’d as of yet and might not be for days. The car is registered to a woman named Stephanie Cross.”

“And you’re ready to get the little one in your custody out of your hair,” he said.

“Did I say that?” The high-pitched shrill quality to her voice told him the degree to which he'd just messed up. This was bad. "No. I didn't. For your information, sir, I'd happily spend all the time necessary with this angel. However, I've already severely broken the rules by bringing her to my home and could end up fired, so there's that."

Blaize let her speak without interruption. "Carys. Is that your name?"

"Yes."

"You sound like a decent human being going out of your way to protect a child while putting your job on the line." The fact that she'd broken the rules said she cared more about doing what was right than staying employed. He applauded her for the move. Integrity like that didn't come around as often as it should.

"I'd like to think so," she said, some of the defensiveness eased from her tone.

"Here's my problem." He waited a couple of beats. "There's no possible way that I'm the father."

"Your name is on the birth certificate, sir."

"Call me Blaize. My name is Blaize."

"It won't make a difference what I call you," she said. "You're still the only name I have to work with."

He issued a sharp sigh. "Is there no other choice? Just me?"

"I can't find a list of next of kin for the mother, if that's what you're asking," she said. "These things can take time."

"You can release the baby to me if I agree?" How was that even possible?

"Yes."

"What's the mother's name again?"

"Stephanie Cross."

Blaize still drew a blank. "How old is this baby?"

"Three months," she said.

That young? What was he supposed to do with an infant?

Thunder boomed, shaking the house as he walked into the kitchen to get a drink of water. Sitting at the table nursing a cup of coffee was the answer. "Hold on a second, okay?"

"Sure," Carys said, drawing out the word.

He moved the phone from his ear and caught his grandmother's attention. "How are you with babies?"

Her eyebrows shot up. "Why do you ask?"

"A friend needs a sitter, possibly overnight, and I don't have the first clue as to how to take care of a kid."

She smiled. A tiny spark lit her eyes. "Are you asking for my help?"

"I guess I am."

"It's been a long time, but I imagine not too much has changed. They still take bottles and need diaper changes." She shrugged and widened the smile. "Might be nice to have a baby around, even if only for a short while."

"I'll owe you one big time."

She winked before taking a sip and making a production of setting the cup down. "I'll take you up on it someday."

They both knew she wouldn't. She never asked for anything, and he was beginning to see how much he'd neglected this place and her. Guilt punched him. Regret stabbed him in the chest. He might have reason to hate Cormac, but Blaize should have checked on his own grandmother more.

He was here now. He would do better.

Before he got the phone back to his ear, the loud baby cries overrode the thunder cracking outside.

"Carys?"

"You'll have to speak up," she said. "I can barely hear you."

"Should I come to you, or how should we do this?" He had no idea how any of this worked and couldn't be more outside his comfort zone. This baby might not belong to him, but offering a hand was the right thing to do. Call it residual guilt for not being able to save his own wife. He'd never felt more helpless during her long illness. This, he could do.

A voice in the back of his head said, *You were of no use then, and you'll be pointless now.* Choosing to ignore it and the knot tightening in his chest, he said, "I'm ready to do what I can to help."

"What? I'm sorry—I can't hear you."

He practically had to shout the words a second time.

"Send me your address," she said. "I'll come to you."

He agreed and then ended the call.

Kit clucked her tongue. “Is there something you need to tell me?”

“Funny story.” He poured a cup of coffee and joined her at the table after texting the address to the ranch. “A person I’ve never heard of before put my name down on a birth certificate.”

“What?” Kit’s eyes saucers.

“I know. Strange, isn’t it?” A crack of thunder rumbled in the distance. The storm was intensifying. So much for grilling outside.

“And you’re sure you’ve never met the woman?”

“Not to my knowledge.” He took a sip of coffee. “And I sure as hell didn’t sleep around. Not with everything going on with…”

Blaize clamped his mouth shut.

Kit reached across the table and patted his hand. Her frail, bony fingers were small by comparison. “Of course, you don’t owe me any explanations.” She caught his gaze. “You know that, right?”

He nodded.

“I just wish you would talk about what happened with someone. Doesn’t have to be me.”

Rain battered the roof. A drip sounded behind him.

He bit back a curse as he pushed up to standing. “I’ll keep that in mind. Right now, I need to fix a leak before we need swimsuits to be in this old house.”

She opened her mouth to speak before clamping it shut again. “I’ll get a bucket.”

RAIN POUNDED THE front windshield to the point where the windshield wipers were essentially just decorations. Carys white-knuckled the steering wheel. The car ride seemed to upset the baby this time. Thunder boomed and lightning streaked the sky. Almost-black clouds rolled across the velvet canopy. No stars were out.

This was a bad omen.

Winds kicked up, shaking the sedan. Debris flew across the road in the form of branches and trash. An actual trash can slammed into the hood of her sedan, then bounced off. *We're not in Kansas anymore, Dorothy.*

The thought of a tornado ripping through the streets was enough to fry her last nerve. She was closer to the ranch than her home, so it made the most sense to keep going. Winds howled louder than the baby's cries.

This was not good. So not good.

I choose to be strong. She repeated the mantra that had gotten her through a few very rough years when she was younger, including surviving an overbearing father after her mother died.

She glanced in the rearview mirror at the red-faced baby. "I understand what you're about to go through better than you realize, Rue. You aren't the only one who lost a mother before you could remember anything about her."

Carys didn't wish death on anyone. For Rue's sake, she hoped the driver wasn't Stephanie Cross. The odds were most definitely against it being the case, but she could hold on to the thought until proven otherwise.

Holding on to the steering wheel for dear life as winds pushed the vehicle around, she navigated onto the farm road leading to the ranch. Gravel spewed behind her tires as she pushed the vehicle to go faster.

Branches flew in front of the windshield. Being out here was dangerous. She should have asked Blaize to meet her at her home instead. What had she been thinking? *You weren't. You were in emergency mode.*

Carys repeated the mantra moments before slamming on the brakes. She careened sideways, narrowly missing a tree trunk.

Her first instinct was to hop out of the driver's side and comfort the child. The baby's loud cries said her lungs were still working as Carys slipped into the back seat. Rain pelted her face and torso. Her button-down shirt needed to be wrung out by the time she slammed the door shut behind her. Her second instinct was to lock the doors as the tiny hairs on the back of her neck pricked.

She glanced around, searching for signs of someone being out here. The feeling they weren't alone nearly overwhelmed her. A second later, she could have sworn a shadow passed by on the passenger side of the car.

An involutory shiver rocked her body as icy fingers gripped her spine. *I choose to be strong.*

Blowing out a calming breath, she refocused on the baby. The buckles on the car seat were not the easiest to navigate. She noticed how shaky her own hands were as she tried to unclick the chest clip holding the straps in place.

"I'm sorry that I'm so bad at this, little Rue," she said, mustering as soothing a voice as she possibly could while under duress. "It'll be okay."

How many times had she wished her own father would have said those words to her while growing up? Instead, he'd overprotected her to the point of stifling her. He'd become obsessed with keeping her safe, which meant never letting her out of the house except for school and school-related activities. She'd joined pretty much every club in high school just to have an excuse to leave the house. He'd denied sleepover requests. *What if the girl has a brother who'd abuse you in the middle of the night or a father who has bad intentions?*

The closer college came, the more he bore down on her, making any kind of life impossible. By her senior year of high school, she'd had it.

I'm moving to campus, she'd said. *And there's nothing you can do to stop me.* It was the first time in her life that she'd stood up for herself and gone against him. Pushing back against the person who raised you—no matter how hard they'd made your life—was the hardest thing to do.

Then I'm not responsible for you had been his comeback.

True to his words, he cut her off financially. They'd had a huge dustup over the move, not because she was mad about the money. She could—and did!—take out loans to get through her four years of school. She'd worked double shifts and crashed on a friend's couch after the required first year of dorm living to save money.

Her father couldn't handle her independence. He threw every name in the book at her when she dug her heels in. He'd accused her of being a harlot—the nicer-sounding word for slut—even though she'd never had sex, let alone a boyfriend.

The fight, the horrible words he'd called her, caused her to lose her father more than the decision to leave did. Because she wanted nothing to do with him after the way he talked to her.

The wall that had come up between them had become impenetrable and strong as steel. She'd contacted him before graduation, humbled herself, and asked him to be there.

He never responded to her text, never showed.

Fine. She decided not to lose sleep over it. Her stubborn streak, it turned out, came from her father.

The car seat's chest clip finally opened. *Thank the stars for small miracles.*

Carys gently wrapped her hands around the little girl and lifted. The crying nearly broke Carys's heart.

"I'm here, little one," she soothed, bringing the baby toward her until the little girl was against Carys's chest. She looked down at the pitiful creature who was so upset. It struck her that Rue had a binky earlier. "Do you need your binky?" She managed to find it in the seat. The second the rubber tip touched the baby's cheek, she rooted for the comfort item.

It was then Carys realized the kid might be hungry.

At least the binky quieted the cries. A sense of satisfaction replaced the deep-seeded failure from moments ago.

Carys didn't want kids. Barely in her mid-twenties, she hardly wanted a boyfriend. Though, after the last one, she needed a minute to regroup. Jack had too many of her father's tendencies. After two months of dating, he wanted the password to her cell phone so he could check texts for her.

Like she needed a gatekeeper for her messages. His jealous streak turned ugly fast, and she couldn't move on quick enough. Weeks after the breakup, if you could even call it that since they'd never had a conversation about being in a relationship, he still showed up in the parking lot with flowers.

Then there was Leonard. He'd been older, which she'd assumed meant wiser. At almost forty, he'd been surprisingly less emotionally mature than some of the teens she worked with since taking the CPS job.

Suddenly, something or someone dashed across the headlights. Panic gripped Carys as a male figure came toward her side of the vehicle, moving directly at her.

She reached for anything she could use as a weapon and double-checked that she'd locked the doors.

With nothing to defend herself with, she and Rue would be at the mercy of anyone who got inside the vehicle with them.

Carys recited a silent protection prayer she'd learned in religious school as a kid and hoped like hell it would be enough to keep them safe. And then she remembered where she was and what she had. She fumbled her phone, then managed to tap the most recent call.

The second Blaize answered, she said, "Help!"

Chapter Three

The panic in Carys's voice against the backdrop of severe weather caused the stress knot to tighten in his chest. "Where are you?"

"No idea," she said.

Not at all helpful.

"I was on my way to your ranch and turned off onto a gravel farm road after the highway."

Better.

A loud crack sounded. She screamed.

The call dropped.

Back to not good.

Blaize turned toward the kitchen door. Kit stood there, blocking his exit.

"Where do you think you're going in this mess?" she asked. Her gaze shot to the set of keys hanging next to the door.

"I have to go." He started toward her.

She stepped aside. "In this? Be reasonable, Blaize. You could get hurt out there. You're no match for a storm this size."

Wind howled. A few seconds later, something substantial slammed against the side of the house as though punctuating her sentence. It was not lost on him that flying debris killed far too many people in weather like this.

"You could get hurt or worse, Blaize. I'm serious."

"Someone could die if I don't go," he said.

Kit gave a small nod. She, of all people, would understand his need to help someone in need. It was the ranching way, ingrained in all of them since birth. Somehow it had skipped a generation with Cormac, but that was another story.

"If you have to do this, be careful out there," Kit said, a worry wrinkle adding to the ones already scoring her forehead.

"You know I will."

With that, he grabbed the keys to his old Jeep and headed out the door. The second he stepped outside rain pelted him like BBs. He tucked his chin to his chest and made a beeline to his Jeep that was parked on the pad next to the one-story ranch-style house.

Once inside, he claimed the driver's seat and started the ignition. The Jeep would fare better than other types of vehicles in this mess of a storm. Texas weather in the spring was as unpredictable as serious illness. Some folks' DNA was a ticking time bomb that, once unleashed, could get out of control fast. At least, that had been the case for Lynn. She'd gone from being the most alive person he'd ever met to sick and sicker in a matter of months.

Storms like this one always reminded him of Lynn. She'd left this world, and him, on a night much like this one.

He navigated down the lane and toward the farm road, face wet with a mix of rain and hot tears—tears that had taken too long to fall. They burned as they rolled down his cheek and dripped onto his shirt. Blaize never wanted to feel that helpless again in this lifetime. An image of Lynn stamped his thoughts. Not sick, almost-dying Lynn. But the one he'd fallen head over heels for.

A thump on the side of the Jeep cleared every distraction, bringing his focus back to the stretch of road in front of him.

Potholes on the lane had him bouncing around, but he didn't care. He needed to get to Carys and the baby girl.

Trying to call back did no good as he was being tossed around like a fishing boat in a storm and he'd lost cell coverage. He muttered a few choice words under his breath as he navigated toward the spot he was certain Carys was stuck.

Barreling down the lane, he turned onto the farm road. Panic struck, causing the stress knot to tighten even more. He had no idea if her vehicle had been struck or if she'd had to abandon it altogether.

The thought of her stuck outside with no shelter sat hard on his chest. Add an infant into the equation and the boulder on his chest dug in deeper. Mud kicked up, splattering on the windows. The windshield wipers couldn't keep up with the barrage.

It had been a long time since he'd been on this road. Muscle memory kicked in as he gripped the steering wheel with both hands. He should be coming up on the spot he believed Carys to be stranded.

Stranded and in trouble—a dangerous combination.

LIGHTING SHOT ACROSS the sky. Carys strained to get a good look out the driver's-side window. A figure, dressed in all black with a hoodie over their head, stood tall. Arms raised, Carys couldn't tell what the person was holding, but it seemed obvious what they were about to do.

An object landed with a thud against the pane. A crack?

The phone had slipped from Carys's hand while she'd been trying to maneuver the child back into the carrier. She muttered a curse as she felt around on the floorboard for the device while keeping one hand on Rue. She calmed with physical contact and a binky. Since Carys had no way to heat a bottle and no idea if the baby could drink formula cold, she needed to do whatever she could to keep the child calm until she could be turned over to her father.

Another thud snapped her back to the person trying to break into the vehicle. Carys had never felt more defenseless in her life. If it was just her, she could slip out the passenger-side door and run for her life. She might not be considered tall, but she could run. Running was one of the extra curriculars that got her out of the house at five o'clock in the morning during the school year when home had become a prison.

Headlights bounced up and down. The hooded figure ran off and disappeared.

A Jeep roared up next to her vehicle. A substantial male immediately jumped out of the driver's side. This had to be Blaize. For one, he came from the correct direction. Who else would be out here in this mess? The man made a beeline toward her.

Carys unlocked the door as the baby stirred.

He opened it but didn't make a move to get inside. After introducing himself, he said, "Let's get you two moved into my Jeep."

"Okay," she said, setting the baby in the carrier before handing her over to Blaize. She glanced around as she unhooked the base. "But someone was trying to break into my vehicle, so be careful."

"What the hell?" he asked as he took the carrier and then immediately got the baby inside the Jeep with Carys's help. Next, he shielded Carys as she exited her sedan after clumsily grabbing her purse and locating her cell on the floor.

He stood next to her while she secured the base. She immediately climbed into the back seat after shouldering the diaper bag and grabbed the carrier once settled.

She scanned the area, but it was pitch black outside, way too dark to see anything. The occasional lightning bolt lit up the sky, but not long enough to see anything clearly. This area was rural, and trees lined the farm road.

"Thank you for coming out in this," she said to Blaize as he took the driver's seat. She could only imagine what he must've thought of her. She was supposed to take care of Rue, not place the little girl in harm's way even further. "I should have stayed home to ride it out."

He waved her off like it was nothing as he banked a U-turn back toward his ranch. "You were acting in the best interest of the kid."

"Was I? Bringing her out in this?" She was still shaking from the encounter with the person intent on harming them. "Not to mention the person who..."

An involuntary shiver rocked her body.

"Speaking of that, did you get a description?" He had to raise his voice to speak over the thunder booms.

Rue spit out her binky and started crying.

"That might be the most pitiful sound I've ever heard in my life," Blaize said, glancing at them through the rearview mirror.

He had the most interesting shade of blue-green eyes she'd ever seen. They were like staring into deep turquoise pools. After standing next to him, she knew he had to be at least six feet two inches, maybe a little more. He had a substantial build. Carys told herself she only noticed because of the threat of danger a few moments ago. On a basic, biological level, she needed to know he could protect her while she was vulnerable. Being with a baby had never made her feel more helpless. You couldn't run from danger while finagling an infant in your arms. You couldn't fight back. She felt defenseless.

Carys had a new understanding and a whole new respect for what mothers must go through on a daily basis. She didn't mean in the physical danger sense because what had just happened was rare. Trying to protect something so tiny and fragile, despite the lung capacity, would be a full-time job.

The baby kept up the crying as they pulled beside a ranch-style farmhouse that looked severely in need of TLC. Part of her job was to evaluate environments and people. She'd been a CPS worker for the past two years. Enough time to get a feel for people and places within a few minutes of meeting them or entering their space.

Blaize over the phone caused a lot of alarm bells to sound. She gave him grace for the fact he was finding out that he was a father from a stranger—not exactly an ideal situation. He claimed there was no possible way he fathered Rue. She needed to have a conversation with him about that before leaving her with him.

But first. Quiet the baby. Then? Coffee.

"What can I do to help?" Blaize asked as he pulled the lever that made the driver's seat go up so she could exit the Jeep.

"Take her," she said, handing over the carrier once more. Carys climbed out of the back seat and rushed toward the back door a half step behind Blaize. He stopped a little too suddenly, causing her to walk right into his back—a very muscled, brick-wall-type back. "Sorry."

If he noticed, he didn't say a word. Instead, he opened the door for her and ushered her inside.

Water dripped into a bucket a foot away from the fridge. The place was old and small but tidy.

A grandmotherly figure hopped up from her spot at the kitchen table, eyes as bright as her smile. "I can heat up water in the kettle."

"That would be amazing," Carys said. "Thank you."

The older woman practically beamed. "Call me Kit."

"I'm Carys."

Blaize set the baby carrier on top of the kitchen table, away from the *splunk* sounds coming from the bucket.

With all three of them working, Rue had a bottle in her mouth, happily sucking the milk within a matter of minutes with Kit doing the honors.

Carys cornered Blaize near the sink. "Thank you for rescuing us, by the way."

"Don't mention it." He issued a sharp sigh. "I'm concerned about the person on the loose who attacked your vehicle. You're sure they were trying to get to you?"

"What other option is there?"

"I don't know." He shrugged massive shoulders. "Maybe they thought you were trapped and couldn't unlock the door?"

She was already shaking her head before he could finish that sentence. "I was in plain sight."

"But you didn't get a description of them?"

"Not with the dark clothing and hoodie they were wearing."

"Male or female?"

"It was impossible to tell." Frustrating as hell, too. "It was dark, and they were wearing oversized clothing that basically made it impossible to make out any shapes other than a general description of, like, they were a human being."

She issued a sharp sigh. "How's that for helpful?"

"The road will be washed out from the rain, so getting footprints or tire tracks won't happen, either." He took a sip of coffee.

"Which means whoever was there remains anonymous until they strike again."

"We'll get the sheriff involved," he said. "That'll get more eyes on the case."

It wasn't exactly progress, but she couldn't be picky under the circumstances. She was still beating herself up for not checking the weather before leaving the house. What kind of parent would she make? Not that she wanted children at this point in her life, or possibly ever. Ruling them out didn't feel like the right move.

She glanced over at Rue, who seemed the most content in Kit's arms.

"She's a good baby," Kit said, practically beaming. "All she needed was a meal and a diaper change to be happy."

"I think you're selling yourself short, Kit. She's comfortable with you. She was screaming the whole time I held her." Not technically the whole time, but it sure felt like it.

Kit issued a grunt. "She's probably worn out from crying, then."

"Do you want to sit down?" Blaize asked.

"Yes." She had questions for the gorgeous man. But something told her that he wouldn't have the answers she needed to hear to be able to walk away from Rue.

Chapter Four

"Do you want a refill?" Blaize nodded toward Carys's empty mug.

"Yes, please." She smiled, and it lit up her face, stirring something in his chest. An attraction wasn't just inconvenient; it was out of the question.

He fixed her a cup and joined them at the table, sitting across from her.

"Thank you," she said before taking a sip. The little mewl that passed over those pink heart-shaped lips stirred him in other places.

Great job, Wilde! Way to keep it in check.

"You are convinced that you're not the father," Carys started after a furtive glance toward Kit.

"I'm absolutely sure." No question.

"May I ask how?"

"How old is she?" he asked.

"Three months."

"And how long does it take for one of those things to cook?"

Carys's eyebrow shot up. "Forty weeks if the pregnancy goes to full term." Her finger absently traced around the rim of the mug as she studied him, head tilted to one side.

He performed a mental calculation. "So, basically, a week more than nine months."

"That sounds right," she said. "I don't have personal experience to draw from, but it checks out with my mental math."

"For me to be the father, I would have had to have sex with the mother almost exactly this day last year."

Kit coughed at the outright mention of sex.

He glanced her way. "Forgive me for being direct."

Her cheeks flushed and she giggled. "I've heard worse. You just caught me off guard."

Turning his attention back toward Carys, whose crimson cheeks were sexy as hell, he said, "I'm certain that I didn't father a child because that would require having sex with a stranger not long after I buried my wife. I got to know one person during that time, but believe me when I say nothing came of it."

Carys brought her hand up to cover a gasp. "I'm so sorry. I had no idea."

"Now you know." He didn't normally shout his business from the rooftop. Blaize wasn't exactly the sharing type.

Kit's girlish smile wiped from her face. "I thought she left you."

He shook his head. Now his private business was out there for anyone to see. Great.

"Why didn't you tell me?" Kit asked.

"Lynn had been sick for a while." He shrugged. "It was something we were going through."

His wife had been fiery, opinionated, and almost wholly unpredictable. The first time he'd drummed up the courage to call her after a week of texting, the phone shook in his hands.

Lynn had been beautiful and carefree. She'd been the opposite of the women he'd gone for in the past. His exes were country down to their souls. Lynn was adventure and excitement. Falling for her hadn't taken but a minute.

As they got to know each other, he uncovered a different side to her—serious and more calculated. A side that thought about every move intensely before making it. The dual sides of her personality had thrown him for a loop at first. But he'd already fallen for her and figured he would never be bored loving someone like her.

The truth had been a little more brutal when the first diagnosis came. Bipolar disorder wasn't something he was familiar with, but Lynn's highs and lows along with her risk-taking behavior made more sense to him once he educated himself on the disorder. Lynn was charismatic like no one he'd ever known on the highs, and she hit rock bottom on the lows.

Blaize and her doctor had gotten his wife on a good regimen with her meds. Life began to resemble something that looked a lot like normal. He'd let himself wonder if the two of them could think about starting a family together. Until the worst diagnosis came the next year. The one that was rarely survivable. The one there was no good medication for. The one that hit hard and fast. They'd tried everything they could think of to slow the illness down and wipe it out. Looking back, he'd tried. Lynn had gone along with whatever he said. The experimental drug didn't work, nor did the clinical trial. Traditional Chinese medicine had no good answers. Acupuncture was a bust as well as half a dozen other far-fetched therapies. No amount of yoga, hypnotherapy, or Reiki could fix her.

They ran out of options. But Lynn had given up almost the day she'd learned about her illness. Part of him still resented her for it.

He looked up and realized he had two pairs of eyes trained on him, waiting for his response. "What good would it have done to bring anyone else down?"

"You wouldn't have had to go through it alone," Kit said in practically a whisper with the kind of reverence normally reserved for talking during church service.

"I knew you were there if I needed you." Those words rang hollow. He had wallowed in self-pity for too many months after Lynn's death. He'd cursed everyone and everything that had once been sacred to him.

"That's not the same thing, and you know it." Kit's scolding tone struck a chord.

"You're right," he said. "I should have told you everything."

"I knew Lynn was sick and that you'd had your ups and downs, but I didn't know it was..." Her voice trailed up as she looked at him with the sincerest eyes. "Explains a lot about the last couple of years."

He nodded. He knew she was talking about the way he'd withdrawn from her and everyone else. The lack of communication with his family. The way he'd treated brothers who didn't take his calls now.

A dawn of understanding passed behind Kit's eyes.

Rather than keep going down a path that couldn't be undone, he shifted the conversation to the real reason Carys was here. "I'm confident that I wasn't sleeping around a year ago. And now you know the reason. But that leaves this little girl in limbo, doesn't it?"

"Officially? Yes."

"What about unofficially?"

"You haven't taken a paternity test to prove you're not the biological father so I have no reason to disregard your name on the birth certificate." She put a hand up to stop him from protesting. "I'm not saying you are. I believe you're being honest. However, I have a government document that implicates you as the father and no DNA test to disprove it." She looked at him with pleading eyes. "If you are officially not the father, then Rue goes to a seriously understaffed orphanage while I hunt down next of kin. You are a good person. You came to the aid of a stranger in this horrific storm. Not many people would risk their own safety under these circumstances. In fact, most wouldn't have called back."

"The name Stephanie Cross suddenly rings a bell," he said, catching on and appreciating the show of confidence in him. If he could buy some time for Carys to find a suitable home for Rue, he wouldn't stand in the way. It felt like he could finally do something good for someone else. He felt useful for the first time in a long time.

Carys shot him a look. "What are you saying?"

"I was hitting a lot of bars a year ago. Drinking more than my fair share." His admission got a stern look from Kit. "I'm not proud of it, but I figure honesty is the best policy."

"And this is true?" Carys asked.

He raised his right hand with three middle fingers extended

while his thumb held down his pinky finger in the Scout Sign. "Hand to god."

"Okay, I can work with that narrative," she said on a slow exhale, needing to revise her report.

Blaize caught Kit's gaze. "You okay with a baby staying here for…what?" He looked to Carys.

"A couple of days, maybe more," she said. "Next of kin will have to be found, then notified of Stephanie's death if that proves to be the case, and I can screen them for suitability. This girl is too young to remember anything that we do for her, but believe me when I say it'll matter in the long run more than you can know."

The heaviness in those words struck Blaize. Had Carys lost someone important to her at a young age?

"IT'LL BE NICE to have a little one around again," Kit said. "We haven't had a crib in this house in a lot of years. Your father got rid of everything I kept for you and your brothers. Said this wasn't a storage facility."

Carys noted the tick in Blaize's jaw at the mention of his father. She would mention that safety standards were different now and it wasn't advised to use cribs and such that were decades old if that would make it better. Based on his tense expression, it wouldn't. This conversation was bigger and had more weight. It was about casually throwing away memories. She got it. Her father hadn't been any better. He'd gotten rid of all Carys's memorabilia, too.

"You'll have to tell me when you're ready to take the DNA test," she said to Blaize. "I appreciate you buying time for me."

Thunder cracked.

"Do you want to settle in for the night?" Kit asked, surprising Carys with the question.

"I don't have any clothes or supplies for myself," she stammered. "I'm sure the storm will blow over, and then maybe…"

When she really thought about it, she needed to stay. Kit would be fine taking care of Rue. Still, leaving felt strangely like abandonment. Was it because paternity hadn't been established? Was that the niggling feeling in the back of Carys's mind warning her to stick close to Rue? Did it have to do with guilt for pushing an infant on a family where she didn't technically belong?

Definitely all of those things. She couldn't imagine walking out that door, going home, and getting any sleep tonight. Especially not after what happened. Was her car even drivable?

"On second thought, I'd love to take you up on your generosity," she said. "Thank you for your hospitality."

Kit smiled as her gaze bounced from Carys to Blaize and back. "It sure is nice to have a few more females in the house for a change." She seemed to catch the implication of her casual comment when she shook her head. She flashed her eyes at Blaize. "I don't think that came out right."

"No offense taken," he said warmly. He clearly cared a great deal about his grandmother. He'd lost a wife. It hadn't dawned on Carys to ask if he had any other children.

Kit motioned for help with the baby. Blaize was by her side, helping her place Rue in the carrier. For a man of his size, he was surprisingly gentle with his grandmother and the baby.

For a split second, Carys was sure she saw something in his eyes that looked a lot like longing when he looked down at Rue. Had to be a mistake on her part.

When Kit left the room, Carys figured it was a good time to ask the questions on her mind. She remembered how much her father drank on certain days that she would later realize was her mother's birthday and their wedding anniversary. Forget major holidays. Those were never the same.

"I wouldn't be doing my job properly if I didn't ask a couple of questions," she said, wincing. They'd extended hospitality to her and Rue. The last thing she wanted to do was slap them in the face with rude questions.

"Okay-y-y."

"It's just…the thing is…"

Wow, she was really winning with words, wasn't she?

"Were you serious about going out drinking this time last year?"

"Yes," he said. It dawned on him where she was going with

this. "I can admit that I drank too much when I was swimming in loss and self-pity."

"Where did you hang out?"

"Austin bars mostly," he said.

"Do you mind making a list?"

"What good would that do?" His right eyebrow hiked up.

"I need to track down information about Stephanie and—"

"You think it's possible I was so drunk that I don't remember having sex with her." The disappointment in his voice stabbed her.

"It's nothing personal," she said, hearing the defensiveness in her own voice. "If she listed you on the birth certificate, you must have had some contact with her."

He exhaled a slow breath. His eyebrows pinched together as he pursed thick, kissable lips. "That's a reasonable guess."

Carys cleared the sudden dryness in her throat. "I'm at a loss as to figuring out who her relatives are. I'll take any thread I can get no matter how loose it might be."

"What are you saying?" he asked. "Stephanie Cross might be a cover?"

"It could be that or someone who wanted to disappear," she said. "It's not impossible to create an identity. Forgers are amazing with identification nowadays."

"Is that what you really think?"

"I have no list of next of kin and a name on a birth certificate for a father who swears he's never heard of this person," she said. "I don't know what to think but Rue deserves for me to do everything I can to make sure her mother isn't alive somewhere, hiding."

"What do you make of the person you said was trying to get inside your vehicle?" he asked.

Carys was just now letting herself begin to think about the possibilities there. "Could have been someone stranded in the storm and panicking."

He nodded. Then he stared out the window. "It's possible. I didn't see a vehicle anywhere near."

"I don't remember passing a stranded car, either."

"Someone is out there and could be watching the house," he said.

Creepy crawlies ran wild up and down her spine at the thought.

"It's time to make that call to the sheriff," he said.

Did that mean she wasn't safe here?

Chapter Five

Blaize listened intently as Carys recounted the story of what happened on her way to the ranch on the phone with the sheriff. This place's bad luck seemed to be rubbing off on everyone who came near. It also occurred to him that he should try calling his brothers again. They needed to be part of the decision-making process when it came to all things dealing with the ranch, which would be happening soon if they were going to keep this place up and running.

He highly doubted Raiden or Phoenix would care about their father's death. Not one of the man's sons could stand to be in the same room with him. Cormac was a piece of work. From the initial look of things, he would create about as much havoc in death as he did in life.

Inheritances were tricky, especially when you were handed something broken. The one thing that was worth saving on this place was Kit. She deserved the world. More of that familiar guilt zinged him at the thought of how badly he'd shut everyone out of his life. Updates on social media weren't his thing, either. He didn't live his life for "likes" or any other type of approval. Hell, he barely used his phone's camera.

One thing was certain—he needed to quit licking his wounds over losing Lynn. He needed to figure out how to put that chapter of his life behind him. Because he'd blacked out a couple of times after a drinking binge last year. Always woke up fully dressed but not always in his own apartment. A park bench? Yes. The back seat of his Jeep? Affirmative.

Was he proud of this?

No.

He tuned into Carys as she concluded her statement to the sheriff. The call ended with Carys promising to call or text with any updates of if the mystery person appeared again. Blaize had paid close attention to the names she'd given the sheriff. Three men.

"What was that about?" he asked.

"What?"

"The names?" He probably shouldn't press the issue, but she'd gotten up close and personal with his business. Turnabout seemed like fair play.

"The sheriff asked about the last person I dated and anyone who asked me out but was refused, with a special note toward anyone who persisted."

"Sounds like he believes this could be personal," Blaize said.

She nodded. "Apparently most crimes against women are committed by someone they know and trust."

The thought of a man hurting the person he was supposed to care about burned him from the inside out. "Makes me sick to think about what happens to women at the hands of men."

"Agreed," she said, a little of the fight gone from her voice. It was replaced with something that sounded a lot like sorrow.

His hands fisted at the thought of someone harming her.

"And what do you think?" he asked, forcing a calm he didn't feel. "Could this mystery person be someone you know?" A stalker?

Carys issued a sharp sigh. "Anything's possible, I guess." She hugged her arms to her chest. "I'd hate to think someone I know would follow me…track my moves." She shivered. "That's awful."

Unfortunately, it wasn't just possible, it was likely. He made a mental note of the names she'd mentioned to the sheriff: James Gray. Ethan York. Gabe Hutchins. Blaize would do a little digging on the internet later. See what he could find out about these men.

"It's a reality that shouldn't exist," he said. "Women should be able to leave their doors unlocked and not have to worry. They sure as hell shouldn't have to live their lives in fear of the opposite sex." Too many times, they did. And it angered him beyond belief.

He glanced at the clock, realized it was dinner time. "Are you hungry?"

"I should probably try to eat something," she said. "Wish I'd been more prepared. I hate to be a burden."

"You couldn't be." He waved a hand, dismissing the idea. Since going out to the grocery wasn't an option, he checked the fridge to see what he could pull together. "We might have to get creative since I got in late last night and haven't had a chance to go to the store."

She blinked at him. "You don't normally live here?"

"I do now," he said before shaking his head. "It's complicated."

"I'm sure I can understand."

"My father passed away and left this place to his three sons." That was it in a nutshell.

"I'm sorry."

"About my father? Don't be."

Again she blinked, looking unsure what to say or where to begin. And then she said, "I totally understand complicated family dynamics. You don't have to explain further if you don't want to, but I'm here if you want someone to listen."

He thought about it for a second, decided it might be a welcome change of topic from the stresses of the day for her. But first, "How do you like breakfast for dinner?"

"Is that a serious question?" She laughed. The sound was almost musical.

"I guess not."

He started pulling out what little supplies were there. Knowing this was all the food in the house brought on more of that guilt that he'd been so focused on his own sorrow that he hadn't been making sure Kit was okay. He would never forgive himself if she went to bed hungry because he was too wrapped up in his own life to notice. Cormac sure as hell couldn't take care of anyone else.

Blaize should have known better. He should have stopped by to make sure Kit had everything she needed.

It didn't take long to whip up the omelets. He toasted bagels that looked dangerously close to being too old. He set out an almost-empty jar of jelly. There were a few hot dogs left that subbed for sausage. He cut them up and served them alongside breakfast. Lastly, he had one can of pork and beans.

"This is a feast," Carys said. "What can I do to help?"

"Set out the plates and then fill yours." He motioned toward the cabinet, thinking how nice it was to have someone who was eager to do their part. From day one, he'd taken care of Lynn. He'd overheard her bragging to a friend that she didn't have to lift a finger around the house. Looking back, she'd allowed him to step in and do everything since for her. He never knew which version of her would show up in a given hour. He'd loved her and made a commitment when he said his vows. So, no regrets.

"Thank you for pitching in, by the way," he said to Carys.

"I literally did nothing." She shook her head, but the way the corners of her mouth upturned made him grin.

Kit waltzed in. "Something smells good in here."

"I was just about to call for you," he said as he cut off the stovetop. "You have perfect timing." He motioned toward the table. "Take a seat."

Kit smiled before doing as asked. "Guess I get the princess treatment today."

Carys put down placemats and set the table, put on a fresh pot of coffee, and joined them. "This does smell amazing."

Those words caused his chest to puff up with pride. He glanced around the table and couldn't help thinking this was what he'd had in mind years ago when he thought about having a family.

Whoa! Talk about putting the cart before the horse.

This seemed like a good time to remind himself this wasn't

his family with the exception of Kit. The kid wasn't his, and Carys was just doing her job.

If that had to become a mantra, so be it.

IT WAS A shame Blaize might not be Rue's father. Sitting here at the table with him and Kit gave Carys all the warm-and-fuzzy feelings she hoped for when she walked into a place where she had to make an assessment and leave a child.

The need for repairs made more sense now that she knew Blaize drove in last night after learning his father had recently passed. The house had a homey quality despite the disrepair. Places had a feeling, and it had everything to do with the people occupying the space. In two years on the job, she'd walked into filth. This place was tidy.

One glance at the way Blaize looked at his grandmother told Carys everything she needed to know about how much he respected her. And she adored her grandson right back. Even without her mother in the picture, this would have been an amazing place for Rue to grow up.

Carys believed Blaize would get this home in tip-top shape. All it needed was a hammer, some nails, and a little elbow grease—sweat equity.

"Thanks for cooking, Blaize." Kit stood up. She must've moved a little too fast because she swayed. Before she could fall, Carys was at her side with a firm hand on the older woman's back.

"Are you okay?" The concern in Blaize's voice melted a little more of the ice encasing Carys's heart.

"I'm fine." Kit tried to play it off like it was nothing. "Here, let me help with dishes."

"Sorry, no can do," Carys said. "I'm on dish duty. Gotta earn my keep if I'm going to stay the night."

"Don't be silly. You're a guest." Kit grabbed onto Carys's hand as she took a step back from the table.

"It would make me feel better about imposing if you let me take this one." Carys helped Kit across the room. "Plus, it's way too early to end your princess treatment. How often does this come around?"

Kit smiled. "My head would swell so big we'd have to cut holes in the doors if I was treated like this every day."

"Exactly, so you might as well enjoy it while it lasts." Carys returned the smile, hiding her concern for the older woman. "Tell me where we're headed, and it would be my honor to escort you, Your Highness."

"Into the living room, if you don't mind," Kit said, mustering a voice that was surely meant to sound royal.

Carys made a production out of helping her into the next room and into a worn leather recliner. A TV tray with remote and a book sat next to the chair. "Can I get you anything before I take my leave, Highness?"

"This'll do for now, but thank you." Kit winked and then picked up the remote. "I'm hooked on a crime series."

"I'll leave you to your binge-watching." Carys gave a little curtsy before leaving the room and rejoining a concerned-looking Blaize.

His face was ghost white as he stood with his backside against the bullnose counter. He white-knuckled the edge.

Carys studied him for a moment before speaking. "I got your grandmother settled."

Sounds from the TV drifted in from the next room.

"I appreciate it," he said in barely more than a whisper. The tension in his tone said he was stressed to the gills and ready to snap. "She didn't say anything about being sick."

"It's possible she just stood up too fast, don't you think?"

A muscle ticked in his jaw. His gaze dropped to the ground. Tension radiated off him in palpable waves.

"I don't know, and I highly doubt she'll tell me now that she knows about Lynn." He barely ground out the words.

"Why would you think that?" Carys asked, keeping her tone as calm and neutral as possible.

"She would believe she is only adding to my stress," he said.

"Those are very different situations," she said.

Shaking his head, he said, "She won't see it that way." He compressed his lips, forming a severe line. "My gut tells me that she is hiding a serious medical condition."

Could be fear or a form of PTSD after losing his wife to illness. As much as she wanted to offer some type of comforting words, she didn't want to give false hope. Kit might've been sick. Or her age might've been catching up to her. Or she might've just been tired. All three were plausible reasons for her moments of weakness.

The storm had created a lot of excitement.

"Is Kit your grandmother on your father's side?" she asked.

"Yes, but I don't see how that…"

He stopped midsentence as though a few dots were connecting that her loss coupled with the stress of all the changes coming could have thrown her off balance.

"She might not be sleeping well," Carys said. "I know when I'm tired, I wobble. Actually, it's very much like me to walk into walls in the morning before I get my first cup of coffee down."

Losing his grandmother after losing a wife and a father would be too much for anyone. Blaize might not have been close to his father or care one way or another whether the man lived or died, but unresolved relationships were almost worse. She couldn't imagine losing the person you were meant to spend the rest of your life with, especially while still so young.

Carys closed the distance between them in a couple of quick strides. Witnessing the pain in his eyes up close was going to be a mistake. It caused her to reach for his hand. He tugged her toward him, keeping his gaze locked onto hers.

Were they two broken souls who recognized each other from a place somewhere deep?

"I'm sorry for everything you've been through, Blaize."

He gave a slight nod.

"And I would very much like to ask for a kiss right now."

"What's stopping you?" he asked.

"Fear that you'll say no."

He took in a slow breath. "You don't ever have to be afraid of me." His voice was low, gravelly, sexy.

Kissing him would be unprofessional if he turned out to be Rue's father.

"Is it okay if I do this?" he asked, bringing his hands up to frame her face. His eyes glistened with something that looked a whole lot like need.

"Yes."

His tongue slicked across his bottom lip. The man was sexy as hell.

"About that kiss," he said.

"What about it?"

"I'm going to need your clear permission first."

"Yes. Definitely yes. One hundred percent yes," she said.

It was all the encouragement he needed. A small smile toyed with the corners of his lips—those perfect lips. The top of which formed a perfect Cupid's bow.

In the next second, his mouth pressed so tenderly against hers it robbed her breath and dissolved the last bit of resolve she had left.

Chapter Six

Blaize grazed his teeth across Carys's bottom lip. The little mewl that escaped her mouth was tinder to fire. He teased his tongue inside her mouth. She tasted like dark roast coffee and honey, his new favorite flavor.

He dropped his hands, splaying them across her back instead. She arched, pressing full breasts against his chest. Pulling back enough to catch his breath, he leaned his forehead against hers.

Her hands came up to his shoulders, fingernails digging in as though she needed to anchor herself.

"Kissing you is the best thing that's happened to me in too long" came out in a rasp as he tried, and failed, to catch his breath. Need welled up like a rogue spring storm, threatening to devastate everything in its wake.

The moment of pause brought on a wave of guilt. He bit back a curse. A child's future hung in the balance, and he could scarcely keep his hands off her caretaker. Did that make him a jerk? Or did it make him human?

"What is it? What's wrong?" Carys asked, as if sensing the mental debate going on in his head.

"It sure as hell isn't you," he said, hoping that gave her enough clarification to drop the subject without hurt feelings.

She took a step back; a sudden chill sat between them. She folded her arms and challenged him with her glare. "Don't bother with the 'it's me and not you' speech. That would hurt my feelings."

Blaize let out a sharp sigh. "Can I make a confession?"

"Please do." She shifted in posture like she was steeling herself to absorb a punch.

Dammit. He hadn't meant for something this mind-blowing to turn into an insult.

"You're the best thing that's happened to me in a very long time, and I don't want to do anything to screw that up." His honesty caught him off guard. "That…and my choices in love haven't exactly paid dividends." Should he tell her the feelings he had for her were as foreign as a poetry slam? That he'd loved his wife but never felt this mix of excitement and ease when they'd first started dating?

"You're a dangerous man, Blaize."

That was all she said before she turned around and walked off. He heard her voice in the next room as she talked with Kit. And then all he could hear was the TV.

Blaize walked over to the sleeping baby in the carrier. She was an angel with just a hint of dark hair. This little girl deserved a loving home. She deserved the world but was an orphan for the time being.

It nearly broke his heart when she took in a breath. Her face crunched like she was about to wind up to cry again like a pitcher at the plate, but then she settled. Her eyes remained closed. There'd been so much excitement, he'd forgotten to ask for a picture of Stephanie Cross. If the woman named him on her daughter's birth certificate, it stood to reason he knew her. The name drew a blank. Cross could be her married name. Did he know any Stephanies?

He had to reach all the way back to high school to pull out a name: Stephanie Ambler. Seemed like everyone had a social media page these days. Could he find her? He picked up his cell and pulled up the most popular one, figuring he'd start there.

Stephanie Ambler, now Smith, posted pictures regularly on her account. A quick flip before the app told him he needed to log in to continue revealed she had three children. The oldest one had a pimply face and looked to be in his early teens. Two daughters, twins, who looked to be a couple years younger than their brother rounded out the family.

While there, he looked up the names he'd overheard Carys provide to the sheriff. No James Gray in the immediate area that he could find. Since Blaize didn't do social media, he couldn't exactly label anyone else who didn't a serial killer. The only app he'd used was for dating. It had been the way he met his wife.

Next he checked Ethan Hutchins. A few names came up, none in this area. Same for Gabe York.

He closed the app.

Glancing over at the spot where he and Carys had shared a kiss so laced with promise and pleasure brought back the memory of it—a memory that set the bar for all future kisses.

Guilt stabbed him. The same pang he felt every time he laughed or thought about moving on with life after Lynn's death. Getting a handle on the ranch might be just the win he needed. He could use a new lease on life.

Blaize started out of the room, made it halfway across before he froze. Was he allowed to leave the baby alone in a room?

Taking her into the living room might wake her up. She was sleeping so peacefully. He didn't want to do anything to disturb her peace. He also needed a shower and at least a few hours of sleep. Watching over Lynn, he'd gotten used to running on five hours if he could close his eyes for twenty minutes here and there.

Since he wasn't sure he could leave the baby and he didn't want to call for Kit, he sat down at the table. Head in hands, he shut his eyes. The image of the kiss was burned into the backs of his lids.

More of that inconvenient need welled up.

Carys was intelligent and caring. Her beauty was beyond anything he'd witnessed before, inside and out. She had a way of looking at him that stripped him bare.

On a practical level, she was probably a decade younger and just getting started in her career. Having a family most likely wasn't on her radar. He'd stopped considering having one when Lynn became sick. At thirty-five, he figured the window was closing since he didn't see himself marrying again. It was all too hard. The vow *for better or worse* meant the world to him. When he gave his word, he didn't take it back.

Even if a relationship could happen between him and Carys—and that was a big *if*—they were in different places in life.

Damn, Wilde. You really went down a rabbit hole. Time to suck it up and get realistic. A kiss like the one they shared needed to be a one-off event. Period. Plus, she was already breaking too many rules as it was. He didn't need to add to it or cost her job. He'd overstepped with the kiss. No matter how much he wanted it to happen again, it couldn't.

EMBARRASSMENT STILL HEATED Carys's cheeks despite the long shower. Kit had laid out clean clothes in the guest bedroom, which were lifesavers. Never underestimate the power of light joggers and an oversized T-shirt when it came to comfort clothes. They were basically a cotton hug.

The kiss she shared—*No! Asked for*—still burned on her lips in the best possible way, like he'd marked her as his. The rejection afterward stung worse than falling onto a fire ant mound.

Carys needed to pluck up the courage to go back into the kitchen and check on Rue. She listened in case the baby needed her. Everything was quiet. Peaceful. Except for the chirps of crickets and other insects outside the window. The noise used to freak her out when she'd first moved out of the city. Now? They were like a lullaby.

Going into the kitchen might mean facing Blaize again. So soon?

Carys had learned over the years to rip off the Band-Aid when faced with something that might be uncomfortable. Why was that suddenly a problem now?

Blaize. The man stirred foreign feelings—feelings that had her asking to kiss the father of her ward. How was that for professionalism? The worst part was that she couldn't stop thinking about what it felt like when their mouths fused together. She'd never believed a relationship could complete her. She was already a fully formed human who didn't need another half to feel whole. This thing between her and Blaize was something else, something deeper.

Giving herself a mental headshake to clear those thoughts, she headed toward the kitchen.

Kit had fallen asleep in front of the TV. Carys grabbed the blanket off the back of the couch and placed it on top of Kit, who instantly relaxed. The AC window unit in the living room was still on, in addition to a ceiling fan. Kit would end up sick at this rate.

Considering the lack of noise, she wondered if Blaize had gone to bed. Would he leave the kitchen light on? The baby unattended?

Rounding the corner, she stopped mid-step as her gaze landed on the image in front of her. Blaize had his arm extended over the table, his head resting on it, using it as a pillow. His eyes were closed, and his even breathing said he was asleep.

Rue was still in the carrier that he'd placed on the floor and scooted next to him. It was a shame Blaize didn't believe he was the girl's father. Between this scene and the longing she'd seen in his eyes earlier when he'd looked at the baby, he was more than ready to be a father.

Instead, he'd lost a wife. Life played some seriously cruel jokes sometimes. She'd walked into plenty of houses with kids where the father figure was so checked out he could barely be forced to step away from the TV screen to meet with her. She was a basketball fan. She understood team loyalty. She also knew how easy it was to record a game and save it for later.

Having walked into dozens of families' lives in her two years on the job, she'd seen the highest and the lowest forms of parenting. The worst of them neglected their children and provided filthy homes with just enough food to get by. The best of them provided loving, caring environments that allowed the children to find their passions and know they always had support.

What was that like?

Her father had become a tyrant and a warden. On some basic level, Carys realized he'd become overprotective after losing the love of his life. He'd overcorrected and become detached. Based on the few pictures she'd seen from before she was born, it was hard to believe he was the same person. Pain had an interesting effect on people. In her father's case, it hardened him. His fear came out as anger. She knew that now.

Still, it was difficult to forgive him for all the damage he caused. It didn't help matters that he hadn't tried to reach out or make their relationship right. Once she walked out the door, he stuck to his threat of disowning her and cutting her off.

Families were complicated. And yet she couldn't help but wonder how different her life might have been had her mother been alive. Would she have made a difference in the manner in which Carys had been brought up?

Would there have been laughter in the house? Holidays with large Christmas trees that they would have decorated together? Hot chocolate by a fireplace?

Would her father smile more? Or at all?

Would she know what it was like to have someone fight for her in parent-teacher meetings rather than ice her out on the way home if she got one bad report?

A crash outside caused her to gasp. Blaize's head popped up. He wiped his eyes.

"What happened?" he asked.

She flipped off the kitchen light, crouched low, and nodded toward the back door. "Someone's out there."

Blaize was on his feet and making a beeline for the back door in two seconds flat. He grabbed a butcher knife out of the block on the countertop before exiting.

Carys was torn between going to the baby or following Blaize. Based on his size and physical strength, he could handle himself in pretty much any situation. What if he brought a knife to a gun fight?

That would be a problem she couldn't solve with her presence.

What if he was surprised? Caught off guard? In a physical fight with someone much larger than he was?

What if someone slipped inside and stole the baby?

Rue was in Carys's charge. She crawled to the baby and sat next to the carrier. It dawned on her that she might need a weapon.

Panic gripped her as she popped up long enough to get a knife. It occurred to her that she should have checked to see if the front door was locked. The sheriff's questions nailed her. *Have you interacted with anyone lately who might want to do you harm? Have you been in a disagreement with anyone? Have you rejected anyone?*

Three names had come to mind. The first was a father who'd lost custody of his child based on her recommendation. Veiled threats in this job were becoming surprisingly commonplace. Gabe Hutchins hadn't threatened her with words. There was no evidence or no way to prove he was out for her. It was more in the way he'd stood there, arms crossed, pure evil in his eyes. The slight sneer. The way he picked her apart with his gaze.

Feeling threatened by someone's presence wasn't the same as being threatened. She'd confided in Harrison, and he'd basically patted her on top of the head and told her not to let her imagination get the best of her.

The next person, James Gray, was someone she'd dated who couldn't seem to let go. They'd gone out a few times after both had swiped on each other's dating profile. The whole situation had been casual for her until she realized he was building a narrative about them being in a relationship. A handful of dates didn't equate to being a couple. James confused the situation despite her being upfront about not being open to anything serious at the time. She was interested in casual dating, good dinner conversation, and that was about it. With the right person, she'd consider adding sex to the equation. She wasn't in a hurry for a relationship while she was busy building a career. Swiping on James's profile turned out to be a huge mistake. It had been quiet lately, though. She thought he'd gotten the hint.

And then there was Ethan York. He came to mind almost immediately when the sheriff asked if there was anyone she felt threatened by. One of her first cases, she'd helped him get into a halfway house as he timed out of the system. She'd graduated college at twenty-two years old. Ethan had just turned eighteen. He had obsessive-compulsive tendencies and had developed the belief that the two of them were destined to be together. He'd mistaken her sympathy for his situation for a love connection.

He was impulsive and had poor emotional regulation, coupled with low self-esteem. If she could go back, there was so much she would do differently this time. She'd been green, a newbie, and it had cost her.

Last Carys heard, he was in jail after being caught with drugs. Maybe it was time to check his status, see if he got released.

Any of those three could fit the vague description of the person wearing the hoodie earlier.

She listened for any signs of a fight outside as more panic gripped her. It was quiet. Too quiet. What the hell was happening out there?

Should she turn around and alert Kit to the potential danger?

The baby stirred.

No. No. No. This is not a good time to draw attention to the kitchen.

Moving her might wake her up. At this point, there was a chance she would stay asleep.

One look at the baby said otherwise. Rue's face twisted, scrunched, before she sucked in a deep breath and then belted out an ear-splitting cry.

Chapter Seven

Blaize slipped around the perimeter of the house, searching for any signs of life. Crickets chirped along with the usual sounds of night in the country. He didn't see any movement other than trees bending to the heavy wind gusts. Stacks of old paint cans next to the back door had been scattered like bowling pins. He couldn't remember if it had been like that earlier but suspected it wasn't.

Heavy rain meant wet soil, making footprints next to impossible to stick. Besides, he would have walked all over them by now anyway. The mud would mold them together.

And that was *if* someone was out here. His thoughts snapped to the hoodie-wearing individual from earlier. This person made the most sense. And then he considered the names Carys had given the sheriff as possible suspects.

He made a mental note to ask more about them in the morning.

Everyone needed to get a good night of sleep so they could wake up early and get cracking. If the threat had moved closer to the house, he intended to figure out who the hell was behind it and stop them before someone got hurt. He would never forgive himself if harm came to Kit. Carys might've been a firecracker on the outside, but her devotion to protecting a child she didn't know more than twenty-four hours ago said she had a soft side that the hard shell was no doubt meant to protect.

Sounds of the baby crying penetrated through the back door as he opened it. He resisted the urge to run toward her. Instead, he glanced around the room, surprised when he didn't see Carys next to the child. His eyes had adjusted to the dark, making it easy to see clearly.

It dawned on him that someone could be inside the house. They could be holding Carys hostage. She wouldn't leave the baby alone, crying without good reason.

Taking a step inside, the floorboard creaked underneath his weight.

From the corner of his eye, he saw a figure leaping at him from around the bottom cabinet. The glint of metal caught his eye. A knife.

Survival instinct took over. He brought his forearm up to block his face.

Carys's face came into view, a panicked look in her eyes. It was as though her brain and hand disconnected. Her face read *Stop*. Her arm kept going.

Blaize ducked in time to miss the swipe. He sidestepped her, grabbing her wrist after her hand passed above his hair.

"Are you trying to give me a haircut?" He managed to growl the words at her. On some level, he realized that she was in full-on defensive mode. He'd seen how protective she'd been with the baby first and then his grandmother. Still. She'd known he was outside and would then presumably come back in. She should've been more careful because he had no intention of ending up in the hospital. "Or brain surgery?"

"I'm sorry," she said through a gasp. "I didn't know it was you, and I wasn't sure if anything happened. And then Rue started crying." Her gaze darted from him to the baby. She held up a hand before rushing over to console the little thing.

For something so tiny, she sure had a great pair of lungs.

She plugged the kid up with some type of rubber contraption. He's seen them before but had no idea what they were called. This was one of many reasons he probably shouldn't be a father.

When his wife became sick, the possibility had been stripped from him. He'd made his peace with it, figuring he would never love again. A family was a lot of work. To his mind, he knew he couldn't keep a kid alive for the first few years without a partner to do it with. He had a ton of respect for anyone doing it alone. Single parents were rock stars in his book.

"There," Carys said with a satisfied smile, bringing his thoughts back to the present. She bit back a yawn.

"You should get some sleep," he said, hearing the grumpy tone in his own voice. Damn if she didn't rattle him in ways he wasn't ready to face. Better to snap at her than kiss her again because the temptation was a real threat. From now on, he'd maintain a safe distance. Physically. Emotionally. Mentally.

"You, too," Carys said softly, still staring at the baby. "She's an angel."

His gaze stayed trained on Carys. "I couldn't agree more."

He thought about telling her about looking for a picture of Stephanie Cross on social media to jog a memory and decided the update could wait until morning. "How often does one of those things wake up in the middle of the night?"

Carys exhaled a slow breath. "I have no idea. I guess we'll figure it out together."

He liked the sound of those words a little too much for his own good. "Will you take her to bed with you?"

"I think that's best for tonight."

Kit yelled out in her sleep from the living room. Blaize made a beeline for his grandmother. He checked her over as her eyelids fluttered, couldn't find anything immediately concerning. A bad dream?

He should get her to her own room where she'd be more comfortable. As he scooped her up, he realized she'd had an accident. The back of her pants was wet.

He'd seen worse. Cleaned up worse.

Kit's eyes fluttered open. Her face soured. "Cormac. What's going on with you? Who is here with you?"

"It's your grandson Blaize. Remember?" There was no way he wanted her thinking her son was here. Cormac couldn't keep a cactus alive in the sun.

"What?" Kit tried to focus her eyes but appeared to be struggling. "What are you doing here?"

He carried her to a secondary bedroom. Cormac had moved her once he took over the ranch, and it was one of many reasons Blaize and his brothers didn't visit. They didn't like setting foot in Cormac's home. When Blaize stopped by before Lynn got sick, he would stay outside for the duration of the visit. If he did step in the house, it was to go to the bathroom or grab a cup of coffee in the kitchen.

The thought of his grandmother being kicked out of her own bedroom made him angry to this day. *Your mother deserved better from you, asshole.*

If Blaize's mother had been interested in more than a drinking buddy, he would have done anything for the woman. By age seventeen, he'd lost track of her. She'd gotten into harder substances and didn't exactly keep up a social media page or a steady phone number for that matter. She had, however, tracked him down on his nineteenth birthday to ask for a loan. Made some excuse about not getting paid for another week and needing food.

Fool that he'd been at that age, he had believed she remembered his birthday and called for that reason. Nope. She wanted money. Wanted him to send it via an app. He ended the call telling her not to reach out again. She hadn't.

He cut across the hallway to the adjacent bathroom. The air was still moist from the shower Carys had taken earlier, and the scent of lavender shampoo filled his senses. He balanced on one leg and managed to close the commode lid before setting Kit down.

"Go on. I can manage from here," she instructed. Was she embarrassed to get undressed in front of him? Of course she was. Kit was prideful.

How could he manage to help her and salvage her pride—pride that had no doubt taken a hit when she lost her bladder. It wasn't a big deal to him, but he understood.

"What can I grab for you from the bedroom?" he asked, realizing she would dig her heels in.

"My gowns are in the top drawer and my undergarments

are in the smaller one right below it." She sat with her back straight despite being mortified. Her tell came in the form of her chin quivering. Eyes straight ahead, she refused to look directly at him.

Telling her that he understood would do no good. So, he excused himself to head across the hall.

Carys was already pulling out the items. She held them out. "Here you go."

Damned if he didn't have to fight himself to keep from kissing her again.

STANDING IN A bedroom alone with Blaize shouldn't have been the most intimate moment she'd had in too long. But it was.

As Carys handed over the clothing, their fingers grazed. An electric jolt shocked her, sending volts shooting through her hand, her wrist, up her arm. Warming her. Blaize was pure sex. Everything about him was perfection. Like how his hands were calloused and rough but surprisingly tender to the touch.

He stood there for a moment like he was trying to process what had just happened, too.

And then he turned and walked out, hanging his head low. Shame?

She hoped he didn't feel remorse for the attraction that was happening between them. Hadn't she read something about survivor's guilt in cases like his? She remembered the person could feel guilty for secretly being glad their loved one's pain was over. Could meeting someone trigger more guilt? Sharing a kiss?

It dawned on her that theirs might have been the first one since losing his wife.

Rather than try to figure out what someone else was thinking, she moved next door to where she'd left a sleeping Rue.

Carys climbed underneath the covers, closed her eyes, and then crashed.

By the time she opened her eyes again hours later, sun filtered through the slats in the mini blinds. How long had she been asleep?

She immediately sat up to check on Rue. The baby's carrier was gone, the baby gone with it.

A moment of panic slammed into her. The door was closed. She threw the covers off and opened it before stepping into the hall and listening.

The low hum of voices drifted toward her from the kitchen. There was not a peep from Rue.

Carys headed straight toward the bathroom, almost tripped over the neatly folded clothes at her feet. What was this? She picked them up. Her clothes? Washed, dried, and folded?

She headed into the bathroom, used the facilities, and cleaned up before dressing. A toothbrush had been laid out for her, along with toothpaste. Basically, heaven.

As soon as she dressed, she moved to the kitchen. The smell of fresh brew hit her senses from halfway down the hall. Her stomach growled. She couldn't remember the last time she'd slept so deeply or woken up so starved.

Rounding the corner to the kitchen, her heart skipped a couple of beats. She stopped, put a hand on the wall to steady herself. Seeing Blaize hold Rue while he talked quietly with an adoring grandmother caused her ovaries to squeeze. It would be helpful if the man could be more of a jerk.

"Morning," she said as she walked into the room.

"Morning to you," Blaize said with a smile that released half a dozen butterflies in her stomach. He had on jeans and a black T-shirt.

"Hello," Kit practically chirped. Her mood had drastically improved. "Grab some coffee and come sit with us."

Carys wasn't so sure that was a good idea. It felt a little too much like a family scene. Considering her background, she would probably say or do something to mess it up. Plus, she needed to get her CPS agent hat back on.

"Mind if I talk a walk first?" she asked, stalling for time so she could come up with a better reason. The last thing she wanted to do was hurt Kit's feelings. The woman had been nothing but welcoming and kind.

Blaize shot a look. The reason dawned on her. He didn't

think it was safe for her to be outside alone. He stood up and gently handed Rue over to Kit.

"Finally my turn with this sweet little girl." Kit beamed.

"I'll go with you," he said.

She knew better than to argue if she wanted to stretch her legs to counter all the sitting she'd done yesterday. Normally, she would go on a run in the morning, but she didn't know the area. A walk was more manageable. How lost could she get?

Of course, Blaize would know the area.

"One sec," he said before leaving the room. When he came back, he had a gun tucked inside a waist holster that was clipped onto his jeans. The reminder of the danger they were in sobered her. "Ready?"

As much as she'd ever be.

"Let's go," she said, leading the way out the back door.

Once outside, she saw paint cans scattered around the back of the house.

"They might have been the cause of the noise last night," Blaize said after following her gaze. "Could have been a raccoon trying to climb them or searching for food."

"Makes sense."

They walked quietly for a while.

"I tried to find her last night and came up empty," he said. "Stephanie Cross isn't on social media that I could find, but that could be a married name."

"You don't remember anyone named Stephanie?"

"No."

They walked around the perimeter of the yard. A cool breeze caused her to shiver. If the weather dipped below seventy-five degrees, she threw on a sweater. Growing up in south Texas had a way of making you a wimp when it came to colder temperatures.

"Given it's Saturday, I'm at a loss as to getting more information about her," she said. "I'm waiting on the sheriff's report, but with the...*conditions* of the crash, we might never get a positive ID."

"That doesn't leave Rue in limbo?"

"It would only matter if a parent claimed her, which I was

hoping you would do, but since you admitted to not having sex during that time Rue's status is up in the air."

"What if I just let it ride?"

"You mean keep her?" she asked, not hiding her shock. "You would do that?"

"Do you have a better idea?"

After the way she'd seen him with Rue this morning, it was a thought. She'd already bent the rules in this case. Could she look the other way on something as big as paternity?

No. Now what?

Chapter Eight

"I wish I could, but—"

Blaize put a hand up to stop Carys from finishing her sentence. "It was the first thing that popped into my mind. Forget I said it."

"I thought it was noble," she said, cracking another layer of ice that encased his heart. At this rate, he'd have no defense left before the weekend was over. "And very sweet."

"I'm not sweet." If only she knew what a jerk he could be. She would change her mind faster than a spring hailstorm tore through a town.

Carys smiled. "Fair enough."

"What will happen to her?"

"The orphanage." She frowned. "It's not a terrible place, but it is understaffed at the moment and I hate the thought of someone so little falling through the cracks." She was quick to add, "They wouldn't do it on purpose. Their mission is good, and they try to do their best. There are some out there I wouldn't trust as far as I could throw. This isn't one of those."

"They can't find good people?"

"Not enough for the demand."

"There has to be another way." He couldn't stand the thought of Rue spending a night at the orphanage. The little girl perked Kit up, too. "Adoption?"

"You?"

Blaize shook his head. "Right. Bad idea. I have to figure out a way to turn this place around. Money is tight, and I can't let Kit lose her home, no matter what else happens. I might need to hire someone to look after her while I work on getting the ranch back in order, which will use up what little money I have left. I was hoping my brothers would answer my calls, but it's been crickets from them so far."

He didn't normally talk so much. Talking to Carys came as naturally as honey to a bee. He didn't have to force words. It was a nice change. When Lynn was in a good place, talking came easier, but it was nowhere near this easy. Carys had a way about her that made him want to open up.

Damned if he could figure out why.

"Did you get into a fight?" She cocked her head to one side.

"I pushed everyone away when Lynn first got sick. Even before that, if I'm honest. I told myself I was protecting her. She had bipolar disorder and wouldn't have wanted anyone to see her darker sides."

"That must have been hell."

"She was a trouper," he said.

Carys's eyebrow flew up. "I meant for you."

"You can't do that. You can't go there on the self-pity thing." It was a downward spiral that led to nowhere good. He knew firsthand.

"I'm not trying to come off as patronizing, but when do you ever prioritize your needs?"

Those words struck like an arrow to the center of his chest. Bull's-eye.

He tried to laugh it off. "I've never minded taking care of someone else."

"You're the oldest in your family, aren't you?"

"Yes, but what does that have to do with anything?" He was genuinely perplexed.

"I read this article about birth order and how it affects someone's personality," she said. "I'd say you're a classic firstborn."

"Because?"

"You take care of everyone else because you're used to being put in charge." Her tone wasn't accusing or coming off as judging, just factual. "You have two brothers, correct?"

"That's right."

"So, the middle one is likely the negotiator and the youngest—well, everyone always caters to the baby," she said. "They usually grow up with the most freedom and know how to push the envelope."

"No one was catered to by Cormac," he corrected.

"These are loose definitions." She studied him. "Do you disagree with the assessments? There's supposedly a ton of research out there on the subject."

"Raiden is the middle child of the family, and I can see where he is the peacemaker or the negotiator," Blaize said. "Or, at least, when he *was* talking to me. Growing up, he was the one who stepped in between our younger brother and me when there was an argument." He cracked a smile. "I was always right, of course."

She smiled right back. "Goes without saying."

"Raiden certainly kept a calm demeanor when I butted heads with Cormac," he said. "Which was probably more often that it should have been."

"And the youngest?"

"Phoenix definitely got the wild-child gene, but nothing like our father. Phoenix marches to his own drum and never cared what anyone else thought about him. He's grown now, but he sure ran with the wild mustangs, if you will, when we were younger. Not party-boy wild. More like a wild horse that didn't want to be tamed. In fact, there was a stint when we thought he would run off to join the rodeo." He thought about how different their mothers were. "All three of us come from different relationships, so I'm sure that influenced our personalities as well."

"You're how many years apart?"

"There's two years between Raiden and me, then one between him and Phoenix." Cormac was clearly "busy" in his younger days. Busy being a jerk who treated women like they were expendable. Blaize had learned how not to treat the opposite sex by watching dear old dad.

"Yikes."

"Yep." That was Cormac. "Classy, right?"

"It's hard to forgive your parents, isn't it?" Carys asked after a thoughtful pause. "They're human, and you kind of remember that. But they can hurt you the most out of anyone else, and their actions shape you for better or worse."

This sounded like more admission and commiseration than a comment about his life.

"It is next to impossible to forgive the bad ones," he said. "No one expects them to be perfect. Not as adults anyway. I've seen it done right. Take Kit, for example."

"She is close to perfection."

He smiled. "I would agree there."

"And easy to love."

"It's strange how her son came out so opposite," he said. "All Cormac cared about was a good party. I'm still scratching my head as to why my grandfather left him the responsibility of the ranch."

"Do you think it's possible your grandfather believed his son might change with the right amount of responsibility or motivation? Grow into the role?"

"It's hard to know what the man's thoughts were. He was the silent type. We always knew he loved us, even though I can't recall ever hearing him say the words. It was just his way. He did things like help Kit make our lunches before heading out for a long day working cattle. Or check in with us at night after we were ready for bed to ask if we'd eaten. We had and he knew the dinner routine. It was his way of making sure we knew he cared."

"Kit is so outgoing," Carys said. "Guess it is true what they say about opposites attracting."

He barked out a laugh at that one. It had been true in his marriage. He'd been the steady stream while Lynn had taken the roll of hurricane. "That's not always a positive."

"I hear you," she said, surprising him with her honesty. "I dated someone I thought was smart, maybe almost too smart, and he became clingy. Thought we were in a serious relationship when we weren't. I gave his name to the sheriff when he asked, but I haven't seen or heard from James in a couple of months."

"What do you mean by clingy?" He had no right to be jealous of her ex. Yet there was an undeniable twinge.

"I would turn the aisle at a grocery store and he'd be at the other end, hiding and spying," she said. "He wasn't good at it. Other times he'd suddenly be standing beside me while I was distracted looking in the meat case. Used to freak me right out."

"Did you file a complaint with the law?"

"No." She shook her head. "He never tried to harm me or attack me in any way. Just left a rose on top of the hood of my car. Or a note saying he missed me and wanted to see me again. Small things like that, along with being in the same place at the same time. All of it used to creep me out. When someone says no, they mean no."

"Some people need to be taught the meaning of that word."

Blaize didn't like the sound of this one bit. James might have been stewing in his anger, plotting, over these past weeks. And now, what? He showed up during a storm because he'd been watching her house? It was plausible. At least the sheriff had James's name now. The man could be investigated and vetted. The sheriff would want to know if James had an alibi for yesterday.

Maybe Blaize could do a little more digging into James's background now that he had a name to work with and possibly a motive.

Carys's gaze shifted to the right, focused on something. A worry line creased her forehead.

"What is it?" he asked.

"I'm not sure, but I intend to find out," she said, starting in the direction of the object that had her concerned.

CARYS SAW A glint of metal on the ground in the tree line. She didn't want to get too ahead of herself, but it looked like it could be some kind of sharp object. A blade of some kind. A weapon?

Fear that the person from last night had tracked her here and came to spy on her was all-consuming. Could it be James? Would he have followed her here to the ranch? Knowing him, he would say that he was trying to protect her since she'd gone out into the storm, that he was following her just in case she needed him. Wasn't that a line he'd used before?

Her skin felt like dozens of fire ants had been let loose on it as she neared the object, realized it was a grill fork. It had a long handle and two sharp, sturdy prongs.

The image of her or Blaize being stabbed with it stamped her thoughts, causing icy fingers to grip her spine.

Blaize glanced over at the barbecue pit and back.

"This could do a lot of damage to someone if they were stabbed with it," she said to him. She searched her memory bank to remember when the kiss had happened versus the crashing sound outside. The kiss came first. She was certain. The thought that James, or some other creep, could have been watching through a window was enough to add a dozen more fire ants biting her skin.

"It sure could," Blaize said. "The raccoon theory is losing its appeal."

She picked up a stick and then used it to scoop up the grill fork by the small leather strap. "I seriously doubt the sheriff will be able to lift any usable DNA or prints after the storm we had. Still, I'd like to hold on to this."

"We can't be sure anyone was even here," Blaize said. He was right. She glanced around. The ranch was in need of serious TLC. "But we can try."

Carys nodded. And then something dawned on her. "Isn't this a cattle ranch?"

"Yes."

"Where's the cattle?" She looked around, surveying the land.

"They aren't here," he said. "But you figured that out already. A neighbor came over and took all of them so we could sort out Cormac's affairs and get Kit settled."

"That's nice of them."

"It's the way ranchers work. It's ingrained to help each other out. I still don't know how all this skipped a generation with Cormac. But my grandfather was a good person and never hesitated to lend a helping hand if someone needed him. People love Kit."

"I can see why," she said. "Where I used to live, the big push was to keep the place weird. But no one showed up in your time of need, if you know what I mean."

"Austin can be fun," he said with a laugh. She liked his smile and the way his eyes lit up and how the change in conversation broke some of the tension tightening her chest. "Do they still sell those *Keep Austin Weird* T-shirts?"

"Yes. Everywhere. If anything, people have doubled down." They were sold at coffee shops, gas stations, and street corners.

"Sounds about right for Austin. It's more of a vibe than a city. Good music. After Lynn died, I would drive in and hit up a few places on the regular."

Carys made a mental note to check with bartenders once they got a positive ID on Stephanie Cross. There had to be a picture of her somewhere they could take around to find out how she might have come into contact with Blaize.

"Speaking of weird, it's strange that someone I can't remember and am certain I don't know would put my name on her child's birth certificate." His tone was serious, matching the intensity of his gaze. "But these are strange times."

"I can think of a few reasons." None that she wanted to say out loud. He was kind, if rough around the edges. He would make a great dad. Was someone banking on the fact he wouldn't remember if they'd slept together or not? Hedging a bet that he would treat her child like a princess if he believed the girl was also his? Or that because of his kindness, her daughter would be safer with him if something happened to her?

Questions and speculation swirled with no easy answers.

"Are you going to explain that comment, or do I have to guess?" he asked, his tone lighter.

"I saw you with Rue earlier. Speaking of which, we should probably go inside," she said, needing time to let those thoughts seed. "And my brain won't work much longer without caffeine. Or breakfast, for that matter. And a glass of water sounds good, too." Using the stick, she set the grill fork down. "This is useless, isn't it?"

"Yes." He confirmed what she already suspected. The heavy rains would have washed away any evidence. If, in fact, anyone had been out there. The racoon really was the most likely culprit. Her imagination was running wild after the incident with her vehicle. “Oh, and I need to get to my car soon so I can survey the damage in the daylight.”

Blaize’s smile faded. And she hated being the one to put the frown on his face.

Chapter Nine

Blaize called the sheriff for the second time in two days. Standing at Carys's vehicle, he couldn't help but wonder if someone was listening in on her conversations or tracking her by phone. "Did you talk to anyone and tell them about your plans to come here before you came out to see me with Rue yesterday?"

"Um, no. Why?" She walked around her four-door sedan, assessing the damage.

She gasped and caught his stare before he could respond.

"You're saying someone might be listening in on my calls and conversations, aren't you?" she asked.

"I'm exploring all possibilities."

She paused, seemingly to regain her bearings after the realization. "Well, let's see, I had a conversation with one of my co-workers about not wanting to take Rue to Sister's Love," she said. "Harrison is his name."

"When the sheriff drops by to pick up the barbecue fork, you might want to give him the name," he said, then watched as half a dozen emotions passed over her face and behind her eyes. There was confusion, sadness, frustration, and a couple others before resignation.

"I seriously doubt Harrison would follow me," she said. "Or want to hurt me in any way."

"He might be fixated on you."

"You think?" Her face puckered. She shook her head as though physically rejecting the idea. "No… I mean, he was complaining about Rue crying and wanted me to get her out of the office because he said…"

Another gasp.

"He said the walls were paper thin," she said.

"Meaning he could be listening to your calls all day, personal and private."

"Even if he was, what would he have to gain by attacking me last night?" Her gaze unfocused like she was looking inside herself for the answer.

"Has he ever asked you out?"

"Harrison? No," she quickly said. "I'm pretty certain that I annoy him. Also, I've always thought he wasn't interested in women."

"Do you know much about his private life?"

"Well, to be honest, not really. No. Huh." She stood there for a long moment. "I guess we made small talk at the office. *How many cases are you working? Did you have a good weekend?* That type of surface-level conversation. He never asked me out on a date or even to grab a drink after work."

"Doesn't mean he isn't harboring feelings," he said. Another stab of jealousy landed.

"You're right, I guess." Her face scrunched again. "I'm just not seeing it. You usually know when someone is interested in you. I guess I never got that vibe from Harrison."

Coming from his perspective, Blaize agreed. When he was interested in someone, he made his intentions clear. Dating. Damn. He could only imagine how much rituals had changed since the last time he was in the dating pool. Folks used apps back in his day, but they seemed a whole lot more prevalent now. He'd also heard tell of folks getting tired of them. Something about app fatigue. It was understandable. You both swiped. You started a chat. Someone ghosted. Rinse. Repeat.

Lynn had been the first person he met on an app. Both stopped talking to other people shortly after. Three years later, he asked her to marry him. So, he didn't have a lot of experience to draw from.

Carys walked the perimeter of her vehicle, assessing the damage while he checked the area for any possible footprints. The chances he'd find any were slim to none. Still, he checked. The person who'd dropped the barbecue fork was sloppy, an inexperienced criminal.

The tree trunk lying across the road would have been too planned for someone like that. Right?

Or had the person intended to stop her so they could ambush her all along? Someone would have had to drive out here, move the trunk onto the road, and then what? Wait? The position of the log made it next to impossible to drive around. Was it random? Placed there?

Any tire tracks were washed away at this point. The heavy rain did a great job of erasing evidence. Was that calculated on the attacker's part? Had this person been waiting, biding his time?

And what, if any, links could there be to Stephanie Cross?

"Let me hop in and start the engine," she said. "Then I'll help you move the log."

He nodded. The parched earth soaked up most of the rain, so driving on mud wouldn't be an issue.

The vehicle started up. Carys didn't smile. She looked relieved.

The stalker theory was gaining steam in his mind. Could be James or Harrison. Or the two other names she'd mentioned to the law. He needed to ask her about the others and what role they might play in her life.

"We should head back soon," he said to her as she exited the vehicle. "Kit and Rue were taking a nap when we left, but you never know when one will wake up."

"True," she said. "And you still haven't gotten any sleep."

"I power napped."

"It's not the same thing." She shot him a warning look that told him not to argue. It made him laugh.

It had been a long time since someone had been concerned about him. The nurses handed over pamphlets with support group names and numbers on them. He'd shot down their concerns, saying he was fine. Saying that he could handle it. Taking care of his wife was not a strain since Lynn was the one suffering. All he wanted to do was be there for her to make the road easier. Funny. You never really thought they were going to die. You held out unrealistic hope that a miracle cure would happen. You held on to stories of others who were knocking on death's door suddenly cured and back to a normal life, as if anything after an experience like this could go back to normal. And you held on to that hope until they took their last breath.

Then you sat in your disbelief when they were gone.

"Everything okay?" Carys asked. She'd walked up beside him.

"Fine."

"You sure about that?" Her left eyebrow arched.

"Do I seem like I'm not okay?" he snapped, realizing his tone came out a helluva lot harsher than intended. He put a hand up to stop her from responding. "I didn't mean that."

"I know." She folded her arms and leaned her hip against the car. "And I realize we have to get back to the house as soon as possible. But…do you want to talk about it?"

Did he?

Could he?

Blaize let out a sharp sigh. "If I did talk about it… I'd want it to be with you."

She took a tentative step toward him. "I'm right here, Blaize. And it's okay to still be hurting."

He exhaled, slower this time.

She came closer and then reached for his wrists. Then she took a final step, closing the gap between them. "Is it okay if I touch you?"

"Yes." Damned if he wasn't falling down a rabbit hole with Carys. Would he recover this time?

CARYS TOOK BLAIZE'S wrists in her hands and then positioned his arms around her body. This close, she breathed in his spicy, dark-roast scent. She locked their gazes, searching his eyes to make sure that she wasn't overstepping her bounds. Touching him sent electrical impulses racing through her body. Her breath quickened.

"I've been thinking a lot about the kiss from yesterday," he said, his voice low and gravelly with something that sounded a whole lot like need. And something else. Regret?

"And?" She flinched, preparing for the worst.

"You're the first person I've kissed since…"

Carys sure as hell wasn't expecting those words. An ache formed low in her belly. Her fingers itched to outline every muscle on his beautiful body. A small smile toyed with the corners of her lips at thinking of him in terms of being beautiful. He wouldn't see it that way even though he had those hard planes and angles down pat. His jawline could crack concrete. He would laugh at those descriptions, too. And those full lips over straight, white teeth. Warmth pooled between her thighs.

"I'm honored," she finally said. Her throat suddenly dried, so she swallowed to ease some of it. Did he regret it? "I hope it didn't disappoint."

His tongue slicked across his bottom lip. She stared at the silky trail it left behind.

"I know we agreed it shouldn't happen again, but I would very much like to ask your permission to kiss you one more time."

Standing this close, her body craved more of his touch. Kissing him complicated matters, but she was tired of refusing to give her body what it desperately wanted and needed…to be touched by Blaize.

Her only hesitation was that she knew one time wouldn't be enough.

Could she pull back at this point?

A nearby rustling of leaves made the decision for her. Both of their attention snapped to the sound. Blaize took a step in front of her, placing his body in between her and the noise, forming a human shield.

Their movement caused a squirrel to bolt across the street. They stood there for a long moment, waiting, watching.

"That was not a smart move on my part," Blaize said, shame in his tone.

"I did that, Blaize. Not you." She noticed his habit of blaming himself every time something went wrong. An eldest-child fault? Or did he blame himself in some way for his wife's death? "If you ever want to talk about it, I'm here."

"For how long?" he asked, his tone so low she almost didn't hear him.

"I'm right here," she said in the most reassuring tone possible. After what he'd been through, it wouldn't surprise her if he was afraid deep down to get close to anyone for fear of losing them. That fear would bubble to the surface in comments like the one he just made.

He surveyed the area. His muscles were so tense if they were cords they would have snapped by now.

"Do you want to sit in my car for a few minutes before we drive back?" she asked.

"Let's move this barrier first."

With both of them working, it took all of five minutes to clear the road.

He walked over to the driver's side and opened the door for her. She took a seat. Blaize rounded the front of the vehicle before settling in the passenger side. She rolled the windows down a crack. Just enough to keep fresh air flowing, while making it easier to hear if someone came up to surprise them.

Blaize kept his gaze focused on the stretch of road in front of them. They sat there, quiet, for a long moment. Pushing him to speak would only cause him to withdraw further. In her two years on the job, she'd witnessed people who experienced trauma. They needed space. They needed a gentle nudge.

He was a good person, someone who took care of everyone around him without asking anything in return. It might not have been her job to help him, but she could be there for him. She could lend an ear. But only if he wanted to take that step.

She'd also learned on the job that she couldn't fix other people. They had to want to fix themselves.

"Holding my wife's hand while she faded was the hardest thing I'll ever be asked to do," he said.

"I have nothing to compare it to," she said quietly, reverently. "And I can't begin to fathom how that would feel."

"There was so much medication by the end," he said. "She was doped up all the time to stay out of pain. One night, the lights were low. I sat next to her, head down, eyes on the phone. And I missed it. I had a work email that I was writing a response to. She said my name a few minutes earlier, and I just kept staring at the screen. Held my finger up to tell her that I'd be with her in a second. By the time I looked up, she was gone."

Damn.

Carys exhaled a slow breath as the weight of those words descended around her, cloaked her. The amount of guilt he carried around made even more sense now.

"You were by her side," she said to him. "That would matter the most."

"What did she want to say to me?" he asked slowly. "What did I miss? Was she in pain? Was there something I could have done to ease it? To help? Did she need something from me? Or did she want to tell me that she loved me one more time, and I robbed both of us of the pleasure of hearing those words out loud?"

Carys didn't respond. Those questions were rhetorical. It was him thinking out loud. Needing to say those words to someone.

"I spent so much time with her and missed the most important moment of her life." He was beating himself up. Words of encouragement wouldn't help right now, so she tucked them away for when he might be ready to hear them.

Reality nailed her.

Once Rue was settled wherever she was supposed to be, Carys and Blaize would likely lose contact. They lived in two different worlds, and he had the responsibility of turning the ranch around along with the self-imposed duty of taking care of Kit for the rest of her life.

She hoped his grandmother would be around for a very long time. Kit was wonderful. And yet Carys wished Blaize could have time to heal from taking care of his wife. It was obvious he loved her. And no matter how strong the attraction was between Carys and Blaize, she would never be able to compete with a ghost.

An emptiness she'd never experienced before filled her chest, and suddenly all the oxygen sucked out of the vehicle.

Chapter Ten

Blaize never talked about Lynn. He thought about her every day, almost every minute of every day. But he didn't talk about her.

Until now.

Saying those words out loud chipped some of the thousand-pound weight off his shoulders.

"Ever notice how we're always harder on ourselves than we are on other people?" Carys asked.

He nodded. She'd been quiet.

"If you knew someone going through what you just described, someone who was being a dying person's sole support…what would you say to them?" she asked.

"I'd tell them to do the best they could and savor each moment," he said. "I'd tell them to try to find humor together in small things. And I'd remind them to take care of themselves, too." It dawned on him why she'd asked the question as he heard his own response. "And you're wondering why I don't give myself that same advice."

"No," she said. "Just observing how hard we are on ourselves and how much softer we are on others, especially when someone we care about is going through hell."

He barked a laugh. Yes. He could relate. "I'm still not letting myself off the hook."

"You don't have to," she said. "No judgment here."

Blaize sat there for a long moment, letting those words really sink in. They'd been gone for a while, longer than he intended. "We should really get back to Kit and the baby."

"Okay."

He didn't realize he'd tensed up so much before her response until he exhaled. With Lynn, almost everything became a challenge or an outright fight. Carys's demeanor had a calming effect on people, on him. Even when they stood close and his body was an exploding minefield of electricity and need, he felt a sense of peace that was foreign.

Growing up in a battleground with Cormac, then with Lynn's bipolar disorder, he'd gotten used to always being ready for a fight.

Carys drove them to the house since the damage on her car was thankfully just cosmetic. Frustrating as all hell, but nothing a good dent-repair shop couldn't handle. Mechanically, the car was sound. Tires were good. He'd half feared the attacker would return and rupture them. Too risky?

Damned if he wasn't already thinking about the kiss from yesterday again. How it was unlike any others.

They pulled up. Carys parked next to his Jeep. Both vehicles could use a good hosing off.

"I can find someone to fix the damage to your vehicle," he said after opening her door for her. It looked as though someone had taken a baseball bat to it.

"Thanks, but I can look up a place just as easy." She held out her phone. "You can find almost anything on one of these."

"And have it delivered," he joked. "Just not out here."

"Leaving the city was definitely an adjustment," she said.

"Why did you come all the way out here to Maverick Pass?" He opened the back door for her after unlocking it.

"For a job. They aren't exactly easy to get."

"Austin can be a tough place to find work, but the medical options are standout," he said. There would come a day when he didn't know who the best bipolar doctor was or bone-cancer specialist. A year had passed since Lynn's death, and he still checked his calendar for appointments out of habit.

"The job market was brutal, even for the kind of work I do."

They entered the kitchen. He listened for sounds coming from the bedroom. Kit had insisted on having Rue stay with her.

"Blaize!" Kit hollered.

And then the baby wound up and wailed.

Heart in his throat, he blew past Carys. The door was still locked, but this old house would be easy to break into. All the latches and locks were too old. Hell, the windows were ancient. No one expected crime all the way out here.

"Are you—"

He stopped midsentence the second he entered the doorway, rushed to Kit, who was lying on her side and curled into a ball.

"What happened?" he asked before taking a knee beside her. He scanned her for obvious signs of injury—blood or a bone sticking out through her skin. He couldn't find anything from this angle.

He could barely hear himself think over the crying baby. Carys was there in the next second, picking up the little girl and offering a soothing tone.

"I'll take her into the next room," she said before disappearing. Her voice might be calm, but panic was written all over her features.

"Can I help you sit up?" he asked Kit when the crying subsided.

"I think so," she said, issuing a frustrated grunt. "I was trying to get to the bathroom, and I lost my balance. Hit my head on the dresser."

"Where?" he asked as he wrapped an arm around her and gently guided her to sit up.

She leaned against the dresser as she brought her hand up to feel around the crown of her head. "Here." She took his hand and placed it on the spot.

A pump knot was already forming.

"We need to get you to the ER," he said, doing his level best to tamp down the panic rising in his chest.

"You'll do no such thing," Kit protested. "My name is Kit Wilde, short for Katherine." She rattled off a couple other facts to prove she was lucid. Facts like the day of the week, her birthday, and the address.

"Then at least allow me to grab an ice pack," he said. It could help with any pain.

"That I can live with." Kit smiled with that grandmotherly warmth in her eyes. "I'm sorry to be such a pain."

"You couldn't be."

"I've been thinking about what you said about Lynn. It couldn't have been easy on you, and I'm figuring you took care of your wife all by your lonesome."

He nodded, unsure where this was going.

"You shouldn't have to step in and take care of an old lady like me," she said. "It's time you live your life for yourself, Blaize. I mean it, and I believe the others will agree."

"Not a chance." There was no way Kit was leaving the home she'd built. He frowned. "Are you trying to kick me out?"

Kit laughed.

"Would you go?" she asked.

"Nah. Probably not." He smiled. "You raised me and my brothers. I may not have heard back from them yet, but I will. And they'll agree with me, by the way."

She folded her arms across her chest and pouted.

"What can I say? We love you, and it's your turn to be taken care of. And it's high time you reclaimed your bedroom." He shook his head. "I have no idea what Cormac was thinking, but if he was alive, I'd..." One look at her said he was hurting her feelings by insulting her son. "I'm sorry, Kit. What he's done to this place burns me up."

"You don't know what happened to Cormac to turn him that way."

What?

CARYS GAVE A self-satisfied smile after successfully changing a diaper and feeding Rue a bottle. Now the baby was happily stretching her hands out in front of her, cooing, and basically looking at this world like everything was miraculous. Carys couldn't remember the last time she felt that way about anything in life. As a child, she'd been suffocated, miserable. Taking charge of her life meant being cut off by her father, a choice no person should've had to make.

She exhaled a slow breath and refocused. It was Saturday, her day off from work. She could turn her phone off and not worry about her boss figuring out what she'd done. At least, not today. That would be Monday's problem, if it surfaced at all. Could she hide all this from work?

Relinquishing custody of a child to their parent was something Carys did on a regular basis. Technically, there was no proof that Blaize wasn't the biological father. Sure, a simple spit test would do the trick in a matter of hours, but she hadn't filed her report yet and so there was no reason for work to question that she'd done the right thing.

There were a few wrong things to worry about. For instance, staying overnight. That was out of the bounds of her job description and could be scrutinized should this case go to court. The storm could explain being stranded. Blaize offered shelter in said storm. The kiss they'd shared might be a bigger issue if questioned about developing a personal relationship with the father of her charge.

That would be the point the case could go south faster than a beginner skater on ice.

Wanting Blaize wasn't an issue. Her body craved his touch. She'd dreamt about his hands on her last night. The kiss they'd shared had been soul-defining. It also caused her to question what she knew about attraction. Had she been settling for partners who either couldn't commit to a relationship or were too clingy? Finding middle ground seemed impossible. Finding someone who saw her through Blaize's eyes seemed unthinkable. Finding someone who made her want things like a real love with a person who loved her back was unimaginable.

Keeping everyone at arm's length was her superpower. Who was she without it?

She listened for signs from the bedroom that Kit was all right. Seeing her lying on the floor, curled up on her side, had caused Carys's stress levels to shoot through the roof. The distraction of caring for Rue kept Carys's nerves at a level above panic.

Considering Carys never saw herself as the "get married

and have kids" type, the satisfaction she got from calming the baby took her by surprise.

Maybe she could consider getting a cat? Or should start small with trying to keep a houseplant alive? The responsibility of day-to-day care would be different than her little win this afternoon.

All this was a distraction from her real purpose—finding Rue's birth father. To do that, she needed to know more about Stephanie Cross. Once Kit's status was confirmed as healthy, Carys could regroup with Blaize.

Hunger pangs got the best of her. She missed those days in Austin when she could just pull up an app on her phone and have food delivered to her door. It was expensive but worth every penny on days like this.

Living in Maverick Pass had honed her cooking skills. She could do more than butter toast, which was good. Thank the stars for online recipes and cooking tips. She would be lost without the internet. Didn't make her a true chef by any means. At least she could feed herself with relative ease. Eating at home had other benefits. She ate healthier.

A noise from the hallway drew her attention back to the present. Blaize walked into the kitchen.

One look at him had her standing up. "More coffee?"

"Yes, please." He rubbed the day-old scruff on his chin.

"Coming right up." She fixed two after settling Rue on the blanket placed on the floor.

Blaize's toe snagged the rain bucket, causing water to slosh and a few droplets to spill. He muttered a curse, glanced at Rue, and then apologized.

"Think she can understand you?" Carys handed over a fresh cup of black coffee.

"No," he said. "I don't want her to get used to those words. I'm convinced the subconscious picks up more than we realize, even in little ones. While around her, I want to do better with language."

The word *while* shouldn't hit hard. Its temporary nature reminded her just how short this visit would be. She needed to go home because there was no way she could sell staying with him over an entire weekend in court should it come to that.

"If Stephanie listed you as Rue's father and it's a blatant lie, she either doesn't know who he is or did and was keeping the baby from him for a reason," she said as they took seats at the kitchen table.

"My mind goes to some pretty dark places when it comes to keeping paternity from a father," he said.

"For instance?"

"Maybe she was being abused and didn't want that life for her daughter," he said. "Or the father was a criminal and she didn't want her daughter brought up in that lifestyle."

"Both are logical reasons." She took a sip of coffee. "Kids change people, don't they?"

"How so?"

She leaned her elbows against the table. "Stephanie could have been fine with a wild lifestyle before this little darling was born. During her pregnancy, she might have realized she needed to change. Rue deserves better. So, she hatched a plan to escape. She sneaks away before her boyfriend or husband, whatever the case may be, knows she's carrying his baby and then writes your name down on the birth certificate to throw him off the trail."

"If she really made a plan like this, it stands to reason she would change her identity, too."

"I should get a report on Monday," she said. "It's sad that her life was cut short after all that scheming and planning, not to mention she wouldn't have planned on leaving Rue an orphan."

"She's not an orphan," he said with finality. "If the father turns out to be a disaster like we think, we'll figure something else out. Stephanie Cross, the person who put my name on that birth certificate trusted me to do the right thing. I won't let her or Rue down."

Blaize was the most honorable person Carys had ever met. She understood why someone would choose him even though it wasn't fair to put him in that position. *You didn't expect to need him, did you, Stephanie?* A picture emerged of a desperate pregnant woman who needed to escape her situation and have a backup plan should the worst happen.

And the worst did happen.

"Are you hungry?" he asked after her stomach growled.

"Yes."

"We could head out to eat since there isn't much left here," he said.

Being seen out and about with Blaize and the baby would definitely not be a good move. But hiding made her feel like she was doing something wrong.

Was she?

Chapter Eleven

"I have a picture of Stephanie Cross."

The announcement caught Blaize off guard. He crossed the kitchen in a few quick strides to where Carys had been perched for the past hour on her laptop. Kit and the baby were resting before dinner, so he was alone with Carys.

"Does she look familiar?" She angled the screen toward him as he took the seat next to her. Their outer thighs brushed, causing electricity to pulse up his leg, his body's reaction to her amplified by the length of time it had been since he'd had sex. It was the only explanation that made sense. Blaize was no stranger to sex within the bounds of a relationship, but no one had stirred a reaction like this one.

He studied the screen. Kinky red hair. Too much makeup. Mole on her right cheek. The mole resonated, but she had on so much makeup it was hard to tell what features were hidden underneath the mask. "There is something familiar about her."

"Makeup can do wonders to change someone's appearance. She has used contouring makeup just about everywhere on her face. For instance, see here." She pointed to Stephanie's nose. "This is making her nose look thinner than it is."

"The hair is throwing me off."

"Looks like she has a perm, and it's possible she colored it. That doesn't look like a natural redhead."

"I'd have to see her in person to know for certain, which is clearly not possible under the circumstances."

"Well, no, but we could visit some of the bars you used to frequent in Austin and ask around. Maybe a bartender will know her and be able to provide a name," she said.

"What would we do with Rue?"

"Kit needs someone here for support in case she falls again," she said. "Maybe they can watch over Rue?"

"My grandmother might have someone who can step in for a day while we head to Austin," he said.

"Right. Ranchers are the rare breed who still watch out for each other. Too bad everyone isn't like that."

"Many of us still do." He thought about what Kit said to him earlier about not knowing what made Cormac turn out the way he had. If the man started out being a good human, it must have been something horrific to turn him into the person he became. Someone who'd lost touch with his roots, his humanity.

Did Blaize really want to know what happened? Would it do any good? You couldn't go back and change the past. He learned the lesson a long time ago. Didn't everyone have some kind of trauma in their background? There was no excuse for the way Cormac treated people.

"We should make a list of the bars you used to go to." Carys's voice cut into his heavy thoughts.

"That's easy. There were three—Deep Roots Bar, Peggie Hays, Chord Street Bar." He'd stopped off at a handful of others. Not long enough for someone to remember his name unless this Stephanie or whatever her name was figured out another way.

Nope. Not possible. He always used cash at bars. No one needed to know his business, and credit cards could be traced. He didn't appreciate how easy it was to stalk someone online or memorize their habits. A determined criminal could get most everything they wanted to know about a person online.

With social media, folks volunteered personal information about their lives on an almost daily basis. Where they ate. What night was date night. What their family looked like. Where they went on vacation. What school their kids attended. Information was endless, which made Stephanie more interesting since there wasn't a profile for her anywhere near Maverick Pass or Austin.

Blaize had one too many a couple of times at bars. Not enough to sleep with a stranger, and especially not enough to sleep with a stranger and then forget it happened. He would have remembered. He hadn't kissed anyone in the past year except for Carys.

"When Kit wakes, I'll have her reach out to a neighbor to see if they can come sit with her and Rue. It's Saturday night, so the bars will be open late. We can make the drive and hit all three in one night if traffic obliges."

Carys glanced at the time on the computer. "We'll have to leave soon."

"I know."

The sound of gravel crunching underneath tires got Blaize up and moving to the window. He grabbed a knife on the way. It might've been the sheriff finally showing up to pick up the barbecue fork, but he couldn't be sure.

Nope.

He didn't recognize the dark blue pickup. The driver, on the other hand, was Raiden.

"Who is it?" Carys asked, walking up beside him.

"My brother." Blaize set the knife on the counter and headed toward the back door. He didn't have the first clue if Raiden would be happy to see him. Time to find out and see if the damage done to their relationship could be repaired.

"Should I wait here in case Kit or Rue needs something?" Carys asked.

"Would you mind?" he asked. "I'm not sure what kind of reunion this is going to be. Might be better on both fronts if I go by myself to face my brother before introducing him to you."

"I'll be right here if you need me." She touched his arm as he walked past. The contact sent electrical impulses zinging through him. "You got this."

"Thank you," he said. Her gentle support seeded a sense of calm in a place deep inside him. Denying it wouldn't make it any less true.

Raiden parked. He hopped out of the driver's seat and came

flying at Blaize. He tensed up for a fight. Instead, his brother wrapped him in a bear hug.

"Hey, man. I'm so sorry about Lynn. I would have been there for you if I'd known," Raiden said. It dawned on Blaize that he wasn't the only one making calls to Raiden and Phoenix. Raiden must have had a conversation with Kit.

"There wasn't anything anyone else could do," Blaize said, embracing his brother.

"Bull hockey. We could have been your support system. Phoenix would have been there, too. We both feel like jerks for not taking your calls. Or, maybe I should say that I know he feels like a jerk since I haven't heard back from him." Maybe there was something to this birth-order bit. Raiden was being the go-between for Blaize and their youngest brother.

He cracked a smile. "You're here now. Kit needs all three of us. This ranch needs all three of us if we're going to keep it in the family."

"I'm just here for the weekend, man. Came to tell you that Phoenix and I think we should dump this place," Raiden said.

Blaize took a step away from his brother. "You talked to each other without including me?"

"Not in the last forty-eight hours. The last time I spoke to our brother, we made a pact. Plus, you made your position clear, Blaize."

"And so you just left me out of the conversation altogether?" His temper was getting the best of him.

"That's why I'm here now," Raiden said. "That and to tell you how sorry I am."

"So, you'd toss Kit out on her ear? Make her lose the only home she's known for her entire adult life? The home she built?"

Raiden stood there, studying, listening. "You want to know the truth?" he asked.

"What kind of question is that? Of course I want to know the truth."

"Kit is the one who urged me to sell. Said you are being hardheaded and that I needed to find Phoenix so we could both show up and convince you to do the right thing and dump this… what did she call it…shanty."

Wait. What?

To say he felt blindsided was an understatement. What was Kit thinking?

"Said it was falling apart at the seams and that you, being you, wanted to fix it up for her but it's too much work, and we all have our own lives. Said she didn't want to get in the way."

"And you believed her?" Blaize asked, incredulous.

"She sounded sincere, man. What am I supposed to think? Kit is a firecracker and knows herself. Said she doesn't want to live in a place that's falling apart anymore."

Color Blaize confused. "Did she mention that she tripped and fell last night?"

Raiden shook his head.

"Hit her head on the dresser and ended up with a pump knot."

Raiden stood there, brows furrowed. He crossed his arms over his chest as he listened.

"She needs us more than ever, Raiden. Can you rightly see kicking her out of here?"

"The place needs a lot of work, Blaize."

"Nothing the three of us can't handle." Was he being overly optimistic? He didn't think so. It would take dedication and time.

"What about the financials?" Raiden asked.

"They are as bad as you think they might be."

"Kit said you'd try to talk me out of my stance," Raiden said. "She was one hundred percent right."

Why would Kit do that? Why would she push them to sell? It made no sense to Blaize. "I don't care what she said. Kit loves this place. Leaving here would be like losing her husband all over again."

"Did she tell you to sell?"

"Yes."

"Why don't you take her word for it?" Raiden asked. It was a reasonable question, and he didn't have a great answer.

"Can you honestly say that you believe her?"

"She was pretty convincing on the phone," he said. "I'm here to talk to you in person like we should have done when you first got Lynn's diagnosis. And I want to be able to look Kit in the eye when she argues her case."

There was more than a hint of doubt in Raiden's tone. Blaize could work with that. If his brother's mind was already made up, there would be no use discussing the subject further. One trait all three brothers inherited was a stubborn streak a mile long and stronger than a bull's.

"Why don't you come inside and have a cup of coffee," Blaize said. His plans to head to Austin tonight just tanked.

KIT WALKED INTO the kitchen and straight to the window. "Raiden is here. Good."

Carys wasn't so sure she liked the tone of Kit's voice. "Everything all right?"

"It is now," the older woman said, confusing her further.

Since she would find out what that meant soon enough, she rinsed out her coffee cup and set it in the sink.

Blaize followed his brother inside. The family resemblance showed in height and build. Raiden would be considered hot by most standards. His hair was a little longer, with wispy curls at the ends. In her opinion, Blaize was the best looking. No contest.

"I'm Raiden," he said to her after greeting Kit and giving his grandmother a warm hug. So far, the Wilde men were the most grounded she'd met in Maverick Pass. They were the hottest, too, but that was a different story.

"Carys," she said. "It's nice to meet you."

"My brother said you work for CPS," Raiden said.

"That's right."

"And that you brought a baby here believing she belonged to Blaize," he said.

She nodded. "Sure did."

"I'm sure you two will get to the bottom of it," he said.

"Thanks. I hope so." She glanced at Blaize. "Are we still good to head to Austin soon?"

"Now that my brother is here, I should probably not—"

"Go ahead," Kit insisted. "We'll be just fine."

"I don't know," Blaize said. Eyebrows drawn together combined with the worry line etched in his forehead told Carys he was seriously contemplating their next move.

"Is the kid here now?" Raiden glanced around the room.

"She's sleeping," Kit said.

"How hard can it be to watch over a little thing that sleeps most of the time?" he asked.

Carys laughed at the same time Blaize did, and equally hard.

"What?" Raiden asked.

"You have no idea until you know," Blaize said.

"Go and do what you need to do," Kit interjected. "We'll be fine. Isn't that right, Raiden?"

"We've got this," he confirmed.

"There's enough formula and diapers to last a couple of days," Carys supplied.

One look at Blaize said he'd made up his mind. He gave a slight nod as he locked gazes with Carys. Checking to see if she was on the same page?

"Let's do this." She could think of no better reason to put her job on the line than to help Rue find a real home. If going to Austin got them one step closer to that, so be it.

"I'll grab an overnight bag."

"Can we stop off at my place on the way out of town?" she asked. "I need a change of clothes."

"Sure," he said.

The thought of spending the night with Blaize in a hotel room should probably freak her right out. It didn't. Sure, the sexual current running between them showed no signs of dimming. However, they were adults capable of restraint. Her body wanted to argue against what her mind realized...having any type of relationship with Blaize beyond professional would shatter her once it ended.

"It was good to meet you," she said to Raiden as Blaize excused himself to grab his bag.

Raiden's gaze bounced from Carys to Kit and back. "I apologize if I'm stepping out of line here, but Blaize seems different with you around."

"Our relationship is strictly professional," she countered a little too quickly. Had she just showed her hand to Blaize's family?

"I'm here because of Rue. Your brother has been great, though. And we're going to get to the bottom of paternity." Wow, had she really just rambled on?

Great. Way to keep cool.

"I understand," Raiden said with a layered look. "I'm sure the two of you will figure it out soon."

"In the meantime, I sure have enjoyed having another woman in the house," Kit interrupted. "I hope you'll stay on a little longer when you return from Austin." She glanced at Raiden. "Don't get me wrong—I love my boys. But the house can use more feminine energy."

Her smile lit up her eyes.

Carys laughed.

Blaize walked into the room. He stopped and studied everyone's faces. He opened his mouth to speak and then snapped it shut before focusing on Carys. "Ready?"

Probably not, but they needed to go anyway.

Chapter Twelve

Carys had been quiet on the ride to her apartment. Too quiet. Blaize had half a mind to ask what his family might have said to her. He decided to let it ride instead.

He parked on the street in front of her bungalow.

The crease in her forehead when she glanced at him concerned him.

"What's wrong?" he asked.

A beat passed. "Maybe nothing. I'm not sure. I think the trash can has been scooted closer to the window. I don't leave it there."

"Do you want to come with me to check it out or stay in the Jeep while I take a look?" he asked, reaching for the door handle.

"I'm coming." She was out the passenger side before he could open the door for her.

Carys took the lead as he scanned the area for any unusual activity.

The trash can had been pushed against the wall underneath what looked like a kitchen window. Nothing else seemed out of the ordinary. "The storm could have blown it over or tossed it down the street. A well-meaning neighbor might have returned it."

"That's a good point," she said. "Mind if we take a walk

around the house before going in? Just to be sure nothing else feels funny?"

"I'm right behind you." He was behind her and a little bit to the side so he could block her using his body should anything come flying at them. A stalker made more and more sense as they walked. She turned the second corner, looked at the window, and froze.

"The window is cracked open." She pointed. "See that?"

"I sure do," he said. "Do you ever leave them like that?"

"Not usually. I don't normally leave the house without checking."

"You had Rue with you. Right?" It was possible she might have forgotten.

"True." She shook her head. "I'm probably searching for something that just isn't there, you know? My mind is tuned to finding something because of the trash can. You're most likely right about it. The storms were fierce. It's highly likely the wind tossed it around while I was gone. It wouldn't be the first time that happened."

"We'll check every inch of the house before we let our guards down," he said.

"Sounds like a plan." She walked to the back door, opened it, and entered the kitchen. The place was simple, orderly, and clean. It looked like she put everything in its place with care. A *You Had Me at Merlot* dish towel was draped over the oven handle. Under different circumstances, he would have chuckled. Right now, he was focused on ensuring no one was hiding in a closet somewhere.

Room by room, he cleared the house. The bedroom window—the cracked one—was last. "No one is hiding here. I've checked every nook and cranny." That was the good news. Her unsettled feeling had him concerned. It was never a good idea to ignore intuition. "If someone was here, they're gone now." He stopped short of saying they were safe. "Does anything look out of place?"

The living room consisted of a small sofa with a matching chair, a coffee table with a book on top, and a side table with a lamp. A blanket had been tossed onto the couch, and the pillows were messy. It looked like someone had been sitting here, relaxing, and then had to get up in a hurry with no time to straighten up. The Rue effect?

"I don't remember. It's hard to say. Everything is usually in its place, but having a little one around really changes things."

He let himself smirk—Rue effect.

"All I could think about was her and how pitiful she sounded," she said. "Hearing a baby cry and being helpless to stop it is the worst possible feeling in the world."

"Agreed."

"I'll just grab a few things, and we can head out," she said before disappearing through a doorway in between the living and dining room.

"Okay." He took a step and heard a rattle. He withdrew his foot as though a snake bit him. A memory punched him. Damned if he hadn't suppressed it until now. Until looking down and seeing the baby's rattle on the carpet. He bent over and picked it up, studied it. Moisture pooled in his eyes. He'd been so focused on Lynn that he'd forced the memory out of his mind, pushed it down somewhere deep where it couldn't surface without the right trigger.

"Hey." Carys's voice caught him off guard. He didn't realize that she'd walked back into the room.

Blaize grunted, set the toy on top of the coffee table, and then headed toward the front door. "Lock up so we can get on the road."

He didn't look back. Didn't want her to see the emotion pooling in his eyes, threatening to spill over.

Dammit.

Blaize walked right past Carys, not stopping until he was seated on the driver's side of his Jeep. He turned the engine on, and waited. She took a few minutes to appear. For a second, he wondered if he'd offended her.

When she set her bag in the back seat, she didn't make eye contact. Her demeanor was calm. Too calm? Part of him wanted her to get mad. Hell, cuss him out.

Instead, she took the passenger seat and said, "Ready when you are."

He banked a U-turn after setting the GPS toward Austin.

They drove for a while before she cleared her throat and asked, "What about the baby's rattle upset you?"

"Nothing."

"You don't have to tell me," she said. "I've been picking up on something…call it a vibe. And it's been causing me to wonder how you feel about starting a family."

"What do you mean?"

"The way you look at Rue when no one is watching," she said.

Blaize clamped his mouth shut rather than bite out a retort. She was spot-on with her observation. The rattle dislodged a memory. One he'd been holding in for a long time. Too long?

Opening up felt like cutting open a vein. Stuffing it down felt like a time bomb waiting to explode.

"Have I mentioned Lynn had bipolar disorder?"

"You have."

"Right." *Here goes…*

"She was pregnant once," he said. "She showed me one of those home pregnancy tests."

"What happened?"

"I was thrilled when I saw the result," he said. "For some reason, a rattle just like Rue's came to mind. It was the first thing I wanted to buy. But Lynn started crying, and they weren't exactly happy tears. She unraveled, said she needed to stay with a friend to clear her head."

"That must have been hard for you, and her."

"It was. She shut me out during a difficult time for both of us."

"What happened?"

"Lynn turned up three days later. I came home from work to find her sitting on the couch drinking wine straight from the bottle." The memory threatened to burn a hole in his chest. Talking about it tamped down some of the blaze. "Said all the stress must have made her lose the pregnancy but that she was relieved because she didn't want kids with me anyway.

"I lost it," he said. "I'm not proud of my actions, but my

temper got the best of me. I said words that I wish I could take back." Guilt punched him again like it happened yesterday.

"I'm sorry, Blaize. For both of you." A few beats passed. "Did she say why? You obviously wanted the child. Had you ever talked about having a family with her?"

"Yes," he said. "We wanted kids, or so I thought. She said the possibility of carrying a child woke her up to the fact she didn't actually want kids. Before that, she'd wanted two, a boy and a girl. I didn't care. She said she couldn't risk passing on the disorder to children. Said it wouldn't be fair to them or to me. Said she was enough of a hot mess without adding to the equation."

"I bet that was hard to hear from someone you loved so much."

"It was." He could admit that much. "So, if you catch me looking at Rue and thinking about what might have been, you're probably catching a weak moment."

"That's not weak, Blaize. You are the strongest person I know." She reached over and touched his hand, sending warmth spreading through him. "The more I get to know you, the more respect I have for you. Life hasn't been easy. Has it?"

"I never expected easy," he said. "I'd hoped for fair instead."

CARYS DIDN'T WANT to like Blaize more than she already did. She was already treading dangerous waters, barely keeping her head above water when it came to the man. His raw honesty wasn't helping her keep an emotional distance.

"Fair isn't always on the table, is it?" she asked.

"We've talked too much about me. What about you?" He turned the tables. "You lost your mother at a young age."

"That's right. I already shared that with you." Where did she begin with her other parental relationship? "As far as my father is concerned, we haven't spoken more than two words in six years. He cut me off when we disagreed about my future. Told me to go away and not worry about coming back. That he no longer had a daughter."

"That's harsh. You didn't deserve that."

"No one does," she agreed. "I get that he was hurting after

my mom died. But his reaction made it like losing two parents in one blow. You know?"

"I can see that."

"Losing her caused him to double down on protecting me. His grip was so tight, I was tempted to rebel. I didn't. I guess it made me want to help others even more, especially kids."

It made her think about Rue. "What's going to happen to that little girl back at your house if her father turns out to be a criminal? Or if we never uncover his identity? The courts would never give her to me. Plus, I wouldn't know the first thing about taking care of a baby full time. I was an only child. And I might have had responsibilities around the house, but I was never responsible for a human life. I've never even kept a plant alive. I don't even want children, which is part of the reason I chose this profession. I can help them without the day in, day out responsibility that I have no idea if I'll ever be ready for."

"Parents do a real number on kids sometimes, don't they?" It was a rhetorical question.

"Thank you for listening," she said after catching her breath. "And not judging me or telling me that I'm supposed to want kids and a family."

"Why would I do that?" he asked with genuine care and authenticity in his voice.

She shrugged. "Isn't it supposed to be natural to want to have a baby?"

"Every person has a right and responsibility to make that decision for themselves."

"I couldn't agree more." Since most of the trip had been heavy with conversation, she changed course. "You know what sounds good right now to me?"

"What's that?"

"Ice cream."

Blaize laughed. "How about Amy's Ice Cream?"

"Is there a better place?"

"Not as long as Mexican Vanilla is on the menu," he said. She appreciated him going with the flow. Talking to him was a little too easy, and she needed to pull back before the connection deepened. She was already swimming in new territory and needed to get her sea legs.

The very real threat of being sucked out by a strong current and drowned slammed into her. As much as her heart wanted to lean into Blaize, rational thought took over, warning her not to get too close.

"Mexican Vanilla happens to be my favorite, too," she admitted, wishing they didn't have so much in common. It would be easier to walk away if she didn't like him so much.

The rest of the short drive to Amy's was spent in silence. They needed to recalibrate and come up with a plan of attack for the bars. They had time. Ten o'clock was early for the bar scene.

Now that they had a picture of Stephanie, they could ask questions. If she was a regular, a good bartender would know it.

After getting ice cream that Blaize had insisted on paying for, they found a spot at one of the outdoor picnic tables and sat down. He took the seat across from her and leaned in. It was next to impossible not to feel like they were on some kind of date, especially since he paid.

Carys pushed those thoughts aside, tried not to focus on those gorgeous full lips of his—and more importantly, what they could do to her!—and forced a calm over her that she didn't feel.

Fake it till you make it was the worst advice she'd ever heard. It ranked right up there with saying things to yourself in a mirror that you didn't believe. Somewhere deep in the back of your mind, you would know that you were faking it. Except when it came to smiling. Someone had once told her to smile, even when she was in a bad mood, and that worked miracles.

She'd faked being happy to make her father worry less for too much of her life. It didn't work on him, either. Maybe Blaize was onto something about Rue recording the world around her deep in the back of her mind.

"Are you okay?" Blaize's voice brought her attention back.

"Yes," she said, faking it. Too bad it didn't work like the smile. They had three bars to visit. "Where do you want to go first?"

Chapter Thirteen

"Peggie Hayes is the closest. We should start there first." Being back in Austin brought back a flood of memories. He'd lived here with Lynn, stayed a couple of weeks after she died. Then he moved out closer to his job, where he oversaw the making of custom saddles. There were benefits to growing up on a small cattle ranch. He knew horses and everything that went along with riding or taking care of them. During the summers he gave riding instructions on the weekends at various campsites to bring in extra money.

Money might not make you happy, but lack of it sure as hell didn't help. Medication was expensive, so were doctor bills. Insurance only covered a portion of the costs.

After marrying Lynn, Blaize had drifted away from the handful of friends he'd made over the years. A few of them married and started families. When she got sick, he isolated himself from everyone but her. Work had to be scheduled around doctor appointments. His world shrank. Despite all the hardships during his marriage, he'd loved his wife. It might not have been the same as the stirring he felt from deep within when he was with Carys, but it was love.

"You got quiet," Carys said as they returned to the Jeep.

"Being back here…let's say being here is loaded and leave it at that." He'd talked enough earlier to become a talk show host.

"Quiet's good."

Neither said much between Amy's and Peggie Hayes. Being in each other's company didn't require words. They sat in comfortable silence, not needing to fill the space.

Peggie Hayes Bar was as funky as it sounded. The walls were covered in graffiti, inside and out. The place was small, the bar big. A dance floor the size of a postage stamp took up the back corner of the room with a jukebox. There was no sawdust on the floor, but country music was as common as mainstream and commercial. Tables had games on them, like trivia, meant for group play.

He parked and then circled around to open her door. They both knew she was fully capable of opening her own door, but he liked doing little things for her, and she smiled and thanked him in response. Her face lit up and his heart galloped.

"Shall we go inside?" he asked. The music thumped. Though crowds hadn't quite formed yet. This would be a good time to hit up the bartender, before business boomed.

"Let's do this," she said with a look of solidarity.

He reached for her hand at the same time she reached for his. They crashed into each other at first, but then their fingers wound through each other's as they fell into step, walking side by side.

Inside, not much had changed. Eleven o'clock was still on the early end for Austin nightlife. He recognized the bartender and saw it as a good sign.

"What can I get you?" the bartender asked, tossing a pair of customized drink coasters onto the bar in front of them. They landed almost perfectly next to each other.

There were half a dozen folks huddled at the opposite end of the bar. A couple of the tables were full. And there were a few stragglers who'd sidled up to the bar. It was a manageable crowd for one bartender and a barback. The bartender resembled a blond Tom Cruise with a similar height and build. His resemblance to the famous actor was the reason Blaize remembered him.

"Can I ask a question while I decide?" Carys jumped right in.

"Shoot." The bartender stepped a little closer and leaned in as Carys pulled out her phone.

"Any chance you recognize her?" She tilted the screen so he could see.

He backed away and put his hands in the air, palms out. His gaze bounced from Carys to Blaize and back. "I don't want anything to do with whatever you two are up to."

Based on his reaction, Blaize suspected the bartender thought this was an affair situation.

"It's not what you think," he said.

"Look, if you're not here for a drink, then you don't need me."

"I'll take a glass of merlot."

Blaize almost smirked as he thought back to the hand towel. Of course she would take merlot. He made a mental note to buy a bottle for her to celebrate when this was all over and Rue was in good hands.

"Coming right up," Blond Tom Cruise said.

He returned a few moments later with a clean glass and a bottle of wine.

"We're trying to find information about her to locate her next of kin," Blaize said.

"Are you cops?"

"Nothing like that," Blaize said. "Carys works for CPS and wants to reunite Stephanie—that's her name—with her daughter, if we can find her or her family." He searched for a flicker of recognition when he mentioned the name.

No such luck.

"Okay, show me the picture again."

Carys did.

He studied it for a long moment. "I'm sorry, guys. I've never seen this woman before in my life. Even without all the makeup, I don't know who she could be."

Blaize pulled out a twenty and set it on the bar as he stood up. "Thanks. We appreciate your time."

"No problem," Blond Tom Cruise said. "Wish I could be more of a help."

After stepping outside, Carys asked, "Do you think he was lying?"

"No," Blaize confirmed. "I watched for his reactions when I said her name and you showed him the picture. He was drawing a blank, unless he's the best poker player in Texas, in which case he could make a lot more money on the circuit than slinging drinks."

It was a dead end.

"Onto Chord Street," he said.

"All right, then." She reached for his hand, and he linked their fingers as they walked back to the Jeep.

Within a few minutes, they were on the road, navigating through the always rush-hour-like traffic Austin was infamous for. A ten-minute drive in most places could take thirty-five or longer in Texas's capital. Bumper-to-bumper, horns honking, Austin had a rhythm of its own. Still weird. Just more crowded.

The drive took twenty-five minutes. Finding parking took another fifteen. It was nearing midnight by the time they walked into Chord Street Bar.

Two working bartenders manned the clients sitting at the bar. One was dedicated to the waitstaff, who were already blowing and going. Chord Street was livelier. It was larger with a crush of people standing around bar-height tabletops with no stools. The bar was the center of the establishment.

"Do you want me to send you the picture of Stephanie so we can divide and conquer?" Carys asked after taking in the scene.

"Sounds reasonable."

She let go of his hand and sent the pic. He went left. She went right.

He didn't recognize the bartenders, but this place was larger and there could have been turnover in the last year. A smaller place like Peggie Hayes might have had a better chance of keeping their bartending staff since it had a more family-owned feel.

This was a better place to get lost, blend in, and not be remembered.

Stephanie could have been an employee or a patron. Her name might not even be Stephanie. If she committed to the name change, it made sense that she might've kept at least the first letter of her name for when she signed papers. It wouldn't surprise him if her name was Stephanie or Sarah or in that ballpark.

He moved across the bar from the bartender. She perked up.

"What can I get you?" she asked. She had purple streaks in her hair and tattooed arm sleeves. A nose piercing topped off her look. She might not've been his type or able to hold a candle to Carys, but the look worked for her.

"I'm looking for someone," he said.

She laughed. "Look around, handsome. I'm sure you'll find plenty of 'someones,' based on the looks you're getting."

He wasn't paying attention. "I'm hoping you can help me."

"Okay-y-y-y," she said, moving closer and leaning across the bar. "What can I do for you?"

Someone tried to flag her down from four seats away.

"Be right with you," she said without turning her head.

He pulled up the pic and showed her the screen.

She stared at it for a long moment like she was trying to look beyond the heavy makeup. Her barback walked up and glanced at the screen as he made his way to restock ice, but Blaize was more focused on gauging the bartender's reaction.

"I'm sorry," she finally said. She threw her hands into the air. "I got nothing."

And then she was gone.

Blaize had lost visual on Carys. Panic nailed him as fast as a sucker punch. He pushed off the bar to standing and turned away.

"Excuse me, sir," came an unfamiliar voice.

THE ROOM WAS wall-to-wall people, all looking to have a good time. Carys was completely out of her element here. Having been overprotected as a child caused you to go one of two paths: hog wild or afraid of every new experience. She had fallen into the second category. That fear was probably the reason she couldn't shake the feeling someone had been inside her home. This was a good time to remind herself that fear was irrational. Having a healthy dose was good. It kept you alive. Too much and it paralyzed you. Stopped you from really living or embracing anything unfamiliar.

She'd been out of her father's home for more than six years now, but you didn't easily shake off the ideals that had been ingrained in you.

A slow exhale helped as she navigated her way through the growing crush of people toward the bar.

This side had a male bartender. She squeezed in between two ladies who had their backs to each other and caught his attention. Her phone was already in hand, so she went for it.

"Do you know this person?" she asked.

He barely glanced at the screen. "Nope. What can I get for you?"

"Are you sure about that?"

"A little busy here," he said. "Do you want a drink or not?"

She gave a small headshake and frowned, unable to shake the feeling of eyes on her from somewhere else in the room. Was she being paranoid?

The busy bartender stared at her for a long moment, issued a grunt, and said, "Hold up. Let me take a closer look."

Again, she held out the phone. He studied the pic this time.

"Still no," he said.

"Thank you for your time," she said.

"No problem. Have you been in here before?"

The question caught her off guard considering how rude he'd been a few moments ago.

"No," she said. "Why?"

"Never mind," he said. "I would have remembered you."

Was that a come-on? Because seriously? *Maybe try being less rude when someone first approaches.*

He was five foot ten, maybe eleven. He had sandy-blond hair and gray eyes with a slightly pointed nose—not bad looking by most standards. She was spoiled by Blaize. Now her standards were ridiculously high. Good looks alone didn't do the trick for her. There had to be substance underneath, holding it up. Worse yet, Blaize had that in spades. Again, he'd raised the standard so high that it would be next to impossible for anyone else to measure up to his looks, him as a person, and certainly the kiss they'd shared. A kiss her body craved to repeat.

Not an option, Carys.

"Thanks for checking out the pic," she said, turning to leave.

"If I'd said that I knew her, would you have stuck around a little longer?"

Gross.

The line didn't deserve a comeback.

When she turned all the way, she practically slammed into Blaize's chest.

"There you are, babe," he said before planting a bone-melting kiss onto her lips, imprinting on her, marking her as his. When he pulled back, he searched her gaze and said, "I was beginning to think I lost you."

A huff sound came from behind the bar.

Carys took Blaize's hand and walked out.

Once outside, he said, "I'm sorry about what I did in there. I thought it was the fastest way to stop him from pestering you." Was there a hint of possessiveness in his tone? Or was she hearing what she wanted to hear instead of what was there?

"Thank you," she said. "The bad part is that he had no idea who Stephanie was, so I didn't make any progress. How did you do?"

He didn't answer right away as they walked through the maze of people on the sidewalk beginning to line up for the bar scene. This was a popular street with several bars and taco joints running along it.

When they reached the Jeep, he turned toward her, glanced around, and said, "The barback asked me to come back closer to closing. Said he would be able to slip me a note."

Carys didn't like it. They could be walking into some kind of ambush.

Or was that old fear creeping in again?

Chapter Fourteen

"Do you want to take a walk or wait here?" They'd been sitting on the ride over, and Blaize wanted to stretch his sore legs.

"I'd like to move," Carys said.

He locked up the Jeep, and they headed east on Chord. Austin was the equivalent of an ant farm of students. They were everywhere, which kept the area safer since there was so much foot traffic. Unhoused folks stayed to themselves, not harassing anyone. It was an easy place to take a walk anytime night or day.

They must have walked, hand in hand, for an hour before stopping for a late-night snack. Blaize bit back a yawn.

"You didn't get much sleep last night," she said. "You must be exhausted."

"All I need is a power nap."

"We can head back to the Jeep after we eat these tacos. I can entertain myself and keep watch while you close your eyes." She checked the time on her phone. "We still have a couple of hours before closing."

He bit back another yawn. "That might not be a bad idea."

Booking a room north of Austin in Round Rock seemed like a bad idea now. He'd intended to keep them north so they could get out of traffic easily tomorrow morning. Being back in Maverick Pass these past days reminded him just how much he loved space. Not much could beat looking up at a Texas sky at night.

The expansiveness. The sheer number of stars that he never got to see when he lived in the city thanks to light pollution.

With Cormac gone, he also found a sense of peace at the ranch. Blaize hadn't been expecting to feel anything, especially not like he was right where he belonged. Raiden and Phoenix didn't think the same way. Could he propose a plan to buy them out? Would the bank even give him a loan on the place?

Or could he get his siblings to bet on him? Give them a share if they didn't force him to sell, then pay dividends once he got the place up and profitable? He tucked the idea away for later, hoping for no more unexpected twists in the meantime. Talk about surprises—Kit trying to force the sale had shocked the hell out of him. Had to be her pride talking or a misguided sense of loyalty to her grandsons. Every one of them would have to give up a career in order to move back to the ranch. Blaize's mind was made up. He could start his own business doing what he loved, making custom saddles. He hadn't talked to Phoenix, but according to Raiden their minds were made up, too. Would they listen to Kit?

It dawned on him that she'd called Raiden after learning about Lynn. It would be just like Kit to think of herself as an unfair burden.

Blaize wanted to do this for her. Kit was different from Lynn. Kit appreciated everything he did for her. She always had his best interest at heart. Lynn had become bitter. She'd been frustrated with how her life turned out, which he understood. He'd been a soft pillow for her to throw punches at. He was strong—physically, mentally, and emotionally. He could take it.

"Are you going to eat that?" Carys asked, staring at his untouched taco.

"Do you want it?"

"No. I could always order my own. I thought you were hungry, and you only ate one taco. I know you can eat more than that, so I'm wondering if you're too tired."

He picked up the taco and took a bite. "Torchy's or Velvet?"

"Velvet. Obviously for their chicken tikka tacos."

He laughed. The great Austin debate over the homegrown favorite, Torchy's, versus the Dallas-originated Velvet had a clear winner. They were in agreement, and it was clear that there was no contest in either of their minds.

"Agreed."

"This fried egg on top might be messy, but it's chef's kiss," she said with a smile.

After polishing off the last of his taco, he washed his hands and headed back to the Jeep. All he needed was twenty minutes of shut-eye to grab his second wind. With the activity on the street, he figured they could get away with sitting in the Jeep out in the open without causing any type of disturbance.

Once seated, he leaned his chair back. Carys followed suit, turning onto her left side, facing him, while she studied her cell.

Blaize closed his eyes. A minute later, he drifted off.

TAP. TAP. TAP.

Blaize sat bolt upright. His leg came up, jamming his thigh on the steering wheel. Carys gasped.

A cop stood at the driver's side window, face almost pressing against the glass as he peered inside the Jeep.

Slowly, Blaize lifted his hands and placed them on the wheel in the ten-and-two position so the officer could see them.

"Roll down your window, sir." The cop was squatty, with a ruddy complexion and a serious expression.

With careful movements, Blaize rolled down his manual-crank window.

"I didn't even see him come up," Carys whispered.

A bright light nearly blinded Blaize. He squinted. The officer ran a flashlight over the interior of the Jeep, no doubt checking for weapons or a reason to arrest them like open containers or visible drugs.

"How can I help you, Officer?"

The man's nameplate read *Officer Marcum*.

"You can start by telling me what you're doing here," Officer Marcum said. His gaze shifted to Carys.

"I'm sorry, sir. This is my fault," she said, taking the lead. She reached over to touch Blaize's arm. "My fiancé didn't get much sleep last night after me being in the hospital, so I asked him if we could stop off and rest before making the drive back to Dallas."

Blaize had no idea where any of this was coming from, but he wasn't about to argue.

Marcum's gaze shifted from Carys to him. "Are you aware that it's not advisable to sleep in a parking lot?"

"Yes, sir. I am now." He rubbed his eyes.

Carys patted her stomach. "We had a scare. I started spotting, and we thought…" Her chin quivered. "That maybe we were about to lose this little bean."

Damn. She was good at this.

"Sorry to hear that, ma'am." Marcum's intensity scaled down a few notches.

"Is there a convenient place to grab coffee for my fiancé nearby before we head out?" she asked. She played the role to perfection. Blaize needed to ask if she had any acting in her background.

"Convenience store is on the corner," he said. "Go straight this way."

"Will do. Thanks."

Officer Marcum turned to Blaize. "License and insurance, please. Before you head out."

"My insurance is on my phone. Hold on." He grabbed his cell and then located the card before showing the officer the screen. When Marcum nodded, Blaize fished out his wallet and then produced his license.

The cop took it and examined it. He excused himself and walked back to his vehicle. He was punching in the information on a laptop that looked like it was attached to the dashboard on a moveable tray. He must have been satisfied with what he found because he strolled over and handed the ID back. "Y'all be safe on the road."

"Will do." Carys beamed. "Thank you, Officer."

Marcum gave a small salute before disappearing around the back of the Jeep and back to his own vehicle. Blaize turned on the engine after rolling up his window.

"What should we do?" she asked.

"Circle the block a few times. Park farther from the bar. He was probably expecting one or both of us to be drunk and unable to drive." He navigated out of the parking lot and onto the road, moving in the direction of the convenience store the officer had mentioned to make it look good. The cop sat in his vehicle, typing away on the laptop as they drove off.

Avoiding a second encounter with the same officer would be ideal. There were enough people around they should be able to blend in.

"You don't think we're being set up, do you?" Carys asked as he turned right at the end of the street. "By the barback?"

"We should come up with a plan, just in case."

"You're right," she said.

"How long was I asleep?" He glanced at the time, muttered a curse. Too long. They only had twenty minutes until the meetup. "We'll have to figure out a parking spot fast and a plan even faster." Parking was a joke in downtown Austin. Try parking illegally and you could end up towed. Not having transportation would be complicated, especially if this was a setup.

"Tell me again what happened," she said. After the cop encounter, he realized how good she was at thinking under pressure. "We can start there."

"A young guy, early twenties, walked past while I was showing Stephanie's picture to the female bartender. I noticed him because he seemed interested. He came around the bar and caught my arm when I walked toward your side. Said he couldn't talk right now but that I should meet him closer to closing time."

"I don't like this," she said.

"He wants me to meet. He's not a big guy. If it's just him, I'm not worried."

"If he has information about Stephanie, why ask you to come back? Why not tell you what he knows right then?"

"Those are good questions," he said, banking a left. "I don't have answers. All I have is someone who wants to tell me something about the person in the picture. With two of us, we can figure out a failsafe if the guy is up to something."

"This whole meetup makes me nervous." Carys twisted her

fingers together in her lap. "There are too many what-ifs and no proof this person has useful information."

"At least we know there are a lot of cops around if this thing goes south."

Carys shook her head. "Maybe this isn't such a good idea."

"It's all we have."

"We still have one bar left," she said.

"Which isn't as good of a lead."

"We don't know that," she said. "All we know for certain is that someone asked to meet after work. How far away from the picture was he?"

"A foot behind the bartender." If that much.

"And you said he walked past. As in, he kept going."

"That's correct."

"Which means he barely got a glance at the picture," she said.

"I wouldn't say that." Blaize had a good feeling about the guy. "What reason could he have for speaking up? Why not just let me walk out the door? The bartender didn't know anything. Why raise suspicion?"

"THAT'S A GOOD POINT." *Breathe.* They might've been getting close to a breakthrough. "I'm freaking out over your safety." And the general feeling of not being able to control the situation. Turned out being overly protected as a kid could cause you to need to control everything.

"I'll be careful." Blaize's reassurance sent a wave of calm washing over her and through her. "Believe it or not, I'm pretty good at keeping myself alive. There've been plenty of times that I've been out on the land, staring down wild hogs capable of killing me on the spot and had to come up with an escape plan. I've faced down poachers and survived. I'll take any and every threat seriously, but I didn't get that kind of vibe from this guy. He looked concerned and maybe a little scared to speak to me. Does any of this help ease your concerns?"

He pulled into a newly available street-side parking spot. That was lucky.

"It does," she said before reaching out to touch his arm. The contact was electric, as she was beginning to expect whenever they touched. It was also tender enough to cause her breath to catch in her throat and her stomach to freefall like she'd just base jumped. "A surprising amount actually."

"Good." He leaned over. "Because I'll be careful and you'll be watching my back. We have no reason to believe the barback saw us together in that crowd."

It had been shoulder-to-shoulder in the room.

"Why do you think he might be scared?" she asked. "If you had to guess."

"Could be for a lot of reasons." If he leaned any closer, they would be within kissing range. "Like he knows why she ended up in a fiery car crash."

"As far as we know, it was a lone vehicle accident." She hadn't considered this could be a murder investigation. So far, she assumed Stephanie was hiding both herself and her child from a potentially abusive relationship.

Would the father of her child have murdered her?

"Without a murder investigation, the sheriff won't look into her text messages," she said after taking a moment to think. A thought struck. "I've been going back and forth on whether she's alive or gone but that might be wishful thinking for Rue's sake. Do you think there's a possibility Stephanie Cross is alive?"

"No," Blaize said. "Although I learned a long time ago to never say *never*."

Carys let the thought sit before trying to unpack it.

All they had right now was very little information and a whole mess of speculation. Going down a trail of what-ifs with this little to go on could be counterproductive and end up getting them lost.

They needed to stick to what they knew was fact, despite how much her brain wanted to fill in the holes. She also needed to tread lightly on this case and not leave a digital or paperwork trail that could come back to bite her in the backside.

Besides, there were too many questions in this case.

With this barback, they might get answers.

Chapter Fifteen

Blaize sat on a step two doors down from the bar in the back alley. The barback would have to empty the trash as part of his closing duties. This spot would give Blaize an advantage. He could clearly see the door from this vantage point. From farther down the alley, Carys could keep watch over him. She had a tire iron from his Jeep to use as a weapon or, better yet, figure out how to give to him if something went south.

The door opened. He tried not to move a muscle or breathe. The barback stepped outside with a full trash bag, as anticipated. He kicked a bucket over to stop the door from closing. It must've locked automatically.

Blaize scanned the area in search of any suspicious movement. The barback hadn't explicitly asked Blaize to meet outside. In fact, he probably expected a visit in the bar before closing like he'd requested. A thin crowd meant the possibility of eyes on them, exposing the barback for possible retribution. The guy came across like he was sticking his neck out. Blaize wanted to honor it.

"Pssst," he hissed in an attempt to get the guy's attention without freaking him out.

"Hey, Thomas." The male bartender stepped outside and lit a smoke. "Why didn't you stock the glasses under the bar like

I told you to? Now it'll take even more time to close out, and I can't leave here until everything is stocked."

Thomas. Blaize had a first name to work with now.

Thomas's gaze flicked over toward the spot where Blaize was sitting. Did the guy just give them away?

"We were slammed all night," Thomas said, pushing back. "Last I checked, I only have two hands and you kept me hopping all night. Or don't you remember?"

Thomas was skinny and in need of a haircut. He had blond hair and light eyes, looked to be a freshman in college or maybe a sophomore at most.

"Excuses," the bartender said, leaning his back against the bricks. He brought his foot up, sole flat against the wall. "Just because you're Angel's nephew doesn't mean you can't get fired."

"Go ahead, then," Thomas said, unfazed. "Tell my uncle that I'm doing a bad job and you want me gone. See how that works out for you while you're out here smoking instead of pitching in. You know, we'll lock up a hell of a lot faster if you put out that cigarette and get back to work."

The bartender flinched like he was about to throw a punch.

"Go ahead and do it," Thomas teased. "Or get out of my way so I can toss the trash into the dumpster, dude."

Blaize liked the kid's spunk. He took note of the fact that the guy's uncle was important to the bar. Manager? Owner?

A squad car turned down the alley.

If the same cop from a little while ago was behind the wheel, Blaize was busted. How much trouble could he get into for being caught lying to an officer? He needed to signal Carys to get out of there. She was positioned down the alley far enough to slip into the groups of folks walking around or standing in line at one of the nearby taco food trucks lining the street.

Could he slip away unseen? Join her?

A quick glance revealed her coming toward him with her back against the wall. *No, no, no.*

From the corner of his eye, he caught the bartender dropping the cigarette butt before crushing it underneath his shoe. He slipped inside and, like the jerk he was proving to be, tapped the bucket away, causing the door to close and lock.

"What are you doing?" he whispered to Carys as she approached. "You had a chance to escape." There was a slim possibility the officer—if it was him—wouldn't have recognized Blaize without her. With her, it was almost a given.

Instead of responding, she fisted his shirt and tugged him up to standing. Then she pressed up to her tiptoes, turned them so that her back was against the wall, and pulled him toward her until their mouths fused.

The cop car crept down the alley, coming toward them, but for a split second, Blaize lost all sense of time and place. The second her lips met his, fireworks exploded in his chest, the world tilted on its axis, and he felt like he was right where he was supposed to be.

With great effort, Blaize forced his attention back to the alley and out of the blissful fog of need.

He heard Thomas swearing along with the sounds of the oversized trash bag being forced into an already-full dumpster.

Next came the hum of the vehicle's engine. It stopped. A window rolled down.

"You can't stay here. Move on." The officer's unfamiliar voice caused Blaize to exhale.

"Sorry," he said, moving to take Carys by the hand and heading toward Thomas without making eye contact.

The squad car sat idle. The officer was likely assessing whether he believed they were sober. They must have passed because the engine hummed and rocks crunched underneath the tires.

Thomas cursed as he tried the door.

"Hey," Blaize said as they approached, hand in hand.

Thomas whirled around, his hands fisted. Right. He probably couldn't make out the sound of Blaize's voice over the loud noises in the bar earlier where voices fought to be heard over the music.

"It's me," Blaize said.

Thomas sighed relief. "You scared the sh—" His gaze bounced

from Blaize to Carys and back. "Anyway, I wasn't sure if you would show."

"I'm here. What did you want to tell me?"

The kid looked around, eyes wild, like he half expected someone to jump out from behind a dumpster. "I could get into a lot of trouble for this." He caught Blaize's gaze. "Like, serious trouble."

"I appreciate you trusting me, Thomas. But you haven't said anything yet. Do you want to see the pic again?"

"No," Thomas said, looking taken aback with the fact Blaize said his name. "I never liked how my uncle treated her, you know?"

"Sure." Blaize had no idea.

Thomas hesitated.

"Before long, another cop is going to drive down the alley or someone is going to open that door to see what's taking you so long to close up," Blaize said. "You'll save us all a lot of angst if you'll spit it out." All kinds of scenarios came to mind, none he liked. Blaize needed to hear the truth before his imagination got the best of him.

"She worked here about a year ago," Thomas said. "Nice lady. I overheard her arguing with my uncle."

He glanced around like the man might jump out and say, *Boo!* He sucked in a breath before continuing. "Two days later, she disappeared, and I haven't seen her since."

"Did you hear what they were saying?" Carys jumped in.

"No, but my uncle isn't exactly… He runs this place on the up and up, but this isn't his only business. People come in and out of here. And it's not good."

"Got it," Blaize said. The timing of her going missing matched with her pregnancy. Was Angel the baby's father?

"What's her name? The woman in the picture?" Carys asked.

"Sharon Clark," Thomas said. "Her roommate got her the job. I sneaked into my uncle's office after you left." He pulled a slip of paper out of his apron pocket and handed it to Blaize. "It's their address. Or, at least, it was. Haley quit about a month after Sharon."

A random person shouted, and the sound echoed. It was

enough to spook Thomas. "I've gotta go. I just hope you find her and that she's okay."

"Why are you helping us?" Carys asked.

"Because she was nice to me and doesn't deserve to have anything bad happen to her," Thomas said. He took off running around the line of buildings. "Keep me out of it."

The back door to the bar creaked before it opened. The noise gave them enough time to dive behind the dumpster and out of view.

"Thomas. Where the hell did you go?" The bartender's voice was familiar. He cursed and then shut the door. The lock clicked.

Blaize tucked the paper into his front jeans pocket, reached for Carys's hand, and then sprinted in the opposite direction of Thomas.

CARYS'S THIGHS BURNED and her side cramped. Blaize was a faster runner. She strained to keep up as he practically dragged her along, urging her to keep pace with every forward step.

They came to a hard stop at the Jeep. She bent forward, clutched her side, and gasped for air.

"Are you okay?" he asked, moving beside her and placing his hand on the small of her back.

"I will be," she managed to say through breaths. Standing up straight, she motioned toward his pocket.

He nodded before pulling the piece of paper out of his pocket. Why wasn't he breathing hard? To say the man was in good shape was a lot like saying butter melted on warm toast.

"Here's the address." He showed it to her.

Carys pulled out her phone and mapped the location. "MLK Boulevard. I know the area."

"I do, too," he said.

"We should get some rest," he said. "Investigating the house now will cast suspicion that we can't afford."

"The cop ran your license." That was tricky. "We'll have to be even more careful moving forward now that there's a record of us being here."

"That was bad luck."

A shower and sleep sounded like heaven right now. Carys checked the location of the hotel. "We're not far."

Blaize walked her to the passenger side and then opened the door. "For what it's worth, you're the bravest person I know."

She highly doubted that. Didn't the man have a mirror? Talk about bravery. She couldn't imagine holding your loved one's hand as they slowly slipped away from you. "You're pretty amazing yourself."

"I wasn't fishing for a compliment." He hesitated. "I get the sense you're uncomfortable with being told how great you are. And how beautiful you are."

She really blushed now.

"As long as you're around me, I hope you'll get used to hearing it."

Blaize wasn't making it any easier *not* to fall for him. He needed to stop before she asked for another kiss—a kiss that was forbidden. Not to mention they'd agreed kissing would be a bad idea.

"We should get going," she managed to say through a throat suddenly as dry as Texas soil in August. "I need a shower and a bed."

He hesitated, looked like he was about to say something else, then closed her door and walked around the front of the Jeep wearing the sexiest smirk. He shook his head before claiming the driver's seat and didn't say a word to her on the way to the hotel or when they checked in.

The standard room had one bed—king size, a desk, and a comfy-looking chair with a reading lamp positioned behind it. The bed looked more like a cloud and was plenty large enough for the two of them to sleep without touching each other. Blaize could take up two-thirds, and there would still be plenty of room left for her.

"You take the shower first," he said.

"Are you sure?"

"Go ahead. Take your time."

Carys carried her overnight bag into the bathroom. The bag made her think of home. The feeling someone had been inside her house returned as she set it down on the counter, stripped, and then eased into the shower.

What was up with the feeling and why did she feel off?

Carys almost laughed out loud. The answer came quickly. Everything. Rue turned her life upside down in a heartbeat.

No regrets.

She'd made a promise to herself a long time ago when she first moved away from her father and to college. Whatever mistakes she made from then on belonged to her and no one else. She would no longer have her father to blame if life wasn't going the way she'd hoped it would. She would no longer have a failsafe to offer a soft landing. And she would no longer have an excuse to be unhappy.

From then on, she'd decided, her mistakes were just going to be part of the tapestry of her life. More importantly, they would be *hers*. And she was okay with that.

Which meant no regrets.

Did the same apply about Blaize? Or could she ask him for a kiss tonight after all?

Chapter Sixteen

Blaize didn't need the naked image of Carys in the shower with beads of water rolling down her silky skin stamped in his thoughts. It had been a long day. They needed rest. That was probably the reason his emotions took the wheel, defied logic, and refused to stop thinking about her.

The best way to stop thinking about someone was with a good workout. His muscles were stiff from all the sitting on the drive to Austin. Then there'd been driving around Austin. They'd walked a little and run a bit—not nearly enough movement to fulfill his body's needs.

The water cut off. He shouldered his backpack.

When the bathroom door opened and Carys walked out, he realized how unprepared he was to see her in pajama shorts and a soft cotton T-shirt. The thin material hinted at revealing her full breasts.

Blood flew south as he stood up, walked past, and then exhaled when he closed the bathroom door behind him. A workout could wait. A shower could ease some of the muscle tension. It wasn't taking all his considerable willpower to force his body not to act on its own accord.

Would she welcome his touch? His kiss?

Rather than fall down that rabbit hole, he took a cold shower and threw on a pair of pajama pants. Normally, he wore boxers to bed. He'd packed the lounge pants for her sake.

Blaize cut off the light as he opened the door and realized he was in complete darkness. It was fine. He'd memorized the layout and could navigate getting to bed all right without tripping over anything as long as he kept one hand on the wall.

His phone sat on the desk. He made his way over without bumping a shin—a miracle. Carys's soft, steady breathing said she was already asleep. She probably conked out the second her head hit the pillow.

After dimming his screen, he slipped underneath the covers. The temptation to pull her into his arms was a physical ache.

He closed his eyes and refocused. Tires. Those were the least sexy things he could think about. He needed to get new tires on his Jeep in the near future.

As though sensing his mental battle, Carys rolled over and settled into the crook of his arm. She slung her leg over his. He was thankful for the thin layers of material preventing skin from touching bare skin. That would be his undoing.

Eventually, he drifted off.

THE SUN PEEKED through the small slit in the curtains Blaize had kept open. Blackout curtains threw him off too much. He didn't know when to open his eyes if they were closed all the way. It was disorienting. He needed the sun as much as he needed the expansive Texas sky.

Carys's warm limbs entwined with his. Her hair splayed across the pillow. She smelled like a field of wildflowers.

Caffeine. Blaize needed to untangle himself or risk waking her, and he sure as hell couldn't stay there while his fingers burned to touch every curve of that beautiful body.

With effort, he managed to slide away and out from underneath the covers. A glance at his phone said it was half past nine in the morning. He couldn't remember the last time he'd slept this late no matter what time he went to bed.

The sun was bright. He moved quietly through the room, made coffee, and washed up. After a cup, he could figure out what to do about food. There was probably a power bar in his backpack tucked in the front pocket. He usually kept that or a small bag of trail mix for easy access to keep from starving.

After sitting down to nurse his coffee, he checked the address again. He looked it up using the map feature on his phone. The house was listed on a popular real estate site five years ago. The pictures were still up. The two-bedroom light yellow house had a one-vehicle carport and black metal bars on the windows. Electric cables ran on the street out front. The yard was small, not giving much separation from the busy street. A small tree blocked much of the house from view.

Inside, the front door led straight into the living room. The kitchen was eat-in. Both bedrooms were in the back of the house. The place was surrounded by low trees that could offer some coverage as they approached.

If the occupants had a dog, they would be busted walking up. Could he and Carys come up with a reason for being there? Knock on the front door? Put on some type of maintenance jumper?

Where would they get one? It wasn't like they sold uniforms at the local big-box store.

Then again, he wouldn't know. It wasn't like he spent a lot of time in those places. He got in and out as fast as possible on the occasion he needed to go inside one.

Back to the phone screen, he studied the layout of the home. He "walked" the neighborhood as best as he could to get the lay of the land. Once on the ground, they needed to appear they knew what they were doing or risk drawing attention. Could they walk down the street holding hands? Pretend to be a couple like they had last night? The move was starting to feel a little too natural with Carys, like they had a rhythm and had been together in another lifetime. Or something like that.

Hell, he didn't normally go full-on romantic. She had a way of bringing out a different side to him. Or maybe he was just trying to rationalize an attraction that was never meant to be understood.

It had been so long since he'd been on a date, would he even know what one looked like now? Not to mention the fact Carys was almost ten years younger than him. Were they too far apart in age? Did they want different things at this point in their lives?

Funny. He didn't want anything except to save the ranch and keep Kit where she belonged. Forty-eight hours made a helluva difference in life. With Lynn, he was reminded that life could change on a dime. With Carys, he saw that as a good thing.

"What time is it?" Carys asked, sitting up and gently rubbing her eyes.

He glanced at the clock. "Ten fifteen."

"I overslept," she said, pushing the covers off and throwing long legs over the side. He couldn't help but remember how good it felt when she'd entwined them with his.

"No, it's fine."

"Are you sure? You must be starving by now," she said as she stretched. He forced his gaze away from the way the cotton pressed against her breasts.

"I'm good. I haven't been awake for very long. This is my first cup of coffee, and I'm about to make my second. Would you like one, or do you need food first?"

"What do you think about ordering room service?"

"We might be too late for breakfast."

"A hamburger and fries sound amazing to me right now," she said, a sleepy smile tugging at the corners of her mouth. Damned if the knot didn't tighten in his chest.

He picked up the menu. "Consider it done."

"What can I do to help?"

"Let me spoil you for a change," he said, and he meant every word. "I like doing things for you that make your life easier."

Was it a mistake to admit that to her?

CARYS SMILED ON her way to the bathroom. "I'm not going to tell you no."

As she brushed her teeth, she heard Blaize on the phone ordering from the lunch menu. Her systems were turned upside down. Her body didn't know day from night at this point. It wanted protein. Besides, she didn't know when she'd get a chance to eat again. Her schedule was all over the place until this case resolved.

Speaking of days of the week, she thought for a moment and realized it was already Sunday. How could she go into the office on Monday if she still had Rue in her custody? *That's tomorrow-Carys's problem.* Besides, she had plenty to focus on today.

Practically, they could investigate the house and get back to the ranch by dinner. They had a new name to work with—Sharon Clark.

She thought about the name Stephanie Cross…a potential fake name. *Were you hiding from this Angel person? What was he to you? An ex-boyfriend?*

Thomas didn't explain what he meant about not liking how his uncle treated her. And now they knew she used to work at the bar. This was like being expected to put together a five-hundred-piece puzzle with a couple of pieces and none of the rest.

These things take time.

Did she have any?

Carys dressed in yoga pants, a sports bra, and a tank top. She pulled her hair off her face into a ponytail. Push come to shove, she could pass for someone being out on a jog. Being a college town, Austin was a lively place, especially the downtown area. Joggers could be seen throughout the day, seven days a week. She should fit right in.

A knock on the door told her she'd been in the bathroom way longer than expected or that room service in this hotel was speedy.

She waited until Blaize answered, then came out of the bathroom once the server was gone since the doors would clash otherwise.

"Food's here," Blaize said in that oh-so-sexy deep timbre of his. That man could read the contents of a cereal box and make women want to start peeling off their clothes.

She laughed.

"What's that about?" He studied her, perplexed.

No way was she sharing that little tidbit.

"Nothing," she said. "This food smells amazing."

"You're probably starving, which helps." He finished setting up the makeshift table and chairs. He directed her to sit in the office-like chair while he took the bed.

She picked up the metal lid and was hit with a waft of awesomeness. "Yes to all of this."

He chuckled. "Do you always go full force at life?"

She had a bite of food in her mouth that she almost spit out from laughing. Once she chewed and swallowed, she said, "Since I moved out. I was kept locked up basically my entire childhood. Once I adjusted to college life, I decided to just run at life full-steam-ahead style. I own my mistakes and do my best to learn from them."

"It's a good philosophy," he said.

"I'm so much happier now. Even when I screw up, and believe me, I have royally done so. Knowing my missteps are my own has its own healing energy attached. Being under someone's thumb is the worst kind of existence."

"I can partially relate. It's no life."

"That's why I feel so sorry for Stephanie or Sharon, whatever her name is." She took a sip of the coffee he'd fixed for her. "This happened to me when I was young. Plus, it was my father. He may have broken our relationship, but he does love me. Or did. I haven't talked to him in too long to know where he stands now. It was misguided love—don't get me wrong. It was action born out of loss and sadness and fear. But I never once doubted that he loved me."

Blaize listened. Truly listened. He didn't try to fix things, like guys she'd dated. And because of that, she felt seen.

"Would you ever want to reach out to see if anything has changed between the two of you?" he asked. "No pressure. I'm just curious."

"I've thought about it. A lot of time has passed. More than six years." She took a bite of hamburger and chewed. "I'm not ready yet to handle the disappointment if he didn't change. The last thing I want is to reopen an old wound just to throw salt in it. You know? Does that make sense?"

"Sure, it does. You would want to have a relationship if he has changed and grown over the years, but sometimes not knowing is better than suffering more disappointment."

"That's it exactly. What if he remarried and has another

family? What if he rejects me and doesn't have a new family? What if he just doesn't care what happens to me?"

Blaize nodded.

They settled into eating and polishing off his second and her first cup of coffee.

"What will your work do when they find out you didn't take Rue to the orphanage?" he asked as he stacked plates on the rollaway tray.

"That depends."

"On what?"

"What happens between now and Monday morning."

"Then let's make sure you don't lose your job over helping an innocent baby," he said with the kind of finality that made her believe him. "I'll just be a minute while I get dressed."

"I'll scoot the cart into the hallway now that we're finished."

He reached for her hand, stopped her from moving the cart. "Might be safer to leave it inside while we get ready. The less we open and close doors, the better."

"Do you think someone followed us?"

"I'd rather not find out the hard way. I didn't tell Thomas my name, and I paid with cash at the first bar on purpose. Still. Taking a chance doesn't seem like the right play here."

He was right. Of course he was. For a moment, she felt imprisoned again. Beyond her father's tight grip, she'd endured everything from being locked in closets by babysitters to being threatened within an inch of her life if she "ratted" out the ones having sex on her father's bed or drinking to the point of passing out while he had to be away on business.

From a young age, Carys understood the fact that her father's job kept food on the table. He worked long hours balancing the finances so he could pay his workers while keeping a roof over her head. She caught glimpses of him looking run down—and an emotion that looked a whole lot like guilt—but he always put up a strong front when she was in the room. Telling him about the babysitters would have only added to his stress. Besides, she'd learned to keep emergency supplies in the form of a flashlight, book, and a chocolate bar in a couple of the closets just to be safe and stave off boredom.

As much as she shouldn't care about anyone else rubber-stamping her life decisions, her relationship with her father was tricky. The urge to make him proud constantly warred with her need to prove her independence, causing a ton of friction in her high school years.

Families and relationships were complicated. No one knew that better than Blaize.

Shake it off.

Mentally, she had to readjust. This was not the past. She was free to go wherever she wanted to go and do whatever she wanted to do. Her father still lived near Austin as far as she knew.

Carys, of all people, knew what it was like to be trapped by someone hell-bent on controlling her and being surrounded by people who carried out that person's bidding.

Is this how you felt, Sharon?

Chapter Seventeen

A simple spit test was all it would take to prove Blaize wasn't Rue's father. So why couldn't he bring himself to stop by a pharmacy and pick up a test? It was more than Rue's safety he was concerned about.

Taking the test meant closing the door on being the one legally allowed to raise her. Could he see himself as a single father? What about the ranch? Kit? Was there any way possible to fit all the pieces together and be a family?

And what about this Stephanie/Sharon person. His mind was all over the place. One part said she died in the crash and they were awaiting confirmation. Another part said she went into hiding and faked her death. Yet another part wondered if she'd gone into Witness Protection. Or did she simply disappear once she learned about the crash?

Creating a fake identity was possible with computers.

What about Thomas? He seemed like a good person. Could he be trusted? He'd said his uncle was connected to Stephanie/Sharon. How? Why?

Too many questions. Not nearly enough answers.

Blaize should be used to life throwing him twists by this point. Unless he uncovered a hidden tackle box full of cash at the ranch, he wasn't sure how to save it. His brothers were united against him. Kit, of all people, had been the one to convince them to sell.

What was she thinking?

Maybe he should jump at the opportunity to rid himself of the responsibility of the ranch. He couldn't. Taking away Kit's home felt like the worst kind of wrong. He knew in his heart that she didn't want that to happen.

Could he make his brothers see it, too?

Cormac Wilde's death might have brought Blaize back to Maverick Pass, Texas, where Blaize had grown up, but raising a daughter might make him decide to stick around once the dust settled.

Damn that he'd lost touch with his brother and pushed Kit away. Guilt punched him again. If he'd done a better job of staying in touch, he might not have been blindsided by the state of the ranch.

Kit had dropped a bomb on him about his father. He needed to have a sit-down with her to find out what in Cormac's past could possibly excuse his behavior. *Complicated* didn't begin to describe Blaize's emotions since hearing of the man's passing. His brothers must've been in the same boat. They all had a difficult relationship with their father, if *difficult* was the right word.

Digging into Stephanie/Sharon's background could stir up big trouble based on Thomas's reaction. It dawned on Blaize that the car attacker from the other night might have been related to her and not someone from Carys's past.

Speaking of Carys. Blaize hadn't felt an emotional pull this strong since…well…ever. The redheaded beauty challenged every belief he ever held about how deep an attraction could run and how impossible it could be to fight against it. This one was stronger than he dared admit to himself or anyone else. Seeing her hold the child stirred up a whole bunch of feelings that had been dormant. Becoming a father had been put in the *For Other People* category once Lynn closed the door to the possibility. After the terminal diagnosis, any thoughts of changing her mind had to be put on the backburner so he could care for Lynn. She'd been dead set against adoption, too. Said she couldn't see putting a child through her mood swings.

Blaize had had the same concern even though he hadn't owned up to it with her.

Now that being a parent might not just be possible but could be a safety net for a little girl, too, he needed to deal with feelings that had been shoved down so deep he wondered if they could be resurrected.

There was another consideration. If he didn't take the spit test, could Carys let him keep Rue and then walk away like he'd never argued against the idea of her being his biological child?

She might've been one to bend the rules when necessary but that was big.

He was getting ahead of himself. They needed to figure out who this Stephanie/Sharon person really was, and they had a solid lead.

Blaize finished getting dressed and packed up the few clothing and supplies he'd brought, tabling those thoughts for the time being.

"Are you ready to roll?" Blaize asked Carys.

She smiled and raised her eyebrows. "As ready as I'll ever be."

"Let's go," he said, taking the lead after shouldering his backpack.

Once safely in the Jeep, Carys asked, "Should we check on how things are going back home?"

She probably meant home as in Maverick Pass and not home as in the ranch. He still liked hearing how the word rolled off her tongue so easily and how natural it sounded in conversation.

"I texted earlier, but a phone call would be good." He motioned toward his phone, which he'd placed inside the cupholder. "Do you mind? They won't pick up if you call. Kit is trained not to answer calls from strangers." He chuckled. "It goes against her nature."

"Sounds like Kit." She picked up the phone. The screen came to life. "You don't password protect your cell?"

"No need. I live alone and I work alone." Why did that make him sound so lonely all of a sudden?

Speaking of lonely, he remembered one of the people he'd spent time talking to at Deep Roots Bar. Sierra Jones. She'd walked up to the stool beside him and asked to sit. The fact that she was alone and not with girlfriends didn't raise any big red flags. Deep Roots was the kind of place where folks showed up when they didn't want to be alone and didn't necessarily have to talk to anyone. It was dimly lit inside, a place where conversations were more like a quiet hum.

The first night Sierra had walked up beside him, he barely noticed her. Would she be considered beautiful by most standards? She was tall with long legs. Her long straight dark hair fell between her shoulder blades. She always wore a skirt that hugged her hips and highlighted one of her best features, her legs. She had almond-shaped, catlike green eyes accented with black eyeliner. She smelled of expensive perfume and carried a handbag that he was sure was designer. Yet she had a salt-of-the-earth quality that made her easy to talk to. Or maybe it was the whiskey. Hell, he didn't know.

"No answer," Carys said.

"We'll try again in a few minutes."

"Do you think everything is all right?" she asked.

"I hope so. We'll give it a minute."

Carys set the phone down and stared out the window, looking lost in her own thoughts. As for his, they drifted back to Sierra. She'd been the one to strike up a conversation first. Blaize swore to himself that he wouldn't fall in love again or consider the "marriage and kids" bit. Neither talked about the past. They were two strangers in a bar who slowly started to open up to each other. Or so he thought. Weeks went by and he started looking forward to Tuesday nights at Deep Roots, to seeing Sierra.

He should have looked for the signs, but his guard was down.

Sierra asked him to go to her place for a nightcap. He'd declined.

She didn't show for two weeks. He had no way to reach her to say he hadn't meant to hurt her feelings. She didn't know about Lynn. He talked about work and the fact that he'd been married. That was it. He couldn't bring himself to discuss Lynn's illness or any of the details of their life together. Sierra assumed divorce, and he didn't correct her.

She talked to him about the difficulties of raising her kids essentially alone, a boy and a girl. The twins were nine years old. She talked about carpools and sports, summer camps. She went on about how difficult it was to manage everyone's schedule, including her own. A couple of months passed. They started meeting up twice a week.

This was the early days after Lynn had passed. Sierra said she wasn't looking for a relationship, which worked out great because he didn't have anything left of himself to give.

Then it was three times.

Not exchanging phone numbers should have been his first red flag. He'd be so lost in his own grief that his guard was down. Then he realized he'd slipped up and developed feelings for Sierra.

He convinced himself they weren't strong. Told himself this was a phase and it would pass. The invitation stood, she'd said, to go back to her place any time. He took that as a sign she was developing feelings for him, too.

Blaize didn't do casual sex, not even when he was swimming in grief.

Then he broke their unspoken agreement one night after one too many whiskeys. He opened a vein and said he'd developed feelings for her that were more than bar meetups. Once again, she suggested a hookup.

His thinking wasn't clear. Grief mixed with whiskey didn't do good things to a person's brain or judgment. So, he'd laid his cards out on the table and said he wanted to take her on a dinner date and then another after that. He wanted to see if they had anything in common besides bar stools.

The minute he mentioned that he might be open to a relationship if things went well, Sierra dropped a bombshell on him: She was still married and wouldn't dream of leaving her husband, who traveled a lot, leaving her lonely and with nothing to do to fill the time.

She'd told him that she had an arrangement with her husband

that allowed them both "extracurricular" activities but that she would never risk a divorce.

Blaize had been angry at himself more than anything else for falling into the trap of developing real feelings. Plus, he no longer trusted his judgment if he could so easily be lied to.

He'd bought the lies and never once questioned why she kept insisting on a hookup rather than trying to build something real. Guess he wasn't great at catching red flags while he was drowning in grief.

Was anyone?

"Did you notice the SUV with blacked-out windows following us?" The concern in Carys's voice shocked him back to the present.

He'd been distracted with memories and could have gotten them killed.

Dammit.

A memory came back in a flash. It was hazy. There'd been someone who took the barstool next to him at Deep Root after Sierra left the night of his confession. A blonde. Medium height and build. His memory might be foggy, but she looked familiar.

Could the person have been Stephanie/Sharon?

BLAIZE CHECKED HIS mirrors and frowned. "How long has the SUV been trailing us?"

"Long enough for me to notice, so more than a couple of blocks at this point," Carys said. He'd gone somewhere dark in his mind. She'd seen the wrinkle in his forehead and the way his jaw ticked whenever he was deep in thought.

"I need to get us away from traffic," he said. "If we slow down anymore, they'll be able to get out of their vehicle and walk to us."

Carys had been uncomfortable ever since the phone call that had rolled into voicemail. Maybe a better word was *unsettled.* Something felt off. It was possible Kit was taking a nap along with the baby. Raiden wouldn't answer her phone for her, so it wasn't exactly time to hit the panic button. Still. She was uneasy.

Would Raiden call if something had happened? He should. There was no reason to keep Blaize in the dark.

Her mind had been drifting all over the place until the SUV. Now she studied the sideview mirror, waiting to see if the driver or a passenger made a move. With the sun's glare and the window tint—tint that should've been illegal if it wasn't already—it was impossible to see if there was anyone else in the vehicle other than the driver. The only reason she knew someone sat in the driver's seat was because it made logical sense.

Breathe.

"Slide down in your seat as much as possible in case..."

Carys did as instructed as she finished the sentence in her mind...*they shoot.*

He weaved in and out of traffic like a skilled race-car driver. She did her best not to panic about all the unknowns in this situation.

"Bear with me."

"Okay."

Blaize cut across two lanes of traffic and banked a right with so much speed she could swear they went up on two tires. At the very least, the tires squealed.

"Grab a phone, either one, and look up nearby police substations," he said. "We don't have a reason to call 911. Should that change, you'll have your phone in hand and ready to go."

Carys grabbed his since it was closest. She checked the map feature, half holding her breath as she searched for a substation. He was right, though—a criminal wouldn't likely follow them into the parking lot of a cop station. Officers could be on shift change or drifting in and out of the lot for other reasons.

"You're going to want to take a left at the next light," she said to him after risking a glance out the front windshield to verify.

"Hold on," he said.

Carys braced herself as he cut a hard, last-minute left turn. Her stomach churned, a mix of stress, speed, and being tossed around.

The seat belt locked, cutting into her chest.

"What else?" he asked.

She refocused on the screen. "Did I mention that I get seasick?" Trying to focus on the device made her stomach turn even more. She wished she had one of those motion-sickness patches she'd heard about.

"I'm sorry, Carys."

"I know," she said through measured breaths. "Maybe sitting up would help."

He nodded.

She pushed up enough to ease some of the queasiness. "Go straight through this light. We're a little more than two blocks away."

"Got it," he said, pressing the gas pedal more.

Carys glanced to her right in time to see the SUV coming but not enough to react before…

Crunch!

Chapter Eighteen

Life slowed, as though time warped and Blaize got caught in the wave.

The SUV caught him on the back right passenger side. His tires struggled to gain purchase as he spun out and then slammed into a parked car. He bit out a curse and grabbed hold of the wheel with both hands.

Fighting against momentum, he mashed the brake. His first instinct was to reach over to protect Carys, but he couldn't risk letting go of the wheel if he wanted to come out of this tailspin. If he'd been driving almost any other vehicle, it would have flipped.

Carys let out a yelp. Her hands flew to the dashboard to brace for impact. This particular model was meant for off-roading, so it had only four airbags in total, covering front-impact and seat-mounted side airbags. Despite the impact, they didn't deploy. He was thankful for small miracles and would take whatever good luck he could get. His tires seemed to be fine.

Fighting to stay in control, he finally got the Jeep to cooperate and stop spinning out. The SUV stopped. It was facing the opposite direction. He glimpsed reverse lights. Was the damn thing going to drive backward to slam into them again?

Biting back a curse, Blaize stomped on the gas pedal.

The light changed. Several vehicles turned, blocking the SUV from coming at him again.

"Are you okay?" he asked Carys, not risking taking his eyes off the road even for a second.

"I'm good." Her voice trembled. Was she in shock? Afraid?

"We'll get out of this in one piece." A trip to the police substation was a guarantee at this point. "Just a couple more blocks, right?"

"That's right," she confirmed.

"Can you grab a pic of the license plate?" he asked, figuring the law could track down the driver based on the vehicle's registration.

The drive took a few minutes. The stop cost them two hours of time. As they were being walked out, a law enforcement officer looked up from his computer screen. His nametag read: Sargeant Amber.

"We got a hit on the plate," he said, then frowned. "It was stolen from an elderly couple's vehicle while they were at the grocery. They didn't notice until one of our officers knocked on the door and asked about it." He made a sharp tic of disapproval. "Shame it didn't lead us anywhere."

"We appreciate the update, Sargeant," Blaize said. He shouldn't be surprised at the development. As much as he was convinced the person who'd attacked Carys's vehicle during the storm wasn't an experienced criminal, switching plates before chasing someone didn't take much brilliance. Or a criminal mind. The move fell into the "common sense" category. If you were going to chase someone and possibly ram your vehicle into them, you wouldn't want to advertise your home address via a license plate.

With that, he and Carys headed outside into the late-afternoon sun.

Going to the address Thomas had given them felt like stepping out of the frying pan and into the fire. Since the license was a no-lead, doing nothing meant making no progress.

"Stinks that we didn't make any progress on who is behind this," Carys said after buckling her seat.

"I know."

She rubbed the back of her neck and winced.

"Are you sure about not going to the ER to get checked out?" he asked, concerned she might still be in a mild state of shock, in which case any pain might not have kicked in yet.

"We don't have time."

"We can make time," he said.

"It wouldn't be worth the trip. I'll take ibuprofen after we eat dinner."

He opened his mouth to plead the case for going to the hospital and then clamped it shut. Panic seized him. The knot in the center of his chest tightened. He clenched his back teeth. All his systems went on high alert.

Memories of frequent hospital trips stamped his thoughts, playing out like a slideshow. Images of Lynn in wheelchair after wheelchair in various states of pain and anguish struck him like physical blows.

"I'm okay. I promise." Carys's reassurance did nothing to stem the emotional storm brewing.

After cutting on the engine, he forced an exhale and said, "Promise me one thing."

Her eyebrow shot up. "Let's hear it."

"You'll let me know if the pain worsens or you think for a second you might need to get looked at. Okay?" He couldn't count the times he'd had to respond to Lynn's screams of pain or found her flopped onto the floor because she waited too long to tell him about the pain. Thinking about it now brought on a flood of frustration and stress.

Understanding dawned. It was written on her face in the way her eyes and lips softened, and the muscles in her forehead relaxed.

She dropped her hand and reached across to touch his. "I feel a little stiff in the back of my neck from the jolt during impact. My head doesn't hurt. Just my neck. I fully believe it's temporary and will go away on its own. However, if my vision blurs or I get a headache, you'll be the first to know."

Those words brought his pulse down faster than the temperature dropping on a winter day.

"Thank you," he said to her, locking onto her gaze for a few seconds longer than was probably good for him. "You have no idea how much it means to me to hear you say that."

"Of course," she said. "And I hope you'll do the same. Tell me if anything feels off. Because I'm worried, too."

He hadn't expected that. He'd always been the "strong one" when it came to his relationship with Lynn. He'd been the one offering reassurances and sitting by her side during and after one of her episodes.

"Sounds like a fair deal to me," he said before breaking eye contact and backing out of the parking spot.

The ride to the MLK house was quiet. Not the awkward silence of strangers but two people who didn't need words between them. A lot could be said in the silence.

"I hate the fact that someone knows exactly who we are, and we have no clue about them," Carys said as he drove past the house.

"We're at a tactical disadvantage." The SUV driver had the element of surprise. They could walk right past the person on the street and not recognize them.

Considering how busy the sidewalks in Austin usually were, MLK was a ghost town. This fact wouldn't make it easy to go unnoticed. Circling the block too many times could draw unwanted attention, so he parked instead.

Blaize exhaled. "Are you ready for this?"

So far, Carys had been attacked twice while sitting inside two different vehicles. It almost felt safer to walk outside. "We'll see in a few minutes, won't we?"

Blaize exited the driver's seat and came around to open her door. "Have I told you lately how brave you are?"

Those words stirred up more of those butterflies.

"There's a fine line between bravery and…"

"You're on the right side of the line, believe me," he said.

"Well, then, I'd like to ask for another kiss before we—"

"Done." Blaize leaned in.

Carys closed her eyes and pressed a kiss against his lips. She grabbed fistfuls of his shirt when his tongue dipped inside her mouth. She could kiss this man all day.

He broke apart first and then rested his forehead against hers, as they both took a moment to catch their breath.

"That's a lot better," she said, wishing they could go back to the hotel and just be with each other even if it wouldn't last. For once, Carys wanted to throw caution to the wind and do the thing her body craved…and right now that was Blaize. Every cell in her body craved his touch.

She'd read something about near-death experiences heightening desire. Biology wanted you to procreate as quickly as possible with the next available partner.

Were her already intense feelings toward Blaize on steroids because of this effect? Or was it something simpler than that? Was it down to two souls who recognized each other? Who fit? Who didn't need overanalyzing to know they matched?

Could she trust it?

Could she compete with a ghost?

Shoving those thoughts aside, she reached for his hand. He immediately linked their fingers. Calm washed over her.

Without another word, they headed down the sidewalk and toward the house. She'd seen it online, walked these streets virtually, and done everything she could to prepare herself for what might happen—an ambush.

At least it was daylight and they were out in the open. While there might not have been many pedestrians, there were plenty of cars. That should help in the event of an emergency. She'd been trained to yell the word *fire* instead of *help*. Apparently people couldn't help themselves when it came to checking out a fire. They came to see if they were in danger or any of their property. Yelling *help* didn't have the same response.

She made a mental note to use the word that would draw the most attention in the event of an emergency.

"What do you say we walk past once, check our phones, and then double back like GPS misled us or was recalibrating?" he asked.

"Sounds like a good plan." Speaking of which, they didn't have one beyond getting here and checking out the house.

With every step, her pulse kicked up another notch. Her heart hammered her rib cage from the inside out. They passed the home with the yellow siding and the menacing metal bars on the front windows. No one was getting in or out that way. What were the inhabitants supposed to do if there actually was a fire?

They passed the house once, and then Blaize pulled out his cell. He stopped. Checked the screen. Looked at her with a raised eyebrow and a shrug. Then turned back and let go of her hand long enough to point to the yellow house.

His acting deserved an award.

"Nice job," she said low and under her breath. The crash had set them back on time. They'd lost hours they needed in order to find out who Stephanie/Sharon really was and who might be after her. To find Rue's father in order to determine if he was fit to take the baby. Or, better yet, locate a next of kin who was capable of loving and caring for Rue in the manner she deserved. That would be like hitting the genetic lottery.

If someone like that existed, would Stephanie/Sharon have made arrangements? Would someone have stepped forward by now? A trusted friend? The officer who'd brought Rue to Carys had said the babysitter hadn't mentioned any known family members or friends. She'd been sitting for Rue for a short time and didn't know Stephanie very well. When she'd asked for a second emergency contact, Stephanie had said she would get back to the babysitter and then never did.

Since the cop had nothing to go on, Carys had put all her hopes on the birth-certificate angle. This was the first time she'd run into a person named on a legal document who turned out not to be the actual parent. This territory was uncharted.

Plus, she'd bent rules before, but blatantly breaking them? She was about to trespass on some random person's property in an area that looked like she would have better luck scoring drugs than getting the information they needed. Monday loomed.

Breathe.

Blaize let go of her hand as they walked up the short, cracked concrete walkway to the pair of stairs leading to a block of concrete as a porch. He slipped away, going left. Before she could formulate words to ask what she should do, he disappeared around the corner.

Rather than just stand there, she cut right, half expecting loud, barking dogs to announce their presence. She welcomed the quiet as she searched for cameras in the eaves. If this place was some kind of drug den or human-trafficking site—her imagination was going wild at this point—wouldn't there be some type of security?

She rounded the corner on the carport side, half holding her breath. The parking space was empty. A bucket filled with cleaning supplies and a container of rags were stacked to one side. A couple of miscellaneous containers and boxes littered the back wall, some empty. Trash clung to one corner.

The place wasn't worse than many of the others she'd seen in her time at the agency. And it wasn't the best. She could tell a lot about a person by the way they kept their home. Messy was never automatically bad and meticulous wasn't always good. Hoarders always raised a red flag to her, especially when it was over the top. It signaled a mental condition that required further evaluation. Overly meticulous people who lived in wealthy neighborhoods abused their children at the same rates as folks with less financial means.

Out of the corner of her eye, she saw someone or something move in the house next door. When she turned to look, the curtain closed before she could tell who it was. A kid spying? A nosy neighbor?

She turned around the next corner, expecting to see Blaize. He was gone.

Chapter Nineteen

Blaize circled back to the front yard where he'd left Carys. She wasn't there.

Figuring she must have circled on the carport side, he cut across the small front lawn that was sprinkled with ankle-high weeds. The property had been neglected. Same on the inside of the home, based on what he could see through one of the bedroom windows. Clothes covered old brown carpet. Empty beer and soda cans littered most surfaces. A dresser drawer sat half opened. The others were in various stages of being closed. A shirt looked to have been haphazardly flung toward the piece of bedroom furniture, landing across two drawers.

With an opened, albeit empty, pizza box wedged onto the nightstand, Blaize could only imagine how the room smelled. Or the rest of the house, for that matter. Stale beer and urine came to mind. The occupants didn't have a dog, thankfully, but he'd seen a cat curled up on top of a messy bed. *Poor thing.*

As he circled around the home toward the carport, the next-door neighbor popped out of the front door. An average-height woman in her late twenties stepped outside wearing a jean jumper and her hair in a bandana.

"Hey," Carys whispered as she headed toward him.

The neighbor held the front door open. "Can you come here

for a minute?" She glanced around nervously. "I have something to tell you about that house."

All of his protective instincts flared.

"Would you go wait in the Jeep if I asked you to?" he said to Carys.

"Doesn't seem to be any safer in it than out here," she said.

"Good point." They had just been rammed in the side by an SUV, which had disappeared as fast as it came at them. "Then stick by my side. Okay?" He reached for her hand and linked their fingers.

"Like glue," she said. "I didn't see any security cameras over here. I haven't checked the neighbor's house."

"I was on the opposite side," he said out of the corner of his mouth as they took the first steps toward the stranger.

There was no doubt that he was stronger than the tiny young woman standing on the porch, waving them on. Add Carys to the equation, and the odds that were already nil went into negative numbers.

There were unknowns. Was Bandana alone? Or was someone hiding inside the house, just out of sight? Only half of her body was visible. Was she hiding some type of weapon where they couldn't see it until it was too late? Would a vehicle come roaring up? One like the SUV?

"Hurry," Bandana said, shifting her weight back and forth while looking all around them with wide eyes. That word caused more alarm bells. If they hurried, they wouldn't have time to accurately assess the risks. "It's not safe out here."

All hope she would say what was on her mind while standing outside just died. He squeezed Carys's hand for reassurance the moment she tensed. She clearly had been thinking along the same lines.

"Please," Bandana urged as they approached the porch.

He tucked Carys behind him as they entered the living room.

Bandana shut the door behind them and locked it. Not exactly ideal, but they stood close enough for him to attack while Carys undid the lock.

"She told me to look out for you," Bandana said, staring at

him. "Said if you came poking around, something bad happened to her." She brought her hand to cover her mouth as she stared.

The house was clean and cozy. More importantly, he could see straight through to the sliding glass door from his position next to the door.

"Who told you?" Carys asked before he could.

Bandana's face scrunched. "Sharon, of course."

"Had to make sure we were on the same page," she said. "I'm Carys, by the way." She was better with people than he was by a long shot.

"Rumi," she said in response.

"I'm—"

"I know who you are," Rumi said.

"Right. How?"

"Sharon gave me a message for you." She held up her index finger. "Hold on. I put it in here."

The hand-carved wooden box on the coffee table had an intricate morning-sun-over-the-mountains design.

Carys let go of his hand. "That's a beautiful box."

Rumi smiled up at Carys as she opened it. "My dad made this for me. He loved whittling. Said no one did it anymore."

Blaize resisted the urge to reach out and pull Carys back for her own safety. She was good at reading people. She knew what she was doing. She wouldn't take unnecessary risks.

So he unclenched his hands and tried not to crack a molar from biting down so hard as he let her work her magic.

"He died two years ago," Rumi said, frowning as she rooted through folded-up papers as well as the kind used to roll up a joint.

"I'm really sorry to hear that," Carys said, crouching down to eye level across the coffee table from Rumi. "Sounds like you miss him very much."

"I do," Rumi continued. "More than anyone could ever know. He was the best."

Blaize had the thought that at least someone had a decent dad. There was hope for humanity yet.

Carys was doing more than lowering Rumi's guard. She actually cared about people. It shined through in the way she interacted with them, in the questions she asked, and the way she responded. Beyond that, it came through in her mannerisms, the way she looked at you with a calm reassurance.

He experienced it every time he opened a vein and talked to her about something deeply private. Her compassion came through, making her easy to talk to. Was that the reason he'd opened up to her on such a personal level?

Rumi's eyes lit up. "Here it is. This is the note I was supposed to give you." She held it in the air. "Sharon told me that I wasn't supposed to do anything with this note except hide it unless you showed up. Is she okay?"

Blaize wasn't touching that question with a ten-foot pole. These two had obviously been close at one time.

"We're trying to figure that out right now," Carys said, not lying and not giving anything away, either. Sharon's identity had yet to be confirmed. Technically, Carys wasn't being deceptive. Plus, they needed to get out of there. The Jeep was parked down the street. If anyone next door had anything to do with the SUV, that might be a problem.

"Can I ask how well you know your neighbor?" Carys motioned next door as Rumi handed the note over.

"Not well," Rumi said. Her frown lines deepened. "It wasn't a good place for Sharon, but she didn't go into details."

"Was there physical or mental abuse or something else like she was being trafficked?" Carys asked.

Rumi shook her head. "A bad relationship." She sat back on her heels. "You know how it goes. You meet someone you think is great, move in, and then find out how truly awful they are."

"Angel?"

"Yes, I think that's his name. I didn't see him all that much, to be honest. He works, like, two jobs and left her alone a lot. Sharon wasn't allowed to go out. He had a tracker on her phone and would call to check on her at random times so she couldn't go to the bathroom without having it on her." Her gaze bounced from Carys to Blaize and back.

"How did you two become friends?"

Rumi laughed. "We used to set the cell on the window sill and sit in the carport to talk. I'd make margaritas or we'd do tequila shots. She wore a lot of makeup to cover up the marks he left on her face."

She shook her head in disgust. The note she'd handed Blaize had been tucked inside an envelope and sealed.

An abusive ex. Was he Rue's father? No way in hell would Blaize allow a person like Angel to have custody based on what he knew about the guy so far.

"I miss her so much that I could have sworn I saw her the other day." Rumi sucked in a breath. "I'm sure it was just wishful thinking. It's been too quiet around here since she took off."

"It's hard to lose a close friend," Carys said.

Rumi looked toward the window with soft eyes and a small smile like a memory surfaced. "Can I tell you a secret?" she asked, refocusing on Carys.

"Of course," Carys said in the calmest, most reassuring tone.

"Sharon was seeing somebody else," Rumi said.

"How do you know? Is that what she told you?"

"No." Again, Rumi shook her head. Blaize got the impression she didn't get out much based on how available she'd been for Sharon and how much she seemed to need to get things off her chest even after all this time had passed since she last saw her friend. "I saw him sneaking around the back when Angel was working late."

Sharon had been having an affair? Had Angel found out?

"Did you know him?" Carys asked.

"Yeah, everyone around here does," she said like they would, too. "Silus Vexler."

"*The* Silus Vexler?" Blaize knew about the man by reputation after living in and around Austin.

"That's right."

"And you're certain about that?" he asked.

"One hundred percent," she confirmed.

That was bad.

CARYS SAT IN the passenger seat as Blaize rounded the front of the Jeep. He hadn't opened the note from Stephanie/Sharon yet. His demeanor changed the second he heard the name Silus Vexler.

"Read this to me while I drive?" he asked, holding the note in between them. "We need to get away from this area as fast as possible."

She took the offering.

"Okay, sure. But I'm very curious as to what kind of person could cause a reaction like this in you."

"That's fair," he said. "Let's just say the SUV is the tip of the iceberg of what Silus is capable of inflicting on us."

He attempted to start the engine. Nothing.

Blaize released a string of curses. He hopped out of the vehicle and popped the hood. Poked around a few seconds before swearing again. "It's not going to start. You might as well come out."

"What happened?" She exited the passenger side.

"Someone cut the battery cables. It's not even going to start with a jump." He surveyed the area.

"Which also means someone is nearby, possibly watching us right now."

"Grab your things—we have to go." He followed her to the passenger side so she could grab her handbag from off the floorboard. She tucked the note deep inside her bag for safekeeping.

He took her hand in his and ran toward the nearest houses, aiming for in between them. The realization he was searching for cover hit hard. Losing the Jeep hit hard. And the realization a dangerous person was after them hit hardest.

Would she do all of this again for Rue? Yes. No question.

Dying wouldn't help the little girl. At least Carys understood Stephanie's dilemma now.

They made it in between two houses, away from Rumi.

"Do you think they know about Rumi?" Carys asked, trying to catch her breath as they ducked behind trash cans.

"I'm guessing they do," he said, confirming her fear this Silus person might take out revenge on Rumi or force her to give out information about them. Fortunately, they hadn't exchanged phone numbers. They barely knew each other's identities and were on a first-name-only basis. That should protect her.

Or they might not believe her and think she was withholding information.

"We have to circle back and warn her," Carys said.

"We don't have time, and someone might already be there."

"That's what I'm afraid of," she said.

Blaize looked up at her and away from his screen. "I'm searching for a rental vehicle that's parked nearby to give us a chance to get out of here in one piece. Circling back, as much as we might want to, could put Rumi in more danger. Leaving her alone might be the best way to keep her safe." Rental cars were parked in the street and available for rent based on an app.

He was making good points. She realized that. He was being logical while she was riding on stress and emotion.

"Got one that's two blocks away," he said before locking gazes. "Say the word and we'll head back to Rumi's place. I want her to be safe as much as you do."

"But you don't like the idea of checking on her?"

"Not if it gives her information that would make someone want to torture her or draws more attention to her house," he said.

A pair of male voices that were heading toward them in a hurry made the decision for them.

"There they are," one of them said.

"We have to go," Blaize urged.

Could they make it to the car now?

Chapter Twenty

Blaize was the faster runner. However the men chasing them could have weapons. There was no choice to make. He urged Carys to run in front. This way he could put some mass—himself—in between her and those bastards.

They darted in between houses, making a big zigzag in an attempt to put more distance between the jerks and them. Whoever was chasing them stopped talking. Were these the dudes from the SUV?

It dawned on him that no one was using guns. The night of the storm, the attacker didn't break a window. Was he trying to scare Carys out of the car so he could snatch the baby? Blaize hoped like hell there wasn't some kind of reward out there for anyone who brought the kid safely to Silus. That could bring more criminals out of the woodwork—anyone looking to make a quick buck.

Damn. This thing could escalate quickly. He needed to get a hold of Raiden and bring him up to speed. Whoever followed her to the ranch the other night might have put two-and-two together.

It also dawned on him that Raiden and Kit weren't answering their phones.

Double damn.

Using the phone app, he unlocked the four-door white sedan

as they rounded the corner. It was two vehicles away, and they were coming in on the driver's side.

"Hop into the back seat to save time. Okay?" he said to Carys.

"I was just thinking the same thing," she said.

"Don't hesitate or look around—just go and then duck."

"Got it," she confirmed.

At the car, he slipped into the driver's seat and grabbed the key from underneath the mat on the floorboard. Carys hopped into the back and disappeared. They were looking for a couple, so this move might buy a few extra critical seconds needed to escape.

He started the engine and pulled out of the spot, hating leaving his Jeep behind. Since they'd tampered with his vehicle, they would be able to find his name through his registration. Fortunately, the address was still on the outskirts of Austin. Even if they had someone on the inside who could run his plate, they wouldn't get the ranch.

Hunkering down in his seat to make himself appear shorter, he navigated onto the main street that was thankfully crowded with vehicles. This was the first and only time he would see Austin traffic as a blessing instead of a curse. The white sedan was the most common color and would blend into the environment perfectly.

He glanced into the rearview and then the sideview mirrors. He scanned the vehicles around him, searching for the SUV or anyone who seemed a little too interested in everyone around them. He came up empty.

"It's probably safe for you to sit up now," he said to Carys.

"I'll stay in the back seat so, at first glance, it'll seem like you're a hired driver and I'm a fare."

"That's a good idea," he said. "It'll be safer for you to buckle in in the event we're chased again and it's safer anyway."

She did.

"We need to get in touch with Raiden or Kit," he said, keeping a close eye on the road ahead as well as his surroundings. "I need to have my Jeep towed. I'd hate to leave it sitting out unattended. Who knows how long it'll be before I can get back to it."

"What about the note?" she asked. "Do you want me to read it now?"

With everything that had happened since leaving Rumi's, he'd tucked the note somewhere in the back of his mind. "Might as well."

"Okay. Just a sec." She fumbled around in her handbag before producing the yellowing card-sized envelope. "Here goes." She used a key to open the envelope, then pulled out a folded piece of paper. "Are you ready?"

The secret of how Stephanie/Sharon knew him was about to be revealed. "I guess so."

"It says, 'You probably won't remember me even if you see me again. I'm going red instead of blond, and I'm changing the way I make up my face. I overheard you talking about losing your wife, Lynn, at Deep Roots, and I knew right then and there you were the person I wanted to take care of my baby. I'm starting to show and have to get out of my situation before it's too late and he knows. Anyway, you seem like a nice guy. Like the kind of person my Lark deserves. I've made mistakes. Big ones. But I'll figure something out. If I don't, well, I guess you came looking for answers like I hoped you would. Don't be mad. Whatever happens, please don't let him get hold of her.'"

"There's only one other person I mentioned Lynn to, and that was at Deep Roots not long after she died."

"Guess Sharon was there, too," Carys said.

"Seems so," he said.

"Who is this man anyway?"

"You haven't heard of Silus Vexler?" He figured everyone knew the man, or to avoid him at the very least.

"Why? Should I?"

"His name gets around in Austin for leaning on business owners for so-called protection," he said.

"I didn't realize that was a thing," she admitted. "I just went to school here. I moved away when I got the job in Maverick Pass."

"That's possibly why you would never have crossed paths with him. I used to manage a custom saddle business, and my suppliers had trouble with him since they sourced across the border. I knew he was bad news, but he didn't come knocking on my door."

"Do you still work there?"

"No. After Lynn passed, I spiraled. Went to a dark place. Gave up my job because I couldn't go into work every day and pretend everything was fine. My employees deserved better."

"Do you mind if I ask how you survived financially?"

"By that point, I had stock in the company. Sold most of it to pay for Lynn's treatments that insurance decided not to cover. There was enough left over to live on for a while. That's what I've been doing." He choked out a laugh. "Funny thing about it is that I was about to head back to work. Finally got my head on straight and decided it was time to make some money, pick my life up and find a way to move forward. Then I got the call about Cormac dying. Seems like every time I set off in a direction, the universe laughs and throws me a new twist." He would have said it always went from bad to worse, but then he met her. He couldn't regret that one bit. It also brought him Rue. "If I changed my mind and told you that I'm the little girl's father, would you believe me?"

She sat in silence for a long moment, giving away nothing.

Before she could answer, his cell buzzed.

"Can you answer that for me?" he asked.

"Sure." She leaned forward enough to grab the phone from the cupholder. "It's Raiden."

"THIS IS CARYS. I have you on speaker."

"Blaize? Are you there, too?" The concern in Raiden's voice caused her pulse to race. Rue was crying softly in the background.

"I'm here," Blaize said. "I'm driving, so Carys is helping me out."

Raiden exhaled.

"Is everything okay? Because when no one answered and I didn't hear back from you, I was worried something happened," Blaize said, getting right to the point.

"It's Kit."

Blaize's knuckles turned white on the steering wheel. "What about her?"

"She fell."

"Again?"

"I'm afraid so," Raiden said. "Caught the corner of the dresser this time and had to get stitches."

"Where are you guys now?"

"At the hospital." The strain in Raiden's voice said it had been a long day in Maverick Pass, too.

"Is Kit conscious?" Blaize asked.

"Yes."

"Is that Rue crying in the background?"

"Yes." He cleared his throat. "A nurse is helping me try to calm her so I could call you. The kid has a set of lungs on her, and I'm not cut out to be a parent. I've tried everything I know to do, which isn't a helluva a lot, and none of it works."

All of a sudden, Rue stopped crying.

"What just happened?" Blaize asked.

"The nurse swaddled her."

"Did you change her diaper?" Blaize asked.

"Yes."

"Feed her?"

"Did that, too."

"Does she have a fever?" Blaize asked.

All these questions were spot-on. Carys had no clue why Blaize didn't think he'd be a good father. Now that she knew his background and about his wife, was he afraid to admit he still wanted children?

It would be understandable after all the disappointments he'd endured. Most people would have folded the tent at this point. Not Blaize. He became stronger and more determined with every setback.

"The nurse checked. No, no fever."

"That's a relief." Blaize released some of the tension in his grip on the steering wheel.

"There doesn't seem to be a reason for her to be fussy," Raiden said. "And Kit will be fine, by the way."

"Will she?" Blaize asked.

"She says this is the reason we have to sell and put her in a home."

"And you believe her?"

"I can only go by what she says." Raiden sounded at the end of his rope. He also sounded much less confident than he had when he first arrived. A good sign?

"We're heading back now," Blaize said. "Is Kit being released tonight?"

"That's the plan, according to her doctor."

"Keep me posted, will you?" Blaize frowned. "There's not much I can do from the road, but I'll be there as soon as humanly possible."

"Will do." Raiden paused a beat. "Any guesses as to your ETA?"

"I'm three hours out, if traffic cooperates." He didn't mention the fact they could be derailed by someone determined to take them out. Was it safe to go back to the ranch?

They couldn't leave Rue with Kit and Raiden anymore.

The brothers exchanged goodbyes. Their bond might have been challenged, but Carys could hear how much they cared for each other in their voices. You can't fake something as genuine as that. She'd witnessed people trying to convince her they were a solid unit. She had a special detector for people like that.

"What if whoever cut my battery cable gets to them first?" Blaize said the minute the call ended.

She glanced at the screen to make certain Raiden didn't accidentally hear something he shouldn't. Relief washed over her when the generic screensaver came up. "Everyone should be safe at the hospital."

"What if Kit is released before we get there?"

"That's a possibility. But there's a good chance we'll get there first." The mention of hospitals caused Blaize's muscles to string tight. Having his beloved Kit in one must be the worst feeling.

"There is so much that needs to be done when I get back." He rubbed the two-day-old scruff on his chin. Dark circles cradled his eyes, and yet the man was still sex-on-a-stick gorgeous, looking more like a sculpture than a human.

Carys faked a cough. "I seem to be coming down with something. I could take a couple of days off, just until you get settled. Besides, I need to make a trip to the orphanage to explain why I kept Rue over the weekend."

"Will you have to drop her off?"

"At some point she—"

He gave one finite headshake. "If you don't get me busted for not being her father, the government believes I'm the one at least for now. Correct?"

"I have to establish paternity at some point in the near future. I can't leave it open-ended like this and keep my job. Plus, my boss will catch on and the courts will require proof before establishing custody."

"I'll find a way to adopt her. I'll get a lawyer to intervene. I'll say her mother was my best friend and wanted me to be the guardian."

"Blaize, be reasonable. You can't take care of everyone. Kit needs someone in the house to watch over her. Rue is a full-time job. You heard how tired Raiden is. It's already too much. Add in the fact you need to save the ranch to keep a roof over Kit's head and there's just too much going on for you to be able to take care of an infant."

"I can do it."

Stubborn must've been his middle name. Carys admired his determination. Reality said that he wasn't Superman.

"If anyone could, it would be you." She needed to add a dose of reality into the situation. "The task is impossible, and you would wear yourself down. I can help for a couple of days, but then I'll have to get back to my own schedule. Where does that leave Rue?"

"I need that meeting with my brothers to figure it out. What if they come back? What if everyone takes a shift? We have to have someone home to watch Kit while she's awake anyway. Why not let them assist her in taking care of Rue?"

"That sounds more like a fairy tale than reality."

He bit down on his bottom lip. "Having Rue in the house has made Kit the happiest I've seen her. They always say parents never recover from losing a child. Cormac wasn't a kid, but he was her son and she loved him. So much so, she jumped to his defense when I brought up one or two of his many deficiencies. I barely scratched the surface."

"She loves you, too."

"I guess I can do no wrong in her eyes. Believe me when I say I'm far from perfect." He glanced around. "I can pull over if you want to slide up to the passenger seat."

"It might be safer to stay like this for a while even though we're on the highway now."

"Let me know if you change your mind," he said.

"Okay." She thought about what he said about Kit. "I highly doubt my father would care if I lived or died. It's too bad not every parent is like Kit, protective even when their kids make huge mistakes."

"She's special," he agreed. "Do you think you'll reconnect with your father at some point?"

"Why? So he can remind me how much I disappointed him? Or tell me again that I'm not his daughter? That one stung at eighteen."

Blaize was quiet for a long moment. Based on the wrinkle across his forehead, he was deep in thought. "I would have liked the chance to tell Cormac what a disappointment he was to his face and how much it damaged us growing up. Now? I'll never get the chance."

"I thought you were going to tell me to try to reconcile with my father," she said. His words resonated.

"What would be the point of that?" he asked. The question was rhetorical. "It's far better to be able to reconcile with yourself. Does that make any sense?"

"Actually, yes. It does. A whole lot of sense, actually." When this ordeal was over, could she reach out? Tell her father how she really felt about the way he'd treated her for wanting to live her own life?

Could she open up to Blaize, too? Risk losing him and Rue?

Chapter Twenty-One

The call came when they were twenty minutes away from the hospital. A nurse had agreed to help get Rue strapped into her car seat safely for the ride home since she held certification as a car seat safety tech. The amount of relief in Raiden's voice when Blaize said they would arrive home at close to the same time was almost comical.

"Did you hear that?" he asked Carys.

She laughed, and he'd be damned if it wasn't the most musical sound. Now that he was determined to keep Rue, would Carys bolt at the first opportunity?

His problems were mounting. The last thing he needed to think about was Carys leaving. Or the kisses they'd shared, which had been the highlight of his year, possibly his life.

How was that for being dramatic?

Blaize chuckled. Too much stress had him on the edge, imagining that his heart would shatter when she walked out.

Didn't everyone leave?

Whoa! Did he really believe that? Or was it just his mind searching for reasons to counter what his heart so plainly saw… that Carys was special.

"How could I miss it? Your poor brother is in way over his head and knows it. At least Rue was quiet this time. I felt even worse for him when she was crying." Carys stilled in the back seat. She'd stayed put the whole ride.

Did he have the same feelings for him or was he latching onto something that wasn't there? His mind was clear. He knew what he wanted. And then the universe laughed and threw every possible obstacle in his way.

When he thought about it on a practical level, how was he supposed to save a ranch, take care of Kit, and bring up a baby? Adding a relationship on top seemed impossible.

He was getting ahead of himself. First, he had to convince his brothers that saving the ranch was a good idea. If they refused to move back and pitch in, he would have to figure out a way to do it all himself.

Easy-peasy.

Blaize almost laughed out loud. Was he losing his mind?

Probably.

He parked at the house. Carys exited the car before he did.

"I need to make a work call," she said, walking away. "Do you mind?"

"Stick close enough to see me, just in case."

She gave a quick nod and walked out of earshot. Was she calling her boss? He didn't like the idea of her getting into trouble because of him. If he'd lied about being Rue's father from the get-go, they wouldn't be in this mess.

Not true. The person would have attacked her car. She might still be in trouble.

He kept one eye on her as he stood up and stretched his legs. Working out had been a lifesaver while Lynn was sick. Ranch work would give him plenty of physical labor.

It dawned on him that a screwworm had been reported to be infecting cows across the border. In response, supplies were being cut off so as not to infect cattle here. And that was a long-winded way of saying he could sell at a better price if he took cattle to market now. He'd never seen prices so high. Could a sale buy him some time to straighten out finances on the ranch? Allow him to hire help for Kit, if needed? It was worth a shot.

Carys ended the call, tucked the phone inside her handbag, and frowned as she walked toward him. "That didn't go well."

"What happened?"

"My boss knows about Rue. Called me out for saying I was sick. Told me to take the time away to make sure my priorities are straight." She exhaled and pinched the bridge of her nose. "So, basically, I'm on leave now until I refocus and I have to take Rue to the orphanage tonight. My boss said she would be checking to make sure Rue is at Sister's Love before bed check."

"When is that?" He needed a minute to process and come up with a plan.

"A couple of hours," she said.

Damn.

"I just had a thought," he said. "What if Rue is safer at the orphanage than with us for the time being?"

"It's been hard enough leaving her for the day. How am I supposed to drop her off and walk away?" The hurt and disappointment in her eyes stabbed him. She was right. Being away from Rue had been more difficult than he'd anticipated. The only reason he could fathom leaving her at Sister's Love for the night was due to it being safer than the ranch. Would he worry? Hell yes.

"I know what you mean," he said.

"Plus, if the people who are after us figure us out, they might be tracking our movements," she continued.

"Sure," he said. Every which way they turned, there was risk involved. Their next step would have to be about taking the least-dangerous path. "So far, they haven't tried to shoot at us, which I take to mean they don't want to risk hurting the baby."

"If these bastards are trying to collect a reward or get in good with the head honcho, they can't bring in damaged goods." She quickly added, "I don't see her that way, but she's nothing but a means to an end for them."

"They don't want to get caught," he reasoned. "Isn't there security cameras or some form of failsafe at the orphanage?"

"It's a small place that's out of the way of the mainstream. I doubt they'd do much more than lock the doors and expect to be safe."

"We can go there to investigate. If it doesn't feel right, we'll turn around and bring her back here."

Carys bit down on her lower lip. "I can live with that."

"I'll see if Raiden can stay the night since we can't leave Kit alone."

The crunch of gravel underneath tires and the hum of an engine didn't normally cause his blood pressure to rise. Until he saw it was just his brother's vehicle coming up the path, his stress levels doubled.

Raiden pulled up next to Blaize and parked. Carys immediately went to Rue. She opened the door to the back on the passenger side and unbuckled the carrier.

"Where's your Jeep?" Raiden asked.

"Long story," Blaize said. They had a little time before they needed to get Rue to the orphanage. "I'll tell you over a cup of coffee and a bite of food."

"I'm starving," Carys said, holding on to the baby carrier for dear life. The determined and protective expression on her face said she'd fight anybody who tried to take Rue away.

Rue was lucky to have someone like Carys in her corner.

He focused on helping Kit out of the car. "You gave us another scare. Is there something you're not telling me about a medical condition?"

"Hogwash," Kit said. "I'm peachy."

"Two falls in two days say otherwise." He lowered his voice to a gentler tone.

"All the more reason to sell this place, so you can put me in a home." There was no conviction in those words.

"Are you trying to leave me all alone?"

Raiden opened the back door and let them inside.

"You'll be better off," Kit said. "I'm a burden at this point."

"Like hell you are." He wouldn't let her get away with making it seem like she'd be doing him a favor. "You happen to be one of my favorite people in the world. How could you be anything but amazing?"

Fears she was hiding a serious—terminal?—medical condition intensified. How the hell would he do any of this without Kit?

CARYS CHANGED RUE'S diaper and fed her as Blaize and Raiden prepared a meal. Kit sat at the kitchen table, nursing a glass of water. She'd done a number on her forehead, come home with wound-care instructions that Blaize had her go over with all three of them in the room.

Her heart went out to the baby. With no other relatives and a dry well of foster families, Rue was most likely going to have to spend the night at the orphanage.

Since beating herself up wasn't productive, she started thinking up ways to keep a close eye on Rue. Could she volunteer at the orphanage? She had connections. She knew the director. There was no way she could ask her boss to give them a call and make the recommendation. Still, as a CPS agent, her background had already been picked apart and processed. No job was too small. She would be willing to do janitorial work if it meant being close to Rue until Carys could come up with a plan.

It was too late to redact her statement about Blaize denying paternity. Was it even possible for him to gain custody of Rue without actually taking a paternity test, a test he would surely fail?

After he shared the state of his finances, hiring a hotshot lawyer would be out of the question. She would contribute funds if she had anything left over. Paying living expenses and student loans took a good chunk of her income every month.

It's fine. It'll be fine. Everything is fine. How many times had she repeated the mantra growing up? It had gotten her through difficult years. She could only hope it still held some of its magic.

"Dinner smells good," Kit said, interrupting Carys's thoughts. "What are you boys cooking up?"

Raiden brought over a tray and set it on the table. "Cowboy Chili on Fritos."

Blaize brought over bowls and spoons.

"I thought chili had to slow-cook all day," Carys said.

Raiden laughed. "We have a cheat code to speed it up. Basically, we just doctor already-made chili from the can." He dipped a spoon inside the large bowl and scooped up a Frito before handing it over. "Taste it for yourself."

Rue was asleep in Carys's arms. She tried to finagle taking the spoon.

"Here, let me help." Blaize took over and fed her a bite.

"Mmm. That's amazing."

His self-satisfied smile shouldn't have been as sexy as it was. What could she say? She would never get tired of seeing that man smile or the effect it had on her.

"Do you want me to hold her while you eat?" Blaize asked.

"I'm just scared that if I set her down, I'll never get to hold her again. Is that weird?"

Heads shook around the table as each person offered a look of understanding.

"I'll just put her in her carrier." It was on the floor sitting right next to her. She could eat and keep one eye on the baby. Blaize took a seat on the other side of the carrier, with Rue in between them.

Carys glanced around at the faces at the table as tears welled in her eyes. She blinked them back as she realized this was the first real family meal she'd experienced. An ache formed in her chest as a picture of these people eating dinner with her every evening took form. It caught her off guard how natural it felt and how easily conversation flowed.

Blaize got his brother up to speed over the meal. They traded playful barbs, which thankfully lightened the mood. Kit piped in every once in a while with a quip of her own, making everyone laugh. It was easy to see why Blaize loved his grandmother so much.

The meal ended too soon. It was time to take Rue to the orphanage.

"I should probably give her a bath before we leave." Was she stalling for time? Hell yes.

"That's a good idea," Kit offered.

The prospect of figuring out how to bathe a baby must've contorted her face based on the way everyone looked at her.

"I can help," Kit said. "I used to be quite the hand at taking care of these little ones."

"Is it a good idea for you to get up?" Carys asked, concerned.

"Those doctors can't tell me what to do," the woman quipped.

She pushed up to standing. "See, I'm as fit as a fiddle and sharp as a tack."

The way she'd mentioned the word *doctors* raised alarm bells for Carys. Given everything Blaize had been through, his mind must've been running wild with possibilities. The stress cracks on his forehead said everything she needed to know. He was worried. She didn't blame him.

Kit refocused on Carys. "Are you ready to give that little sweetheart a bath?"

"Yes, I am."

Carys was grateful for the help. She didn't have the first clue of how to take care of a baby. Did you run bath water? That didn't seem right. Did you put them in the sink? No, probably not. Having someone with experience around would keep Carys from panicking.

"Let's take her into the bedroom so we can put her on a soft surface," Kit said.

Carys took note of the way Kit held on to her arm, half guiding, half using it to steady herself. They walked into the guest bedroom where Kit had been sleeping. Carys put the carrier down on the floor.

"We'll need a towel and a washcloth from the bathroom," Kit said.

"Got it."

She returned with both in a matter of seconds.

"Let's put the towel on top of the comforter and spread it out."

Carys did.

"I'll let you pick Rue up since I'm not so steady on my feet these days." Kit sounded more than a little frustrated.

"What did the ER doctor say is happening?" Carys asked as she unbuckled Rue and then put her on top of the towel.

"Inner-ear infection," Kit said. "He wants me to take antibiotics, but I refuse."

"Why is that?"

"They make me too sick," she said. "I'm sure it'll clear up on its own."

"Blaize is worried about you falling again," Carys said. "What if I call your doctor and get a different prescription?"

"There is one that'll help, but it's not covered under insurance," Kit explained. "Blaize has enough on his mind without trying to come up with two hundred dollars on the spot."

"Where is the prescription being held?"

"Pharmacy in town. Why?"

"Just curious." Carys would pay for it out of her own pocket. She also wondered if this was the reason Kit kept pushing to sell. "This land is amazing."

"House needs fixin' up." Based on Kit's tone, Carys struck a chord.

"Nothing a few boards, nails, and paint can't handle."

"Blaize has already sacrificed too much," Kit said. "I wouldn't ask him to do more. He's suffered enough."

"He might suffer more if you don't let him take care of this place. And you."

"My grandson looks like he's aged ten years in the past two. Now I know why."

"He's been through more than his fair share," Carys said. "But he's strong."

Kit's chin came up, proud. "He sure is."

"And you believe in him, don't you?"

"I sure do."

"Then maybe let him fix this place up and get it running again," Carys said. "It'll do him good to see the results."

Kit studied Carys like she was looking through her to the core of who she was.

"He's different with you," she said. "It's the first time I've seen him happy."

What was Carys supposed to do with that?

Chapter Twenty-Two

Blaize parked in the lot next to a pickup at Sister's Love. He exited the rental car and opened the door for Carys. Working like a team, they freed the carrier from the seat belt and grabbed the diaper bag. Rue had been in his life for less than forty-eight hours yet had managed to imprint his heart. If he lost her, he would regret it for the rest of his life.

Sister's Love was in need of TLC, much like the ranch. Two stories with peeling paint, it had an almost ominous air to it. The wraparound porch had seen better days. Once he got the ranch up and running again, he could gather a group of volunteers to work on this place.

As they approached the door, it opened from the inside. A short, round woman welcomed them inside.

"I'm Rosie," she said to Blaize. "I'd offer a handshake but yours are full. Can I take her from—"

"Could we sit down for a minute?" Carys asked.

"Of course." Rosie led them from the foyer into a formal living area. The furniture looked to be original to the house. She held out her hand toward the sofa. "Please, sit down."

"I know how challenging it has been with staffing," Carys said, starting right in. "I'd like to volunteer for the next couple of days."

Rosie blinked like she couldn't believe her eyes. "We're always looking for good people. You of all people know that. We'd love to have you. I'll get the paperwork started tomorrow morning."

"I was thinking more like starting tonight," Carys said.

"With paperwork? Nothing can be done until—"

"I know you need the help, Rosie. And I don't feel good about dropping her off and running when I know how short-staffed you are."

"I appreciate your willingness to drop everything else in your life and help." Rosie sat up a little straighter. "I can assure that we can handle every situation that comes through that door."

"You sure about that?"

Carys's words landed like bullets.

Rosie stood up, shot a glare, and grabbed the handle to the carrier. The hallway was too dark to make anything out clearly. Blaize saw the outline of someone lingering. Was she waiting to take Rue?

"Hold on, Rosie. I didn't mean it to come out like that." Carys's tone was pleading.

Blaize reached over and took her hand in his. It was then he realized hers was trembling. Watching Rosie take Rue away and hand her off hit hard.

Carys stood. He followed suit. She squeezed his fingers.

The baby was then given to the silhouette.

Rosie turned around, blocking their view of the hallway. "Shall I walk you out, or do you want me to call the authorities?"

"There's no need to do anything like that," Blaize said, a little shocked at the threat. "We're heading out now."

Carys hesitated. He squeezed her hand gently for reassurance. Thankfully, she followed him out the front door without an argument. The last thing they needed to do tonight was get the sheriff involved. Carys didn't need another hit on her performance record.

"We'll figure something out," he said as soon as they were in the clear and walking toward the rental car.

Out of the corner of his eye, he saw a streak of red behind the building.

Nah. Couldn't be.

What the hell?

"I think she's here," Blaize said.

"Who?" Carys's forehead wrinkled with confusion. And then it dawned on her. Her mouth snapped open and shut. "Sharon?"

He signaled toward the back of the house. Then took off running.

The front door opened, and Rosie came out in a hurry. "Carys. Don't leave yet. Can I speak to you?"

TORN BETWEEN FOLLOWING Blaize and hearing what Rosie had to say, Carys froze.

"Go talk to her," Blaize said before disappearing around back.

"What is it?"

"She was here," Rosie said, waving Carys inside. "Please. Hurry."

Carys jogged over and then followed Rosie into the house, stopping in the foyer. "What's going on, Rosie?"

The woman twisted her fingers together. Beads of sweat formed on her forehead. "There was a man with a gun. He had her."

"Who?"

"Sharon."

"You know her?" Carys didn't bother to hide her shock.

"She came here when she was pregnant," Rosie admitted, working her fingers. "We let her help out off the record. She said she was in trouble and needed our help."

"Blaize just saw red hair," Carys said, trying to process what she was hearing.

"She dyed it so the baby's father wouldn't recognize her."

"You knew all of this and didn't say anything?"

"I helped a pregnant single mother without quizzing her," Rosie said. "It's part of what we do here."

"We have reason to believe she died in a car crash."

"No." Rosie shook her head. "That would be impossible because she was taken out the back door after you handed over the baby."

"You took Rue and delivered her to a criminal," Carys said, her tone accusatory.

"I gave her to her mother." Rosie compressed her lips into a frown. "And now I have no idea what to do."

"Call the sheriff and explain everything you just told me," Carys said.

"Sharon said he would kill her if I did that," she admitted.

"I have to go." Carys started toward the back door. "Blaize is out there. Alone."

A shot fired.

Oh no.

Carys's heart dropped. Rosie grabbed hold of her. The world started to spin. Nausea caused bile to rise up and burn the back of her throat.

Blaize!

"Don't go out there," Rosie said. "You might end up getting shot."

"I can't leave Blaize out there alone to deal with—"

The back door opened so hard it smacked against the wall. Rosie screamed.

"It's me," Blaize said.

Carys bolted around her and into the dark hallway toward the kitchen. The first thing she saw was blood.

"Blaize, you're shot."

"I know. It's okay." It would be just like him to reassure her when he was the one bleeding out. "It's not as bad as it looks."

Blood flowered on his shirt sleeve near his right bicep.

"It's a lot of blood, Blaize."

He was shot, bleeding. Rue was gone. Sharon was somehow alive.

"Help me!" shouted a female voice from outside.

Rosie came running into the kitchen and straight to the door. "It's her."

"Don't open that door," Carys warned. "It could be a trap."

But it was too late. Rosie had already undone the lock. The second she did, the door flung open and smacked her.

"Rosie," the redhead from the picture—Sharon—said with concern in her voice. She scanned the room. "I'm so sorry."

"Where's the baby?" Carys asked.

"He got her," Sharon said.

"We have to get her back. Call the sheriff," Carys said to Rosie. "Now!"

"They'll arrest me," Sharon said.

"Do you want to lose Rue forever?" Carys worked on stemming the blood dripping down Blaize's elbow.

"Who has her?" he asked.

"Silus," Sharon said.

"He came himself?" Blaize asked. He looked to Carys. "I've got this." She'd put enough pressure to stop the bleeding temporarily.

"That's right. He said he couldn't trust anyone else to get the job done or handle a precious package like her and—"

"Lock the door behind me," Blaize said. "I know a shortcut. I can head him off, but I have to go now."

"Not in this condition, you can't." No way was Carys letting him go out there without her. "You're bleeding."

He shrugged it off like it was nothing.

"Then I'm coming."

"Too risky."

She shot her best *do not argue with me* look and followed him out the back door after he heaved a sigh and then jumped into action. The lock snicked the moment they were outside. Good that Rosie took it seriously. Not so good that they couldn't turn around and go back inside if Silus was out here.

Blaize took off running toward a wooded area. She did her best to keep up as she fumbled with her cell. Rosie might not call law enforcement due to Sharon's request, but Carys had no problem doing it. If the woman ended up in jail, so be it. For Rue's sake, Carys hoped the courts would go easy on Sharon.

Silus was a different story altogether. That man needed to rot in a burning—

Dammit.

Carys dropped her cell. It was black as pitch out here. There was no way she could keep going and find it.

"Do you have your phone on you?" she asked Blaize as they half hopped, half ran through scrub brush, zigzagging in and out of trees. Branches slapped her face and torso as they bolted through the woods.

They ran long past her thighs burning. She was lost. It was dark. What if they ended up stuck out here overnight?

The shock of seeing Sharon alive and of Blaize being shot was something she might never recover from.

A glimpse of red taillights stopped Blaize so fast that Carys ran into his back.

As they moved closer, a familiar sound pierced her chest like a bullet through armor. Rue's cries broke Carys's heart.

From this distance, they could see that the driver's-side door was open. Had he fled, leaving his daughter to fend for herself?

The question they should have asked was *Why would Silus abandon the vehicle?* They didn't. Emotion overtook logic when it came to Rue.

"Stay here," Blaize warned.

"Like hell I will."

Carys bolted around Blaize on his right side and ran like hell toward Rue.

Chapter Twenty-Three

Anything that happened next would be on Blaize. He shouldn't have brought Carys out here into the thicket. He shouldn't have gone after Silus half-cocked with no weapon or plan. And he shouldn't have let Carys get past him just now.

She'd chosen his injured side, so he couldn't stop her from running toward Rue. He couldn't blame Carys. He wanted to do the exact same thing.

It wasn't the best move.

He winced as he expected to hear another round being fired. Either way, he wouldn't wait. He took off after Carys and toward the abandoned vehicle.

The engine idled.

Silus had taken off in a hurry. What did that mean?

The answer came in the form of a downed tree lying across the road, blocking it. There was no way the vehicle could drive over it. He could have in his Jeep. But Silus would never get the sedan over the massive trunk.

Maybe his luck was turning. He'd had enough bad luck to last a lifetime. Were the powers that be finally giving him a break?

Carys got to the vehicle first. The loss of blood made him dizzy and move slower. He was halfway there when the crack of a bullet split the air. The world stilled, and everything moved in slow motion.

Carys dropped to the ground. Hit?

He instinctively dove for cover, then army-crawled toward her despite the biting pain in his arm.

"Did it…"

He couldn't manage to finish the question. Then he didn't need to. She rolled onto her side, and he saw a red dot flowering on her upper thigh.

Blaize cursed the heavens and earth.

He immediately stripped off his shirt.

"No. You need that," she said, eyes wide in a state of mild shock.

"You need it more." If they didn't stem the bleeding, she might bleed out. Now that he'd found her, he couldn't lose her. Not her, too.

He wrapped the shirt around her thigh slightly above the wound and tightened the knot enough to slow the bleeding, if not stop it altogether. "Let's get you in the back seat."

Could he hop into the front and turn this vehicle around? Head back to the house?

There wasn't much of a choice, was there? Neither of them were in any condition to run back to the house. Add the weight of carrying the baby and it would be next to impossible.

The nagging question of why Silus abandoned the car and baby niggled at the back of his mind. All he could focus on right now was getting the three of them to safety.

He helped Carys into the back. "Stay down. Okay?"

"Okay," she parroted.

Another nagging question surfaced. Why only one shot? They were out in the open. Did Silus know he'd hit both his targets and figured it was a matter of time before they bled out? Problem solved without even having to get his hands dirty? Or was he saving bullets until he could get in closer range in case he'd missed?

Would he panic and take off? The shots meant to stop anyone from following? Silus wasn't normally the one to get his hands dirty, was he?

Blaize took the driver's seat and closed the door. He sank as low as possible into the seat, not bothering to put on his seat belt. The smaller the target he made, the better.

Rather than turn the vehicle around, he put the gearshift in reverse and sped backward until it seemed safe. Only then did he turn the vehicle around for the rest of the drive to the house. The only other road meant driving by the house again. So be it.

"How are you doing back there?" he asked Carys.

Rue had stopped crying, and it was far too quiet in the back seat as far as he was concerned. He glanced at the rearview. Carys's head was lying against the headrest, bobbling back and forth on the gravelly road.

"I'm okay," she said, her voice weak.

Could he get back to the house and call for emergency medical treatment? Or should he risk getting on the road? There were probably some supplies back at the house. Had the makeshift torniquet's knot come loose? Had the bullet hit an artery?

"Stay with me," he said to her, more plea than request. "I can't lose you, Carys. I love you." He risked a glance. "You should know that I've fallen in love with you and I can't imagine spending another minute without you."

He couldn't lose Carys.

Did she hear him?

Was she conscious?

The fact she hadn't responded made the decision to stop at the house clear. She might not make it to the hospital. At the house, she had a fighting chance.

He couldn't lose Carys.

Blaize sped to Sister's Love. He pulled up in front, not bothering to park. He couldn't get out of the driver's seat fast enough. He immediately pulled Carys from the car. Her head fell to one side. No. Not a good sign.

He couldn't lose Carys.

The front door opened, and Rosie stumbled onto the porch. Eyes wide, mouth open, her look of shock and sudden jerk forward said she was pushed from behind. Sharon came out next in similar fashion.

And then Silus came partially into view. He stood behind the ladies.

"Turn your head," he said to Sharon.

She winced as he forced her to comply, revealing that he had the barrel of a gun pressed to the back of her head. The redhead was crying as she mouthed the words *I'm sorry.*

She couldn't have known any of this was going to happen. Blaize couldn't blame her for trying to survive and make a better life for her child.

A desperate person took desperation actions.

"Give us the baby and walk away," Silus said.

"The woman with me needs medical care, or she's going to die," Blaize said. "If she dies, that makes you a murderer."

"Hand over the baby," Silus said, his voice reaching an almost hysterical pitch. The man was agitated.

Sharon subtly shook her head and mouthed the word *no.*

"Do as I say, or I'll shoot you both," Silus demanded.

"How should we do this?" Blaize asked.

"Get her out of my car and step away," he said. "I'll take it from there."

"How do you plan to get out of this, Silus? What comes next?" Blaize realized the man wouldn't want to leave witnesses. There were four, with himself and Carys being the wild cards in the equation. "This hasn't gone so far that you can't walk away. Let me get her inside and stop the bleeding before it's too late."

"Once you step away from the vehicle, you can do anything you want. Now, do what I said or I'll start shooting beginning with Sharon."

"You don't want to shoot the mother of your child," Blaize warned. If he did as Silus asked, the man could disappear with Sharon and the baby into his criminal network. The two might not surface for years, if they did at all. He would likely shoot Rosie if he took her along for the ride. Dump the body somewhere it might never be found.

Silus was known for pressuring business owners into paying protection money. He had enough ties to thugs to hide behind them for ages. He could skip across the border, run his business from there. Force Sharon to live in horror with the threat of taking her daughter away.

No wonder she disappeared, changed her name, and then tried to fake her death. At some point, CPS would have linked Stephanie to Sharon, Rue would be in safe hands—his!—and then Sharon could have come back to retrieve her daughter once the dust settled. She could have started a new life in another place.

"I said now!" Silus was growing more desperate.

This wasn't good.

"Okay, just give me a minute to get her out of the car safely," he said, stalling for time. Once Silus got everyone into the car, it would be much easier to slip away and disappear. The law didn't have a great track record of shutting the man's business down. No, Silus had figured out how to get around the legal system. He knew how to fly under the radar, using others to do the heavy lifting for him.

At this point, Sharon would likely testify under oath that she wanted to go with Silus of her own free will. The shooting could be chalked up to accidents. Who the hell knew what this man was capable of pulling off.

Slowly, carefully, he wrapped arms around Carys and gently pulled her from the vehicle.

Her eyes opened for a few seconds, locking onto his. Was she conscious?

He could have sworn she winked at him, but he was probably just seeing what he wanted to instead of the reality that he was losing her with every second that ticked by.

Silus knocked Sharon forward another step. Rosie gasped.

"Shut the hell up, woman, or I'll shoot every last one of you." The threat rang hollow to Blaize. Silus couldn't afford to shoot everyone, but Rosie panicked. She brought her hand up to cover her mouth and tried to step away.

He pistol-whipped her across the cheek. The older woman let out a pitiful yelp.

"Don't hurt her," Sharon said, panicked. "I'll do whatever you want, but leave Rosie out of this."

"That woman kept you from me while you were carrying my child," Silus bit out through clenched teeth. "She doesn't deserve to—"

"Please, Silus," Sharon begged. "She didn't know that I was your girl."

Those last two words were fingernails on a chalkboard to Blaize. First of all, Sharon was not a girl, she was a grown woman. And secondly, she didn't belong to anyone except herself.

The trio moved toward them. Silus kept the gun firmly pointed to the back of Sharon's head. Based on the panic in her eyes, he would shoot if pushed too far.

Blaize held Carys in his arms, taking another step back.

"Move," Silus insisted.

Blaize took another step. He was too far away to make a move without risking Silus accidently squeezing the trigger mechanism. He bit back a few choice words.

"Get in first," Silus said to Rosie, kicking her as she turned toward the back driver's-side door. It was still open, and there was blood on the seat and floorboard. At least they were leaving a DNA trail that would be next to impossible to cover. *If* the police could catch up to Silus before he torched the vehicle.

It dawned on Blaize why Sharon would have "died" in a fiery crash. The fire would erase all DNA evidence. It also made the driver impossible to positively ID. If Sharon wasn't in the vehicle, who was? Did she murder someone? Drug them and then set the car ablaze?

Sharon might end up in jail for murder the rest of her life when Blaize turned Silus in. Where would that leave Rue?

As Silus passed by, Carys's body seized. For a split second, Blaize feared she might be dying, but then she opened her eyes and was surprisingly lucid.

Her foot, however, landed on Silus's ribs. She kicked so hard, he flew into the driver's-side door. Caught by surprise, the gun flew out of his hand.

Sharon screamed, processed what had just happened, and before Silus could regain his balance, she went wild on him, kicking and punching and screaming.

Carys bucked out of Blaize's arms. As much as he tried to balance her, she still landed on the ground half on her side.

Something cracked. Her wrist, maybe, as she planted her hand down to break her fall.

The time to act was now or never.

Chapter Twenty-Four

Carys landed hard on the unforgiving earth. She'd seen an opening a few seconds ago, so she'd taken it. Blood loss or not, she wasn't letting Silus leave with Rue. She would have to be unconscious or dead for that to happen.

Something cracked. Her wrist?

Thank the stars for adrenaline. For the moment, the pain was negligible. So, she took advantage of the momentary reprieve and crawled on her knees and one good hand toward Silus and Sharon. She was putting up a good fight, but he was stronger and meaner.

Blaize dove over top of her, scoring a direct hit with Silus's midsection and one-arming him.

Sharon was now out of the way and stumbled a couple of steps to her left and then caught herself on the vehicle. She managed to stay on her feet.

Silus was a flurry of fists and kicks. The only reason he was landing any punches or kicks was because Blaize was in a weakened state. Carys had no doubt he would easily take care of Silus in a fair fight.

The amount of blood on Blaize's shirt was concerning. Plus, he'd been exerting himself. He was far from full strength.

Sharon dropped by her side, essentially blocking her from helping Blaize. "Where do you think you're going?"

Rosie turned. "We can lock the doors and call 911. Let's get inside the house."

"I'm not leaving him." Carys's tone must have been finite because Rosie shrugged before turning her attention toward Sharon.

"Hurry. Before he—"

"I'm staying right here, Rosie. These people took care of my girl. I'm not leaving them when they need me." The sincerity in Sharon's tone touched a nerve with Carys. And she appreciated Sharon not turning her back.

"I'm going," Rosie said.

"Do you what you need to do." Sharon reached for Carys's hand.

The woman bolted toward the house.

"Thank you," Sharon said, helping Carys to her feet. "Let's stop this guy together."

"Let's go!"

Blaize was holding his own, but when Carys saw an opportunity to slam the opened door into Silus's head, she took it.

He immediately went limp.

Blaize took the opportunity to roll the man over, forcing him face down while he hoisted Silus's hands behind his back.

Carys couldn't go any longer. "I need to sit."

That was all she could get out of her mouth before she plopped down, back against the vehicle, and then blacked out.

SIXTY SECONDS WAS all it took for everything to change. A flood of activity happened as law enforcement and EMTs roared up to the scene. But all Blaize could focus on was Carys, leaning with her back against the car, limp. Her eyes were closed, and from his position it looked like her breathing was shallow.

Fighting exhaustion, fatigue, and a wave of nausea so huge it threatened to bend him in two, he yelled for someone to take over so he could go to her. With every fiber of his being, he needed to see that she was alive.

The stress knot in his chest tightened as a deputy took over. Blaize rolled onto his back, needing to catch his breath and gather enough strength to stand up so he could walk to Carys.

"Sir, I need to examine you. Okay?" an EMT with the name *Andrew* sewn onto his pocket asked after coming into view.

Blaize shook his head as he forced himself to sit up. He saw stars. The world spun faster.

"Hey, let me help you," Andrew said. "I'll get you fixed up and feeling better in no time."

A stretcher was already being brought over by another EMT—Andrew's partner, no doubt.

Another worked on Carys, blocking his view.

Blaize craned his neck in an unproductive attempt to get eyes on her. He attempted to stand up, landed hard on his backside, and bit back a string of curses.

"Whoa, there," Andrew said, immediately jumping into action to keep Blaize from slamming his head on a tree trunk. "What are you trying to do?"

"Carys," he said, again vainly attempting to get a visual on her. "I need to know her status."

"I can check if you promise to sit tight." The EMT looked resigned.

"Promise."

Andrew studied Blaize for a long moment, like he was deciding if he could trust the answer. "Okay. I'll be right back. Stay here."

"Got it."

He jogged over and took a knee next to the EMT working on Carys. It was all Blaize could do to stop himself from following. Out of the corner of his eye, he saw Silus regaining consciousness while being cuffed. A deputy was espousing Silus's rights, including the one to remain silent.

Silus spit dirt out of his mouth as he was hoisted up. He glared at Sharon, who stood a few feet away with Rue in her arms. Her attention was on Carys.

"You bitch," Silus ground out as the deputy led him away and toward the back of his SUV.

"Mind your language when you're speaking to a lady," the deputy said.

Silus scowled. He was going to be locked away for a very long time once all his crimes came to light.

Unfortunately, Sharon would face justice too. It was a shame the lengths she had to go to in order to feel safe from Silus. She'd protected her daughter, though, and Blaize would see to it Rue knew her mother.

Thinking clearly while he didn't know if Carys would live or die wasn't an option. He would figure the rest out later.

Andrew came jogging back. "I'll give you the update if you let me check out that arm of yours."

"That's blackmail."

"I know." He shot a look of apology. "It's also the only way I'll convince you to let me help."

"Fine." Blaize rolled up his shirt sleeve.

Andrew went to work as Carys was lifted onto the stretcher. A neck brace caught his attention. And, of course, the blood. There was so much blood.

Rosie had joined Sharon, both giving statements. From this distance, he heard Sharon admit to the sheriff she'd been the one to attack Carys's vehicle the other night, thinking she would scare her into running away from the car and leaving the baby. Sharon would then take her daughter and disappear. She'd made up the name Stephanie Cross, stitching together a new identity after learning she was pregnant. One that wouldn't raise flags for a life that didn't yet exist. If everyone believed Sharon was dead, no one would come looking for her after she grabbed her child and ran. The fiery crash had been a setup. Desperate, she'd taken advantage of a stranger's misfortune and accelerated the plan. The woman perished at some point overnight. Sharon had come across the deceased person on a park bench, and then seized the opportunity. It had all happened so fast. The moves had been meant to ensure Rue's safety. Sharon had also been the one to break into Carys's place to poke around.

"Can you hurry?" he asked, hearing the impatience in his own voice.

He winced as Andrew put pressure on the wound.

"Sorry about that," Andrew said, working his magic.

"It's fine." Blaize might have said the words, but if he lost

Carys, nothing would ever be fine again. She needed to know how he felt.

Would he get the chance to tell her?

CARYS BLINKED HER eyes open. Her first thought? Blaize. Her second? Rue.

"Hey." Blaize's masculine voice sent ripples of awareness through her.

She exhaled. "You're here?"

"Right here," he said, squeezing her hand. It was then she realized he'd been holding it.

She was groggy and felt disconnected to her body until the warmth of his hand brought sensation back. "Where's Rue?"

"She's safe." He was quiet for a moment, then said, "Kit told me about the medication she needed, so Raiden picked it up. Thank you for asking her, by the way."

"I'm just happy that worked out." She reached for water with her free hand, her mouth was as dry as dirt in a draught and her tongue felt like sandpaper.

A few sips of water helped. Moving hurt like hell.

"I can get whatever you want," he said, studying her as she winced. "You don't have to move."

"Water's good," she said as she looked at him. *Really* looked at him. Dark circles cradled his eyes. Had he slept at all? "How long have I been out?"

"Thirty-seven hours and..." He checked his watch. "Forty-two minutes."

"I lost a whole day?"

"You've been in and out since surgery."

"Right." She had a vague memory of needing to remove bullet fragments out of her upper thigh. "What about Sharon?"

"She turned herself in this morning. She's been staying at the ranch, helping out. The sheriff said he would release her with an ankle bracelet until her court date since there was an abusive situation. We worked out a deal for her to keep an eye on Kit in exchange for room and board."

"That's a relief," she said. "It seems like you'll get the help you need while you focus on the ranch. That's great." Was this the end of the road for the two of them? Because her heart squeezed so hard she could barely breathe at the thought of losing him. "Everything is working out for the best."

"Not everything." He locked gazes with her and butterflies released in her stomach. "Carys, we've only known each other a short time, but it feels like so much longer. Like we met before in some alternate space and time and we're reconnecting now." He paused a beat. "I don't want you to feel any pressure, but I've fallen hard for you. I have never felt this deeply or connected to anyone else. What we have is special to me, and I don't want to lose you. I'm in love with you, Carys, heart and soul. And I would very much be honored if you would consider marrying me."

Carys's mouth dropped open.

"You don't have to decide today or anytime soon," he said when she couldn't formulate words adequate to express her emotions. Had he misread her? Because she loved this man. "I just wanted you to know how I feel. No, I needed you to know how I feel and what my intentions are." His thumb drew circles in her palm, and it was the most tender, most sensual act. "I can't imagine spending another day without you, but I'll wait until you're ready. I'd wait an eternity for you."

"You won't have to, Blaize," she said, finally able to find the words. "Because I'm head over heels in love with you. I think I was from the moment we met. It was like some deep-down part of me recognized you, and I've felt the pull ever since. The more I'm around you, the stronger the force. I love you, Blaize. And I want to do forever with you."

A hot tear streaked down her cheek. He thumbed it away.

"But there's one condition," she said. "And then you have my full heart and soul."

"Name it."

The fact that he didn't hesitate gave her hope.

"I want to be foster parents to Rue until Sharon gets out of trouble and back on her feet," she said.

"Already done," he said. A smile toyed with the corners of those full, sexy lips. "Does that mean you'll put up with me for the rest of our lives?"

"You couldn't chase me away if you tried."

Carys had found the one place she felt like she belonged. She found her person.

"There's one more thing," he said after pressing a tender kiss to her lips.

"More surprises?"

"I hope this is a good one," he said, pushing up to standing.

She cocked her head to one side. "What are you up to, Blaize?"

"I tracked down your father. After being with Rue, seeing what a parent goes through, I decided he should know what happened to his daughter."

"And?" She didn't want to give away the sudden blossom of hope inside her that the relationship between her and her father could be reconciled.

"He dropped everything and drove here," Blaize said. "He's been sitting out in the hallway ever since. Do you want to see him?"

Those words sprouted wings in her soul.

"Yes," she said.

"Hold on." Blaize stepped to the door, cracked it open, and waved.

A few seconds later, her father walked into the room. His steps were tentative. His gaze unsure.

"Hi, Dad."

He broke down into tears. "My baby girl. I'm so sorry for the way I've treated you. But I've missed you every day since you walked out the front door with that beaten-up suitcase. Can you ever forgive me?"

Carys smiled through tears. "Already done, Dad. Come sit with me for a while."

The two most important men in Carys's life were right in front of her, so close she could reach out and touch them.

So, she did.

"Thank you for coming, Dad."

"This is long overdue, my girl," he said. "And I have a lot to make up for, if you'll let me."

"Everyone deserves a second chance if they're serious about making amends."

Blaize moved beside her and took her by the hand. In that moment, she knew she'd found home. And she planned to hang on to him for the rest of her life and whatever came next because if she lived a hundred lives, she would want every one of them to be with him.

* * * * *

Keep reading for an excerpt of a new title
from the Romantic Suspense series,
PRIVATE BODYGUARD by Veronica Forand

Chapter One

Quinn Martinsson stared out the window of AxionMind's headquarters, fuming over the latest setback to his company's launch of what could change artificial intelligence for the better. As the countdown to launch day ticked closer, encrypted files went missing, systems crashed without warning, and there were whispers among the engineers of backdoor access points embedded deep within the code. The further the engineers dug, the more it looked like someone on the inside was sabotaging the launch from within. Quinn sighed, turning away from the window.

On the other side of his desk, Kate Mercer, his COO and most trusted ally, paced back and forth, adding to his uneasiness. "This isn't the team being paranoid. They found solid evidence that someone's trying to sabotage the launch of Project Zeus." She stopped to face him. "You need to take this seriously."

"We've handled worse."

"Not like this," she said. "It's all too coordinated." She crossed her arms, and stared him down with none of the hesitance in her actions that other employees revealed when around Quinn. He respected that about her. "I've hired a security firm to add more safeguards to this facility, and to protect you as well."

Quinn rubbed his temples, his lack of sleep catching up to him. Exhaustion had followed him around for years, pushing him to prove himself, especially to his father. The coward divorced Quinn's dying mother because he couldn't "handle the heartache." As if a sixteen-year-old could handle it better. At her funeral, his father showed up with his new wife, not to offer comfort and support, but to blame Quinn for failing her. Then he disappeared again. He only reached out a few years ago after Quinn's IPO transformed AxionMind from a small start-up to an international technology giant. Perfect timing for dear old dad and a hundred other people from his past to try to cash in. He'd created this technology himself and later with his handpicked team. The idea of needing anyone outside of his closest circle, especially a bodyguard to shield him from this threat, made him ill. He hadn't needed anyone to protect him during his screwed-up past, he didn't need someone now. "I don't want some gorilla in a paramilitary outfit following me around."

"You're too visible and some of the threats are directed at you personally. If you go down, the company goes down with you."

He clenched his jaw. "I'm not someone who hides behind security details. I built this company with my bare hands, and I'll protect it the same way."

"Despite your daily workouts, I'm pretty sure it was your mind that built this company, not your brawn," she replied, shaking her head. "But I can't protect that genius of yours if you're dead. That's why I hired Fresh Pond Security."

He froze. "Fresh Pond Security? How did you get their name? And why didn't you run it by me?"

"You had it listed on a piece of paper on your desk. I researched it to make sure they were legitimate and found they're the best of the best."

He hadn't looked into the firm for their ability to carry a concealed weapon, he'd looked into it for information on one particular person... Meaghan Knight. He couldn't explain to Kate that he kept track of a woman from his past. Not that Meaghan had ever been anything to him. She'd caught his eye and a small piece of his heart back in school, but she'd never showed any interest in him. When he left college early to pursue a start-up venture, he never forgot her. Every so often, he found himself checking in on her, more out of curiosity than anything else he'd dare to admit. Kate hiring Meaghan's firm, however, was too much proximity to his college roommate's sister.

"Tell them we don't need them." He'd only been curious about Meaghan, not obsessed, and he couldn't stand people following him around.

Most of his house staff had to leave before he arrived home to give him privacy. He could not endure a team of bodyguards. He would not live his life in a cage.

"At least give them a chance."

The sun had set, and the lights around the parking lot turned on. Blending into the darkness was something that changed all his priorities in an instant. A column of black smoke coming from the direction of their warehouse. "Kate…do we have anyone over at the warehouse right now?"

She followed his gaze, then grabbed her phone, already making calls, as a cold chill slid down his spine.

After she hung up, she turned to him. "Three employees were leaving when the fire started. They all got out and managed to call the fire department."

He nodded, processing her words. This was getting out of control. He currently only had six security guards who rotated through headquarters, the plant and the warehouse. Fresh Pond Security had over forty personnel, according to his research, so the chances of him ever coming face-to-face with Meaghan were slim to none. He could hear the wailing coming closer and distant red lights were growing brighter. "Fine. We'll go with Fresh Pond Security. Have them focus on protecting the company and our employees, and you can have one bodyguard assigned to me. One."